A TOM WAGNER ADVENTURE

THE MEDUSA SECRET

THRILLER

FROM THE BESTSELLING AUTHORS
ROBERTS & MACLAY

Copyright © 2023 by Roberts & Maclay (Roberts & Maclay Publishing). All rights reserved. No part of this book may be reproduced in any form or by any electronic or mechanical means, including information storage and retrieval systems, without written permission from the authors, except for the use of brief quotations in a book review.

Translator: Edwin Miles / Copyeditor: Philip Yaeger

Imprint: Independently published / Paperback ISBN 9798378914692, Hardcover ISBN 9798378914722

Cover Art by reinhardfenzl.com

Cover Art was created with photos from: depositphotos.com, freepik.com

This is a work of fiction. Names, characters, businesses, places, events and incidents are either the products of the author's imagination or used in a fictitious manner. Any resemblance to actual persons, living or dead, or actual events is purely coincidental.

www.robertsmaclay.com

office@robertsmaclay.com

"In theory, there is one potential means to perfect happiness: To believe in something indestructible within oneself, and not to strive for it."

Franz Kafka

CHAPTER 1

A SUITE IN THE TASCHENBERGPALAIS HOTEL, DRESDEN, GERMANY

She woke first, as she always did. An inner restlessness forced her out of bed every morning at five, regardless of what had happened the night before. And the night before had been intense.

She opened her eyes. It took her a few seconds for her memory to return, but then the uneasiness came. She hated being physically close to someone in situations like this, just as she hated intimacy when she wasn't the one in control. She turned and looked at the naked young man beside her. She frowned. No one, seeing her at that moment, could have known from her expression what she was feeling. Pride, perhaps? Disgust? Amusement? The man was well built. He lay on his back, fast asleep. No wonder, considering everything they'd put into their bodies the night before. He still looked good to her. A powerful, downy chest. The hint of a sixpack. Well-endowed, too—*that* was still fresh in her memory, even as he slept. And he had known how to use what he had.

She felt a sudden movement on the other side of the bed. She'd almost forgotten the second man. But only almost, because he was in no way inferior to the first. He lay on his stomach and snored softly, so softly that it did not bother her. She hated men who snored.

It was time to go.

Cautiously, she pushed her naked body inch by inch toward the foot of the bed, careful not to touch either man. She knew herself. If she touched one of them now, her sexual appetite might be reawakened from one second to the next. And that was the last thing she needed right now.

Gradually, as if in slow motion, she rose from the bed and rearranged her tousled, raven-black hair, tumbling almost to her bottom. For a few seconds, she stood and looked at the sleeping young men. They lay before her like Greek gods, and she sensed the all-too-familiar desire stirring in her belly.

It had been an outstanding night, even by her standards. And she had had two men, sometimes more, in her bed countless times. Everyone had gotten what they wanted.

She turned her eyes away from the bed and scanned the room, unable to suppress a smile. A rock band with a clutch of groupies could hardly have made a bigger mess. Two empty bottles of Dom Pérignon, a few more of Kristall vodka, crushed Red Bull cans, glasses lying on their sides, the scraps of midnight snacks. Countless items of clothing lay strewn around the room, as if someone had thrown a bomb into a laundry.

And then there were the toys.

Not that the three of them had actually needed any extras to have fun, but why deny yourself if you didn't need to? Handcuffs, leather straps, a ball gag, dildos in a wild array of shapes and sizes—and not only for her. There were many different ways to take cocaine, each a little different in its effect. It never ceased to surprise her what men were willing to do when driven by lust.

She tiptoed to the window and looked out over the still-sleeping city. She loved these morning moments. The city had an innocence about it that would soon give way to the hustle and bustle of the day.

She began to gather her things. She slipped into her thong and was just arranging her bra when her cellphone vibrated. A glance at the screen, and her expression changed. Her face grew stony and her eyes cold when she read the subject line: "Trinitas."

She scanned the few lines of the message, then reached into her handbag and slid out a Glock 44. Calmly, she screwed a B&T small-caliber suppressor to the front of the barrel.

Her eyes narrowed; her pulse quickened. She felt her arousal grow. This was a fire no man in the world could ignite in her, a fire that blazed only when she killed.

Slowly, she returned to the bed and the first man, sleeping soundly on his back. Her eyes wandered a final time over his flawless body, his broad shoulders, his muscular stomach, his cock.

If she were not the professional she was, her arousal would have made her tremble, sexual excitement pumping adrenalin through her body. But her hand remained steady. She took aim at the man's head and, without hesitation, squeezed the trigger twice.

Blood sprayed across the sheet, spattering the man who lay on his stomach on the other side. The suppressor muffled the gunshots, to be sure, but the second man still woke. He sat up, looking around in confusion, and saw the bloody body on the bed beside him. Then he saw the woman pointing a pistol at him.

What is going through his mind right now? she wondered. She looked at the man's distressed face for a moment before again pulling the trigger twice. The man fell back on the bed, dead. They were both dead.

She let the suppressor cool for a few seconds as she studied her handiwork. Then she unscrewed it from the pistol and put both away in her handbag.

She had orgasmed several times the night before, but none came close to the climax she felt when she killed.

She checked her watch and saw that she still had a little time. She went into the bathroom, showered, made up her face, dressed.

A final look at her victims before she left the room. For her, death followed sex. Every time. They didn't call her "the Mantis" for nothing.

CHAPTER 2

CHAMBERS OF THE TENNŌ, IMPERIAL RESIDENCE, CHIYODA CITY, TOKYO

Almost as one, Tom, Hellen and Cloutard bowed before the emperor. They had just entered the audience chamber, and Tom looked around in fascination. He'd been expecting pomp, luxury and opulence, but instead they had walked into an exceptionally minimalist room. It made Tom think of the simple chamber in which Pope Sixtus VI had lived. It seemed to be true: those who wielded true power had little concern for material wealth.

His face turned to the floor, Tom stretched both hands out in front of him. He was holding an old linen sack, beige-colored and entirely unexceptional. The emperor murmured something that might have included "*arigato*." He took the small sack and hefted it for a long moment in his hand, as if wanting to be certain that what was inside was, in fact, what he was expecting. A barely perceptible smile flickered across the monarch's face.

"The last of the *ryō* coins from the Ezo treasure," said a voice behind Tom in flawless, unaccented Japanese. Tom had almost forgotten that their employer, the billionaire Eon van Rensburg, was there with them.

Until a few weeks earlier, Tom had never heard of Ezo.

As Hellen had explained, Ezo had been a short-lived republic in Japan, proclaimed by separatists in the nineteenth century. Its political structure had been based on that of the United States. Admiral Enomoto Takeaki and his two-and-a-half thousand soldiers had declared their republic on the island of Ezo, known today as Hokkaido, but they had quickly realized that they had no chance against the Empire. They surrendered, accepting the rule of Emperor Meiji instead, but part of the republic's treasury of old, oval-shaped ryō coins had never been retrieved.

Over the years, van Rensburg had tracked down leads and clues to the whereabouts of the remaining coins, which were of great importance to Japan's emperor, and Tom, Hellen, and Cloutard had finally managed to recover them from the fortress of Goryōkaku.

"*Merde*. Do you have any idea how much these coins would bring on the black market?" Cloutard had grumbled when they finally had them in their possession. "I know a collector who would give us five million for them without a second thought, cash in hand." Hellen had been about to respond, but Cloutard had already raised his hands in surrender. "I know, we are the good guys. We are not looters. We are working for van Rensburg, and he alone knows why he wants to return the coins to someone who already has everything he could ever possibly want," he'd muttered as they left the fortress and Tom was messaging van Rensburg about their discovery. Cloutard was therefore doubly interested to find out what game van Rensburg was playing.

The emperor and van Rensburg exchanged a few words in Japanese, van Rensburg bowing at least a hundred times as they spoke. At least, it seemed like that many to Cloutard.

Without warning, the emperor barked a sharp command. Moments later a servant appeared in the room carrying a rosewood casket. Bowing deeply, he presented the casket to the emperor.

Tom, Hellen and Cloutard saw a gleam appear in van Rensburg's eyes. He was practically drooling as he stared at the casket.

"My preciousssss," Tom whispered, earning a jab in the ribs from Hellen. Fortunately, the emperor didn't notice.

"The Royal Danish egg, crafted by Peter Carl Fabergé for Tsar Nicholas II and presented to his mother to mark the fortieth anniversary of her father's accession to the throne," said the emperor in heavily accented English as he opened the casket.

Cloutard raised an eyebrow when he saw the pale-blue egg set with precious stones. He recognized it instantly. The top section displayed the coat of arms of the Danish royal family, supported on both sides by Danish heraldic lions. At the very top stood a figure of the Order of the Elephant, Denmark's ancient chivalric fraternity.

"Only three eggs missing," Cloutard said, louder than intended.

Van Rensburg accepted the casket with reverence, his hands trembling slightly.

"What does he want with that?" Tom murmured when they had once again left the emperor's chambers and said goodbye to van Rensburg. He was in a hurry—he had to attend to the multimillion-dollar purchase of a tech start-up in London.

"No idea," said Hellen. "But for some reason, he's tracking down all the lost Fabergé eggs."

"Perhaps you have forgotten, but everything we went through to find Anne Bonny's treasure was just so he could get his hands on an egg," Cloutard added, with a trace of sarcasm. "He is planning something with them."

"And I'm sure we'll find out what it is soon enough," said Tom. He pulled Hellen closer. "But right now, we've earned a few days' vacation."

"So, you are returning to Vienna?" Cloutard asked.

Hellen and Tom nodded eagerly. "What about you?" Tom asked.

"Back home to Tabarka. Fabio and Adalgisa are paying me a visit. They have something they want to discuss."

Tom raised his hands. "No details, please, or we'll have to arrest you," he said with a grin.

"Not on your life," the Frenchman countered.

The three friends shared a farewell embrace, and when Hellen was alone with Tom in their car, heading for Tokyo-Narita airport, she asked, "Do you also get the feeling François has been acting a little ... strange lately?"

"Yeah. Something's going on. He usually plays his cards close to the chest, but this is different," said Tom, at the wheel. Both of them were looking forward to getting home.

CHAPTER 3

HOTEL ROOM, THE MOZART PRAGUE HOTEL, CZECH REPUBLIC

"Who is it?" called Meinrad Richter, director of Vienna's Museum of Fine Arts. He got up and went to the door. He was not expecting visitors. The congress at the Czech Academy of Sciences began the following day, but this time he had no presentations to make. He was there as a guest, no more.

He opened the door. The pretty face of a young woman peeked tentatively back at him through the gap.

"Sorry to disturb you, Doctor Richter," the young woman said shyly. She was wearing a brightly colored and decidedly low-cut summer dress, and her raven-black hair was tied back in a ponytail that fell to her hips. A pair of horn-rimmed glasses sat a little too far forward on the tip of her petite nose.

"What is it?" Richter said, instantly squaring his shoulders. It was not every day that a beautiful young woman found her way to his hotel room.

"I apologize for barging in like this, but I'm in a bit of an awkward situation . . ." the woman said in a soft, almost timid voice.

Nor was Richter used to pretty women in awkward situations turning to him for help. He felt a little out of his depth. "No problem at all. Come in, please. How can I help?" he asked, ushering her inside and gesturing for her to sit.

He took the chair at the small desk, while she sat opposite in the leather armchair. "Thank you," she said. She looked up, pushing her glasses slowly up on her nose with a fingertip. "I'm Elsa Cutter. My boss asked me to come and see you. I've just arrived from Greece. We need your help—or rather, your expertise."

"My expertise?" Richter asked, unable to contain a smile.

"As one of the leading experts in Greek history and mythology."

"'Leading' is perhaps an exaggeration," Richter said modestly, but he was clearly flattered.

"An artifact has been discovered that falls squarely into your field." The woman retrieved a photograph from her handbag and pushed it across the coffee table between them. Richter took it and studied the picture for a moment. The woman saw his eyes widen.

"The amphora in that picture was found a week ago in Akrini, in northern Greece," she said, leaning forward. Richter's eyes shifted momentarily from the photo to her low neckline, then, embarrassed, back to the photo. Well aware of her charms and willing to use them, the young woman leaned back again.

Richter did his best not to let it show, but his interest had definitely been aroused. And not only in the amphora.

"I've been sent to ask you to come and examine the artifact today."

Richter hesitated. "Today?" He twisted nervously on his chair and glanced at his old Oriosa watch. "But . . . that's impossible. I have to be up early tomorrow . . . uh . . . so many interesting talks, and . . ." he stammered. His defenses were already crumbling.

"We are naturally prepared to pay you an appropriate fee for your trouble." The woman opened her handbag again, took out a check, and leaned farther forward than before to pass it across to Richter. This time, he allowed his eyes to wander a little lower. "You won't need to arrange anything. We'd just like you to answer a few questions and confirm our hypothesis," the young woman continued.

"Hypothesis? What hypothesis?" Richter reached for the check, but the woman held it back.

"It would mean a lot to me if you could help," she said, almost tenderly, looking deep into Richter's eyes. Then she withdrew her hand, leaving the check on the table.

Richter swallowed hard. His eyes were still fixed on the young woman, who leaned back with exaggerated slowness and smiled at him. Only now did Richter look down at the check. He could hardly believe his eyes. "Fifty thousand euros" was written on it, in words and numbers. He looked up and gaped in disbelief at the young woman.

"And when you're finished, there'll be another check for the same amount," she said. He was hooked. She knew it. He was practically eating out of her hand. "Shall we go?" Without waiting for an answer, she stood and moved toward the door.

CHAPTER 4
TOM AND HELLEN'S HOUSEBOAT, DANUBE RIVER, VIENNA

"A completely different world," Hellen said to Tom as they climbed out of the taxi.

Tom grabbed their bags from the trunk and tramped with them to the houseboat door. For years, his family had owned a small property in the heart of the Danube-Auen National Park, a conservation area to the east of Vienna. Tom had anchored his houseboat there around ten years earlier.

His floating home was a symbol of his lifestyle, his need for freedom, and his distaste for convention.

"And a completely different life," he added, opening the door—unlocked, as always. They stepped inside, and the memories came streaming back.

They had not shared many hours together there, but the houseboat had left its mark on both of them. The time they had spent together on board was one of the things that bound them together so strongly—even when they had been apart, neither of them wanting anything to do with the other.

"Do you remember our first night here?" said Hellen, as she picked up one of the few photos standing in the small living room. It showed the two of them with the Austrian chancellor just after they had found the "Stone of Destiny"—the Florentine Diamond—in Schönbrunn Palace. The picture showed all three of them, holding the diamond up proudly for the camera. It was the same photograph that had graced the front pages of every daily newspaper at the time, but the papers had only showed Hellen and the chancellor. At the time, Tom had still been an officer in Austria's antiterror unit, the Cobra, and his face could not be shown in the media.

Tom wrapped his arms around Hellen from behind and rested his chin gently on her shoulder as they looked at the picture.

"How could I forget? Our first adventure together," he said, and he kissed her on the cheek.

"Back when the world made sense," she said, and Tom heard a trace of melancholy in her voice. He knew what she meant, of course, and what had changed since then. "One day, Tom . . . one day I'd like to know," she continued. She put the picture back in its place and went out onto the small terrace with its unmatched view over the Danube. One of the freight barges so common on the river was chugging past just then, probably on its way to the Danube-Black Sea Canal.

"What would you like to know one day?" Tom asked.

Hellen tilted her head to one side and looked at Tom a little reproachfully. "Don't play dumb, darling," she said. "I'd like to know who killed my father, on whose orders they were acting, and most importantly: why?"

Tom's expression darkened.

"It's not because I want revenge. My father was not a good man. Of course, no one deserves to be killed for that . . . but his death brought a lot of horrible things to an end."

Tom nodded. He sensed that Hellen had worked her way

through the subject completely. She spoke earnestly, without wavering, and he heard no sadness or other negative emotions in her words.

"I just want to know. I want to know the who and the why of it. Because it's very possible that the subject hasn't been laid to rest yet, not completely," she said. She began absently unpacking their travel bags.

"I know that pretty much every law enforcement agency in Europe and the States is busy right now cleaning up the mess AF left behind," Tom said. "From what I've heard, Hagen is in charge, and several second-rank leaders have already been taken into custody." He wished—for Hellen's sake, especially—that they could finally be done with Absolute Freedom.

"Still, someone ordered someone to assassinate my father. One day, I'll ask you to help me find out who it was," Hellen said. She put her arms around Tom and hugged him tightly.

As if on cue, the houseboat door swung open and Theresia de Mey, Hellen's mother, stepped inside, putting an end to the somber scene. Hellen ran to her, the two women embraced, and a flood of greetings and chatter washed over Tom. Suddenly animated, they talked about what had been happening in their lives in recent months. Hellen in particular had a lot to relate, what with Anne Bonny's treasure and the *ryō* coins.

"A Caribbean pirate treasure in West Africa?" said Theresia. "The more I hear, the more incredible it sounds." She pointed to Tom. "And this fellow you've caught here—it's never going to be boring with him around, is it?" she said with a touch of irony, and she went to Tom and gave him a hug.

"I love you, too," Tom quipped.

"You two aren't the only ones with stories to tell, you

know. I've had a lot going on myself since you left on your extended honeymoon," Theresia said, sipping at the cup of coffee Hellen had prepared in the meantime.

"Well, don't keep us in suspense. You were so secretive on the phone," Hellen said.

All three were sitting on the terrace now, watching the sun set.

"The Metropolitan Museum of Art in New York wants me to be their new director," Theresia announced with no preamble, as dryly as if saying she had to go buy milk.

Hellen almost choked on her coffee. "The Met? My God, mother, that's the Olympus of museums."

"Well, now, let's not blow things out of proportion. You'd be doing very well for yourself at the Museum of Fine Arts if your career had taken a slightly different path." She smiled, casting Tom a sidelong look. "That's not exactly a backwater."

"Yes, sure, but you're talking about the Met! When do you start?" Hellen pressed. She had shuffled her chair a little closer to her mother's and was looking at her intently.

"I don't even know if I'm going to accept their offer," Theresia said in the same indifferent tone.

"What? Why not?" Hellen placed her hand on her mother's forehead as if checking her temperature. "Are you okay? Are you out of your mind? This is the MET, for God's sake! The *MET*!"

Theresia grinned. She could understand her daughter's enthusiasm only too well.

"It is. And I've been wondering if my energies wouldn't be better spent doing something more humanitarian, or maybe in the environmental branch. The Met would just be more politics, meetings, and bureaucracy. I want to make a difference, just like the two of you."

Tom raised his eyebrows. *A compliment, though a little*

indirect? Was Hellen's mother expressing admiration for what Hellen, Cloutard and he did? That would be new. Theresia had never made a secret of her distaste for the methods their little gang used, especially Tom's. But he squelched any sort of triumphant reaction and nodded attentively.

"And?" Theresia looked around, her expression turning to a frown of disdain. The niceties were over. *That was quick*, Tom thought. He already knew what was coming. "How much longer are you going to go on living on this tub?" Theresia said. Her tone had turned about ten degrees cooler. "It's a bit cramped, isn't it?"

"Mama! Not now," said Hellen reprovingly, waving off her mother's suggestion.

"Oh, excuse me. I didn't realize you hadn't discussed this yet," Theresia said, although Tom could detect no regret in her voice.

"Discussed what?" Tom said, looking at the two women.

"Moving, of course. A normal person can't lead a normal life here," Theresia said with glee, waving her hand disparagingly at the terrace and the rest of the little houseboat.

Then again, we're not normal people, Tom thought.

CHAPTER 5
PRAGUE

The whole thing was fishy from the start. He should have known better, and he knew it. A serious request of a researcher as prominent as himself would have been made differently.

Director Richter only accepted the assignment as impulsively as he did because the money was so tempting. He was juggling a series of private research projects that were all in urgent need of a cash injection, and he was always looking for patrons and sponsors. Asking for money was exhausting work, and Richter found it fundamentally repugnant. The fee the woman was offering would be a godsend.

But his alarm bells began ringing loudly when he saw the small army of bodyguards that accompanied them from the moment they left the hotel.

He and the young woman were being driven somewhere in a limousine, and Richter realized in an instant that there was money involved here—and a lot of it. He knew people like these from his fundraising events. The nouveau-riche, with their status symbols and vain ostentation. Even the bodyguards were wearing designer suits.

And then there was the woman...

Richter had never been much of a ladies' man. His wife had died young, and he'd been more or less asexual ever since, concentrating on his research and his career. But this woman was sparking his interest, stimulating his imagination in unfamiliar ways. He hadn't been the morose type as a young man, and he'd been anything but prudish . . . but the pictures flashing in his mind when he looked at the woman astonished him.

"Where are we going?" he asked, his voice uncertain, almost breaking. *What's wrong with me, damn it?* he immediately thought.

"To the Four Seasons Hotel. It isn't far," the woman said softly. "It's beside the Vltava River, and it has a *very* romantic view," she murmured. Richter felt his heart beat faster. Then her tone suddenly changed. "You'll find out more when we get there. You might even meet my employer, Apostolos Ibis."

"Should I know the name?" Richter asked. He knew practically every researcher of note who dealt with the ancient Greeks and their mythology, but "Apostolos Ibis" was new to him.

"Mr. Ibis prefers to avoid publicity," the woman replied. Her voice was forceful, almost domineering, but there was also a sweetness in it that made Richter break into a sweat. And there was more: she was sitting opposite him, and every time she crossed and uncrossed her endless legs, he caught himself staring where he knew he shouldn't. It wasn't that he wanted to, but he couldn't stop himself. And the way she smoothed her skirt after crossing her legs almost drove him crazy. He felt a stirring in his crotch and shook his head, but his eyes never left her. Her sexual allure was almost hypnotic.

Richter was glad when they reached the hotel. He had made up his mind to find out what he could about this

"Apostolos" as soon as he could. He found the whole scenario highly suspicious.

The limousine drove directly into the underground garage. From there, they went straight to the Royal Suite Villa, situated on the banks of the Vltava in front of the hotel.

"What's your real name?" Richter suddenly asked, although he wasn't really sure why. They had barely spoken on the short drive to the hotel.

"What makes you think Elsa Cutter isn't my real name?" the woman asked.

"In German, 'Cutter' would be 'Schneider,' and Elsa Schneider is a character from 'Indiana Jones and the Last Crusade.'"

"You're a clever man," the woman said. "Perhaps too clever." She smiled and placed a hand on his shoulder. "My real name doesn't matter," she said. She leaned close and spoke into his ear, as if she did not want the flanking bodyguards to hear. "But sometimes they call me the Mantis," She left a pregnant pause, then added, "You should focus on your task, Professor Richter." Her voice was a whisper, and her lips brushed his ear as she spoke.

Richter shuddered. His pulse doubled, and his body suddenly pumped an overdose of blood to his loins. The woman seemed to notice. Her hand drifted from his shoulder to his crotch, and he felt her fingers glide casually over the bulge in his trousers. "Now, now, Professor. That's not very professional." The villa doors opened, and she steered Richter inside. "Take a seat. I'll be back for you in a moment," she said, and she left the room, leaving Richter utterly perplexed.

He sat, a semi-hard-on in his pants, his mind racing. What was he doing there? Was he in some kind of danger? Was he being kidnapped? For a second, his thoughts turned to his secret, a secret he and all his predecessors as director of the Museum of Fine Arts had guarded closely for more than a century. Could that be why he'd been brought here?

He shook his head. No, impossible. Nobody knew about that. He hadn't mentioned it to a soul, and the previous director had been dead more than a decade. He was the only one who knew about it. It had to be something else.

"I'm sorry, Professor," the woman said, returning to the salon. "Apostolos can't join us right now. He has an important meeting with Damjan Mandalov. I'm sure you've heard of him."

Richter nodded. Mandalov was a name he knew, of course. He was the *enfant terrible* of the scene. His discoveries and his insights into Greek antiquity were groundbreaking, but no serious scientific institute wanted anything to do with the man. His writings on Greek mythology and the truths they allegedly contained were simply too absurd.

"Apostolos has given me the honor of discussing the matter with you myself. What I'm about to show you is very special."

Without waiting for Richter to respond, she placed a leather file on the table before him. Apparently, it contained the papers he was supposed to examine.

"What's really going on here? What do you expect from me? I thought I was here to date an amphora," Richter said, as he leaned forward and opened the file.

"Just look at the papers," the woman said, with a trace of impatience that, to Richter, suddenly sounded more than threatening.

Richter scanned the first lines, then stopped and looked up. "I hope you don't think these are originals. They're far too recent to have come from antiquity. That much is obvious at a glance."

"Read the text, Professor. Tell me what you think." The

woman's voice was more than a request, now. It was an order, and one that would brook no dissent.

Richter's disquiet grew. What had he gotten himself into? With a worried sigh, he began to read. After the first page, his breath caught in his chest, and his heart felt as if it skipped several beats. He made an effort to hide his dismay. What he was reading could spell disaster. But what did she want from him? Why had they brought *him* into this? Yes, it was written in sloppy, almost illegible ancient Greek, but he was far from the only expert who had mastered the language.

His terrible suspicion intensified. Whoever Apostolos Ibis was, he must have somehow learned Richter's secret—a secret he'd kept faithfully for years. His encounter with the woman could serve only one purpose: to make him lower his guard. He had to get home, fast.

CHAPTER 6

UNKNOWN LOCATION, ONE MONTH EARLIER

The man took a few deep breaths. His plan was not simple, and his particular situation meant that he faced many more obstacles than he would have otherwise.

But there was no problem he could not overcome. The obstacles were no more than minor hindrances, small stumbling blocks on the road to ultimate triumph. But he was still a long way from that. His plan was almost perfect, but for one major flaw: in the long run, the project had to be visible. Nothing he was planning would happen from one day to the next, although the way people thought these days would play into his hands.

Events of recent years had shown him how easy it was to steer people in a certain direction. In the past, dictators spent years working to build their empires, step by laborious step. Today, the same could be achieved with one good YouTube video.

The man stood and checked his equipment one more time.

The lights were positioned so that his face would not be visible, and he made sure that the rest of the room was so dark that even the best technicians would be unable to work out where the video had been made. The room itself was soundproof, which meant the analysts from the CIA, FBI, and all the other agencies would pick up no extraneous sounds that might give him away. And listening in from outside was completely impossible. No sound made it in or out. He had gone to great lengths to make sure of that—especially in light of his present situation.

He checked the proxy server and VPN connections one last time. He would use these to upload the video to YouTube, Facebook, Instagram, TikTok and many other portals.

He had set up his system so that the hundreds of fake accounts he operated across the portals would share and reshare the video hundreds of thousands of times in short order, augmented by bots and auto-reposting tools. All the usual Internet conspiracy groups would pounce on it like vultures. He ran two dozen discussion groups on Facebook himself, with several hundred thousand members.

Within hours, real accounts and bots would drive views of the video into the millions, signaling to the algorithms on YouTube and Facebook that it contained important content that deserved a wider audience. When that happened, he could sit back and watch social media take over.

Brave new world, the man thought, and he read a final time through the script that millions would soon be hearing, reading, and seeing for themselves.

The recording would be filtered through a series of AI text-to-speech apps, rendering voice analysis impossible.

A beep announced a new message coming in from the dark web chat. One of his employees informed him that the website was also ready. The first blog articles had been written, and distribution deals with relevant forums, influencers and conspiracy sites around the world were locked in. A lot of money had changed hands, but that was the least of his worries.

In a few days, the entire world would know about the Medusa cult. It would be talked about in the same breath as Q-Anon and other conspiracy theories.

Last of all, he checked the list of celebrities he had on board. It was pitiful to see how far pathetic, C-list celebs would go to see their names back in the headlines. He had actors, singers, models, motivational speakers, politicians, and a large number of so-called influencers on his payroll, all of whom would soon be spreading fear and terror of the Medusa cult. They would give interviews, appear on talk shows, use their own social media channels and God knew what else to make the world believe that the Medusa cult could mean the end of the world as we know it. Some of the celebrities would even be doing it for free, just to get people talking about them again.

The man smiled and shook his head. Even after all these years, it still amazed him how easy it was to plant crazy theories and obscure fears in people's heads.

He was already looking forward to the media circus when the pop diva a little past her prime, normally so well-behaved, started talking about the ruthlessness of the Medusa cult. Or when the populist politician facing a raft of scandals started warning people about the evil Medusa cult, hoping to generate enough political currency to win reelection; or when the actress whose third plastic surgery had left her so disfigured that not even "I'm a Celebrity" would have her back on began talking about the Medusa cult and its hold on Hollywood. He particularly enjoyed the story about the casting-couch brainwashing.

Long ago, people had fought with swords and spears. Today it was the Internet, its algorithms, and the fact that you could get into everybody's apartments, houses, and even heads in real time. And with very little effort, without them even noticing, without it looking like propaganda.

Brave new world, the man thought again. Then he switched off the light and hit "record."

CHAPTER 7
DIRECTOR RICHTER'S HOUSE, DÖBLING DISTRICT, VIENNA

Rain rattled onto the roof of the taxi as it pulled to a stop. Richter, who had been checking his watch practically once a minute and drumming his fingers on the door handle the whole way from the train station, handed the driver fifty euros, said "Keep the change," and climbed out. He opened the wrought-iron front gate, hurried up the path to his sizeable house, and unlocked the front door.

Absently tossing his keys onto the sideboard in the entry, he turned left into his library. Heavy old bookshelves lined the longest wall from floor to ceiling, filled with ancient folios, encyclopedias, scientific treatises, and countless minor historical works from all around the world.

A small stepladder stood beside the leather wing chair. He pulled it over and moved several books at once from the second shelf from the top to the one beneath it, then repeated the process, gradually revealing a wall safe behind the books. He tapped in a code, opened the steel door, and took out a large folio. This was no ordinary book: the front and back covers were carved wooden panels measuring eighteen by twenty-four inches. The volume was bound with decorative metal hinges and a beautifully ornamented clasp.

He descended the ladder, crossed the room, and placed the oversized book on his antique mahogany desk. Quickly opening the clasp, he turned one fragile parchment page after another.

He knew that his edition was no more than a medieval duplicate, probably created by Cosmas Indicopleustes. Historians couldn't even agree on the authenticity of the thirty-five dialogues attributed to Plato, to say nothing of these reports—whether they were in fact the work of the great philosopher was heavily disputed.

From his pocket, Richter took the photograph the young woman had given him in his hotel room, the one she had used to lure him under false pretenses to the Four Seasons. He put aside the check she had given him, which he'd taken out along with the photograph. Then he placed the photo beside an illustration, comparing the two. He slumped back in his leather armchair.

The thoughts running through his mind were insane. *Where could they have gotten their information? This would change everything. It's not only dangerous, but it brings with it a brand-new problem.*

Richter closed the book and pushed it aside, leaned back in his chair. He had to act, and fast. *It* was no longer safe in Vienna. Under no circumstances could he allow these people to discover where he kept it. They already knew too much. But how? Over the years, he had turned down countless international job offers, just so he could stay in Vienna. The task passed onto him by his predecessor was too important. The secret needed to be protected at all costs.

He reached for his phone and called his assistant, Mrs. Gabi, and asked her to find a number for him. He knew of only one person with both the means to equip a place with the required security and the necessary knowledge to help him.

After returning the folio to the safe and replacing the books on the shelves in their original positions, he grabbed his keys from the sideboard. Before he left the house, a portrait of Emperor Franz Joseph of Austria that stood on his desk caught his eye. In the portrait, the monarch was wearing the official vestments of the Order. And yet Richter still found the theory absurd.

On his way out to his car, he shook off these thoughts, took out his phone, and dialed the number his assistant had sent him. The call was swiftly answered.

"You don't know me," Richter began, starting the car and turning out of his driveway. "But we have friends in common. I need your help, and I need it urgently."

In a few words, he explained his situation to the man on the other end, finishing with, "Come alone!"

In his agitation, he failed to notice that another car was following him.

Another possibility occurred to him: he could destroy the artifact. That would solve all of the problems, of course. The moment it was destroyed, all the damage it had done would be undone. But what was required to destroy it . . . that would be far more difficult than simply getting it to safety.

CHAPTER 8
ARLINGTON, VIRGINIA, USA

"Come alone!"

The young Asian-American woman pressed "Stop," rewound the recording, and checked it again at different points.

"... We have friends in common."

She moved the play head a little farther forward, and the voice became incomprehensibly fast.

"... You work with Hellen de Mey, after all..."

"... I have to get something to safety, and you have the best facilities for that..."

"... Can we meet in Vienna?"

"... I can't talk about it on the phone..."

"... a matter of life and death..."

"... Come alone!"

The young woman slipped her headphones off and let them dangle around her neck. She leaned back and stared at the monitor, which was flanked by two more. She had listened to the message three times and still couldn't believe it.

She had been researching the Medusa cult for several weeks—since the day the videos had appeared, to be exact.

Conspiracy theories had always been a hobby of hers, not least because, as she was well aware, some of them contained a kernel of truth. And through her work at the front lines, she had become part of one of those theories herself.

She watched people. Even in college, her hacking skills had raised eyebrows, and had finally led to her being recruited. The saying "nothing to hide, nothing to fear" had become popular in the '80s, with the advent of the widespread collection of personal data, and had only gained in relevance with the Snowden affair, Anonymous's data leaks, and the role social media platforms played in them. But with her, the saying took on a whole new meaning. No computer system, no cell phone was safe from her skills.

Her current employer had tasked her with looking into a tech start-up. It was her job to assemble comprehensive dossiers on the employees and find out what they were working on behind closed doors. Which was also why she was eavesdropping on the conversations of the billionaire interested in the start-up . . . except that this particular call clearly had nothing to do with what she'd been hired for.

In fact, it looked as if she had made a breakthrough in her private research. She had come across the director several times in the course of her "explorations," though more often his position than his name. That had led her back to the opening of the Vienna Museum of Fine Arts in 1891 and, just a year later, to Otto Benndorf's founding of the Austrian Archeological Institute.

It was the piece of the puzzle she'd been missing all along. Now her employer finally had to start taking things seriously. Ever since the appearance of the cult, she'd been trying to impress its urgency on him. She encrypted the files and had just sent them off when a shrill ringing cut into her thoughts.

Akira Seki raced out of her apartment home office and trotted barefoot to the front door. She was wearing cotton short-shorts and a hoodie with a manga character on the front. Her hair was pulled up in a bun and held in place with chopsticks.

"I'm coming, I'm coming!" she called when the doorbell rang again. "Did you forget your key again?" She opened the door without bothering to look through the peephole.

"No, but my hands are full," said a young man, two large shopping bags in his arms, as he pushed past the petite young woman. Akira closed the door and followed him into the kitchen.

Jamie Sanders was a tall, cheerful young man with blond hair. He set the shopping bags on the kitchen counter and began putting things away.

"What goodies did you bring us?" Akira said, stretching up to kiss her boyfriend.

"I was thinking we'd take it easy today, make a nice brunch, then—"

A *ping* interrupted the moment. Akira let go of Jamie and hurried to her office door, which stood ajar. She'd forgotten to close it. She quickly pulled the door closed and tapped a numerical code into the touchpad on the doorknob.

"Sorry," Akira excused herself.

"You know you can trust me."

"Of course I do," Akira said, cuddling close to Jamie again. "But you know what these game developers are like. They're more paranoid than the CIA. If I want to work from home, this is how it has to be. They insist." She went up on tiptoes, put her arms around him, and kissed him again.

Lying to her boyfriend was the only bad thing about her job, especially since she considered it almost a miracle that she had a boyfriend at all. She'd struggled with social interaction all her life. People in general scared her, and as a result, she'd been alone since childhood. It was only much later, when she'd finally been diagnosed with Asperger's Syndrome, that her life became clearer and even a little easier. At first, it had been a shock to discover that she was autistic—though not severely—but it was also a blessing to finally understand why her life was the way it was.

"I'm going to take a quick shower while you make us something good to eat," Akira said. She pulled the chopsticks out of her jet-black hair, and it tumbled down her back. She blew Jamie a kiss and disappeared into the bathroom.

"That smells amazing," she said, when she reappeared from the bathroom half an hour later wearing nothing but a towel. The aroma of fresh coffee, pancakes and bacon filled the air. Akira reached for a slice of the bacon that was arranged neatly on a plate, but Jamie playfully rapped her across her knuckles.

"Patience, Miss Greedy," he said. He picked up the plate and took it to their small dining table and set it beside the sliced fruit and carafe of orange juice.

"Thank God one of us can cook," Akira said, sitting at the table.

"Fried bacon and instant pancakes from a box isn't exactly 'cooking,'" Jamie said. "But thanks for the compliment."

"Hey, I can burn water trying to make tea," Akira joked, looking at him gratefully. She was thankful—not just because he'd done the shopping and cooked, but because he was part of her life at all. She had never dreamed she'd get to know a man like him—a man who loved her the way she was, with all her ragged edges and all the issues that came with her condition.

If Akira hadn't forced herself to leave the house at least once a week, even though it made her break into an anxious sweat, she never would have met Jamie. Her reclusive life had allowed her to push her computer talents to unmatched levels, but it had also caused her already-impaired, barely developed social skills to decline even further. So a few years earlier, on her therapist's advice, she had made up her mind to venture out into the wider world at least once a week. She had bought herself an annual pass for the Smithsonian and spent one afternoon a week indulging her second great passion: art and history. On one of those excursions, as stressful as they were, she had met Jamie.

When they finished eating, Jamie stood up from the table and came back from the kitchen with a bottle of champagne and two glasses.

"Wow, what's this all about? My birthday's still a month away," Akira said.

"Nothing in particular. It . . . it's just that I see you so rarely and I wanted . . . I thought, why not spoil you a little today?" Jamie stammered. He opened the bottle with a loud *pop* and, with a trembling hand, filled the two glasses. Akira smiled shyly. She already felt bad about spending more time in her office than with him. But when she was in her element, she forgot everything around her, and sometimes that included Jamie. They clinked glasses.

Just then, Akira's cell phone began to vibrate. She and Jamie looked at each other. Akira could already see the disappointment in her friend's eyes.

"Don't answer it," Jamie said.

"You know I have to."

She jumped up, ran into the front room where her phone lay, and answered the call.

"Yes, sir. What? No, you know I . . . but sir, our agreement . . . all right, if there's really no other way, I'll be there in thirty minutes," she said, ending the brief conversation.

"I'm so sorry. My boss . . ." said Akira. Jamie sighed.

"It's always 'my boss this, my boss that.' It's Sunday, for God's sake. I hardly see you at all during the week. You're in that damned office day and night." Jamie nodded bitterly toward the locked office door.

Akira went across and sat on his lap, slinging her arms around his neck. His downcast look made it even harder for her to leave the house so abruptly.

"I'll be back faster than you can say 'pancake.' I'll make it up to you, I promise," Akira said with a lascivious smile, batting her eyelids several times.

"Don't look at me like that. It isn't fair. You know I can't be mad at you when you do that."

"You're a treasure." She kissed him and went into the bedroom to get dressed.

Thirty minutes later, she turned her bicycle from Wilson Boulevard on to North Randolph Street. A hundred yards farther, on the left, stood the heavily guarded glass-fronted office building. She dismounted from her mountain bike and stood it with the others in the parking lot. She didn't bother with a lock. No thief would risk stealing anything from here.

She strode quickly past the large sign at the entrance: five large letters on a blue ellipse, crisscrossed with lines of latitude and longitude: DARPA—the Defense Advanced Research Projects Agency.

CHAPTER 9
HAUPTALLEE, PRATER PARK, VIENNA

"Pick me up at the airport in two hours! It's important."

That was about all their boss had said. Van Rensburg had sounded far more severe than usual, almost imperious. Taken aback, Hellen and Tom simply stood and looked at each other.

When his call had come through, they were deep in conversation about moving out of the houseboat. Hellen's mother had broached the subject rather bluntly the previous evening, and it was too important to leave undiscussed for long.

Tom loved his houseboat. Sure, it was small and not particularly luxurious. It was not where you would want to live out your twilight years. In fact, Tom had to admit, it was completely unsuitable for two people to live in for any length of time, especially in the winter. He knew that. But he was happy aboard his boat, and he and Hellen had decided to take a stroll along the Hauptallee—the main pedestrian boulevard through Vienna's huge Prater Park—to talk through their options. Hellen knew she did not want to live like this, but she also knew their work for van Rensburg would keep them on the road at least six months of the year anyway.

"Let's talk about it when we know we'll be spending more time in Vienna," Tom had said, hoping to put off any deeper discussion, at least for a while.

"It won't change anything, Tom," Hellen said. "We have to have somewhere to call home when we come back from a job."

"But we have—" Tom began, but then van Rensburg's call had come in, and Tom put the phone on speaker.

Hellen was frowning deeply when Tom ended the call. Their discussion would have to wait after all.

"Can't the man even arrange a taxi for himself?" she asked angrily. "Are we playing chauffeur for him now, too? Isn't that going just a bit too far?"

Tom knew Hellen when she got wound up. In the past, he might have tried to placate her. Or even, God forbid, to change her mind. But in the meantime, he'd learned when to keep his mouth shut. And right now was one of those moments.

They marched on to the end of the Prater Hauptallee and the building known as the "Lusthaus." The Lusthaus had served as a small hunting lodge as far back as the sixteenth century but had been destroyed in World War II and later rebuilt. Today, it was a national monument and housed a restaurant.

Tom had reserved a table, looking forward to having a romantic lunch with Hellen in the park, but van Rensburg's call had put an end to that idea. He told the headwaiter that they would not be needing the table after all, and a short time later they were sitting in his Mustang, headed for the airport.

"I wonder what van Rensburg's doing in Vienna," Tom said aloud as they climbed out of the car at the private terminal parking lot and went into the arrivals hall. Their boss had already landed, and he waved to them nervously. He seemed worried, looking around apprehensively, checking his watch, and glancing over his shoulder.

"I've never seen him like this," Hellen whispered as they crossed the terminal toward him.

"Let's go. I've got a meeting in the Volksgarten. Can you take me straight there?" van Rensburg said, wasting no time with greetings. Not waiting for a reply, he strode off. "Where's the limo?" Tom and Hellen heard, hurrying after him.

They grinned a little sheepishly and pointed to the Mustang. Van Rensburg shook his head. "Shotgun!" he called. "You, my dear, will have to squeeze in the back, if you can call it that." Hellen sighed and slipped into the back seat.

Half an hour later, Tom turned off the Ring, the boulevard encircling Vienna's city center, then passed the chancellor's and president's offices, and turned into a cul-de-sac between the Volksgarten park and the green expanse of Heldenplatz.

"Wait here. The meeting's at the Temple of Theseus, and I'm supposed to go alone," van Rensburg said. He jumped out of the car and jogged off toward the rose garden in front of the temple.

Tom and Hellen looked at each other in confusion. They had grilled van Rensburg for details on the drive—what he was doing here, who he was meeting, what it was all about—but he had stayed tight-lipped.

"Honestly, I'm a little worried. He's acting pretty weird," Tom said, gazing off across the Volksgarten, which was filled with the usual crowds of tourists. "Even weirder than usual. I guess it's probably another one of those Fabergé eggs. What do you think? Should we follow him?"

"There are hundreds of people here. What could happen?" Hellen said. "This isn't Tehran. Bombs don't go off and people don't get shot in public places, thank God."

"Hmm," Tom murmured, and he pointed in the direction of Heldenplatz. "It wasn't so long ago that bombs were exploding, and people were getting shot just over there."

Hellen thought back to what had taken place there a couple of years earlier. An AF team had forced its way into the Imperial Treasury and stolen the Holy Lance. Tom had done his best to stop them but failed. It was also the first time he and Hellen had seen each other after their break-up two years before.

"I remember it well," Hellen grinned. "And you were insane enough to try to chase Guerra and his men in a horse-drawn carriage!" Hellen tilted her head to one side and smiled at her husband. She loved his crazy ideas, even if they didn't always go as planned.

"I would have caught him, too, if you hadn't thrown a wrench in the works."

"Of course you would have, dear," said Hellen, patting his shoulder in mock consolation, her voice heavy with irony, but Tom had already turned his nervous attention back toward the park. "You know what?" Hellen said. "There's a sausage kiosk just over there, and I could really use a brat and a beer."

Tom raised his eyebrows and glanced at his watch. I was just on twelve. "Isn't it a little early for beer?"

"Think of François," Hellen said. "I'm sure he wouldn't say no."

"That's true," said Tom, and they strolled off to get a sausage.

DARPA Headquarters, Arlington, Virginia

. . .

On the heavy security door hung a sign that read "Authorized Personnel Only." The door buzzed and Akira pulled it open. Beyond it was a depressingly barren security checkpoint. An armed soldier sat at a computer terminal behind a pane of bulletproof glass. His blank gaze settled on Akira for a moment, then he turned his head and nodded toward a security terminal.

"Good morning, Sergeant," Akira said, making an effort to keep eye contact with him as she stepped through the metal detector. "I'm here to see Lieutenant Colonel Weaver."

She placed her backpack on the counter and the soldier looked through it quickly.

These soldiers, she thought, smiling to herself. Even at a boring job like this, they took their tasks so deadly seriously. He might as well have been a robot. The irony was that, in a few years, he might well be replaced by a robot—probably one of the ones they were developing on the third floor. The robotics research they were doing up there was pioneering, decades ahead of any other institute on the planet.

But Akira had nothing to do with that. Her activities, even as a freelancer, fell within the scope of the last word of the DARPA acronym—"Agency." DARPA was just one of many facilities that, together, constituted the Department of Defense's intelligence services.

A buzz and a green light beside the second door interrupted Akira's thoughts and signaled that entry to Lieutenant Colonel Weaver's section had been granted. She picked up her backpack and went through.

Every time she stepped out onto the gallery, her nerdy heart skipped a beat or two. She rested her hand on the railing for a moment and watched the hive of activity below.

Below her lay a hall laid out like a NASA control center,

but as big as a football field. A twelve-foot-high video wall stretched across the entire end wall. Divided into countless smaller screens of various sizes, the wall was a constant feed of information from surveillance cameras, traffic monitors, live news feeds, and YouTube videos from around the world.

In front of the video wall, on different levels, sat analyst after analyst, each with his or her own workstation. Along each side was a row of glass cubicles—conference rooms, offices of the heads of departments, even a small kitchen. Directly below her, opposite the video wall, sat her boss, Lieutenant Colonel Reece Weaver, the man who'd called her in on a Sunday despite their contractual agreement.

As Akira descended the black steel staircase, her cell phone buzzed. She took it out and checked the message Jamie had just sent, which consisted of the word "pancake" followed by a series of hearts. She sighed but did not smile. She could not even tell the man she wanted to spend the rest of her life with what she really did for a living. He thought she was a low-level programmer working for a computer game developer.

She put her phone away again, took a deep breath, and went to Lieutenant Colonel Weaver's office. When he saw her coming, he raised his hand and waved her in.

"Sit," he said, and he pushed a button, instantly turning the glass walls of his office to opaque frosted glass. Reece Weaver was lanky but muscular, an imposing figure even in the "cammies" he always wore. The camouflage uniform and buzzcut accentuated his severe-looking face—his expression suggested he'd seen his share of front-line fighting. Despite his office job, he could be found at the gym or the rifle range at least three times a week.

Akira sat and looked at him expectantly.

"I've been going through your report about this 'dangerous cult,'"—Lieutenant Colonel Weaver made air quotes as he spoke—"that you've been bugging me about for weeks. What's it called again? Yeah, here, the Medusa cult, and I have to say that you've really..."

Weaver paused, and for a fraction of a second, Akira thought he was going to say, "done a great job, keep it up." But Weaver shook his head incredulously, and her hopes evaporated.

"... got a nerve, wasting my time with crap like this. I've told you to drop it several times. This cult's been in the media for weeks, but you just happen to be the one who's uncovered the great conspiracy? Your assignment is clear, isn't it? Surveil startups, analyze what the nerds are inventing, see if it might have a military application. That's it. That's what you were hired for. But you keep coming to me with this BS."

Akira was speechless. Hadn't he read the briefing at all?

"But sir, this call confirms that the billionaire is somehow involved. He works with the former Blue Shield team that specializes in these things, the same team that brought down the Absolute Freedom terror group. Now he's meeting the director of the Museum of Fine Arts, who my research shows is guarding some kind of ancient artifact. And I'm a hundred percent sure it's the same artifact the cult wants to get its hands on. It's all connected, I'm sure of it."

"I don't give a shit whether they found the Ark of the Covenant or the Philosopher's Stone or whatever other mythical crap. This is DARPA. We answer to the Department of Defense, not S.H.I.E.L.D."

"But sir, this could—"

"Enough!" Weaver snapped. "Your so-called sources are a conspiracy blog that makes 'The X-Files' look like a BBC documentary series, and a phone call that could mean just about anything. You need to pull your head out of your... fantasy world and join the rest of us back in reality. We could churn out a dozen novels with the nonsense you keep bringing me. Now take your cult and your delusions and get out of my sight. You come to me with anything like this ever again, and it'll be the last time you work for us. Then you can go and fill out an application for the FBI. Maybe they've got an empty office in the basement, right next to Fox Mulder." With a dismissive wave, he ordered her out and reached for the phone.

When Akira had once again passed through security and was back at her bike, she'd made up her mind. She took her laptop out of her backpack and sat on the ground. It took her just two minutes to find the man she was looking for, a man she knew would appreciate what she'd discovered. A second later, she'd sent the information off.

CHAPTER 10
VOLKSGARTEN, VIENNA

"What was that? It sounded like . . ."

"Gunshots," Tom said, finishing Hellen's thought. "From the Volksgarten," he added, already running for the nearest entrance to the park. Hellen was close behind him. The sausage vendor shouted after them angrily.

In good weather, tourists and locals alike loved to stroll in the magnificent rose garden, and the weather today was excellent. Tom and Hellen stopped beside the fountain at the entrance and looked around. People were running in all directions.

"Over there, by the Temple! That's where he was meeting his contact," Hellen cried. Like Tom, she'd seen where the people were running from. To her left, behind a small stand of trees, stood the colonnaded temple, modeled after the Temple of Hephaestus in the heart of Athens. Tom, his gun in hand, grabbed a fleeing woman by the arm and stopped her.

"I'm with the police. What happened?" he said.

"Someone started shooting back there," said the woman, pointing toward the temple, then she jerked herself free and ran. Tom's eyes scanned the area, looking for anything out of place.

"Go and find van Rensburg. I'll be back," he said, pointing Hellen toward the temple. Then he ran off in a different direction.

"Tom! Where are you going?" Hellen shouted after him.

From the corner of his eye, Tom had spotted a woman in motorcycle leathers, heading south across the lawn. With a large black bag over her shoulder, she was making a beeline for Heldenplatz, in front of the Imperial Palace—walking calmly while everyone else was fleeing in panic. That had caught Tom's eye. But Hellen's shout had drawn her attention. She turned and spotted Tom, running straight across the park toward her. She broke into a run.

Why do I always have to be right? Tom thought. "Freeze!" he shouted. He stopped and tried to get a clear shot at the woman, but there were too many people running in between. Too dangerous. "Shit," he muttered, lowering his gun and taking up the chase. The woman had almost reached the side entrance. Tom thought about her options. If she went left, she'd run straight into the cops guarding the government buildings that way. He flashed back unpleasantly to the indescribable boredom that went with that particular job.

His mind raced. Where were the cops? Hadn't any of them heard the shots? Who was the woman and what did she want? A professional would have used a silencer. He only knew one thing with any certainty: he had to catch her before she reached her motorcycle, which she had presumably parked in the lot at Heldenplatz. Once she was on two wheels, he'd have no chance of stopping her.

The woman ran through the exit and into the cul-de-sac where one of Vienna's most popular dance clubs, also called the Volksgarten, was located. Just as she exited, a police car screeched to a halt directly in front of her, but the woman, barely breaking stride, whipped out a silenced pistol and fired several well-placed shots through the windshield. The two officers inside never had a chance.

"Fuck. Guess she's a pro after all," Tom said aloud, picking up his pace. The woman noticed more police closing on her from the direction of Heldenplatz. She turned right and ran down the middle of the street beside the park, heading for the Ring.

Tom made the turn right behind her and sprinted along the sidewalk in the same direction. A row of cars was all that separated them.

"Out of the way!" Tom cried, gesticulating wildly at passersby, trying to avoid running into anybody. He glanced to his left. He and the woman were neck and neck. Tom sprang onto the hood of one of the parked cars, darted over the roof, and leaped at the woman, his arms outstretched. They hit the pavement hard, and her pistol went skidding across the asphalt. The strap on her bag snapped. Tom managed to roll with the fall, but the woman was back on her feet just as quickly. She went for the bag, but Tom cut her off.

"Not so fast, sweetie," he said.

They stood and glared at each other, standing in the middle of the broad sidewalk and bicycle path that separated the Ring and the Volksgarten.

"Police! Hands in the air!" a voice suddenly snapped behind Tom. Then a bicycle bell let out a shrill ring as a cyclist tried to ride between Tom and the woman.

"Hey, assholes! It's a bike path!" the cyclist shouted. The woman suddenly jumped forward, knocking the man off his bike and into Tom, who stumbled back and landed on top of the cop behind him. The woman took off running again.

Tom got back to his feet and his eyes met the cop's.

"Wagner? Is that you?" It didn't matter where he was or what was happening: if someone mispronounced his family name —using the German "Vahgner," as the officer had—it stung.

"Yeah. Keep an eye on that bag," Tom snapped. He pointed to the large black bag, then jumped over the fallen cyclist and took up the chase. Two hundred yards later, just before the woman reached the arches of the Heldentor, he caught up. He was already reaching to grab her when she turned left to run through the Heldentor, probably to try and vanish among the tourists. But she didn't make it that far.

She turned the corner into the large archway, a *fiaker*, one of the horse-drawn carriages so beloved of tourists, was just rolling out, straight at her. The coachman saw her too late and hauled back on the reins. The woman screamed. The horses reared. Tom was able to dodge clear in time, but the woman was not as fortunate. A hoof struck her in the head, and she crashed to the ground.

"I didn't see 'er at all," the coachman stammered. He'd quickly managed to gain control of the frightened horses and prevent them from injuring the woman more or even dragging the carriage over her. He jumped down from the coach box in distress and ran to Tom.

"Call an ambulance," Tom said as he checked the woman's pulse. The horse had only knocked her out. Within moments, dozens of tourists were crowding the accident scene and taking photos.

"What happened?" said the officer Tom had collided with a minute before. Carrying the bag, he'd run after Tom.

"I know as much as you do," said Tom. "I heard shots in the Volksgarten and saw Catwoman here fleeing the scene."

Two more officers ran up. They pushed the spectators back to make space for the arriving paramedics.

"Let's see what our thief here was carrying," said Tom, reaching out for the bag in the officer's hands.

"Sorry, *Wagner*," the man said, deliberately mispronouncing Tom's name again. "You know how it is. The bag's evidence. I can't just hand it over to a civilian." The officer grinned broadly, and his words dripped sarcasm.

Tom glared at him. Then he turned away and ran back to check on Hellen.

CHAPTER 11
TEMPLE OF THESEUS, VOLKSGARTEN, VIENNA

Crouched out of sight behind a bush, Hellen was watching the temple entrance. She'd realized very quickly why Tom ran off without explanation: he was chasing a woman heading calmly for the exit, unlike everyone around her.

Had that woman been responsible for this chaos?

The area around the temple emptied rapidly, everyone running for their lives. Hellen ran quickly across the open area, then up the wheelchair ramp at the side of the temple. She darted through the row of columns and pressed close to the outer wall of the small chamber that the columns encircled. At one time, the chamber had housed a magnificent statue of Theseus sculpted by Italian artist Antonio Canova. The statue had moved to the Museum of Fine Arts in 1890, and today the small temple served as an exhibition hall for art projects.

Hellen crept slowly along the wall until she reached the corner, and peered around to the entrance. Nothing moved. There was no one in sight.

Tom was right again, she thought, ducking around the corner. At the entrance, she cast a quick, cautious glance inside. To her surprise, apart from an absurd and undefinable sculpture, the room was empty. What now? The temple only had the one entrance. She turned back and went down the stairs to the plaza. She stopped and looked around. There was no sign of van Rensburg at all.

Did he run away with everyone else? But if so, why hadn't he called?

An uneasy feeling came over her. As she looked around the surrounding gardens, she suddenly realized where she was standing. She looked down at the ground. During the Middle Ages, the city had been surrounded by a moat, and she was standing where it used to flow. Because of the moat, when they built the temple, they had had to dig exceptionally deep foundations.

Of course! The crypt! She spun around and looked to the west. The temple had once had a small annex where the trees and bushes fringing the edge of the plaza now grew. From inside the annex, you could descend to the crypt below. Today there was only a manhole cover concealing the entrance.

"Mr. van Rensburg!" Hellen cried when she found him. He was lying motionless in the bushes fifty yards from the temple, beside the open manhole. The opening revealed an iron staircase spiraling out of sight into the depths. She checked van Rensburg's pulse quickly—to her relief, he was still alive. An ugly head wound suggested that he'd been knocked down and was simply unconscious. A few feet away lay a second body: a man, face down. She grasped him by the shoulder and turned him over.

"Director Richter!" Hellen gasped, recoiling. Two gaping holes in his chest left no doubt—Richter had been shot to death.

"Hellen . . ." van Rensburg suddenly groaned, making her jump. Only now did she see the revolver in van Rensburg's hand. Her eyes widened.

"What happened?" Hellen said uncertainly. "Why are you holding a gun?" Van Rensburg let go of the pistol in shock—apparently, he was also seeing it for the first time.

"There was a woman . . . leather jacket, leather pants. She held us at gunpoint and bashed me over the head." His face twisted in pain, and he raised a hand to his head. "Where's Richter?" he asked.

Hellen looked at van Rensburg sadly. "He's dead. He's been shot," she said, and her eyes turned unavoidably toward the pistol beside van Rensburg. He followed her gaze.

"What? No way. It wasn't me. I've never seen that gun before in my life."

"It's okay. I believe you. But what were you even doing here with the director of the Museum of Fine Arts?"

Before van Rensburg could reply, they heard a shout. "Hellen? Where are you?" It was Tom.

Hellen stood up. "We're here," she called, waving him over.

"Holy shit. What happened here?"

"The woman you were following is probably behind this," Hellen said. "Did you catch her?"

"More or less," Tom said. "Long story."

"The bag," van Rensburg groaned.

"Yeah, sorry, that's suddenly become 'evidence.' One of the patrol cops has it and he won't hand it over."

"What was in the bag? And how was Richter involved?" Hellen asked.

"I don't know," van Rensburg said. "Richter called me in London, out of the blue. He asked me to meet him here. He sounded nervous as hell, almost panicking, saying something about a danger to all humanity. He wanted to give me some kind of container, but he couldn't tell me what was in it. Then that woman showed up, and I woke up here."

"Okay, this is all very exciting—but unless we want to spend the rest of the day talking to cops, we should beat it," said Tom. "Come on, help me get him up," he added, turning to Hellen.

Together, they got van Rensburg back on his feet. But just then, a barked order made them freeze.

"Nobody move. Hands in the air!"

Two masked Cobra officers, from the same unit Tom had worked for years ago, had them in their sights.

CHAPTER 12

IN FRONT OF THE TEMPLE OF THESEUS, VOLKSGARTEN, VIENNA

The Volksgarten was in an uproar. Countless uniformed cops, Cobra officers, and forensics specialists had overrun the temple. Barriers were being set up to keep the curious at a distance. Witness statements were being taken, and Tom, Hellen and van Rensburg sat on the temple steps in handcuffs, waiting to be questioned. The two Cobra men watched over them. A paramedic had treated van Rensburg's head wound, and a forensics specialist had swabbed their hands and clothes to see if any of them had fired a gun.

"You guys are really getting a kick out of this, aren't you? You finally got me in cuffs." Tom looked up to his former colleagues, one on each side, leering disparagingly back at him. "You've got your killer already. She's on her way to Vienna General Hospital."

"Tom, Tom, Tom. What have you been up to this time?" one of the Cobras said.

"Nothing," Tom said, a picture of innocence. "She got into a fight with a *fiaker*—and guess who won? If I'd caught her, we wouldn't be in this mess now and we'd be questioning her instead."

"Don't worry, Mr. Wagner," van Rensburg said. "My lawyers will have this sorted out soon enough."

"Let's start at the beginning," Hellen said. "How did you know Director Richter?"

"Until today, I didn't. But I'm not unknown in the art scene. He'd read an article about me, and he knew about my collection and my safe room at the house in South Africa. He also knew that you worked for me."

"Really?" Hellen said, more to herself than the others. She and Richter were not on particularly good terms. When Hellen had worked for Blue Shield, they'd locked horns more than once. And during the search for the Florentine Diamond, Richter had actually been shot by Isaac Hagen.

"But what exactly did he say before that woman showed up?" Tom asked.

"Not much. He was very nervous. Confused, even. I got the impression that something or someone had frightened him to death. We met here and Richter led me down into the crypt. And let me tell you—it wasn't what I'd expected. I knew the crypt used to be used for storage, but what's down there today..."

"What do you mean?"

"There's a modern, high security vault down there, with a retinal scanner. Inside it was a steel case, which is what the police have now. Then he started babbling about the Medusa cult. He said that people were watching him, that the case was no longer safe here. He asked me to take it to South Africa and keep it under lock and key down there. Under no circumstances could it be allowed to fall into the hands of the cult or anyone else. The fate of all humanity depended on it."

"The Medusa cult?" Tom asked. "Mean anything to you?" He looked curiously at Hellen. "Not that weird conspiracy theory that's been going around for the last few weeks?"

Hellen shook her head. "That doesn't sound like something Richter would have been involved with. He was a scientist. He'd never had anything to do with weird events tied to ancient artifacts."

"He didn't tell you what was in the box, did he?"

"No. He never got that far," van Rensburg answered.

Hellen's bewilderment grew. What could Richter have hidden away down there? He specialized in Greek mythology. There was nothing really tangible about the field at all, just a thousand wild stories. And apart from the new conspiracy theories, she'd never heard anything about a Medusa cult, although she was certainly familiar with the mythological Medusa, one of the Gorgons. Originally, she had been a woman of such exceptional beauty that she tempted even Poseidon—which hadn't pleased his niece, Pallas Athene, at all. So abracadabra, Pallas Athene transformed her into a monster with snakes for hair—the Medusa, whose very gaze would turn any mortal to stone. Later, the demigod Perseus had beheaded her.

A grating voice broke through Hellen's train of thought. "Well, well, who do we have here?"

Tom knew that voice only too well. Captain Maierhofer, head of the Cobra unit and Tom's former boss, was standing over them.

"Thomas. Maria. Wagner," said Maierhofer, looking down at him, and to Tom's surprise he used the correct pronunciation. The two Cobra officers smiled maliciously. They couldn't stand Tom, that much was obvious—and they weren't the only ones. None of the Cobras had ever thought much of the reckless lone wolf, even when he'd been part of their unit. The two looked on gleefully, expecting one of their boss's famous tirades. But to their surprise, it never came.

"Uncuff them," the captain instructed his men. Grim but confused, they did as ordered. "Not him," Maierhofer said when they went to unlock van Rensburg's cuffs.

"What? Why?" Hellen said.

"I'm sorry. Mr. van Rensburg's fingerprints are on the murder weapon, and there's gunshot residue on his hand and clothing. We can't ignore that. For now, he's to be detained, pending investigation."

"Call de Waal," van Rensburg said. "He'll inform my lawyers."

Hellen nodded. "Don't worry. We'll find out what's going on here." She turned to Tom and added, "Won't we?"

Tom looked first at Hellen, then at Maierhofer. He swallowed. "We will. Don't worry."

CHAPTER 13

MI6 HEADQUARTERS, LONDON, ENGLAND

In his undercover years among the Absolute Freedom terrorists, Isaac Hagen had had to do a lot of dangerous and despicable things. On his last mission in the field, when his cover had finally been blown, he'd assassinated AF's leader, Edward de Mey, from just over a mile away—an incredible shot with a sniper rifle. Very few people knew this.

Hagen had joined the military straight out of school, and a short time later had been recruited by the SAS and completed his training as a sniper. A few years and countless secret missions later, the Secret Intelligence Service—better known as MI6—recruited him. He'd spent the last five years infiltrating AF for them.

Now that the organization had been dismantled, he was able—or was forced—to be himself again and lead a normal life. It was a task he found far from straightforward. With his invaluable insider knowledge of AF, its members and tactics, he'd been assigned to head a special task force, a collaboration between MI6 and the CIA. The task force's job was to track down AF adherents and accomplices around the world and bring them to justice.

From one day to the next, his once-exciting life had been

replaced by a boring desk job. The last twelve months had been longer and more arduous than all the years before, when he'd lived in constant fear of being discovered. He longed for nothing more than another exciting mission, a shootout, a few explosions . . . anything that would provide a solid hit of adrenalin.

He stood up from his desk, crossed to the window, loosened his tie, and looked out thoughtfully over the city. Broad, dirty, reeking, the Thames flowed through London, directly past the building that housed his office.

"Mr. Hagen," said a young man, dragging him from his thoughts.

"What is it?" he said without turning around.

"We've had an anonymous tip, sir. I'm not sure if someone is having us on or if there's really something to it." The young man was standing in his office doorway, holding a red folder in one hand.

"What makes you think I can judge that any better? You're the analyst, right?" Hagen said, unable to keep the frustration and boredom out of his voice.

"For one thing, it's addressed to you personally. Also, you're the only one here with any first-hand experience with things like this. It's all just hocus-pocus to me," the young man replied.

That got Hagen's attention. He turned around. He'd certainly seen enough hocus-pocus in his undercover years. One of AF's principal directives had been to obtain mythical artifacts for their absurd crusade and to utilize them however they could. "Show me what you've got," he said.

The young man stepped up to Hagen's desk and handed him the file, and Hagen looked through the pages carefully. The analyst stood silently and waited for a reaction from his boss, but nothing came. "See what I mean?" the young man finally prompted. "Crazy, right?"

After a few minutes and with no discernible reaction, Hagen looked up from the pages. "Thank you," he said. "I'll attend to this personally." He patted the file and dismissed the man with a wave.

The young man was taken aback but decided not to say anything. He turned and left the office.

"Close the door behind you," Hagen called after him. Then he opened the file and went through it again. He smiled. This was just what he needed. A mission only he could take on. But he could use a little help.

He pressed a button on his intercom.

"Yes, sir," his assistant's voice came back.

"Prepare the jet. I'm flying to Vienna immediately," Hagen said. He rolled down his sleeves, pulled on his jacket, and marched out with the file under his arm.

CHAPTER 14

VIENNA GENERAL HOSPITAL

"Tell me one thing, Wagner," Maierhofer began. "Why are you always making such a godawful mess?"

Tom and his former boss were standing outside the hospital room of the unknown woman whom Tom had chased through the Volksgarten. The horse's hoof had left a deep gash on her head, and she'd been unconscious ever since. The doctors could say nothing about when—or even if—she would wake up.

"As if I'm the only one making a mess," said Tom. "Last time we were here, *you* got thrown through one of these glass walls." Tom rapped his knuckles against the large glass pane beside them.

"I remember just fine, thank you. But even that was because of one of *your* 'adventures,' indirectly. And I was lucky the guy didn't kill me."

Tom smiled sheepishly. "But you did save Hellen's mother's life in the process. And from what I saw on the surveillance video, you held your own pretty well. But why isn't this woman over in the secure wing?"

"After those two hijackers you caught that time were assassinated despite the tight security, and after the attempt on Theresia's life, they decided to renovate the wing. While they're bringing it up to the latest standards, we have to improvise. She's here in intensive care because we can keep an eye on her here better than anywhere else. I've got one of my people watching her around the clock. They'll inform me the minute she comes around and we can question her."

"Do we know who she is?"

"Not yet. But we've made inquiries with Interpol and the FBI. And the DSN is asking around the secret services, Mossad in particular."

"You know that van Rensburg didn't kill Richter, right? It was this bitch," Tom said, nodding in the woman's direction.

"You may be right. But van Rensburg was found with the murder weapon in his hand. We can't ignore that. All indications are that he pulled the trigger."

Tom shook his head vehemently and tapped his index finger on the glass.

"She did it! She set the whole thing up." Tom paced back and forth. "I've been asking myself all along why a professional like her didn't use a silencer. Now I know. It's because she *wanted* the shots to be heard. She wanted van Rensburg to be found with the gun in his hand. She just didn't count on me showing up."

"Be that as it may, the district attorney practically started drooling when he heard about it. This is the kind of case that could make his career. He's fixed things to keep van Rensburg in custody pending trial. A man with his resources is a serious flight risk."

"Who did the DA put on the case?" Tom asked.

"A guy named Messner, from the homicide division," Maierhofer said. Tom stopped pacing and looked at Maierhofer.

"Shit. He and I butted heads once on a mission. He's a world-class asshole, and he loves to see his picture in the paper. I'll bet he's drooling, too. I won't get anything out of him."

"Why does that not surprise me?" Maierhofer, smiling, shook his head.

"Then you'll have to help." Tom looked Maierhofer in the eye. "Can you get me Richter's phone records? Including the ones from his office? Then we can see for ourselves who he's been in touch with the last few days."

Maierhofer snorted. "Wagner, I've got a really bad feeling about this. Every time you start sniffing around, things tend to blow up."

"No explosions, cross my heart." Tom placed his left hand on the right side of his chest and grinned at Maierhofer, who glared back. Tom looked down. "Oops, got it bass-ackwards." He smiled and quickly laid his right hand on the left side. Even Maierhofer had to grin.

"No explosions? Are those words coming out of your mouth? Impossible. Wagner, you're an idiot, but you deliver results, though I'm still very, very happy you no longer work for *me*." He shook Tom's hand. "Okay. I'll send you the phone records as soon as I can."

"Thank you," Tom said, pushing open the doors to intensive care. "And call me when the bomb-squad guys examine that case. We have to find out what's inside." With that, he was gone.

CHAPTER 15

MUSEUM OF FINE ARTS, VIENNA

Nobody responded when she knocked, so Hellen cautiously opened the door to Richter's office and slipped inside. His secretary, Mrs. Gabi, was not at her desk. *And why would she be?* Hellen thought. Richter won't be coming to work today. And besides, the woman must be devastated . . . if she even knew.

Mrs. Gabi had treated Richter as if he were her son. Hellen remembered the somewhat overweight woman well. She was nearing sixty now, a real old-school secretary. Mrs. Gabi liked Hellen, too, even though her boss hadn't. Hellen and Richter had seldom agreed about anything, and when he'd been appointed to run the Albertina on top of his other duties about three years earlier, they had crossed swords for the last time. For a moment, Hellen paused. Right there, at the opening of her Habsburg exhibition five years earlier, was where she'd first met Tom. She and Richter had fought, as they often had, and she had stormed furiously out of his office and straight into Tom's arms. Although she hadn't particularly liked Richter, she had always respected his knowledge and his academic success. It made her sad. No one deserved to die like that.

She entered the director's office and looked around. She had marched out of that same office several times over the years, always with the words "I quit"—an empty threat, until the day she'd met Tom. Now, she moved around to the other side of the antique desk and sat down. At first glance, she saw nothing out of the ordinary. A few files, a picture of his deceased wife, stationery, his computer. Nothing was disturbed or seemed to be missing. Hellen slid out a drawer and rummaged through its contents. Nothing.

"What the devil is—" Richter's office door flew open, and his secretary stalled in mid-sentence. "Dr. de Mey?" She looked at Hellen in surprise. "What are you doing here?"

"Mrs. Gabi, I'm so terribly sorry," Hellen began.

"Sorry for what? For waltzing in here like this, or that I caught you red-handed?"

Hellen gulped. So she hadn't yet heard about Richter's death...

"Mrs. Gabi, I think you need to sit down," Hellen said. She hurried over to the woman and guided her out to the reception area.

"What do you mean? What's happened?" the older woman said, sitting at her desk.

"I have some bad news," Hellen said, crouching in front of the elderly woman. "Director Richter was murdered today in the Volksgarten."

Mrs. Gabi stared at Hellen. There was silence for a moment.

"What are you saying? I mean . . . no, that's . . ." A sob escaped her, and her eyes filled with tears. Hellen fished a handkerchief out of her handbag and gave it to her. "What . . . it can't be. I just spoke to him on the phone this morning." She blew her nose. "That's why I came in on Sunday, because I thought he might need my help." She paused. "And honestly, I was bored at home." For a moment, a tender smile appeared on both women's faces.

"I'm so sorry. I know how much he meant to you," Hellen said.

"Thank you, my dear," Mrs. Gabi said, and she patted Hellen's shoulder softly. "Is that why you're here?"

"Yes. My husband and I want to find out why he was killed."

"How can I help?" Mrs. Gabi wiped her nose again and squared her shoulders resolutely.

"We have to find out what he did in the last few days, and who he met."

Mrs. Gabi quickly called up the director's appointments on her computer.

"The only thing in his calendar is the congress at the Academy of Sciences in Prague. He's not even supposed to be in Vienna," she said. "Which is why I was so confused when he called me this morning."

"What did he want from you?" Hellen asked.

"A telephone number for a Mr. van Rensburg. He said something had happened in Prague and he had to return to Vienna immediately."

No more than we already know, Hellen thought. Then she had an idea. Tom would kill her if she did it alone, but time was short.

"I know this is a strange request, but do you perhaps have a key for Director Richter's house? Maybe I can find a clue about what happened there."

Mrs. Gabi nodded. She trusted Hellen and had always liked her, and it had saddened her when Hellen finally resigned. She picked up her handbag. "I do. I go over and water his flowers whenever he goes away. Since his wife died, I've been looking after him a little." She took a bunch of keys out of her handbag and passed them to Hellen. "Please find out who did this."

Ten minutes later, when Hellen was sure that the older woman was going to be all right, she was back in her car and tapping Richter's home address into the GPS.

CHAPTER 16

FRANÇOIS CLOUTARD'S HOME, TABARKA FORTRESS, TUNISIA

"Merde. I am *so* out of practice!" Cloutard swore, flinging his crème brûlée torch angrily across the kitchen.

With rolled-up shirtsleeves and a chef's apron, he stood in his enormous kitchen in the basement of Tabarka Fortress, which he'd claimed as a prize many years earlier in a dangerous deal involving Libyan freedom fighters battling Muammar Gaddafi. At the time, Cloutard had supplied the rebels with the cash they needed—money that his own grave-robbing associates had stolen from the Gaddafi family. Cloutard had taken a mischievous pleasure in knowing that Gaddafi had unwittingly financed the rebellion against him. Though the rebellion—sadly—had ultimately failed, Cloutard had managed to hold onto Tabarka. And while he had no idea how the Libyan rebels had got their hands on a Tunisian fortress, he had no real interest today in finding out.

The Gaddafi raids had also brought in enough money to allow him to renovate the neglected fortress, and he had transformed it into a veritable palace. When he had lost the property in the battle with AF, in the person of Ossana Ibori, it had hit him hard. But now he had his medieval fortress back, a fact that had been celebrated properly with Tom and Hellen's wedding.

In the past, Cloutard had regularly thrown lavish banquets, and had played host to some very illustrious guests indeed. Cloutard had never differentiated: art thieves and Mafia bosses, Catholic cardinals and Persian mullahs, counterfeiters, smugglers, double agents from all the world's intelligence services . . . all kinds of people had had the opportunity to savor Cloutard's exquisite culinary skills within the walls of Tabarka. Of course, in the past he'd had a great deal of support in the kitchen. His role had been more that of a little Napoleon, ordering his kitchen staff around.

Today, his guests were his erstwhile accomplices and friends of many years, Fabio and Adalgisa. For such a small party, he had assumed he would be able to conjure a five-course meal easily—and most importantly, unaided.

And until he came to dessert, everything had gone admirably. They had started with soup: Cloutard's famous *consommé double* with a garnish *royale*. This was followed by an hors d'oeuvre of truffled quail eggs, an entrée of *Blanquette de la mer* with fresh North Sea redfish and ling, and an exceptional entrecôte with red cabbage and mushroom polenta for the main course.

Everything had been going smoothly, with Fabio and Adalgisa heaping praise on Cloutard's talents in the kitchen, as the Frenchman was used to. But the *crème brûlée* was a fiasco. Cursing loudly, Cloutard stomped across the kitchen. He sighed as he opened the walk-in refrigerator in search of an adequate alternative.

"What's going on down there, old friend?" he heard Fabio ask as he battled his way through the countless varieties of ice cream he had flown in as needed from the Italian gelateria Venchi—a poor substitute for his planned *crème brûlée*, certainly, but sometimes one had to compromise.

"Nothing, nothing," Cloutard sighed, his breath sending little white clouds of condensation drifting through the refrigerator. "The *crème brûlée* is not what I had hoped it would be. We will have to make do with gelato."

Cloutard stacked up a pile of ice cream boxes and balanced them back into the kitchen.

"You seem a little preoccupied, François. Did that Caribbean affair leave its mark? I heard it was not an easy job. They beat you up rather badly, I heard. And at your age..."

"Where did you hear that?" Cloutard snapped at his friend, more vehemently than intended, and then immediately backpedaled. "*Excuse-moi*, I did not mean to shout, but I had to put up with the same slander from Tom and Hellen, too. I am not some doddering old man. What should I do, shuffle off to a retirement village, where I can spend my days cheating at bingo?"

Fabio raised his hands placatingly. "It's all right, François. I was only asking. I would be happy to do a job with you at the Louvre tomorrow."

Cloutard paused and looked at his friend. "That would certainly be a welcome change of pace. Fun, too," he said with a grin as he filled bowls artfully with the ice cream and decorated them with fruit, whipped cream, and chocolate sprinkles. "*Pas si mal, n'est-ce pas? That does not look too bad, does it?*" he murmured.

"But I'm afraid the Louvre will have to wait, Cloutard. I have to—"

Fabio stopped talking in mid-sentence. He had to take a few deep breaths before he went on. Cloutard was so involved in his ice cream creations that he did not realize how much his old friend was struggling.

"Adalgisa and I...uh...last week, we..."

"What are you stuttering about? *Parle déjà!* Out with it, man!"

"We saw Kendra," Fabio finally whispered.

The ice cream scoop fell from Cloutard's hand and a ball of stracciatella fell with a splat onto the kitchen floor. He gazed at it for a long time, as if waiting for it to melt. Then he looked up at Fabio.

"And?" His voice was decidedly cold, hurt, distanced. "Why are you telling me this? That topic is dead to me." He glared at Fabio, who didn't really know what he was supposed to say.

"But she is . . ." he stammered.

"What?" Cloutard's voice was loud, now. "What is she?"

"What the hell *is* this?" Adalgisa cried, and Cloutard fell silent. The tension filling the air was becoming too much for her.

"Oh, it is nothing," Cloutard finally said, turning back to his ice cream creations.

Fabio frowned and shrugged.

"Then everything is fine," Adalgisa said. But Cloutard could hear that she didn't believe him for a second. "But I have one question . . ." She was standing beside Cloutard now, and she held out an old leather-bound diary for him to see. "Where did you get this?"

Cloutard gave the book a quick glance and grinned. "I spirited that one out of Egypt. It was in the Nazi bunker beneath that pyramid, the one they used as a headquarters for their Egyptian campaign. You remember, when we were searching for the Holy Grail. Why?"

"It contains a few interesting things that might just be connected to the Medusa cult everyone's talking about."

Cloutard raised his eyebrows in astonishment. His interest had been piqued.

"Then let us take a look," he said, as he began flipping the pages.

CHAPTER 17
TOM AND HELLEN'S HOUSEBOAT, DANUBE RIVER, VIENNA

"A new video about the strange Medusa cult is making headlines. Posted online by a secretive group of conspiracy bloggers, the video has accumulated more than a billion views worldwide so far. The group, which first appeared on social media platforms just few weeks ago, has been dominating headlines around the world. Their absurd assertions that a global 'Medusa' cult is trying to take over the world have been met with no more than a weary smile from government officials. 'The whole thing is just a well-made show with no substance behind it,' the White House Press Secretary said at today's briefing. An FBI spokesperson added, 'There is absolutely no evidence of the existence of such a cult.'

"The calls for increased Internet regulation are also growing louder. 'We cannot let fake news and conspiracies spread unchecked. The Internet needs to be regulated once and for all.' Such statements have sparked renewed debates about freedom of expression, data protection, and national security, and have already led to demonstrations and unrest in country after country. Despite official assurances, the videos appearing in recent weeks have caused fear and panic around the world, and demonstrations have repeatedly turned violent."

Tom stared at the screen in disbelief. *Has the world gone completely crazy?* he thought. After leaving Maierhofer at Vienna General, he'd returned to the houseboat. Hellen hadn't yet returned from the museum, so he'd made himself comfortable on the sofa, grabbed his laptop, and was catching up on CNN and their coverage of the Medusa cult. *The world really isn't going to put up with all this social media bullshit much longer*, he thought.

The world had obviously stopped making sense for CNN's anchorman, too. The studio had gone to a reporter interviewing demonstrators on the streets of Washington.

"It's about time someone new took over," said one demonstrator. "We stopped trusting politicians a long time ago."

"You know, with everything going on in the last few years, QAnon, fake news and stuff like that, nothing surprises me anymore," said another.

"People are afraid!" barked a third. "And the politicians are up there laughing about it and plotting to take away our freedom of speech. If things go on like this, it's gonna look like China here soon."

Tom heard the Mustang's engine before it arrived, and he clapped the laptop closed. A moment later, Hellen opened the door. She put her handbag aside, went to Tom, gave him a kiss, and sat beside him on the sofa.

"So how was your trip to your old stomping grounds? Find anything?" Tom asked, already eying the papers in Hellen's hands.

"Richter's secretary couldn't tell me much, so I . . ." Hellen hesitated. "I went to his house."

"What?" Tom yelped. "Why didn't you call me? We don't know the first thing about what's going on, and you went to the victim's house? Alone? What if someone had been waiting there?" Tom scolded. Smiling broadly and rolling her eyes, Hellen let Tom's tirade run its course.

"You're right about someone being there. If you hadn't interrupted me, then I would have told you that a guy from the homicide division, Detective Messner, was already there with his people."

"Great. Another fan. Another dead end, I suppose," Tom said.

"You don't put a lot of trust in your other half, do you? Look at me. No man can resist these charms, certainly not a guy like Messner." Hellen looked sternly at Tom, but she was also smiling. His annoyance evaporated.

"That's my girl," he said, smiling back. "So, what did you turn up?"

"I'm not sure yet. First, I found a check for fifty thousand euros from an account in the name of Apostolos Ibis. Naturally, I checked the name, but Google found approximately nothing. A few things about 'Apostolos' and plenty about 'Ibis,' of course, but nothing at all about a man by that name. Isn't it strange that someone could manage to get the all-seeing eye of the Internet to overlook them?"

Tom nodded. "And who would pay a museum director so much money? More importantly: why?"

"I was wondering the same. It was far too much for a lecture or presentation. But that's not the interesting part. On his desk, beside the check, was a picture of an old Greek amphora. And it had a seal I've only ever seen once before—on the Alexander mosaic they found in Pompeii, which is now on display at the National Archaeological Museum of Naples. But I don't know how a Roman mosaic is connected to a Greek amphora, or why anyone would get killed for it. I'm going to have to do a little research on that. What did you find out at the hospital?"

"Not much. The woman's still out cold and neither Interpol nor the FBI know who she is. At least, not yet."

"The only lead we have points to Prague," said Hellen.

"Prague?" Tom said. But suddenly, there was a knock at the houseboat door. Tom and Hellen turned around. The door opened a crack, and they found themselves staring in disbelief at the face of Isaac Hagen. He was holding a red folder.

"I hope this isn't an awkward time, but I need your help."

"We really need to put a lock on that door," Tom said with a grin.

CHAPTER 18

BOMB DISPOSAL UNIT, COBRA HQ, SOUTHERN VIENNA

As if he were handling a raw egg, but also with the ease of long experience, Peter Steiner lifted the sealed steel case out of the cargo bay of the explosives transport van. He and his young colleague, Lucas Harrer, made up one of nine teams that comprised the Cobra's bomb disposal unit.

"You can relax," Steiner said to his young colleague, who had just turned twenty-five. He stood wide-eyed beside Steiner, not sure if he could do anything to help. He closed the van door a little too hard and pulled over the pushcart they'd brought out earlier. "The bomb-sniffing dogs didn't turn up anything at the site and we've found no explosive residues, so we're pretty sure it's not a bomb," Steiner said, and he saw his colleague's expression relax.

"But we still can't rule out it being some kind of chemical or biological agent, can we?" Lucas piped up.

Steiner smiled and shook his head. "No, we can't. And because it looks as if there's some kind of liquid inside, this is where you come in. As our new biological and chemical expert, you get to examine this thing."

Steiner set the steel case on top of the cart and rolled it

slowly toward the entrance to the laboratory wing. Lucas followed close behind. "Did I hear right?" he asked.

"About what?" said Steiner, using a keycard to unlock the secure door. Lucas held it open, and Steiner rolled the cart through.

"I mean, that he's back. And that he's mixed up in all this?" Lucas said, almost whispering.

"You mean Wagner?"

The younger man nodded. Steiner laughed. "You can say his name, you know. He's not Lord Voldemort."

"It's just, you hear all kinds of freaky stories about Tom Wagner. Is it true he foiled a hijacking in mid-air, unarmed, with just a food trolley? And that he found the Florentine Diamond? And they say he flew a float plane into Barcelona and—"

Steiner had stopped and was about to interrupt the young man's fanboy rhapsodizing, but the harsh voice of Captain Maierhofer beat him to it. The two officers spun around.

"It's all true," Maierhofer said. "He also destroyed the Treasury, endangered hundreds of people by racing through a pedestrian zone in his Mustang, and crashed into St. Stephen's Cathedral. On top of which, he constantly—"

"Yeah, yeah, I know. He constantly defied your orders," Lucas said peevishly.

Captain Maierhofer's face turned an unnerving shade of crimson. Steiner's mouth fell open. Had his young colleague actually interrupted the head of Cobra? Steiner knew there had only ever been one person who could make turn Maierhofer's face turn crimson and make the veins in his forehead bulge like that: Tom Wagner. But it seemed Lucas shared that particular talent.

"Respect was never your strong suit," said Maierhofer. "When we're at work, it's Captain to you, too."

"Yes, Dad. Sorry, Captain," Lucas said, snapping to attention.

Well, that explains a few things, Steiner thought.

"Well, then. Let's see what Voldemort's brought us this time," Maierhofer said, and he smiled at his son. His face had returned to its usual hue.

Steiner swiped his keycard again and all three entered the special lab.

In the center of the lab was another room, or rather a circular steel chamber. About ten feet in diameter, the bulky, windowless object resembled nothing more than an antique vault. There was a large wheel on the door that kept it airtight. Lucas turned the wheel and pulled the heavy door open. Steiner lifted the sealed box from the pushcart, carried it carefully into the chamber, and set it on the table in the center. Then he rejoined Maierhofer and Lucas outside. As well as a special exhaust and filtration system, a sprinkler system, a built-in fire-extinguishing system, and a liquid nitrogen supply to instantly shock-freeze practically any material, the chamber also contained the usual bomb-defusing equipment and the tools needed to carry out biological and chemical tests.

"She's all yours," said Steiner.

Nervous, Lucas pulled on his Level A hazmat suit. It was his first day on the job, and he was being plunged in at the deep end of the pool. Maierhofer checked the suit's seals, then looked at his son through the large window on the front of the hood.

"You're here not because you're my son, but because you were the best-qualified applicant. You've got this. It's a piece of cake," Maierhofer said, and he clapped his son on the shoulder.

"Our first step is to make a few images with the digital X-ray," Steiner added.

81

Lucas gave them a thumbs up and stepped into the room. Maierhofer closed the steel door behind his son, swung the wheel to seal it, then joined Steiner at the computer monitors. Cameras installed inside the chamber let them watch what was happening on the displays.

"Can you hear us?" said Steiner, pressing and holding a small button on the microphone stand in front of him.

"Loud and clear," Lucas replied.

They watched as Lucas connected his suit to an external oxygen system and pulled over the articulated arm that held the X-ray camera. On a computer, he activated the digital X-ray feed, then he brought the arm into position.

The first image appeared in black-and-white on a display. Inside the modern steel case was a container. It looked to be sealed and was probably embedded in foam. It looked much older than the case and appeared to be made of glass surrounded by some kind of metallic cage.

"What the devil . . . ?" said Maierhofer. Like Steiner, he was staring in bewilderment at the monitor. But it wasn't the jar-like container that surprised them.

"What *is* that?" Steiner said, pointing to the countless fine lines that extended like the teeth of a comb away from numerous thicker lines.

Steiner pressed the intercom button again. "Give us a different angle."

The image vanished briefly but reappeared a moment later, as Lucas repositioned the X-ray.

They could see the outlines of the cage—probably made from some kind of lead alloy, because the X-rays couldn't penetrate it at all. In between, they saw more of the comb-like structures. Steiner and Maierhofer leaned back in unison.

"Holy shit," they heard Lucas say over the speaker. "Definitely not a bomb."

"I hope we're recording this?" said Maierhofer. Steiner nodded.

"Are those . . ." Steiner stammered, looking at Maierhofer.

"Are you seeing this? I'm going to boost the power," Lucas said.

A shudder ran through all three as the background became clearer.

"What the hell is that?" Lucas's voice buzzed through the intercom.

"That, my boy, looks to me like a shit-ton of trouble."

CHAPTER 19

TOM AND HELLEN'S HOUSEBOAT, DANUBE RIVER, VIENNA

"He doesn't write, he doesn't call, and after a year of radio silence he shows up on our doorstep, asking for our help." Arms folded, a glowering Tom was on his feet and standing face to face with Hagen at the door. "What do you think, sweetheart? Do we have a few minutes to help out James Bond Lite here?"

"Bad timing, I'm afraid," Hellen began, ignoring Tom's half-hearted attempt at humor. "We're up to our necks in a murder investigation."

"Hellen's right. It's the worst possible timing, actually. Our boss, Eon van Rensburg, is sitting in jail because some crazy femme fatale killer is trying to pin a murder on him. But come in, we can find time for a drink, at least." Tom shook Hagen's hand and closed the door behind him.

Caught a little off guard, Hagen lowered the file. "Sure, no worries. No, this can wait. Anything I can do to help you?"

"Can I talk to you for a minute?" Hellen said to Tom. She threw the papers on the coffee table, went to the terrace door, and pulled it open.

"'Scuse me a minute," Tom apologized to Hagen. He followed Hellen outside.

"I thought we were done with AF, and everything connected to it. We don't have time for this. Van Rensburg needs our help."

"I know, but it can't hurt to hear what it's about. And if he wants to help . . . the guy has contacts we can only dream about."

"Look, I know the two of you are cut from the same cloth, and you know better than I what a man who spent years undercover had to go through . . . but I don't trust him. He tried to kill us a dozen times!"

"But he failed," said Tom. Hellen scowled at him. Tom took her in his arms, and she let him.

"Okay, if he wants to help, he can help," she said.

"And after that, we'll listen to what he has to say," said Tom. "We can still decide if we can help him or not. Sound good?"

Hellen nodded and they went back inside.

"Sorry about that, we had to figure out tomorrow's shopping list. Always the same debate, steak or tofu. You know how it is."

Hagen smiled.

"Sorry, Isaac. This is really important," Hellen said, finally shaking his hand. "But if you help us, maybe we can solve it faster. Then we'll see what we can do for you." Hagen nodded. He put his file aside and listened attentively. "Well, as I was about to say earlier, Richter was in Prague," Hellen said. "He was attending a symposium on Greek history and was originally supposed to return in a few days. But something brought him back earlier. He called his assistant unexpectedly and asked her to find van Rensburg's phone number."

"Five hours later, he was dead," Tom said.

"And we're running out of ideas," said Hellen.

"Would it help to know exactly where he was in Prague?" Hagen asked.

Hellen and Tom looked at each other, then turned to Hagen and nodded.

"Okay. Let me make a few calls."

It took him less than ten minutes to get what he wanted. "The GPS data from his mobile phone shows that he drove to the Four Seasons Hotel late in the evening, and that he returned to Vienna right after that. He didn't even check out at his hotel, The Mozart."

Just then, Tom's phone rang. The conversation lasted only a minute.

"That was Maierhofer. The bomb boys are ready to open the container the Killer Queen tried to steal. Looks like it isn't a bomb."

"Fantastic," said Hellen. "Then at least we'll know what this is really all about."

CHAPTER 20
BOMB DISPOSAL UNIT, COBRA HQ

Tom's Dodge Challenger screeched to a halt in the parking lot at Cobra headquarters. The car had belonged to his uncle, Admiral Scott Wagner, and Tom had had it shipped at great expense from Washington, D.C. to Vienna. He still had his 1967 Ford Mustang Shelby GT500 as well, and the two cars were his pride and joy. But since Hellen had claimed the Mustang for herself, he'd had to make do with the Dodge.

Cobra headquarters consisted of several low buildings arranged in a U-shape in the middle of a densely forested park, impossible to see into from outside. Tom got out of the car, closed the door, and looked across at the building. It had been almost three years since he'd last been here.

Hellen came around beside Tom and looked up at him. "Do you miss it?" she asked.

"Not really. I never really fit in here. I was always the outsider. If Noah hadn't . . ." Tom's voice faltered as he thought of the man he'd called his best friend and partner back then, but who had eventually betrayed them and been responsible for his uncle's death. "Without him there, I probably would have thrown in the towel a lot sooner."

Hellen heard the pain in Tom's voice. She took his hand in hers and squeezed softly.

Hagen had also climbed out and joined them.

"Nice setup. So this is where the snakes train," Hagen said. Tom and Hellen looked at him curiously, and Hagen laughed. "Just a nickname we gave you guys at MI6."

Just then, Captain Maierhofer appeared from inside one of the smaller buildings.

"Thanks for getting here so fast," Maierhofer said, his hand outstretched toward Tom as he approached. "I see you've brought reinforcements." He shook Tom's and Hellen's hands, but his eyes were fixed on Hagen. "What brings MI6 to Vienna?" he said, turning to face the Briton.

Hagen said nothing, but the corners of his mouth twitched upward as the two men shook hands.

"Understood," said Maierhofer with a sly smile. He turned and marched back toward the small building. "You're just in time. We've started trying to open the metal box, but it's proving to be stubborn," he explained as he led them to the special lab.

"What did the X-rays show?" Hellen asked.

"You'll have to see for yourself. If I told you, you wouldn't believe me." He held his keycard against the reader and opened the door to the lab.

"You know Steiner," Maierhofer began, when they were all inside. Tom and Steiner nodded to one another. "And in there is my son, Lucas. He joined our little gang recently, straight out of college." Maierhofer proudly indicated the secure chamber in the center of the room, then pointed at one of the displays, which showed a man in a hazmat suit.

"I didn't know you had a son," Tom said.

"He lives with his mother. Long story," Maierhofer replied, and Tom saw a trace of regret on his old boss's face. *So there's a heart in there after all*, he thought. His relationship with Maierhofer had improved considerably in the last year or so. Tom and Hellen had even invited him to their wedding.

"Can I see the images?" Hellen said, turning to Steiner. He nodded and pulled up a file, and Tom, Hellen and Hagen peered at the monitor.

"Are those . . .?" Hellen asked, pointing at the finer and thicker lines. They looked like spines and ribs.

"Yes. Snakes. But that's not the strangest part." Steiner opened the next file. "Look at this."

Hellen drew a sharp breath.

"It's impossible. That's nothing but a myth," she murmured to herself.

Tom knew that face. "What is it?" he asked, but Hellen ignored him, her eyes scanning the video recording intently.

On the display, behind the skeletons of the numerous small snakes, was the faint outline of a human skull. No one said a word. The only sound was the cooling fans in the computers and other equipment, filling the room with a low, monotonous hum.

"I've got it!" Lucas suddenly exclaimed, breaking the tense silence. Tom, Hellen, and Hagen instinctively turned, but they saw only the huge, windowless chamber.

"On screen," Steiner said with a smile, tapping a monitor. They turned back and watched the activity inside the chamber. Lucas was carefully lifting the lid clear of the steel box.

"Woohoo!" he whooped through the intercom. This was followed by a clang and a scraping noise. Lucas had stumbled back in shock, dropping the lid and banging into a small table on the side.

"All good," he said. "No damage. You won't believe what's inside."

Outside, everyone was transfixed by what was

happening on the monitor. Lucas stepped up to the table again and carefully lifted the glass jar, reinforced with metal ribs, out of the case and set it on the table. As he stepped aside and the camera could get a clear image of the jar, Hellen gasped out loud. She and Tom were cheek to cheek, staring at the screen.

"That . . . that's . . ." Hellen stammered, pointing at the screen with a trembling hand. She looked at Tom. He knew as well as she did what it looked like.

"You want to tell us that's the head of Medusa? Like, Greek mythology Medusa? But that's

. . ." Tom stopped in mid-sentence and shook his head.

Surrounded by small snakes, a gruesome female head, severed roughly at the neck, sat in a cloudy liquid. Its eyes were closed, and the skin on its face hung slack.

"Look at it. What else can it be?"

"The sick artwork of a serial killer?" Steiner suggested.

"*The* Medusa?" Tom paced back and forth behind Hellen. "Turn-you-to-fucking-stone-if-you-look-her-in-the-eye Medusa?"

Hellen shrugged and nodded.

Hagen, standing a short way behind the others, had turned pale.

"This takes bizarre to a new level," Tom said. "But okay. The Medusa's real."

Maierhofer and Steiner shared a look. Hagen stood and watched things unfold.

"It's impossible," Maierhofer said. "The head of Medusa —it's bullshit. It's an ancient Greek bedtime story, that's all."

"That's what we thought about the Nordic sagas, and then we found Siegfried's sword and the cloak of invisibility," Hellen said. "We might have the Internet and Google Maps, but the world is a big place. There's still so much out there we don't know about, let alone comprehend."

"I still think Steiner's serial killer theory's more plausible."

"You really think Richter was a serial killer? And what, that van Rensburg was his accomplice?" Tom said.

"Of course not," said Maierhofer.

"Hey guys, I think the jar is going to be easier to open than the box," Lucas said, interrupting. He was already going to work on the lid. "I've nearly got it."

Hellen stared at the screen and her eyes widened. "No! Don't! Stop!" she screamed.

CHAPTER 21
BOMB DISPOSAL UNIT, COBRA HQ

"The button! You have to press the button," said Steiner, holding down the talk button.

"Lucas, don't! Stop! The eyes!" Hellen yelled, and she looked in dismay at Tom and Hagen.

Tom, gripped by the live-feed monitor, saw the eyes of the severed head begin to move beneath the closed eyelids.

"No sweat, I'll have it in just a second," Lucas said excitedly. "Then we can take a closer look at this thing, and I can do a few tests."

"Lucas, don't!" his father's powerful voice rang out.

Hellen jumped up and ran to the secure room and began turning the wheel to unlock the sealed door. Hagen and Steinerran to help her.

"We have to stop him. He mustn't take the head out of that liquid," Hellen cried.

Maierhofer stared at the monitor. Lucas had managed to open the lid of the large jar and was already reaching inside.

"Where's the fucking talk-button?" Maierhofer growled. "Lucas, no! Wait!"

Lucas was now standing with the head in his outstretched arms. He looked back over his shoulder into one of the cameras. "See, Captain? Nothing happened," he said cheerfully.

Hellen and Hagen pulled the heavy door open as Lucas turned back to face the head. Entering from the opposite side, from across the lab table, they saw the hideous head only from the back, the snakes hanging like slack dreadlocks.

"Lucas, quickly, put it back in the jar."

"But—" Lucas began. But he was cut off by the loud hissing of the snakes, which abruptly straightened on all sides of the head, making it look like a ghastly sea urchin. It was as if the head's nerve cells had suddenly been connected to a power source. Hellen and Hagen froze in mid-step. Tom was now beside them in the room.

"Lucas, don't look at it!" Hellen shouted, but it was too late.

The Medusa's eyes opened and stared at Lucas. Its mouth gaped. But to everyone's amazement, nothing seemed to happen. Seconds passed. Nobody moved.

Then Tom acted. As if vaulting a fence, Tom braced against the edge of the table, swung his legs over, and kicked the head out of Lucas's hands. The snakes instantly fell slack again. Tom grabbed a lab coat hanging on a hook by the door and threw it over the monstrous head, which had come to rest against the wall. Without hesitation, he drew his new Glock 18C, switched to full-automatic mode, and squeezed the trigger. The magazine emptied in less than a second.

"Are you crazy?" Hellen screamed, ducking low, her fingers plugging her ears.

Tom quickly reloaded, stepped closer to the head, and nudged it with his foot. Nothing moved.

"Is everyone okay?" Tom put the gun away and turned around. He looked at Hellen, who was just straightening up again. But her eyes were fixed on Lucas.

"I don't think so," she said, and she nodded toward Maierhofer's son.

Everything had happened so fast that no one had realized that Lucas, since taking the head out of the jar and looking at it, had just been standing there. He was like a statue, arms outstretched, completely motionless on the other side of the table. Horror and panic were frozen onto his face.

Maierhofer charged into the chamber. "Lucas! Lucas!" He pushed Hellen and Hagen aside and stumbled to his son. "Lucas!" he cried, shaking him. No reaction. "What's the matter with him? He's completely stiff." With a jerk of his head, he signaled to Hellen, Tom, and Hagen. "Help me! We've got to get him to the infirmary."

Hellen put her arm around Maierhofer's shoulders and drew him aside, making room for Tom and Hagen.

Steiner was staring inside from the chamber door. "Don't just stand there, call for help!" Hellen snapped at him. Steiner nodded, grabbed a phone, and dialed the emergency number. Tom and Hagen took hold of Lucas, who seemed to be frozen solid, and carried him bodily out of the chamber. Hellen left Maierhofer inside and followed them. The captain didn't move from where he stood.

"But . . ." Maierhofer stammered to himself. "But how is that possible? It's just a myth."

Tom swept one of the lab tables clear and they laid Lucas flat on top.

"We have to get him out of the suit," Hagen said. Tom didn't hesitate, taking out a pocketknife and slicing the hazmat suit open. In seconds, it was no more than a pile of tattered plastic on the floor.

Hellen stepped up to Lucas and checked for a pulse at his wrist and neck, while the others looked on, tense. She shook her head: nothing. Then she shone a small flashlight into his wide-open eyes.

She recoiled sharply.

"What is it?" Tom asked.

"His pupils . . . they're reacting to the light."

"Then he isn't dead?" Hagen said.

"But there's no pulse, and he's completely catatonic," said Hellen.

"I know a few substances that could cause a condition like this, things you can use to simulate death. A superficial examination would make you think the victim was dead," Hagen said.

Just then, two paramedics arrived with a gurney. They took over the examination.

"He's catatonic, pupils reacting, but I can't find a pulse," Hellen briefed them.

"No heart massage, no defibrillator!" Hagen said. "Under no circumstances."

"But we can't—" one of the paramedics replied in amazement.

"Do as he says," Maierhofer said, his voice low but firm.

"Hook him up to an EKG and watch for the slightest sign of a heartbeat. I think his system's just been dialed down as far as it can go. Complete bloodwork, too. All known poisons," Hagen added.

The paramedics nodded, lifted Lucas onto the gurney, and rolled him out.

"Go. We'll be all right," said Tom, seeing Maierhofer's indecision about whether to go with his son. Maierhofer nodded gratefully and followed the paramedics out.

"The head," Hellen suddenly said.

Back in the chamber, Tom, Hellen, and Hagen stared at the shredded lab coat on the floor.

"What now?" said Tom.

"We have to put it back in its jar," Hagen said.

"But I fired an entire magazine into the thing. It's had it."

"I wouldn't be so sure," Hagen said. Hellen looked at him in surprise.

"Then let's take a look, shall we?" Tom crouched beside the coat.

"Careful. Don't—"

"Don't worry. I only have eyes for you," said Tom, grinning cheekily back at her.

"Dork."

Tom picked up the ragged bundle and paused momentarily. Nineteen bullets lay on the floor, each one crushed to a tiny mushroom. "What the fuck?" he murmured. Then, taking care not to look at it, he carried the head to the table and held it over the glass jar. Hellen carefully arranged the tatters of the lab coat around the jar and Tom lowered the head into the liquid.

"And now?"

"I think the liquid offers some kind of protection from its gaze, maybe puts it into a kind of suspended animation. It only opened its eyes after Lucas took it out," Hellen said. She pulled the coat from over the jar, quickly took a sample of the liquid, and replaced the lid.

Tom stood beside her with one eye closed and the other squeezed almost shut, peering carefully at the jar.

"See?" Hellen said. "Nothing happened."

"Yeah. I emptied a magazine into that thing, and it doesn't have a scratch," said Tom. "What now?"

Hellen shrugged and looked around. "Where's Hagen?"

CHAPTER 22
BAR AT THE IMPERIAL HOTEL, VIENNA,
24 HOURS LATER

"The Imperial. Nice. Your task force is splashing out, putting you up here," said Tom, as he entered the hotel bar with Hellen and dropped onto a red Biedermeier chair. Hagen was waiting for them.

Built in 1862 and opened by Emperor Franz Joseph and Empress Elizabeth in 1873, the Imperial Hotel reeked of tradition. When you stepped inside, you could believe that time had stood still. Down to the smallest detail, you felt as if you'd been transported back to the days of the Austro-Hungarian Empire, not least because the "Imperial," as the Viennese fondly referred to it, was one of the last hotels in the world that still offered a butler service. Heads of state, Hollywood greats, sheiks, and captains of industry regularly frequented its corridors.

The hotel was a particular favorite of classical conductors and soloists appearing in the Golden Hall of the adjoining Musikverein—from the rear entrance of the hotel, it was just a few steps to the *Gesellschaft der Musikfreunde in Wien*, as the venerable Vienna concert hall was officially called. Nor was it uncommon to see one of the world's leading conductors wearing tails and hurrying across

Bösendorferstrasse, which was itself named after the maker of the uniquely Viennese concert grand pianos.

"Nice place to live," said Tom, as the white-gloved, tuxedoed waiter served his whiskey sour.

Hellen had ordered her usual White Russian. "I'm not surprised you ran away from the Medusa. I'd much rather be here than at Cobra HQ," she said with a smile.

Tom had just stuffed a few macadamia nuts into his mouth and his eyes were roaming the bar, noting the heavy red velvet curtains, a scarlet carpet woven with gold threads, and a painting of Empress Maria Theresia. It was truly a trip back to Vienna's golden age. All that was missing was for the waiter to bow to Hellen, drop a *"g'schamster Diener, gnä' Frau,"* and retreat behind the bar.

"That wasn't why I took off," Hagen said, raising his glass. "It's time I told you why I'm here."

Tom and Hellen looked at him in anticipation.

"Well, you've seen for yourselves that the Medusa myth is no myth at all."

"We kinda picked up on that, yes," said Tom.

"How's Maierhofer's boy?" Hagen asked.

"No change. The lab tests haven't found a thing. And the analysis of the liquid preserving the head hasn't turned up anything yet, either," Hellen said. "Lucas is in the same catatonic state. I guess that's where the legend comes from, about how you turn to stone if you look the Medusa in the eye."

Hagen screwed up his face. "What I'm about to tell you stays between us. It's officially top secret."

Tom and Hellen leaned closer.

"No doubt you've heard about the Medusa cult conspiracies. And now, with the real Medusa and the ancient cult appearing at the same time . . . frankly, we think it's more than a coincidence."

"Ancient cult?" Hellen asked. "I'm not as conversant with the ancient Greeks as Professor Richter was, but I've never heard of a 'Medusa cult' before."

"But you've heard of the Alexander cult?" Hagen said.

"The Alexander cult? You mean the Ptolemaic cult of Alexander? The one that developed after the death of Alexander the Great, in ancient Egypt's Greek period?"

"That's the one. We believe the cult has persisted down to the present day, and that it worships the Medusa. Or at least, what's left of her."

"You keep saying 'we,'" said Tom. "Who's 'we'?"

"As you may know, I'm heading up a joint CIA and MI6 task force charged with mopping up the mess left by AF. Just recently, we received an anonymous tip that suggested that there's more to this Medusa cult than just bad taste—that it also presents a real, immediate danger."

Tom sipped at his whiskey sour. "So, what do you want from us?"

"I originally wanted to get you on board so we could track down the Medusa cult together and gauge any danger it presents. We believed until recently that the cult was close to finding Medusa's head."

"Until my hero here managed to nip that in the bud," said Hellen. She smiled proudly at Tom and kissed his cheek. "It's good to know that's over with. We've still got to find Richter's murderer and get van Rensburg out of jail."

"Then we're actually working on the same thing," said Tom. "Because we have to assume that the woman in Vienna General was working for the Medusa cult."

"Very likely," Hagen said. "By the way, I know her."

CHAPTER 23

THE PENTAGON, ARLINGTON, VIRGINIA

"Enter," Lieutenant Colonel Reece Weaver heard his commanding officer bark through the door. He squared his shoulders a little and entered the office. "What is it, Reece?" said General Jasper Horne chummily. Despite being several ranks senior to Weaver, the two men had known each other for many years and were fast friends.

"You'll never guess what just landed on my desk," Weaver said. He placed a file in front of Horne and took a seat opposite the general without waiting for an invitation.

"Has your little hacker been ignoring orders again and digging around outside her assignment?" Horne said.

"She has. But I'm pretty sure she got the message this time. She won't be interfering with us anymore. As far as that goes, we're in the clear."

"Let's hope so," Horne said, but he sounded doubtful.

"Don't worry, sir. But there's a new complication. One of the CIA's task forces has placed a little order. And it has the top brass's blessing," Weaver said. Horne had picked up the file and was leafing through it.

Horne frowned and looked up at Weaver. "Am I reading

this right? They're having A GBU50-MOAB IV delivered to White Sands?"

The acronym MOAB stood for "massive ordnance air blast" but the abbreviation was also behind the bomb's nickname: "mother of all bombs." It was the most powerful non-nuclear weapon in the DOD arsenal. Its predecessor had been deployed in Afghanistan in 2017.

Weaver nodded.

"Shit. They're getting serious," Horne murmured.

"Getting serious? About what? Why would they need a weapon with the power of twelve *tons* of TNT?" said Weaver.

"They want to destroy Medusa's head."

Weaver burst out laughing. "And they need a MOAB for that? That's kind of overkill, isn't it?"

"If I can believe the report my contact passed on, I'm not at all sure that a MOAB's enough for the job. And that's what this is all about." Horne stood up, pacing back and forth as he continued. "Those idiots in the White House actually want to let this once-in-a-lifetime opportunity slip through their fingers. The president doesn't seem to have the balls to defy the treaty or stand up to the UN Security Council."

"Treaty, sir?"

"More UN Security Council bullshit. At the end of World War II, with all the stuff they found in the Nazis' hands, the allies agreed that if anyone anywhere finds an artifact that could present a danger to mankind, it must be destroyed immediately. But they're bureaucrats. They don't see the potential. They even gave the treaty a name: the Perseus File," Horne said.

"Perseus?"

"Looks like you slept through Greek mythology at college. Perseus was the Greek hero who cut off Medusa's head."

"I never had much interest in history," the colonel

replied, scowling—Horne's condescension could be turned against him, too.

"The plan was for us to get our hands on the head."

"Yes, sir. But it looks like the task force beat us to it."

"Unacceptable. Completely unacceptable. Having the CIA involved changes everything. We can't let those myopic paper pushers in Langley destroy the head. Do you understand me?"

Weaver nodded curtly and awaited his orders.

"Okay. Take a black-ops team and bring me that thing. Destruction is not an option. I'll talk POTUS around. You have a free hand. Bring me the head of Medusa! Whatever it takes, collateral damage included."

"Are you sure you want to go to that extreme?"

"Why the hell not? That absurd cult is playing into our hands beautifully. If things fall apart, we've got a natural scapegoat. We can blame them for everything."

Weaver jumped to his feet and saluted. "Sir, yes sir!" he snapped, and he turned on his heel and left the general's office.

When Weaver had closed the door behind him, Horne reached for his phone. He had one more loose end to tie up. Weaver's hacker was responsible for the CIA finding out about the plan, he was sure of it. And he hated having a hacker out there who could connect him and Weaver directly to the Medusa. It made things considerably easier that the girl was a civilian, employed through a shell company.

"I've got a job for you," Horne said when the call was answered.

"I'm listening."

"A hacker. Her name is Akira Seki."

"Consider it done."

CHAPTER 24

BAR AT THE IMPERIAL HOTEL, VIENNA

"You know her? How?" Tom asked. Hellen, just as surprised, stared at Hagen.

"Well, 'know' is an overstatement. Our counterterrorism friends at the DSN sent me a photo after her arrest. They wanted to know if we at the CIA had anything on her."

"And do you?"

"Not a thing. We don't know anything about her. She's a ghost. Not even Mossad knows who she really is. Until yesterday, no one had so much as a photograph of her. No one knows her name or where she comes from. Our paths crossed just once during my time with AF, but there are two things I know for certain: she's a stone-cold killer, and she calls herself the 'Mantis.'"

"The people you know," said Tom ironically.

"And before you ask who she's working for, I can't tell you. We have no idea."

Hagen raised his hand and the waiter reappeared.

"What cigars do you have?" Hagen asked in German, earning a weary smile from the waiter.

"*Gnädiger Herr, Sie soiten lieber frog'n, welche wir ned ham,*" the waiter replied in a thick Austrian accent.

Hagen, who had barely understood a word, just looked at him in confusion.

"He's saying they have an excellent selection," Tom translated. "Try a Cohiba Siglo VI. I'll take one, too. Have you ever tried a really good Cuban?"

Hagen smiled. "You know the CIA has some history in Cuba, right??" he said.

The waiter nodded. A moment later, he brought the cigars, a cutter, and a box of long matches.

"Cloutard would love you guys," Hellen said. Tom looked at her and nodded happily.

"Your president, by the way, has expressed his wish that you come with me," Hagen said.

"Come with you? Where?" said Tom, blowing his first smoke ring.

"To the U.S., to monitor the destruction of the Medusa and make sure it really happens."

"Destruction?" Tom and Hellen said in unison.

"Yes. You already know that AF grew out of the remnants of Hitler's and Himmler's *'Ahnenforscher,'* their cultural heritage research group. They were tasked with finding artifacts that would ensure final victory for the Nazis. The Americans' Monument Men found their share of potentially dangerous mythical artifacts, too. This led the Allies to adopt a secret treaty at the end of the Second World War that says that any discoveries that could represent a global danger to humanity are to be destroyed immediately. Since then, the treaty has been signed by all NATO states and the EU. The agreement, incidentally, is also included in a secret addendum to your Austrian State Treaty," Hagen explained.

Tom and Hellen looked at him as if they had a thousand questions, but Hagen raised his hands defensively. "That's all I can tell you, and I shouldn't even have told you that much." He took a long pull at his Cohiba. "While you've been searching for proof of van Rensburg's innocence, I've tried several times to destroy the head at Cobra headquarters—with the consent of the Austrian officials, of course. We shot it with rifles, a pump-action shotgun, and a fifty-caliber machine gun. We doused it in petrol and set it on fire. We stuffed hand grenades down its throat. Nothing. Nothing left a mark, not even a block of C4." Hagen threw his arms up helplessly. "The thing is basically indestructible. We need more firepower, and we have that at our missile range in New Mexico."

Tom looked first at Hagen, then at Hellen. Then he shook his head vigorously. "No. We have to find Richter's killer. I can't leave Vienna now. We're meeting François in Prague tomorrow."

"A new lead?" Hagen asked.

"Yes," Hellen said. "Cloutard sent me something very interesting." She took her iPad out of her handbag. "He emailed me this yesterday. He found a few clues in an old diary kept by a Nazi librarian. Apparently, the Nazis were also looking for Medusa's head. A lot of what's in the diary uses similar wording to that turning up in the blog articles and videos about the Medusa cult."

"So do you see why I can't come with you?" Tom said to Hagen. "We have to find Richter's killer. And that guy from the homicide division, Messner? He couldn't find a Krügerl in the Schweizerhaus."

Hagen had no idea what he was talking about, so Hellen translated: "The Schweizerhaus is Vienna's most famous beer garden, and a Krügerl is Austrian for a half-liter glass of beer."

"Maybe I have another argument to persuade you to come," Hagen said, draining his glass of Kentucky Owl Batch 9.

Tom looked up with interest.

"General Horne is the DOD liaison to DARPA."

Tom suddenly broke out in a fit of coughing. "General Jasper Tiberius Horne?"

"Who's that?" Hellen asked. She clearly did not know the name.

"My dead uncle's arch-enemy. Horne sat in on every presidential briefing, and he and my uncle were at each other's throats constantly. Their shouting matches in the Situation Room were legendary. Not even the former president could hold them back." Tom took a swig of his whiskey sour. He caught the barkeeper's eye and twirled his finger in the air, ordering another round. "If Horne had had his way, the U.S.A. would have started World War III several times over. According to my uncle, the guy was constantly railing about nuclear first strikes and all kinds of awful stuff."

Hagen nodded in agreement. "Yeah, Horne's as sick as they come. For him, the United States *is* the world. That's why they shunted him off to DARPA. They figured it was where he could do the least damage."

"But how is DARPA involved? Don't they just make robots?" Hellen asked.

"That too," Hagen said. "That's what the outside world knows. But they're involved in all kinds of developments for the armed forces. We'll be using a DARPA prototype to try to destroy the Medusa. And if they know about it, then Horne does, too." Hagen paused for a moment, then continued. "And if Horne knows about it—and we're assuming he does—he's not going to sit around and watch the Medusa be destroyed. He's going to try to get his hands on it," he said, looking intently at Tom.

Tom stared into his glass and twirled the ice cubes with his straw. After what felt like an eternity, he turned and looked at Hellen.

"You don't need to say a word, darling," she said. "If

Uncle Scott thought the man was dangerous, it makes more sense for you to go with Isaac. I'll still have my personal Monsieur Poirot here. We'll solve Richter's murder without you."

Tom held her face in his hands and kissed her tenderly. "Thank you. Be careful," he whispered, before turning back to Hagen. "All right. When do we leave?"

"Right away. My jet's fueled up and the head is already packed."

Tom slapped his thighs and was about to stand up, but Hellen stopped him.

"There's one thing I still don't understand," Hellen said, looking at Hagen. "Yes, the Medusa is dangerous. But she's not a weapon of mass destruction. Why is everyone going out of their minds about her?"

"That, my dear, I can't answer. We don't know enough about it. But I know one thing: if this many people are after the head, that usually means trouble," Hagen said. "My gut is telling me there's a lot more going on here than we currently know."

"The Medusa Secret," Tom suddenly said. Hellen and Hagen looked at him in surprise. "What? It would be a cool title for a film."

CHAPTER 25

VIENNA GENERAL HOSPITAL

The fluorescent light burned painfully into her eyes. Her head was buzzing. *Where am I?* the woman thought. She looked down at herself. Tubes and cables crossed her body, ending at an IV bag and the EKG machine beside her bed. She tried to lift her right hand and made an unpleasant discovery: she was handcuffed to the side rail of the hospital bed. But her left hand was free. She looked around. Through the closed curtains, she saw the silhouette of a man in front of her room. A guard?

Gradually, her memory began to return. The last thing she remembered was horses and a man who had been chasing her. She raised her left hand to her head and discovered a bandage.

She looked at the handcuff again. *Fuck*, she thought. She would need more than a length of wire or a pin to get it open. She needed the key.

She had to figure out a way out of there, and the sooner the better. She had to finish her mission.

. . .

The Cobra officer Captain Maierhofer had posted to watch the suspect tapped away in boredom at his phone. It wasn't exactly according to regulations, but the woman was in a coma. *What could possibly happen?* he thought.

A loud crash distracted him from his game, and he almost dropped his phone. He looked left and right, but the corridor was empty. No doctors, no nurses. He put the phone away, dropped his hand to his pistol, and edged open the door to the woman's room. He peeked inside through the gap. The woman lay motionless on the bed, as expected. He looked down. To his surprise, a side table lay on its side in front of the bed. He approached the bed slowly, keeping one eye on the unconscious woman. The silent EKG machine displayed a regular heartbeat.

She was a very attractive woman, even in her condition. *Hard to believe she's a killer*, the man thought. His grip on the pistol eased. He rattled the handcuff, checking that it was still firmly attached.

That was his mistake. He had no chance to react. The woman grabbed hold of the hand on the cuff, then rapidly swung her long, athletic legs around the officer's neck and pressed him down onto the bed. With a single sharp jerk, she snapped his neck. But she didn't release him, not yet. With her left hand, she swiftly searched his breast pockets as he hung backward from the bed, his neck pinned between her legs. She found the small key and freed herself from the handcuff. Then she slid the infusion needle out of her arm. Only now did she slacken her legs around the man's neck, grabbing him instead with both hands and hauling him bodily onto the bed. She straddled his body and began removing his clothes, and had to smile. She usually killed her victims *after* undressing them, although as she soon discovered, he wasn't exactly her "size."

Minutes later, she was wearing the man's uniform. It

wasn't a perfect disguise, but it would stand up to a casual glance. Now she had to find out what had become of her package, and fast. Too much was at stake. The Cobra officer had died so suddenly that his eyes were still wide open, and she took his phone and held it in front of his face. It unlocked instantly.

She tapped in a number and pressed the call button. She didn't have to wait long. "Barkley, I need your help," the Mantis said.

CHAPTER 26
CHARLES BRIDGE, PRAGUE, CZECH REPUBLIC

François Cloutard leaned on the railing beside the statue of Saint Wenceslaus and gazed out over the Vltava River and beyond it, to the old part of Prague.

He had been to the city countless times, and had often stood there on the Charles Bridge, the city's most famous landmark, contemplating the many crowned heads that had crossed it as they followed the route known as the Royal Road. For centuries, it led the Czech kings to St. Vitus Cathedral, where their coronation took place.

He had often felt like a king himself in the city. He had ruled over his own realm there for many years, after all. Cloutard shook his head, angry at himself for his gloomy thoughts. Yes, they had been good times, but they were over now, and there was no point dwelling on the good old days. Now, with Tom and Hellen, he had a new direction. And although he found his thoughts returning again and again to the break-ins, the raids, the cons, and the smuggling operations, he also found it strangely satisfying to know that he was now part of something unique—something that not only enriched him personally, but also, every now and then, benefited all of humanity.

He reached into the inside pocket of his seersucker jacket and took out his faithful hip flask. He unscrewed the lid and raised the flask as if in a toast to the entire Old City of Prague. Then he pushed his Panama hat back a little on his head and took a large gulp of Hennessy Louis XIII.

"Drinking alone is a bad sign," he heard a voice behind him say, and he smiled.

"*Ma chérie*, you are more than welcome to drink with me," he said, offering the flask to Hellen.

"It's ten in the morning, François. Let me at least wait until after lunch," she said, embracing the aging gentleman thief and basking in the affable, almost fatherly warmth he radiated. She had grown especially fond of the old rogue since they had first met a few years ago.

"Enough cuddling," he said wryly. "We're not here for fun, but to catch a murderer."

"I hope we didn't interrupt anything important in Tabarka," Hellen said.

Cloutard shook his head. "Not at all. I leave Tabarka around this time every year anyway. The olive trees there will be blooming soon, and I am terribly allergic to them."

"Allergic to olive blossoms? And you live in Tunisia voluntarily?"

"It is only a few weeks of the year when it is really unbearable, but of course I must also avoid Turkey, Spain and Greece in that brief season, or my nose falls off," he said, and he wrinkled it in revulsion. "And you may think it strange, but I do not suffer at all in Italy. My nose just has its own peculiar style, even for allergies."

Hellen rolled her eyes. Cloutard simply could not conceal his inner snob, wherever he was. "I could spend hours talking with you about your nose, but that's not why we're here," she said. "And I'm sure you have a plan for how we can squeeze a little information out of the concierge at Richter's hotel, don't you?" She hooked her arm in his and they strolled along the bridge, heading east toward The Mozart.

Ahead of them, suddenly, they saw blue flashing lights and a large crowd carrying banners and shouting slogans.

"Another one of those demonstrations calling for action against the Medusa cult," Hellen said. "The Internet is a dangerous medium."

"In the past, there would have been one or two articles in the papers and people would have forgotten about it. Now they find something to be outraged about every day on Facebook, YouTube, and Instagram," said Cloutard, scratching his chin.

"It's almost as if someone's deliberately fanning the flames," Hellen said as she pulled Cloutard aside to let them pass. The chanting protesters trudged across the bridge, their police escort looking as if they were expecting violence at any moment. "Everyone's so on edge right now. But we can't do anything about that. We need to focus on our job."

"*Bien sûr!* So, back to the concierge. Like a sailor with a girl in every port, and me being the old crook that I am, I have my contacts in every big city," Cloutard said, stroking his moustache a little too smugly. "The concierge at The Mozart has a weakness for the ponies and spends every minute he can at the Velká Chuchle racecourse. Unfortunately for him, he has no talent for picking a winning horse. He has built up a sizeable debt." He reached into his jacket pocket for a slip of paper, which he held up like a trophy. "I called in a few favors. This is one of his markers. We should be able to exchange it for a little information," he said as they entered the lobby.

"Welcome to The Mozart. Can I help you?"

The man was in his mid-forties and was doing his best to cover his balding scalp with the few strands of hair he had left. It was a hopeless task, but it did not stop him from constantly sweeping the remaining strands across the top of his head.

"*Mon ami*, we would like to ask you a question or two." Cloutard held the IOU up in front of him. The man recognized it instantly and paled. "Not to worry," Cloutard continued. "We are not here for money. I know you are as broke as Boris Becker. But if you can assist us a little, this IOU is a thing of the past."

The man looked a little dubious.

"A few days ago, this man stayed here," Hellen said. She held out her phone to the concierge, a picture of Director Richter on the screen. "Remember him? He's Professor Meinrad Richter, director of the Museum of Fine Arts in Vienna."

The concierge studied the photo and nodded. "Yes. A very attractive woman visited him late in the evening." The man grinned enthusiastically. "Richter left the hotel that same night and never returned."

"We know that he drove to the Four Seasons," Hellen said.

"Call the staff there," Cloutard said. "See to it that you find out something useful. Most importantly, who it was that he met." He waved the man's marker in the air one more time.

The man twisted his mouth to one side. "I will see what I can do. Give me a few minutes."

He reached for his desk telephone but paused and looked at Hellen and Cloutard.

"Ah. You need a little privacy," Cloutard said.

They stepped away a short distance and let the man make his call.

"The concierges of the great hotels have maintained a powerful, worldwide network since time immemorial. Information is exchanged, favors called in, secrets leaked, and much more. It is almost a kind of mini-Mafia," Cloutard whispered to Hellen.

A few minutes later, the concierge waved them back over. "The professor arrived at the hotel with the woman," he said. "And they were shown to the Riverside Villa."

"The Riverside Villa?" Cloutard asked.

"A small villa located in front of the hotel, directly beside the Vltava. The villa was booked in the name of Apostolos Ibis. My Four Seasons associate never actually saw Mr. Ibis, but he believes Richter met with Ibis at the villa."

He paused momentarily and looked around, as if to be certain no one was listening. "But he also said that he thought the professor and Apostolos Ibis had some kind of disagreement. Director Richter left the Four Seasons not long after he arrived. Apparently, he seemed quite fearful, even distraught, as my associate called for a taxi to take him to the train station."

Hellen's phone pinged, but she ignored it.

The concierge glanced at the IOU still in Cloutard's hand. Cloutard smiled and pushed the slip of paper across the counter. The man swiftly reached for it, but Cloutard did not let it go.

"I am sure there was more," Cloutard said, although it was more suspicion than certainty.

"Okay, okay, okay. Another man also visited Apostolos Ibis in the villa before Richter arrived. My associate doesn't know his name and doesn't know if he also spoke to Richter, but he was certainly in the villa just before the professor."

"And?" Cloutard pressed, growing impatient.

"The man stood out, my colleague says, because he had . . . he had an air of dignity, even grandeur, that one rarely sees these days. He had a special aura, a radiance, as if he embodied the wisdom of centuries. A very special person indeed, he said." The concierge saw the astonishment on Hellen's and Cloutard's faces. "Remarkable, I know, but what can I say? Those were my associate's words."

"What did the man look like?" Cloutard asked.

"Rather nondescript, actually. He was at least eighty years old and walked with a cane. A worn tweed jacket, an argyle sweater-vest, and corduroy trousers. Very 1970s, stylewise. But despite his shabby appearance, he carried himself like a monarch."

Cloutard looked intently at the concierge, who raised his hands defensively.

"That's all. I don't know any more than that." He sighed. "I have used up all my favors for you now," he said in resignation.

Hellen looked at Cloutard, who shrugged.

"Really?" Cloutard asked. "That is everything?"

The man nodded.

Cloutard looked the man in the eye for a few seconds, then turned to Hellen. "Give me a minute, please," he said. Hellen understood. She left Cloutard and sauntered back outside through the lobby.

After a brief exchange of words, Cloutard finally handed over the IOU. "*Merci beaucoup*," he said amicably, and the man let out a relieved sigh. Cloutard left the hotel and rejoined Hellen, who was waiting out the front.

"The Four Seasons has security cameras," Cloutard said.

"And we'll get the recordings?" said Hellen.

"*Bien sûr , ma chère*. And I already know how we will do it."

Hellen suddenly remembered the message that had come in a few minutes before, and she fished her phone out of her handbag. Quickly scanning the display, she read slower and slower until she finally came to a stop. She looked up and glared at Cloutard.

"Are you so hard up that you have to sell information to conspiracy bloggers now?"

CHAPTER 27

A BOUTIQUE IN THE FIRST DISTRICT, VIENNA

The Mantis studied herself in the mirror. In the basin of the small kitchen lay trimmed hair and the remains of the bleach that, with a heavy heart, she had applied to disguise her long black hair, now shoulder-length and the color of copper. She had had no time to do more, although she had at least managed to apply enough makeup to cover the bruises on her face. A pair of sunglasses would cover the rest.

She took off the police uniform and stepped over the body of the young boutique owner. Cool and calm, as if out for a day's shopping, she rummaged through the clothes racks until she found an outfit she liked. Then she dressed, pushed the Cobra's pistol and spare magazine into the back of her jeans, and pulled on a baseball cap. She wiped away any possible fingerprints and packed the uniform and everything else she'd brought into a bag.

She had entered the shop an hour before and almost immediately murdered the owner and locked the front door. Now she exited through the back.

Able to move more freely now, she hot-wired a parked car in an alleyway. She climbed in and took out the mobile phone that the boutique owner had been kind enough to unlock for her before she died. *Normal people will do anything with a gun to their head*, the woman thought. But their survival instinct was playing a sick joke on them. Did they really believe they'd live if they did what was demanded of them? The young woman had found out for herself how delusional that was.

The Mantis opened Google Maps and typed in the address she'd found using the cop's phone in the hospital. She drove off. Along the way, she stopped at Vienna Central Station to retrieve her go-bag—she kept one in every important city in the world for just such an eventuality. She parked the car in the parking garage and made her way to the lockers. When she punched in the code on the keypad and the door swung open, she thought of the parcel she'd deposited in a similar locker at the train station in Syracuse —her final destination, the goal of all her work.

Back in the car, she could finally breathe easily again. In the go-bag was cash, a gun, credit cards, and a few passports for her numerous aliases.

Her phone vibrated. She picked it up and read the message Barkley had sent: "Palais Modena in one hour."

With a satisfied smile, she put the phone aside and drove off.

CHAPTER 28
AUSTRIAN MINISTRY OF THE INTERIOR, PALAIS MODENA, VIENNA

The Mantis straightened her glasses and aimed her nicest smile at the man at the security desk while he checked her press accreditation. He compared her passport with the details on his display, then handed the woman a lanyard with an ID card.

I can always rely on Barkley, the woman thought. She nodded gratefully to the man and arranged the lanyard around her neck, then followed the rest of the media representatives upstairs.

The Interior Minister made a brief address to the gathered press, then handed them over to a detective from the state criminal police, Major Messner, who explained the current status of the investigation. After Messner, Captain Maierhofer, head of the Cobra, stepped up to the microphone.

"First, I would like to express my sincere condolences to those Director Richter leaves behind. It is a tragic situation, and as you have already heard from my colleague, it is the number one priority both for his department and the district attorney's office.

"Captain Maierhofer, what can you tell us about the

suspect your men arrested in the Volksgarten?" a journalist asked.

"As Major Messner has already explained, we cannot provide any information about the ongoing investigation at this point."

"Is there anything to the rumors that the second suspect has fled Vienna General and also murdered one of your officers?" a second journalist asked.

The Mantis, at the back of the crowd of reporters, could not resist a smile.

"That's something else I cannot comment on at this stage." Maierhofer raised his hand as the journalist was about to ask a follow-up question. "And to pre-empt your next question: I can safely say there is no truth to any stories of an attempted bombing. We did secure a steel case, but it did not contain a bomb. However, I can't provide any further details at this point about what the case contained."

The Mantis pricked up her ears. This brought her a step closer—the case was in the hands of the Cobra.

"Given that the murder took place close to the Temple of Theseus," another journalist called out, "is there a connection between the attack and the Medusa cult causing demonstrations and civil unrest around the world?

"We have no information about that."

"Is it true that your son was injured while examining the case?"

Maierhofer's face turned scarlet. He had to make a huge effort to stop himself from exploding before the assembled press.

"That will be all for today," he said after a few seconds. Shuffling his notes together, he stepped back from the podium.

While the crowd of reporters shouted more questions, the Mantis kept her eye on Maierhofer. She wandered toward a side door through which the Interior Minister and Messner had already passed, but a security man in a black suit blocked her path.

"You can't leave this way. Please exit the room the same way you entered."

"Sorry, it's my first time here. I was just looking for the bathroom," she said with an innocent smile, which had its desired effect on the guard.

She only vaguely took in what the guard was telling her. Her attention was really on Captain Maierhofer, who was standing just ten feet away and reading the riot act to a young man. She could tell from the dynamic between them that the younger man was Maierhofer's assistant.

"How do they know about my son?" Maierhofer growled. "Find out who leaked that. I want their head on a pike." His face was still an unhealthy shade of red.

"I'm sorry, Captain," the young man stammered. "I'll look into it immediately. Oh, one more thing." He stepped closer to his boss. "I'm supposed to tell you from Wagner that Project Perseus is going according to plan."

"Koller, are you out of your mind? Why don't you just put it on the front page of the paper?" Maierhofer grabbed the young man by his arm and dragged him out through the door.

"Thank you, I'm sure I'll find it," said the woman, and she smiled again at the guard who had just explained in excruciating detail how to find the toilets.

Perseus, the woman thought, as she followed the journalists back out. The name made her smile inside—these secret services and their painfully obvious codenames. Still, the codename didn't tell her much by itself, and she lacked the computer skills to hack a secret service. Maierhofer's assistant, however, was easy prey. And now she knew his name and face.

She didn't even have to wait half an hour. She recognized the young officer the moment he came out and went to his car. She got out of hers and went after him, and when Koller reached his car, she was right behind him. She jammed her pistol into his back and forced him to get into the car. Then she climbed into the back seat.

"Drive, Mr. Koller," the woman said in heavily accented German. "We're going to have a frank discussion about Perseus."

CHAPTER 29

WHITE SANDS MISSILE RANGE, TULAROSA BASIN, NEW MEXICO, U.S.A.

"Wow. It really *is* cold," Tom said, letting the fine, white sand trickle through his fingers.

White Sands Missile Range was about 40 miles from nearby Holloman Air Force Base, where they'd landed three hours earlier on a special flight with their extraordinary cargo.

"Yes. It's the unique mineral composition of the sand," said Hagen. "It's a relic of the last ice age, the world's biggest—"

"Enough already, Mr. Wikipedia," Tom interrupted him. "You're starting to sound like Hellen." He stood up and brushed the sand from his hands. "Can't we just soak up this magnificent view for a minute?" He spread his arms wide. All around, snow-white dunes glittered in the sunlight. Encircled by distant mountains, the natural spectacle covered almost three hundred square miles of the Tularosa Basin. "It feels like you're on another planet here, right?"

Hagen rolled his eyes. "Okay, enough soaking. Time to come back down to earth. We've got a job to finish," he said.

"Spoilsport."

"Sirs? We're ready," said the Air Force Lieutenant who had just approached.

Tom and Hagen turned around. Not far from the Humvees they'd arrived in, a kind of platform had been erected, above which a massive bomb was hanging. The platform was surrounded by several vehicles, and a swarm of technicians were at work on the bomb, which was thirty feet long and more than three feet in diameter. It hung nose down, with its tip waist-high above the platform. The team had spent the last twenty-four hours preparing the bomb as they had been ordered.

"We've set the MOAB up so that we can detonate it remotely," the lieutenant said.

"Fantastic. Then let's blow this thing back to Olympus," said Tom.

"Sir, if I may ask . . ." the lieutenant began tentatively, ". . . what exactly are we doing here? What's this all about?"

Hagen and Tom looked at the man.

"Sorry, soldier. That's—" But an all-too-familiar sound interrupted Tom.

The three men turned around in unison as the sound grew louder and louder. An ultra-modern helicopter with an oval logo on the side was approaching, already beginning its descent. The sandstorm created by the rotors engulfed them momentarily, and Tom, Hagen and the lieutenant raised their hands to protect their faces. Because of the crystal-white sand and the merciless midday sun, all of those at the site were wearing sunglasses with side covers to protect their eyes—not only from the glare but also from flying sand. The soldiers and technicians looked upwards as the chopper descended. Tom's gut told him something was off. He and Hagen shared a look. The British agent was as unsettled as Tom by the turn of events.

"What the hell is this?" Hagen shouted to make himself heard over the noise of the rotors.

"You deal with our visitors, I'll take care of the Medusa," Tom shouted back, and he hurried away to the Humvees. He opened the door and pushed his duffel bag aside to get to the code-locked, high-security flight case holding the glass jar that contained Medusa's head.

Even before the pilot had brought the helicopter down completely, eight men jumped clear of the side doors, left and right. Only one of them wore a uniform. The others looked to Tom like private contractors or a black-ops team: jeans, t-shirts, baseball caps, tactical vests with built-in holsters, and the mandatory sunglasses.

Moving upright, not ducking the way most people did when they moved beneath helicopter blades, the eight men approached Hagen and the lieutenant. Tom had just lifted the flight case out of the car and was carrying it toward the missile platform, but his eyes were on the newcomers as they took up positions. They seemed to be securing the area, and Tom had a strong feeling that he knew why. Seconds later, his suspicions were confirmed.

"Stop that man," the uniformed soldier shouted, pointing toward Tom. Two of his men immediately ran to Tom and blocked his path. Hands resting demonstratively on their pistols, they told Tom to come with them. In the meantime, the uniformed man had planted himself in front of Hagen and raised his hand in a half-hearted salute. He was wearing camouflage gear, a beret, Swisseye Raptor sunglasses, and a holster with a chromed revolver strapped to his thigh. "WEAVER" was embroidered on a Velcro label on his chest.

"Lieutenant Colonel Reece Weaver," said the man.

"Lieutenant Manning," the soldier beside Hagen said, standing to attention and saluting, but Weaver was far more interested in Hagen. A man in civvies at an operation like this normally meant one thing: secret service.

"Isaac Hagen, MI6. What can I do for you, Lieutenant Colonel?" Hagen said in his unmistakable British accent. The realization that he was standing face to face with a foreign agent did not seem to please the lieutenant colonel at all, as Hagen immediately saw. He had said MI6 deliberately, rather than CIA, to provoke a reaction from Weaver.

Weaver's disdainful glare turned to Tom, who joined them escorted by Weaver's men. "And you would be . . .?" Weaver asked.

"Tom Wagner, adventurer," said Tom flippantly. He put the flight case down and, wearing a put-on grin, held out his hand to Weaver. "What's DARPA doing here? Did one of your robot dogs run away?"

Weaver scowled and ignored the offered hand. He looked Tom up and down. "Wagner? Any relation to Admiral Scott Wagner?" he asked.

"Yes, sir. He was my uncle."

Weaver said nothing but kept staring at Tom.

"Lieutenant Colonel, what are you doing here?" Tom asked. "This is a top-secret operation."

"Yes, Project Perseus. As you can see, we're well informed." Weaver looked down at the flight case that Tom had set on the ground at his feet.

"We're representing the UN Security Council," Hagen said. "You have no authority here."

Weaver snorted with contempt. "That's where you're sorely mistaken, my British friend. You're on U.S. soil, and in my world that means that you're the ones with no authority. Like you, I have my orders. But unlike you, I only take orders from one person: the President of the United States."

Hagen and Tom looked at one another.

"Manning, give me the detonator," said Weaver to the

lieutenant, and the young man hesitantly handed it over. "Now get everyone out of here." His men reacted immediately, getting the soldiers and technicians into their vehicles and making sure they cleared the area. Two of Weaver's men drove off in each of the Humvees.

"These two are coming with me," Weaver said, pointing to Tom and Hagen, then the chopper.

Minutes later and three miles from the MOAB, Weaver, without warning, flipped up the red security flap to reveal the trigger, and detonated the bomb with no hesitation at all. For a split-second, an enormous fireball rose into the sky above the white desert, followed by an even larger mushroom cloud of dust.

"Well, fancy that," Weaver said. "Mission complete. The target was successfully destroyed. Now if you'd be so kind as to tell me the code for the case, I'll get out of your hair."

CHAPTER 30
UNKNOWN LOCATION

It was a strange sensation. He tried desperately to get used to it, but he simply could not.

He held in his hands the threads connecting so many things. He made his marionettes dance as he saw fit, and yet he had to accept that he could not reveal himself. For the moment, he had to make do with directing, maneuvering, manipulating. He had to let others play the active roles. But that would also change.

He had learned patience over the last few years, and he had learned it from the very best. Most importantly, he'd learned that gentle pressure would suffice to achieve his goals—and without drawing attention.

He'd learned that the true wars were not fought on the battlefield between soldiers, that the true weapons were not rifles, rockets, or nuclear warheads.

The true power was the Internet, and true weapons consisted of bits and bytes. The opportunities to wage war had become endless. You needed no armies, no supplies. No ammunition, aircraft carriers, or marines. You needed a computer, and you needed to know how people ticked. And the convenient thing about that was that people ticked fundamentally the same wherever in the world they were.

He laughed, unable to help himself. He thought of Joseph Goebbels, Hitler's brilliant propaganda minister. There was so much to learn from Goebbels, even today. If Goebbels had had today's resources, the Nazis would be ruling the world. He would only have had to snap his fingers. He had been a natural talent when it came to manipulating the masses.

But what was exciting about Goebbels was that his goal had not been to manipulate people's thoughts. True manipulation consisted not of forcing people into a particular school of thought, religion, or political ideology. It consisted of what was known as agenda setting: the specific content of the manipulation was less important than the influence you had on what people talked about.

Communications science had realized only decades later that it isn't content that influences people, but the power to decide what they think about—to decide what occupies the space in their heads.

The diabolical part was that you only had to tell people what they were supposed to think, talk, debate about—and they would invent their own nightmares. And for that, he knew, the Medusa was perfect.

Toppling a few delicately balanced dominoes was enough to make the subsequent mass panic unstoppable. Fear would be stoked by all the freeloaders who saw in it the money, fame, Facebook likes, or YouTube views they craved. It had all become so simple once he'd understood how the world worked. Reality was dead; it was whatever was breaking the Internet right now. And that kind of reality could be invented, then trumpeted loud and long on the World Wide Web.

He thought of the many chess pieces out there making their moves on his behalf, doing his work for him, not even aware that they were doing so.

The man was jolted rudely from his thoughts. A knock on the door. Time to eat.

CHAPTER 31
U PARLAMENTU RESTAURANT, PRAGUE

"Fine, François. I believe you. I don't think you leaked anything."

Hellen and Cloutard finished off their glasses of Pilsner Urquell as they recovered from the gigantic portions of *Svíčková na smetaně*, the typical Czech beef tenderloin with steamed vegetables and a thick, garlic-heavy cream sauce, served with dumplings and cranberries.

"Someone must have hacked my email. Who could have guessed that my photos from the Nazi diary would turn up online the very next day?" Cloutard said.

"But what I still don't get is how it all hangs together," said Hellen. "Richter's murder, the Medusa or Alexander cult with its apocalyptic fixation, the actual head of the actual Medusa, and these unknown men Richter is supposed to have met. We know one of them is named Apostolos Ibis, but that's all."

Cloutard wiped beer foam from his lips, then signaled the waiter to bring the bill. "One step at a time," he said. "First, we have to find out who Ibis is."

"I found a check with his signature among Richter's papers, but I couldn't discover anything about him. It would be interesting to know who hired the woman to ambush van Rensburg and Richter. Also, whoever hired her was planning something with the Medusa, but we don't know what."

"Maybe she is working for the cult, whatever you want to call it?"

"Questions and more questions," said Hellen. She stood up and straightened her skimpy skirt and plucked a little at her blouse—cut far too low and revealing much more than she was comfortable with. "Is this really necessary, François?" she asked, looking down at the overly provocative outfit the two had assembled that afternoon on a sortie through Prague's cheaper shops.

"I am glad Tom is not here," Cloutard said, looking down at the five-inch heels that completed Hellen's outfit. He grinned. "He would tear my head off for letting you parade around Prague like that. Think of everything I've had to put up with. The night manager happens to have a weakness for beautiful women."

"Cheap women, more like," Hellen grumbled.

"In the words of Dolly Parton, it costs a lot to look this cheap—so relax."

Hellen nodded in resignation, and they pushed their way out of the crowded pub. Prague's Old City didn't really come to life until after dark. The streets were packed, and the people gathered to laugh and drink in the city's beer gardens. Here and there, in passing, they heard the word "Medusa" and heated discussion surrounding it. A group of young women passed by, and Cloutard nodded after them.

"See, *ma chère*? You are not the only one trying to land a man tonight." The girls' outfits were even more revealing than Hellen's.

"I didn't think it was possible to get any skimpier," she said, watching them walk on.

After picking their way through the narrow, crowded

streets, the Four Seasons Hotel appeared ahead. It was well past midnight; by now, the hotel would have settled down for the night.

"Ready?" said Cloutard.

Hellen pulled her top down a little to reveal even more her cleavage and adjusted her skin-tight skirt upwards. She toyed with a strand of hair, touched her index finger lasciviously to her bottom lip, and murmured in Cloutard's ear, "I was born ready, baby."

They both grinned and Hellen tottered away on her high heels into the hotel lobby.

Cloutard did not have to wait long. He was just about to take a sip from his flask when he saw Hellen leave the hotel with the night manager. *Hollywood missed out on a star there*, Cloutard thought, watching her Oscar-worthy performance. Hellen seemed upset, fearful, almost in a panic. She had her arm around the night manager's and was pulling him away in the direction of Křižovnická, the main street on the other side of the hotel. His initial resistance seemed to have been little more than a façade.

Cloutard could see that his eyes were glued to Hellen's breasts and his right hand was wandering down to her behind. *Tom will kill me when he finds out*, he thought as he entered the lobby.

It was empty, the front desk unattended. He went behind the desk and into the office directly behind it. Inside, he took a small leather pouch out of his pocket, opened it, and examined his burglar's tools with a grin: a set of lockpicks and other precision tools that had literally opened doors for him. Many doors.

Calmly, swiftly, he went to work on the door marked "SECURITY" in large letters.

Not that secure, he thought when it sprang open, and he

was suddenly standing in a room full of monitors. He sat at the computer terminal and typed in the relevant date and time. Seconds later, he'd found the recordings he was looking for.

"I do love well-organized people," he murmured as he played back the video.

Suddenly, he heard Hellen's voice, or rather a high-pitched squeal.

"*Merde*," Cloutard muttered. Hellen and the night manager were already back. But Cloutard had what he wanted, and he saw the man the concierge had described: elderly, a walking stick, worn-out tweed jacket, argyle sweater-vest, and corduroy trousers.

A gloating smile crossed the Frenchman's face. "Damjam Mandalov," he whispered to himself, recognizing the man. He quickly copied the video to a thumb drive.

Now all he had to do was get out of there. As he moved from the office into the reception area, he could hardly believe his eyes. Hellen lay sprawled across one of the large, upholstered armchairs that surrounded a table decorated with a large vase of flowers. The night manager was on top of her, his hands everywhere, with Hellen letting out shrill yelps of protest.

But Cloutard knew what it sounded like when Hellen was really in danger. She was still playing her role. Even so, he moved quickly. He darted out of the office, left the reception area, and crept past the two draped over the armchair. He was almost outside when he turned around.

"Enough!" he heard Hellen say. "No means no." She groped for the vase of flowers on the table beside her and a second later smashed it over the night manager's head. The man slid off of Hellen and slumped unconscious onto the Persian rug on the floor.

"That's what you get when you don't know how to treat a woman," Hellen said accusingly, stepping over the unconscious man. She looked inquiringly at Cloutard.

"Do we have what we need?" she asked. Cloutard nodded. "Then let's go!"

CHAPTER 32
NATIONAL GALLERY OF ART, WASHINGTON, D.C.

As she did whenever she visited the gallery, Akira sat on the dark-gray sofa in the center of the small room. At this time of day, the National Gallery of Art was always quiet, just the way Akira liked it. Dealing with other people had always been difficult for her, and she found crowds positively paralyzing. In recent years, she had learned to live with her condition and cope with it, but still—as far as she was able—she avoided crowds. If she had to go out, she never used public transport, and if something she needed could not be delivered, she took her bicycle or called an Uber.

Now, she simply sat and admired the picture in the corner to her right. It was an 18th century oil painting by the French artist Jean-Honoré Fragonard: *"La Liseuse,"* the "Young Girl Reading." It was her absolute favorite picture. Akira visited the gallery at least once a month, sat on that same sofa in Gallery 54 in the West Building, and studied the young woman sitting and reading in her yellow dress. The picture radiated a sense of peace, but also a loneliness that Akira could understand very well.

Akeem Johnson, the gray-bearded museum guard who

watched over this section of the museum, had come to know Akira quite well. Despite her social phobias, she had had a number of interesting conversations with the warm, elderly man. She liked him. And he was also known to look the other way if Akira had a little snack during her visit—food was against gallery rules. After half an hour, Akira stood up to go.

"Has Jamie proposed yet?" Akeem asked. He was standing at the gallery entrance, keeping an eye on the few visitors.

"No, Mr. Johnson," Akira replied, smiling shyly.

"I believe I'm going to have to have a serious word with that young man. How's he doing, by the way? Since that internship he did here two years ago, I've only seen him a couple of times."

"He's just busy. He's working in a small gallery now."

"I'm glad to hear it. But bring him by next time you come. I'll tell him it's about time he made an honest young woman out of you," Akeem said with a wink.

"I'll do that, Mr. Johnson."

The two said goodbye and Akira left the museum.

She cycled through the National Mall, crossing Jefferson Drive, then rode past the Washington Monument and the Lincoln Memorial Reflecting Pool, around the memorial itself, and across Arlington Memorial Bridge. Twenty minutes later, she reached Clarendon Boulevard and the modern brick building where she lived.

She stowed her bicycle in the basement and took the elevator up to the second floor.

As she exited the elevator, her steps grew slower. Her heart began to race as she walked down the hallway toward her apartment. An inexpressible feeling took hold of her. Her stomach knotted. Even from a distance, she could see that her front door stood ajar. Despite the obvious danger, she edged closer and closer, only stopping when she heard noises from inside. Her hands trembled and she was breathing fast. Her face was chalk-white, and she stood for a moment as if petrified.

Another noise from inside jolted her out into action. She dug frantically in her pocket for her cell phone, but her breath caught in her throat as the phone slipped from her sweaty hands and clattered onto the tiled floor. She snatched it up and ran to the other end of the hallway and around the corner. With jittery fingers, she dialed 911.

"911, what is your emergency?"

"You have to help me. Someone's breaking into my apartment," Akira whispered as she cowered on the floor and peeped around the corner toward her door. She gave her name and address and hung up.

Minutes later, she heard sirens approaching rapidly. She ducked out of sight and clapped her hand over her mouth when her apartment door was jerked open and two men wearing disposable gloves charged out and ran downstairs.

She waited another half a minute, then ran down the hall to her apartment. She gasped at the chaos. Her living room had been turned upside down. The sofa had been slashed open, drawers pulled from cupboards, and their contents dumped on the floor. Shredded books lay everywhere. Her keycode-secured office door had been forced open and her expensive equipment destroyed. A pungent odor stung her nose when she stepped inside. Her drives had been doused with acid. Not even specialists would be able to retrieve the data on them. This was the work of professionals.

She pushed open her bedroom door and slapped her hand over her mouth to stifle a scream. The scene before her was horrific, surreal. She would never be able to wipe it from her memory, as long as she lived. Jamie lay on the rose-petal-strewn bed, with three bullets in his chest. He was dead.

CHAPTER 33
HOLLOMAN AIR FORCE BASE, NEW MEXICO

Weaver was not happy. His face was scarlet with rage as he paced back and forth in the small room, arms crossed over his chest. He had summarily taken Tom, Hagen and all the technicians into custody and had them transported to nearby Holloman Air Force Base. Their loud protests fell on deaf ears.

"I'll ask again: what's the code?" Weaver said through gritted teeth. He knew he was out of line, acting this way, but General Horne's orders had been clear.

"Code? Do *you* know the code?" Tom looked at Hagen in feigned bewilderment.

"I thought *you* had it," Hagen said, joining Tom's game.

"Don't fuck with me," Weaver snapped. His patience was wearing thin.

"We wouldn't dream of it. But we don't know the code," said Tom.

Weaver was close to losing his last scrap of composure, but Tom and Hagen didn't react. They didn't even flinch, not even when Weaver slammed both hands on the table and let fly with, "What's the fucking code?!"

"Okay, Lieutenant Colonel." Tom signaled to him to come

closer. "I'll tell you a secret." Tom leaned forward in Weaver's direction, and Weaver moved expectantly nearer. In a low voice, Tom said, "This is terribly embarrassing for us, really, and I hate to admit it, but we've actually forgotten the code." For a moment, the two men stared at one another until Tom abruptly leaned back and grinned. "Why do you think we needed the MOAB? We couldn't get the case open with C4."

Weaver was boiling over. Hagen looked down at the floor, stifling a laugh.

"For the last time, give me the goddamned code. This order comes from the President of the United States himself."

"Well, see, for one thing I doubt that very much," Hagen said. He pointed at Tom and himself and continued. "And secondly, we're not Americans, so if it's an order from your Demander-in-Chief—who, by the way, is only president because someone offed the last guy—then, to put it nicely, we just . . ." Hagen looked at Tom and they nodded to each other and said together: " . . . don't give a shit."

"We answer to the UN Security Council," Hagen continued, "and unless you want to cause your beloved POTUS some unnecessary headaches, then you'd better let us go."

"Also, my wife is definitely going to be worried, and you do *not* want to tangle with her," Tom added.

Crossing their arms, Tom and Hagen leaned back in their chairs. They had nothing more to say, and Weaver knew it. He glared at them but said nothing and stormed out of the room.

"We need a plan," Hagen said. "We can't let DARPA move the case away from here. It's hard to open, sure, and would probably stand up to a grenade, but sooner or later they're going to get into it. Think about it. An essentially indestructible artifact that makes people de facto incapable of combat would be a godsend for America's number-one weapons lab."

"I realize that. But reverse-engineering a mythical, if not supernatural... *thing* like that isn't going to be easy."

"Which has never stopped people like them from trying."

"Believe me, the whole thing stinks of General Horne," Tom said. "If there's no voice of reason to balance Horne, then I'm not surprised at all that the president's ignoring a seventy-year-old international agreement."

Hagen shrugged. "So, what do we do now? Where's the brilliant Wagner plan that will get us out of this mess?"

Just then, the door flew open, and Weaver came in with two of his men.

"Listen up, gentlemen. As you so eloquently put it, you're not U.S. citizens. And as I've just discovered, you did not enter the country in the usual manner— and, in fact, have no proper visas. So, my men here are going to escort you to El Paso and put you on a plane back to your beloved Europe."

Hagen looked at Tom, and Tom saw the first signs of unease on his face. He gave him a wink.

"Follow me," barked one of Weaver's men.

"I'll have your head for this, and Horne's with it," Hagen said.

"You're welcome to try. Lodge a complaint with the UN, or whoever the fuck you like. By then, Medusa's head will be long gone, buried in the depths of Area 51."

Weaver watched his men lead them out, a broad, smug grin on his face.

"Can we have our things back, at least?" said Tom, as they crossed the parade ground and headed toward an old Ford. "They're still in the Hummer. We're going to need our passports, right?" The Ford was a standard-issue sedan, the same kind used by non-military police.

One of the men nodded, and Tom went over to the Humvee they'd been traveling in since they arrived and opened the rear door. He took out Hagen's backpack and shouldered his own duffel bag. He tossed Hagen his pack and they stowed them in the Ford's trunk. Weaver's men were already holding the doors open for them, and they slid onto the back seat. One of Weaver's men got in behind the wheel, the other on the passenger side. Then they drove off and left the base, heading south.

"What do we do now?" Hagen whispered.

"Don't worry. I've got a plan," Tom whispered back.

CHAPTER 34
ST. PAUL THE APOSTLE AIRPORT, OHRID, NORTH MACEDONIA

It had taken a while for Cloutard to convince first Hellen and then the pilots of van Rensburg's private jet that the trail led to North Macedonia.

Damjam Mandalov, the man he'd recognized on the security cameras, had vanished from the radar years earlier, retiring from the "business."

Mandalov was already a legend when Cloutard was still earning his reputation as a smuggler and art thief. To people in the antiquities trade, the man was a true expert, especially when it came to anything involving Alexander the Great.

"You're sure about this? I've never heard the name before at all," Hellen asked as they disembarked at the airfield. Cloutard had told her everything worth knowing about Mandalov during the flight.

"Almost certainly. My gut tells me it is more than a coincidence," Cloutard said as they headed toward the airport building. He was speaking loudly to make himself heard over the roar of the jet engines cycling down. "Richter is murdered as he's about to hand over Medusa's head to van Rensburg. A weird Medusa cult starts stirring up social media. And just then, a man who just happens to be the leading expert on Alexander the Great reappears."

"And that's what worries me. Mother and I both have excellent contacts among historians, and I've never heard a thing about any Damjam Mandalov."

Inside the terminal, Cloutard pulled his Panama hat a little lower over his eyes and leaned closer to Hellen as if to share a secret. "Just because he is not a recognized expert does not mean he does not know more about the ancient Greeks than all of your professors put together. You of all people should know that there is more than one truth in this world."

"And what if he turns out to be this sinister Apostolos Ibis? The name has come up a few times, but the man seems to be a phantom," Hellen said.

Cloutard narrowed his eyes. "Mandalov is certainly eccentric, but hiring assassins is not his style. Although I wouldn't bet my life on it."

Once they were through the entry formalities, they left the airport through the arched entrance that dominated the building. Cloutard flagged a taxi. "To Samuel's Fortress," he said curtly, pressing a twenty-euro bill into the man's hand.

The man nodded happily and sped away. Cloutard leaned forward between the seats. "They say that someone still lives in the fortress," he said

The man laughed out loud and Cloutard saw a gap-toothed smile in the rearview mirror. "Old stories. There is nothing to them," the driver replied in broken French, recognizing Cloutard as a citizen of *La République*.

"I was here many years ago and visited someone in the old ruins." Cloutard paused for a moment to lend his words more weight. "Damjam Mandalov."

The taxi driver scoffed again and shook his head, but

Hellen looked at Cloutard in surprise. "You've been here before?" she asked.

Cloutard turned to her and switched to German. "*Ma chère*, do you really think I would drag you all the way here on a mere suspicion? Twenty years ago, I was invited to a reception that took place at Samuel's Fortress." He smiled almost blissfully at the memory. "And a most illustrious circle it was. I was able to arrange a number of lucrative deals. There, I met Mandalov for the first and last time. I thought he must be dead—he was already an old man then. It surprises me to find that he is still among the living."

The driver turned right and left the main road that passed through the center of Ohrid, a sizable town located not far from the Albanian border beside Lake Ohrid, the second largest lake in the Balkans. The road wound slowly up to the fortress, which was situated on a promontory in front of the city.

"According to legend, there used to be an older fortress here, built by Philip II," Cloutard said, pointing up at the ancient walls.

"Alexander the Great's father?" Hellen asked.

Cloutard nodded.

"And Mandalov still lives here?" she pressed.

"I hope so," Cloutard said. "Even back then, the idea that anyone was living in the old ruins was scoffed at. A ridiculous myth, they said. But I know better."

The taxi driver stopped on the small, cobblestoned plaza. He turned at looked dejectedly at Cloutard. "You will not find anyone here."

Cloutard and Hellen climbed out. Even before the doors closed, the driver was speeding away in a cloud of dust. A large halogen floodlight illuminated the entrance, lending the fortress a spooky air. There was no sound at all apart from the wind blowing in from the sea and whistling through the trees that surrounded the fortress.

A few steps brought them to the inner courtyard. Hellen looked around and groaned. "Seriously, François?" Her arm described a semicircle, demonstrating how impressively empty the courtyard was, surrounded by no more than dilapidated, overgrown walls. "It's a damned ruin. How is anybody supposed to live here?"

Unfazed, Cloutard moved on toward one of the watchtowers. They struggled through bushes and stony rubble until they reached the steps leading up to the battlements above.

Cloutard stopped at the steps, turned left, and moved a few paces along the high defensive wall. He seemed so sure of himself that Hellen's doubts began to fade. Apparently, he knew where he was going. Suddenly he stopped, and Hellen heard him counting softly.

"*Un, deux, trois, quatre . . .*" Cloutard counted the stones on the wall, then pressed on one of them. Nothing appeared to happen. Then he continued along the wall. Hellen followed until they reached some matted bushes. A gap had opened in the wall behind them.

Cloutard pointed to Hellen's backpack. "We will need your flashlight."

She patted his shoulder with admiration and squeezed through the gap behind him into the interior of the structure. A steep stairway led deep into the mountain on which the fortress perched.

"Tsar Samuel of Bulgaria chose Ohrid as the capital of the First Bulgarian Empire and built this place on the foundations of Philip II's fortress. The secret passages that lead down to the sea are reputed to date all the way back to Philip's time," Cloutard said as they descended the hundred or more steps.

When they reached the bottom, the passageway widened into a small hall, at the end of which a pale light gleamed.

Cloutard led the way toward the light. The closer they came, the slower Hellen walked—mostly because of the grim-looking man who had stepped into the dim light in front of a massive door, an HK MP7 submachine gun slung over his shoulder.

"Ζεί ὁ βασιλιάς Αλέξανδρος," Hellen heard the man say.

Cloutard smiled. "Ζεί και βασιλεύει," he replied without hesitation.

Hellen looked at Cloutard with a frown.

"I will explain later," Cloutard whispered.

The guard retrieved a large key from his jacket pocket, inserted it into the antique keyhole, turned it twice, and opened the door.

"*Après toi,*" Cloutard said, and with a sweep of his arm he ushered Hellen ahead. Hellen felt as if she were entering a new world.

CHAPTER 35

ON THE ROAD TO EL PASO, NEW MEXICO

An uncomfortable silence filled the car as it trundled along the almost empty Highway 70 toward Las Cruces at fifty-five miles per hour. Nothing but barren semi-desert rolled past, mile after mile. After half an hour, they passed the turnoff to the Missile Museum and the road snaked up toward San Augustin Pass, with its breathtaking views over the Tularosa Basin and White Sands. In forty minutes, they would reach Las Cruces. From there it was another hour to El Paso International Airport.

Tom, in the back with Hagen, had spent the drive eyeing the men in front, trying to figure them out. They seemed like most "private contractors": too cool for the official armed forces, and often temperamental, impatient, violent, and trigger-happy. Not a good combination, and it left men like these with few options but to work privately, as muscle for hire. He and Hagen could use that to their advantage.

"Are we there yet?" Tom asked, out of the blue. Hagen looked at him and frowned. The two soldiers ignored him. "Did you play 'I Spy' when you were a kid on a long drive with your folks?" Tom chattered away at a mile a minute, at the same time testing cautiously whether the doors could be opened from the inside. No luck. "I always won. But if I think about it now, I think my mom probably just let we win." The electric windows were also deactivated.

Hagen jabbed Tom in the side as the driver glanced in the rearview mirror, checking they were behaving themselves. The driver laughed.

"What, you think you're going to jump out while we're driving? You'd never survive it. This ain't a movie."

"Can we at least open the window a little way? You'd give a dog a little fresh air on a hot day, wouldn't you?" Tom said, watching the men carefully.

The two soldiers exchanged a look and shrugged. Then the man in the passenger seat pressed a switch on the center console. Tom's window dropped a couple of inches.

"Hey, one more thing. Could you pull over somewhere? I always get carsick in the back seat. I don't want to blow chunks down the back of your neck."

The two men didn't respond, but they were obviously getting annoyed.

Tom looked imploringly at Hagen and, with his eyes, motioned toward the two soldiers as inconspicuously as he could, hoping to make his intentions clear without saying a word. Hagen was an experienced undercover agent, after all, and had no doubt found himself in any number of seemingly hopeless situations like this.

"All right, all right. I get it. But can I at least get a bag?" Tom needled. "You know, just in case worse comes to worst?"

The man in the passenger seat glowered grimly back at him. "Time for you to shut your mouth," the man growled.

"I gotta use the can, too. We didn't get a chance to go before we left." Another menacing glare from the soldier.

There was silence for a moment. Then Tom, sitting behind the passenger seat, slid forward a little and leaned his elbows on the armrests of the two front seats. "Say, why are you guys driving so slow? You're allowed to do sixty-five here, and you're creeping along like two senior citizens on the way to bingo. We're going to miss our flight, and Lieutenant Colonel Grumpy sure ain't gonna like that."

Tom had him where he wanted him.

"Sit your ass back on your goddamned seat," the man riding shotgun said. He jammed his pistol under Tom's nose. The driver grinned.

"Okay, okay, Dutch. Take it easy," said Tom, raising his hands defensively. Then without warning, he grabbed the hand with the gun and pushed it upward. At the same time, he circled his right arm around the man's neck and pulled him back against the headrest.

"What the hell?!" the driver yelled. The sudden wrangling made him swing the wheel and he slammed into the guard rail and scraped along it, sending sparks flying.

"The windows!" Tom shouted.

Hagen leaned forward and pressed the window buttons, and the rear windows descended further. Tom slammed the hand holding the gun repeatedly against the roof of the car as he squeezed man's throat tighter and tighter.

The driver managed to get the car back on course. He tried to draw his own pistol, but Hagen was faster, grabbing the man from behind and snatching the gun from his shoulder holster.

Just then, a shot blasted from the passenger side. The driver's blood and brains splattered like a rotten tomato against the side window. He collapsed forward and the weight of his foot pressed on the gas pedal. The car shot forward.

Hagen leaned over and grabbed the steering wheel,

swinging them clear of a semi coming the other way. He was able to prevent a collision, but the sudden swerve sent the car into a sideways skid. It hit the shoulder and rolled several times, finally coming to rest on its roof on the arid sands, a short way off the road.

CHAPTER 36

IN THE CATACOMBS OF SAMUEL'S FORTRESS, OHRID, NORTH MACEDONIA

Hellen let out a sharp cry, and Cloutard grinned. "I thought you might like this," he said.

"Like it? Oh my God, it's paradise."

After giving the correct password, Cloutard and Hellen had entered a hall at least as big as a football field. The room was filled from one end to the other with historical artifacts and statues, an immense array of discoveries dating back thousands of years. Excavated items were arranged meticulously on enormous tables, and thousands of books filled row after row of bookshelves along the walls. Among the antiquities was a collection of technical equipment that would make the world's leading museums salivate. The room was subdivided into several sections with different lighting schemes, bright floodlights giving way to indirect lighting, then to infrared lamps. Large sections of the room, the far end of which Hellen could not even see, were in total darkness.

"Here I was, Doctor de Mey, thinking that after the Library of Alexandria, my collection here would surely no longer impress you." A soft voice almost whispered from the darkness. From behind one of the Doric columns, an electric wheelchair appeared. The man seated in it was very old indeed. A full head of snow-white hair flowed to his shoulders—*astonishing hair for a man his age*, Hellen thought, guessing him to be at least ninety years old.

The high-tech, touchscreen-controlled wheelchair rolled to a stop in front of Hellen and Cloutard. *So, this is Damjam Mandalov*, Hellen thought, studying him. His face was deeply furrowed, amplifying the emotions that played across it, and his clear eyes were full of youthful curiosity. And although the man obviously spent most of his time underground, his face had a healthy color, he was clean-shaven, and his long, white hair was immaculately groomed. Hellen had never seen a man at once so ancient-looking and so attractive.

He smiled at them, then abruptly shook his head in annoyance, braced himself on the chair's armrests, and slowly stood up. "But where are my manners? My name is Mandalov, Damjam Mandalov. I am happy that you have found your way here to my domain." Mandalov swept his arms out wide, then looked down at his wheelchair. "As you can see, I am not very mobile these days, so I thank the gods for this contraption. The passages down here are long, so I have chosen to give myself wheels most of the time." His smile was at once engaging and disarming. If a single human being could embody charisma, then it would be Damjam Mandalov. He had a radiance that took Hellen's breath away.

"Monsieur Cloutard, I'm glad to see that you remember the old Gorgonian password from the last time we met." Hellen's expression showed her confusion. "The Gorgons are figures from Greek mythology," Mandalov explained.

Hellen nodded. "I know that much, but I must admit, Greek antiquity is not among my areas of expertise."

"There is a legend," Mandalov continued, "that the

Gorgons would demand a watchword from passing ships, and the response would decide whether they sank or spared the ship. They asked the ship's crew if Alexander the Great was still alive, to which the only right answer was: 'He lives and rules as king.' Any other answer, and the ship was doomed." Mandalov smiled. "I took the liberty of using their password as my own."

He sat in his wheelchair again and they followed him to a large table that stood in the center of the hall. One of Mandalov's assistants brought three glasses containing a clear fluid.

"Of course, Alexander knew nothing about ouzo, but I love the stuff," Mandalov said, and he raised his glass. Hellen and Cloutard did the same. "A drink to Alexander the Great before we get down to business. I am sure there must be a very special reason you are here. But first: *Jámas!*"

Cloutard and Hellen repeated the traditional toast. They clinked glasses and tossed back the fine, anise-flavored liqueur.

Damjam suddenly grew serious. "I have heard a lot about you, Dr. de Mey, particularly about your discoveries in recent years. Impressive indeed." He looked from Hellen to Cloutard and back. "So, what brings you and Monsieur Cloutard to me?"

"We've come because you were in Prague recently—François saw you on a security camera at the Four Seasons Hotel. My former boss, Professor Richter, the director of the Museum of Fine Arts in Vienna, was in Prague at the same time. He was there to meet someone named Apostolos Ibis, and a short time later, he was murdered. We were hoping that you could perhaps tell us something about Ibis."

Mandalov refilled first Hellen's glass, then Cloutard's, and finally his own with ouzo. He looked pensive, and a little sad.

"I was in Prague, yes, but incognito, of course. No one would allow a madman like me anywhere near a symposium at the illustrious Academy of Sciences. If you don't move in recognized scientific circles, you're nobody," the old man said with a smile.

Cloutard looked at Hellen as if to say, "I told you so," and Hellen nodded, chagrined.

"I was sought out by an exceptionally attractive young woman," Mandalov continued. "She asked me to visit the Four Seasons to examine an amphora that Mr. Ibis had found. She also promised me a chance to read a letter from Plato that had long been considered lost. The fact that these people even knew about Plato's letter told me they had some expertise."

Hellen frowned—she clearly had never heard of such a letter.

"But when I got to the hotel, everything felt very suspicious. I was supposed to analyze the amphora first, and only then would I be able to see the letter. At that point, I said no, and insisted on meeting the mysterious Mr. Ibis, but I was told he was talking with Professor Richter from Vienna just then."

Cloutard and Hellen exchanged a significant look.

"The whole situation felt wrong, so I simply left. That's all I can tell you. I have never met a man named Apostolos Ibis, and I'm afraid I can't offer anything new about Professor Richter's regrettable death. I stayed on briefly in Prague and met with a few people on the fringes of the symposium, then returned here.

Hellen sighed and looked uncertainly at Cloutard, who nodded encouragingly. "I believe we should tell him," he said.

Hellen toyed a little nervously with her glass of ouzo, turning it between her fingers, unsure whether to reveal their secret. Then she summoned up the necessary courage. "Mr. Mandalov, François told me that you were the leading expert on ancient Greece. I must apologize for never having heard of you before, but looking around here, I can see that François was not exaggerating."

"There's no need to apologize for not knowing me. It's how I prefer things to be. A lot of my research has been published, in fact, but all under pseudonyms, so I'm not surprised that you do not know my name. What was it that you wanted to tell me?"

Hellen paused briefly, then said, "Mr. Mandalov, we have found the head of Medusa."

From one second to the next, the color drained from the old man's face. "It had to happen one day," he said softly.

He drained his refilled ouzo and tapped on his wheelchair's touchscreen. A hissing noise sounded, lights came on at the end of the huge hall, and a heavy steel door opened. Mandalov was already rolling toward it.

"Follow me. There is something I think you ought to see."

CHAPTER 37
AKIRA'S APARTMENT BLOCK, ARLINGTON, VIRGINIA

Akira stared at the red point of light. She did not know how long she'd been there. It was dark. She was crouched in a corner, arms hugging her backpack, rocking back and forth. The light had gone out long before and now all she could see was the red glimmer of the LED in the switch. There were gaps in her memory. She did not know how she had gotten to the basement. She only knew that she couldn't deal with the police, so she'd hidden herself away. And now she was sitting there, leaning on the basement door. Her hands shook and the terrible images kept flashing before her inner eye. All that blood. Jamie's lifeless body. The rose petals.

Why?

The question had been circling through her head. The men who broke in hadn't been there for her stuff. They had to have been after her personally. Why else would they destroy her computers? And Jamie—why was Jamie even there? He should have been at the gallery at that time of day. Suddenly, it all fell into place. Sunday, brunch, the champagne. That's why he'd been so upset when she went to see her boss. And the rose petals today. Akira sobbed and began to cry uncontrollably at the thought that Jamie had probably wanted to ask her to marry him.

She squeezed her eyes shut when the light suddenly came on. Her sobbing stopped instantly. She listened. A door opened. Steps. She quickly slipped the stun gun she kept with her at all times for emergencies out of her backpack. She jumped to her feet and attacked. A man she didn't immediately recognize collapsed twitching when she jammed the stun gun into his side. Only then did she realize who he was.

"Oh, God, sorry Mr. Wilson. I didn't know it was you. I'm sorry, I . . ." She tripped over the twitching body of her neighbor where he lay on the floor, got back to her feet, and ran upstairs and out onto the street. She ran and ran until she couldn't run any more.

Out of breath, she found herself at the Marine Corps War Memorial. The iconic monument, inspired by the equally iconic photograph taken at the Battle of Iwo Jima in 1945, showed six Marines raising the American flag. She leaned against one of the marble blocks beside the five steps up to the monument and stared up at it.

What was she supposed to do now? Her boyfriend was dead, murdered in cold blood. Her apartment had been ransacked and her equipment destroyed. *All because of something I did*, she thought. Nothing else made any sense. But why would anyone want to kill her for that? She had to find out what she had stumbled upon as soon as she could. Could it have something to do with the Medusa cult conspiracy? Or with her work for DARPA? She thought feverishly. Her research into the tech company had turned up nothing worth killing for, which left the cult. As absurd as it all was, the conspiracy had led to marches and protests around the world. The men in her apartment had definitely been professionals. She had only seen them for a fraction of a second, but she had seen the gloves they wore and the shoulder holster one of the men had worn under his jacket.

She took out her cell phone and found Lieutenant Colonel Weaver's number, but she hesitated. She'd been reporting to him about the cult for weeks, and less than twenty-four hours after she gave him what she believed was a crucial clue, unknown men had tried to kill her. It could not be a coincidence.

The truth struck her like a bolt of lightning. She smashed her phone on the ground and stomped on it several times, until the display turned black. They could track her through her phone. She looked around fearfully. Were they already here? Were they close? She had to go underground, find somewhere safe. She pulled her hood low over her face and ran around the access road circling the memorial until she reached North Meade Street, where she found a taxi. She told the driver to take her to the National Gallery of Art. The whole way, she kept looking over her shoulder, checking that she was not being followed. The drive seemed to take forever—demonstrations around the Capitol and White House were causing chaos on the streets—and Akira's panic grew.

When she finally reached the museum, she hurried up the steps and ran inside. She passed through the metal detector and held her annual pass to the card reader before passing through the turnstile.

Relief washed over her, and she slowed her pace. The museum was a lot busier now than it had been a few hours before, but she still felt safer in here than outside. She was happy to be away from the mass of demonstrators moving inexorably along the National Mall, the park that stretched for over a mile between the Capitol and the Washington Monument, toward the Capitol.

But she kept looking around. More people than she was comfortable with were strolling beneath the high rotunda. Black marble columns arranged in a circle supported the dome high overhead. She turned right and moved down the sculpture-lined hallway before entering Gallery 54 on her right.

"Twice in one day?" said Mr. Johnson, beaming when he spotted Akira. But he saw right away that something wasn't right. With her hood pulled low, hands clasped together, eyes on the floor, Akira shuffled toward him. Seeing his familiar face calmed her a little. Her adrenalin eased, and suddenly her tears came pouring out.

"What is it, Akira? Has something happened?" Mr. Johnson led the distraught Akira to the sofa in the center of the gallery and sat down beside her. She was sobbing uncontrollably, her gaze still locked on the floor. He went to put his arm around her shoulder, but she shrugged him off.

"Jamie's dead," she stammered, so low Mr. Johnson could hardly hear her. "They killed him."

"What? What are you saying? Who would kill him?"

"I didn't know where else to go."

"All right. Come with me for now," the old man said soothingly. He radioed a colleague to take over his post, then he and Akira walked together back to the hallway and out to the rotunda. "Let's go to the break room. You can tell me everything there."

Akira nodded silently and glanced up at him, a grateful smile on her face.

They were just crossing the circular front hall near the main entrance when the distant beeping of the metal detector made Akira stop and look across the circular space. She instantly recognized the two men flashing IDs and arguing loudly with a security guard. A burst of adrenalin gave her renewed strength.

"They've found me. I don't know how, but they've found me," Akira whispered, staring toward the entrance.

One of the killers spotted Akira in the rotunda and forced his way past the security guard, who hit the floor hard. The two men pushed and shoved their way through the crowd at the entrance, heading straight for her.

"The stairs to the ground floor!" Mr. Johnson said, pointing to the stairway leading down. Akira ran, weaving through the gallery visitors.

The old man tried to stop the two killers, but he had no chance. They simply ran around him. Akira looked back.

"Run, Akira, run!" Mr. Johnson shouted after her.

She took the stairs several at a time, then hooked left at the bottom. Dodging athletically between the tables and chairs in the Garden Café directly underneath the rotunda, she headed west. Her pursuers weren't as careful—tables and chairs went flying, people yelled, and museum staff tried in vain to stop them.

Akira left the central gallery behind her, leaped down the stairs to the side entrance and raced out of the building. She turned south, running toward the National Mall. On both sides of the park were the museums that made up the Smithsonian Institute. A crowd of hundreds of thousands filled the Mall, waving placards and chanting as they streamed toward the Capitol.

Akira pulled up when she saw the sea of people, her adrenalin surging again. Her hands turned moist, her face pale. She turned around. She saw the men some way behind her, but they had lost sight of her for the moment.

She had one way out, one chance to escape the men, and she knew it. If she wanted to live to see tomorrow, she had to summon up all her courage and push through the dark shadow that had dominated her entire life. She pulled off her hoodie and stuffed it into her backpack. Hands trembling, she took a deep breath and edged in among the demonstrators. She risked a final look back and saw her two pursuers, out of breath, pushing through the crowd coming from 7th Street, looking all around before finally retreating again in frustration.

CHAPTER 38
IN THE CATACOMBS OF SAMUEL'S FORTRESS, OHRID, NORTH MACEDONIA

They had to duck to enter the small, secure room. It contained only one item, a yellowed painting behind glass.

"Is that what I think it is?" Hellen said.

Damjam Mandalov nodded. "It is indeed. No doubt you are familiar with the Alexander Mosaic, discovered in Pompeii and now on display in the National Archeological Museum of Naples. This is the original painting on which the mosaic was based."

"But I thought the original was lost!" Hellen said.

Cloutard smiled. "Did I not say that for anything relating to Alexander the Great, we were visiting the right man?"

Carefully, almost reverently, Hellen stepped closer to the faded image. Mandalov had left his wheelchair again and now stood beside Hellen. She studied the painting minutely. "I don't know the Alexander Mosaic in detail, but I could have sworn that here . . ." She let her sentence hang as she pointed to a spot beneath Alexander the Great's head.

"The Alexander Mosaic is a depiction of the Battle of Issus, when Alexander fought the Persian King Darius," Mandalov said. "What you are looking at here is a painting by Philoxenus of Eretria. Now, while the mosaic is based on this painting, the differences, as you have just noticed, are considerable," he explained.

Hellen took out her phone and found an image of the mosaic, her gaze shifting repeatedly from the phone to the painting in front of her and back.

"There are hundreds of differences, in fact," said Mandalov.

"But at least the painting is complete. The mosaic, sadly, was already damaged when it was discovered in Pompeii, and damaged even more when it was transported to Naples," Hellen added knowledgeably.

"Look here." Mandalov pointed to the left third of the picture. Hellen compared it with the mosaic, which was incomplete on that side. "Alexander is holding Medusa's head in his hands," Mandalov said. "But in the mosaic, Medusa's head is much smaller and depicted as no more than an image in the center of his breastplate."

Only now did Hellen realize that Mandalov, although he had turned pale, had not actually seemed very surprised when she told him about discovering Medusa's head.

"Where is the head now?" he asked, as if able to read her thoughts.

"Probably already destroyed," said Cloutard, glancing at his watch. "Tom Wagner, Hellen's husband, was on his way to the United States with it. They were going to try to destroy it there."

Mandalov frowned. "They won't be able to," he said softly, a note of awe in his voice. "Medusa's head is not so easily destroyed."

Hellen looked at Mandalov in surprise. "What do you mean?"

"This will take a little explaining," Mandalov said, lowering himself into his wheelchair again. Hellen and Cloutard pulled up chairs and sat with him. Like two children whose grandfather is telling them a story, they sat wide-eyed before the old man and listened closely.

"You have already seen for yourselves that the legends surrounding the Medusa are true."

Hellen and Cloutard nodded.

"Alexander the Great's father gave him the task of conquering the world, aided by Medusa's head."

"His father? Philip II? But where did he get the head of Medusa?"

"Not Philip II. He was Alexander's adoptive father, that's all."

Hellen, confused, said, "*Adoptive* father?"

"Alexander the Great's true father was none other than Zeus, the father of the gods. And Alexander is known by other names, too. He is also the demigod Perseus—it was he who cut off the Gorgon Medusa's head."

The expressions on Hellen's and Cloutard's faces looked like someone had hit pause at an inopportune moment during a movie. Both their mouths were wide open, gaping at Mandalov as if he'd just told them about little green men from Mars. The old man went on undeterred.

"But to keep the Medusa under control, Zeus provided his demigod son with two objects that gave him power over her. Even the gods were fearful of the terrible creature. Hardly any of them could stand up to her."

After a few shocked seconds, Hellen recalled all the mystical artifacts she herself had recovered in the last few years and she regained her composure. Alexander the Great turning out to be the son of Zeus and planning to conquer the world with Medusa's head was practically par for the course, at this point.

"What objects?" she asked.

Mandalov smiled. He saw that he had piqued Hellen's archaeological curiosity.

"Zeus commanded Hephaestus, the god of fire, to forge a breastplate. The plate, known as the Aegis, was to have a polished, mirror-like panel at its center, centered on the solar plexus."

Hellen tapped the image of the Alexander Mosaic on her phone. "You mean, the Medusa we can see on Alexander's chest is a reflection?"

"Correct, Doctor de Mey. But there was still something missing from the Medusa-proof armor. It was not yet complete." He pointed up at the painting on the wall. "You can see there that Alexander is wearing a kind of cloak, or cape."

Hellen looked at the picture. "You're not suggesting . . ."

"You've guessed it, my dear," Mandalov said triumphantly. "Alexander is wearing the Golden Fleece of the Argonauts as a cloak."

"*Très interessante*," said Cloutard, tuning in again at the mention of the fleece.

Hellen grinned and shook her head. "Typical. The slightest hint of gold and you're back on board."

Cloutard raised his hands in a shrug. "Once a crook, always a crook."

Hellen turned back to Mandalov. "So, you're saying the only way to confront the Medusa is if you are equipped with these objects? It's the only way to withstand her power and destroy her?"

Mandalov nodded. "Nothing else can stop her. The Medusa is a treacherous monster. And the longer she is awake, the more dangerous she will become."

"What do you mean?"

"According to the legend, after Perseus, or Alexander, cut off her head, she only had one goal—to find a body once again. If she does that, she will be invincible. But there is one piece of good news. With the Aegis and the Golden

Fleece, Medusa can be destroyed. Perhaps more importantly, her curse can also be reversed."

"You mean, the people 'petrified' by looking at her will reawaken when she's destroyed?"

"So says the legend, at least," the old man said, leaning back and looking pleased with himself. He gave the impression that everything he had just said was common knowledge.

No one spoke for a few seconds. Hellen looked at Cloutard, who immediately nodded. "That would mean Maierhofer's son would be saved," Hellen said, more to herself than the others.

"Then first we need the Golden Fleece and Hephaestus's breastplate," said Cloutard confidently.

As absurd as it sounded, it felt like a glimmer of hope to Hellen, too. "Mr. Mandalov," she asked cautiously, "would you happen to know where those things might be found?"

"They are probably lying around here somewhere," Cloutard said cynically.

"That would be nice, certainly," Mandalov said. He sighed. "But you are right, Doctor de Mey. As it happens, I *do* know where to find them."

Hellen's expression brightened.

"But I'm afraid that is the only good news. The Golden Fleece and Hephaestus's Aegis are well protected. Both are in a place that has been sought for more than two thousand years—the grave of Alexander the Great."

CHAPTER 39

HOLLOMAN AIR FORCE BASE, NEW MEXICO

The white cloud of smoke from Lieutenant Colonel Weaver's cigar shrouded his face almost completely. He paced impatiently behind one of his men, who was attacking the high-security flight case with an angle grinder, trying to get it open. Sparks sprayed across the workshop and fell to the floor.

"How much longer is this going to take?" Weaver bellowed over the scream of the grinder. The noise suddenly stopped. The man pushed up his safety glasses and turned to Weaver.

"Sorry, sir, these cases are built to withstand—"

"You don't fucking say!" Weaver cut him off. "How stupid do you think I am? Just get the damned thing open and spare me your insights."

The man said nothing. He adjusted his safety glasses and started the grinder again.

"Call me when you get through the lock. Do *not* open it without me!" Weaver yelled. The man merely nodded and kept on grinding.

Weaver stepped out of the workshop. He stuffed the stub

of his cigar in his mouth and bit down on it, then took out his phone and dialed a number.

"We've got it," he said, when the call was answered. "We made it look like the MOAB worked."

"Good."

"There's one small problem. It's inside a high-security case, and we haven't got it open yet. But my men are working on it."

"And the task-force guys?"

"They'll soon be crossing the Atlantic on their way back to Europe. They won't be bothering us anymore."

"Good work," said General Horne. "Get that thing to our lab as fast as you can. We've got no time to lose. I've got POTUS on our side for now, but once the international pressure starts to build, I think we'll lose him."

"Yes, sir," said Weaver, and he hung up.

Weaver puffed contentedly on his cigar. Soon, he'd be heading back to Arlington with his men, and the lab rats could start their analysis. If Horne was right and the artifact truly had the incredible potential he believed it did, then it would give the U.S. military an invaluable long-term advantage.

"Sir, I've got it," a voice behind Weaver said. The mercenary was standing in the workshop doorway. He was covered in sweat but clearly proud of himself.

"Then let's take a closer look at this horror," said Weaver. He threw the last remnant of his cigar on the ground and strode back into the workshop.

"What exactly is supposed to be in there, sir? And why did those guys from the task force want to throw a MOAB at it?" the man asked.

"See for yourself. You probably won't believe it."

Weaver grasped the lid and lifted it. Both men were staring wide-eyed into the case when the workshop door flew open. "What is it?" Weaver roared across the room in fury and indignation.

"Sorry, sir. It's the team taking the two agents to the airport. They haven't called in as agreed. We've been trying to contact them, but there's no response."

"Motherfucking son of a . . ." He looked the man straight in the eye. "Take the chopper and a few men, find those agents, and bring them to me. Don't even think about coming back without them." The man nodded, turned on his heel, and went out.

"This can't be happening!" Weaver bawled, slamming the lid on the empty flight case.

CHAPTER 40
EL PASO INTERNATIONAL AIRPORT

The Mantis stepped smartly through the automatic doors and into the arrivals hall. She was wearing beige, slim-fit pants that accentuated her figure, a white blouse, and black loafers. Her copper-tinted hair was pulled back in a tight ponytail, and a pair of Ray-Ban Aviatorshid her eyes. A Bordeaux-red handbag dangled from one arm, and she towed a small carry-on case behind her.

She quickly spotted a man holding a card with her alias on it among the waiting crowd. A few minutes later, she was standing at the trunk of his car in the parking lot.

"Let's take a look," she said.

The man threw back a blanket and opened what looked like a regular travel case. Inside, embedded in foam, were two Glock 44s with silencers and spare magazines, several knives, and a telescopic baton. She let her experienced fingers glide over the equipment until they stopped at a roughly rectangular object about four inches long. She lifted it out.

"Everything's here," the man said with a trace of smugness.

"And the camera?" the woman asked, as she toyed with

the object in her hand and looked expressionlessly at the man.

"The tripod is back here." He pointed to a bag behind the case. Then he lifted the layer of foam that contained the weapons, revealing a Nikon Coolpix P1000 nestled underneath. The Mantis smiled. With its 3000mm superzoom, you could read a waitress's nametag from a mile away. It was a stalker's dream.

"And my money?" the man asked.

"Your money, right . . ." the Mantis said, taking a step toward him. "This is really a little embarrassing." Her voice was silky, almost erotic. "Is there a cash machine close by?"

"Lady, are you fucking with me?" the man said. He slammed the lid of the trunk without taking his eyes off her. "No money, no honey," he said, and he turned to go.

He heard the click of the Microtech Hera OTF automatic knife, but too late to react. At the press of a small button, a blade shot out of the object she had taken out of the case. Quick as a rattler, she grabbed the man from behind and stabbed him twice in the kidneys before sinking the blade into his ear. He collapsed without a sound. Normally, she would not resort to such methods in public, but time was against her. She was working with someone she didn't know, and she had to improvise. She dragged the man behind another car, dropped her own case in beside the one in the trunk, climbed in, and drove off.

Ninety minutes later, she turned onto Trap Club Road and drove to the end. She ground the car to a halt, kicking up a cloud of dust in front of a small building. When the dust settled, she climbed out and looked around. The empty shooting range lay around half a mile east of Holloman Air Force Base.

She took out her cell phone and read through the message she'd received from an unknown number. *The head is still out there*, it read. Beneath that was a set of coordinates that pointed her to a building in a remote corner of the base—to her surprise, because she was going in that direction anyway. Despite Barkley's best efforts, he had been unable to find out who had sent the message, so she had decided to get to the bottom of it herself. In the course of a strenuous discussion with Captain Maierhofer's assistant, she had learned that Medusa's head had been flown to Holloman. Koller had been brave. At first, he'd refused to reveal anything, but in the end her promise that the pain would stop had convinced him to talk. And he had told her a lot before she released him from his suffering. But the base was big, and the coordinates she'd received out of the blue were just what she needed.

Opening the trunk, the Mantis took out one of the Glock 44s, loaded it, and pushed it under her waistband at the back. Then she took out the camera and tripod, closed the trunk, and circled around to the other side of the run-down weatherboard building. She set up the camera and tripod on the western edge of the range, beside one of the nine roofed firing points, and pointed it toward the coordinates.

She squinted through the viewfinder and pressed "Record." There were a few Humvees, a building, and a helicopter, nothing else. She zoomed in on the helicopter. Four men were standing beside it. They looked like contractors, not regular soldiers. Then she saw the logo on the side of the helicopter.

DARPA? What's DARPA doing here? And why are they using heavily armed mercenaries? the Mantis wondered. *Could the number-one weapons lab in the country be after the head, too? More importantly, did they already have it . . . and were they holding it inside that building?*

A man with a cigar in his mouth came out of the building and made a phone call. The Mantis checked her watch and noted the time. Maybe she could find out later who he was talking to. But who was he? She zoomed closer and spotted a small Velcro patch with his name on it—Weaver—in slightly faded black letters. A silver oak-leaf insignia was sewn onto his collar. The door behind him opened and another mercenary appeared. He and Weaver exchanged words, then both went back inside. She swung the camera back to the men at the chopper. One of them was talking on a radio. Then he ran over to the building and disappeared inside. Moments later, he reappeared and ran back to the helicopter. All four jumped inside and the machine took off, heading southeast.

She swung back to the building. Weaver reemerged. He was clearly not happy. Something had happened. Whatever it was, she had to find out what the man knew.

She packed the equipment away and took out her phone. "Barkley, you need to find out everything you can about a Lieutenant Colonel Weaver. As soon as you can, please. He probably works for DARPA." She glanced at her watch. "And he made a phone call exactly seven minutes ago. I'm sending you his coordinates right now. Trace it. I want to know who he called. And hurry!"

She hung up. Then she climbed into the car and drove to the next town, where she found a room in the White Sands Motel.

CHAPTER 41
THE CATACOMBS OF SAMUEL'S FORTRESS, OHRID, NORTH MACEDONIA

"*Merde*," said Cloutard. Ducking low through the door, he, Hellen and Mandalov left the room containing the painting that had served as the model for the Alexander Mosaic. Back in the cavernous hall, they continued their conversation.

"Since I first became interested in archeology and history, Alexander the Great's tomb has been the most sought-after grave in the world—across all cultures, all races. Not even Cleopatra's final resting place has attracted as much interest," Hellen said. She sounded dubious, even desperate.

"Our chances do not look good at all this time," said Cloutard. "And archeologists and scientists are not the only ones looking for Alexander's tomb. Grave robbers, art thieves, and the biggest dealers in illegal antiquities have all searched for it in vain." The Frenchman reached for the ouzo bottle. He filled his glass, drained it in a single gulp, and filled it again.

"I know there are countless legends about the location of Alexander's tomb," said Hellen.

Mandalov nodded. "The legends are certainly many and

varied. Or rather, *were* many and varied, because a lot of the possible sites have already been ruled out. Every conceivable location in Egypt, Greece, Asia Minor, even India has been searched, and thoroughly. You can take my word for that. I was part of many of those expeditions myself." The old man looked at Cloutard. "If I remember correctly, you and I locked horns a little on one of those expeditions." Mandalov smiled knowingly, as if his own background was not exactly squeaky-clean.

Cloutard nodded. "That is true. My people and I spent years looking for the tomb. We can safely cross Siwa Oasis and the entire Babylon region off the list."

Mandalov sighed. "Memphis and Alexandria, too. There was once an immense mausoleum with a solid gold sarcophagus in Alexandria, but all traces of it have been lost to history."

Hellen smiled at the frustration on Cloutard's face at the mention of a sarcophagus made of gold. He reached for the ouzo again.

"Julius Caesar, Octavian, Septimius Severus, Caligula and Caracalla all visited Alexander's tomb," said Cloutard. "There are endless legends, and many of them tell of how each visitor took away a 'souvenir' from the objects buried with Alexander—every single one of them priceless."

"So we cannot even be certain that the artifacts are still in the tomb?" Hellen said, feeling despondent.

"Anything is possible. We simply don't know what was in the tomb originally and what is still there, assuming it even exists," Mandalov said.

"Have you heard anything from Tom?" Cloutard asked. "They should have blown up the head by now."

"Nothing. No answer to my message yet, either," Hellen said.

"It is impossible to destroy the Medusa," Mandalov said

again. "Without the artifacts to counter her powers, it is absolutely out of the question."

Hellen paced back and forth. Cloutard leaned on one of the large tables. "But there must be a way. Have all the possible locations for the tomb really been searched already?" Hellen asked.

"All of the ones anyone takes seriously," Mandalov said. "However, there are also two theories that have a certain . . . novelty value." It was clear from his voice that he thought little of either one.

Hellen turned and approached the old man. "I don't want to sound impolite. I'm a scientist, like you, and I know how little we think of absurd theories with no basis in reality. But in the last few years, some of those theories have taken us a long way."

Mandalov nodded. "I know, I know. The Sword of Peter, the Ark of the Covenant, the Library of Alexandria, Arthur's Chronicle, even the Holy Grail. And those are only the ones I know you've found."

Mandalov's eyes shifted between Hellen and Cloutard. His respect for both of them was obvious. "Good. Then let me tell you of these theories. The first suggests that Venetian merchants stole a mummy and other artifacts from Alexandria in the eighth century. They believed they had the mortal remains of the apostle Mark. According to this theory, they prepared a tomb for the apostle beneath St. Mark's Basilica in Venice. But it was later realized that the remains could not be St. Mark's, and given the origins of the mummy, some historians believe that the remains now buried beneath the Basilica could be Alexander's."

Mandalov shook his head. His face showed his disdain.

"Alexander the Great in Venice?" Cloutard said with a grin. "As if they did not already have enough problems with tourists."

"And the second theory?" Hellen said.

"Less absurd, to be sure," Mandalov said. "Many important rulers, among them Caesar, Wilhelm II, and Adolf Hitler, were fascinated by Alexander the Great. He was considered the greatest military strategist in human history."

Cloutard and Hellen looked at Mandalov. They sensed there was more to come.

"And there was yet another great commander who was similarly obsessed with Alexander. He even organized a French campaign in Egypt and Syria. He called it the Egyptian Expedition."

"Napoleon Bonaparte?" Hellen and Cloutard said as one.

"Correct. Give me just a moment," Mandalov said, and he trundled away in his wheelchair to the other side of the room. He returned a minute later with an old leather handbook. "The aide-de-camp's report is unambiguous, but only until their arrival in Paris, I'm afraid." He indicated the questionable passages, and Hellen and Cloutard quickly scanned the lines. "He describes how Napoleon found Alexander's tomb. He ordered his soldiers to take everything, pack it all aboard his ships, and transport it to Paris."

"Maybe there is something to it," said Cloutard. "Napoleon was crowned Emperor of France just a few years later."

"But why does the report end before they reached Paris?" Hellen asked.

"Because the man who wrote it died before they arrived," Mandalov said with a sigh.

"So, no one knows where Napoleon took what he'd looted?" Hellen pressed. She found the theory far from absurd.

"No. I stumbled onto this theory myself only recently. But I'm afraid I'm not in any physical condition to go treasure hunting anymore," Mandalov said unhappily.

"Where would you start looking if you were?" Hellen asked.

Mandalov tilted his head left and right thoughtfully. "There are many possibilities. I think I would start at Luxembourg Palace. Napoleon lived there for a time after his return from Egypt."

Hellen's enthusiasm had returned. "Then we'll follow that lead," she said. She placed her hand on the old man's shoulder. "And we'll stay in touch. If we find anything, you'll be the first to know." Then she shook his hand and was already heading for the exit. "François, are you coming?"

Cloutard bowed to Mandalov, then hurried after her. "*Magnifique!*" he said. "I have not been to France for an eternity."

CHAPTER 42

HIGHWAY 70, NEW MEXICO

"Isaac? You okay?" Tom groaned when he came to. They were tangled together on the roof of the upturned car.

"Still alive," Hagen replied. "But I'm a long way from okay. And get your bloody foot out of my face."

"Sorry," said Tom. It was a struggle, but he managed to turn and push one arm out through the open side window. He grabbed the door handle and pulled. The door sprang open, and he crawled out. When Hagen scrabbled through after him, Tom reached out and helped him to his feet.

"Are you out of your mind?" Hagen swung a punch at Tom but missed. Both were still a little unsteady.

"Why are you complaining? We're free," Tom said as he dragged the passenger out of the car.

"What do you think's going to happen now? We've killed two DARPA guys. The DOD'll send God-knows-who after us. They'll hunt us to the ends of the earth."

"One DARPA guy," Tom corrected him. He pointed to the unconscious body he'd just freed from the wreck. "This one's still alive. Although I don't think these guys actually work for DARPA. They look more like black ops to me."

"Horne," they said simultaneously. They looked at each other.

"Besides, this guy here shot his partner, not us." Tom jabbed his foot into the unconscious man's side.

"Semantics."

Tom crawled back into the car and came out with the mercenaries' pistols and spare magazines. He searched the unconscious man and discovered a few more magazines in his pockets. The cell phone, unfortunately, had not survived the crash. Tom threw it aside.

"So here we are," Hagen said. "Middle of nowhere. We've lost the head, they've taken our phones, and it's only a matter of time till the highway patrol or someone else is breathing down our necks."

"When did you get so negative? You've been stuck in that stuffy old office way too long." Tom tossed Hagen one of the pistols and two spare magazines. Hagen caught them a little awkwardly, but he rapidly and expertly checked whether the gun was loaded—years of training had burned the handling of weapons into his brain. "Also, you really need to have a little more faith. Haven't you learned anything from all the times we crossed paths?"

"What exactly am I supposed to have learned? How to get bashed over the head?"

Tom went around to the back of the vehicle. He looked all around to make sure there was no one even remotely close by. Then he took aim at the lock on the trunk and fired. "That you shouldn't underestimate me," he said.

He kicked at the shattered lock and the back opened downward. Everything inside tumbled out onto the ground. Tom picked up Hagen's backpack and handed it to him. Then he picked up his duffel bag. "When the DARPA chopper landed, I got a bad feeling about where things were headed. It seemed pretty obvious to me that not everyone would want the Medusa to be destroyed. And we both know Horne. So, I grabbed the case and pretended I was carrying it over to the bomb. But that was just a show for the new arrivals." He tugged open the cord on the bag and folded down the sides. "I'd already moved the head to my bag. *Et voilà.*"

Hagen's eyes widened. Surrounded by Tom's socks and underpants lay the metal-reinforced jar containing the head of Medusa. A smile appeared on Hagen's face, and he shook his head. "That doesn't mean we're out of the woods," he laughed.

"I know. But I think we can agree that our mission to destroy it was a failure."

Hagen nodded.

"Our first priority is getting this thing to safety, ideally out of the country."

"What do you have in mind?" Hagen asked.

"First, we need some wheels," Tom said. He shouldered his bag and began to walk.

CHAPTER 43

A GRAY CITROËN HY DELIVERY VAN, STREETS OF PARIS, FRANCE

"It's impressive, really, that your Paris contacts are this good. A few calls, and suddenly we're wearing overalls and sitting in an old delivery van on our way to Luxembourg Palace. But I don't see how your plan will work, François."

Hellen's grubby blue overalls covered a checked shirt of indeterminate color. Cloutard, at the wheel, wore a similar outfit, with a tattered, typically French beret on his head and his sleeves rolled up. Under the overalls, however, he wore a shirt and tie.

"*Ma chère*, a little more faith in my talents, please. So much negativity . . . how does Tom put up with it? If there is one thing I know well, it is how to get inside buildings." He had been about to remind Hellen how easily he had "borrowed" the Holy Chalice from St. Mary's Cathedral in Valencia but decided against it.

"Also, if we're going to sneak into Luxembourg Palace as restorers while the French Senate is actually in session, why exactly do you get to be the chief restorer while I have to play second fiddle as your assistant?" Hellen said, annoyed.

"Because, my dear, you look too young. That is all. No one is going to believe that you are an experienced restorer of old and valuable paintings, certainly not as sexy as you look in overalls." Cloutard clucked his tongue and looked Hellen up and down, playfully raising his eyebrows a few times as he did so.

"Why, you old charmer," Hellen laughed, and boxed him playfully in his ribs. "All right, what exactly are we doing?"

The smile vanished from Cloutard's face. "I honestly do not know. In Rue de Vaugirard, to the right of the main palace gate, is the entrance to the inner parking area. Fortunately for us, we are on the gatekeeper's list, and he will let us in." He turned and bowed his head to Hellen. "What are friends for?"

"Look out!" Hellen suddenly shouted, and Cloutard slammed on the brakes.

"*Sale crétin!*" they heard a woman yell from the motorcycle Cloutard had almost crashed into. She was able to swerve clear just in time, flipped them the middle finger, and added a loud "*Gros bouffon!*" for good measure.

Cloutard grinned. "Truly, nothing beats the warmth and friendliness of the French."

At the end of Rue de Tournon, he turned right onto Rue de Vaugirard. Moments later, they pulled up at a boom gate inside the entrance to Luxembourg Palace. Cloutard handed the man at the gate a handful of papers. He consulted his computer, nodded, and a few seconds later the boom rose, and they drove into the courtyard.

"What did you show him?" Hellen asked.

"Documents from the Ministère de la Culture saying that we are here to inspect the seven statues in front of the Chambre du Semicircle."

"Fakes, of course," Hellen murmured.

"*Naturellement*," Cloutard said proudly. He parked the van in the courtyard, but when they climbed out, they were immediately approached by two armed men.

"*Pardon*," one of the men said. "Security. We have to check your vehicle and search you for weapons."

Cloutard explained why they were there, and that apart from a camera and their digital microscope, they had no other equipment with them. The security check did not take long, and they were soon entering the palace through a side entrance and making their way toward the Senate Library.

"*Madame la docteure*, why precisely are we starting our search there?" Cloutard asked.

"We need to take a close look at the paintings on the ceiling. One of them might hold a clue."

Cloutard had to show his forged cultural ministry papers a few more times, but in ten minutes they arrived at the library, closed to visitors just then because the Senate was in session.

Hellen pointed up at one of the paintings in the dome overhead. "Well, François? What do you see?"

"What is this, 'Who Wants to be a Millionaire'?" Cloutard replied. "You tell me, Lady Croft!"

"We are looking at a painting by Eugène Delacroix. It shows Alexander the Great sealing Homer's works inside a gold casket."

"*Bon, d'accord*," said Cloutard. "We are clearly in the right place. Unless I am mistaken, the legends surrounding the Medusa originated from Homer's pen."

"They did indeed," said Hellen. She took a few photographs of the ceiling painting, which she then enlarged on her iPad to study them more closely.

"I have just one question," said Cloutard. He was strolling through the library and was already searching the room for hidden compartments and secret doors.

"And that would be?" said Hellen absently, her focus solely on Delacroix's painting.

"Something does not fit timewise. Mandalov told us that

Alexander was the son of Zeus, and that he is also Perseus, a demigod. But the stories from Greek mythology date from much earlier. Homer lived around five hundred years before Alexander was born. How could anybody write stories about an alleged demigod named Alexander-alias-Perseus if he did not even exist at the time?"

Hellen looked up momentarily from her iPad but returned her attention to it seconds later.

"There is an explanation for that," said Hellen, almost as an aside.

"*Alors* . . . I am all ears," said Cloutard.

CHAPTER 44
ORGAN, NEW MEXICO

A four-mile walk west along Highway 70 brought Tom and Hagen to the top of the San Augustin Pass. Below, the small town of Organ glowed in the late-afternoon sun. They had seen few cars, and those they had seen—unsurprisingly—ignored Hagen's half-hearted attempts to thumb a ride.

No one had witnessed the crash, apart perhaps from the lone trucker, but whether he had seen it or not, he hadn't stopped. It looked as if he hadn't even notified the highway patrol. Just to be on the safe side, Tom and Hagen had tied up the surviving mercenary to stop him from calling for help too soon.

"Hold up, I need a moment," said Hagen, stopping to catch his breath. In the baking sun, the climb through the pass was taking it out of them.

"I know exactly how you feel." Puffing, the two men looked at each other. Tom and Hellen had spent most of the last year enjoying the good life, barely thinking about staying in shape, and Hagen had gone from undercover agent to pencil pusher. The crash, too, had taken its toll. Bumps, bruises, and a handful of cuts and abrasions were making things harder than they otherwise would have been.

"Not the most inviting place," Hagen said, when they passed the first outlying buildings ten minutes later.

"What did you expect? We're in the southwestern United States. There's not much here. This is probably an old mining town."

Tired and beat, they trudged along the main street. At first glance, Organ looked like a ghost town. The windows and doors of an old store were boarded up. Rusty, crooked fences and derelict silos dominated the view. Then a trailer park appeared: the first real sign of civilization.

Another ten minutes, and they reached a flat-roofed building with several cars parked out front. They stopped.

"'Renoo's Thai Time'? Incredible. No shops, no gas station, but they've got a Thai restaurant," said Tom.

"I'd be more interested in fish and chips, myself," Hagen replied.

Tom screwed up his nose. "I'd never claim that America's a land of urbane foodies, but your countrymen could learn a thing or two from them."

"We don't have time to eat in any case," Hagen said. "By now, Weaver knows we've escaped. He probably already has a little pack of his mercenaries heading our way, so we have to make a decision."

"Okay. What decision is that?"

"Which of these fine automobiles we want to borrow."

Four cars were parked in front of the building. Apart from an old sedan that bore an uncanny resemblance to their Ford post-crash, there was a Toyota Prius and two pickups, one of which looked as if it was held together with duct tape. "Easy choice," said Tom, heading for the other pickup. "It's always interesting to see where people put their priorities. Some people live in a crappy house or a run-down trailer, but they drive a seventy-thousand-dollar truck."

Tom ran his hand almost lovingly over the shoulder-high hood of the huge red-and-orange Ford F-150 Raptor.

"Three-point-five liter high-output V6 engine, Fox Racing Shox, all-wheel drive," Tom enthused. He was something of a gearhead, after all, especially when it came to American muscle cars. His Mustang and his Dodge were proof of that. But he had inherited them; he could never have afforded the beautiful beasts on his Cobra salary.

"Should I give you two a moment alone?" Hagen said. He was standing on the other side of the truck, looking around. "Also, how do you plan on hot-wiring this high-tech masterpiece?" he asked. He got no response. "Tom?"

But Tom had vanished.

A moment later, a man charged out of the restaurant, closely followed by Tom.

"What the hell did you do my truck? I hope you're insured, buddy. Do you know how much this baby's worth?" the man shouted. He was on the pudgy side and wearing jeans, a baseball cap, and a checked, short-sleeve shirt. He ran to the back of his pickup.

"Down there." Tom pointed to the bumper and quickly looked around. "I'm real sorry. I just didn't see your car," he said.

"How the hell could you not see thi—" But that was as far as he got. Tom had grabbed him from behind when he leaned down. A well-executed chokehold rendered the man unconscious within seconds, and he slumped to the ground.

"Come on, give me a hand," Tom said to Hagen. Between them, they dragged the man behind the trash cans beside the restaurant's back entrance. Tom knelt beside him and searched his pockets until he found the digital key. Hagen just stared at him and shook his head. "Don't look at me like that," Tom said. "You can't hot-wire a car like this. They've got Keyless Go and alarms. So, where to now?"

"That depends. Where will the head be safest?"

"Well, we sure as hell can't trust the Americans. I say we get back to familiar territory, the sooner the better."

"El Paso airport's out of the question. It's the first place they'll look for us," Hagen said.

"Then we don't have too many choices," said Tom. "Albuquerque to the north or west to Tucson, Arizona. Those are the next closest international airports."

"Or we could go to Mexico," Hagen suggested.

"Juárez is just over the border from El Paso. Isn't that drug-cartel central?"

"Maybe a decade ago. Crime's at a ten-year low," said Hagen. "There are cities here in the States with higher murder rates these days."

"Okay. Still, let's play it safer—Tucson it is."

An hour later, they were following State Road 9 along the Mexican border, heading west. They'd decided to stay off the major roads, like Interstate 10 to the north, hoping to avoid any run-ins with the authorities. Those routes would be the first to be searched.

Nothing much had changed about the landscape, but the expression "deserted" was taking on a whole new significance. Since turning west in Santa Teresa, a suburb of El Paso, they had passed only one other car.

They didn't see the helicopter coming, and when a burst of machine gun fire slammed into the asphalt alongside them and Hagen swung the steering wheel sharply, they almost crashed a second time.

CHAPTER 45
SENATE LIBRARY, LUXEMBOURG PALACE, PARIS

Hellen smiled at Cloutard.

"Oh, please, do not torture me like this. Explain the temporal discrepancy to a poor Frenchman," Cloutard said impatiently.

"One of the most important sources of Greek mythology is the Bibliotheca, also known as the Bibliotheca of Apollodorus, which dates back to the first century A.D."

"You mean someone later rewrote the stories of Homer and whoever else?"

"Or added new ones. Anything's possible. Have you heard of the 'phantom time hypothesis'? The invented Middle Ages? It's based on the theory that almost three hundred years of medieval history were simply made up and later expanded in the history books. Charlemagne, according to this theory, never existed. We also know that the Bible as we know it today was only put together at the First Council of Nicaea in 325 A.D. Since then, it's been rewritten, shortened, expanded, and revised multiple times. Knowing that, it's easy to imagine that someone might have doctored Greek mythology after the fact, too."

Cloutard had just begun to climb one of the ladders

attached to the bookshelves. "That stands to reason," he said, and he began studying the room from his slightly raised vantage point. "I fear we are going to be here a long time." Cloutard peered along the extensive bookshelves, like a captain standing on the bridge of his ship and giving his crew orders.

"*Monsieur le Capitaine*, come back down. We need to take a more strategic approach," Hellen said so sternly that Cloutard immediately climbed down.

"Fine. So Napoleon lived here. Logically, he would not have parked any artifacts from Alexander's tomb here in the library. It would be highly unlikely, at least," Cloutard said.

Together, they turned their attention back to the painting on the ceiling.

"I was thinking the painting might provide us with some kind of clue," Hellen said. "Like we found that time at St. John's Co-Cathedral in Malta." Her brow furrowed. "But so far, nothing's jumped out at me."

She handed the iPad to Cloutard, who also began to go over the painting inch by inch. "We see Alexander laying the works of Homer in a golden box. An angel is flying overhead, and in the background are Alexander's armies. But I also see nothing that really points to Greek mythology," Cloutard said.

Hellen shook her head. "Eugène Delacroix was considered one of the pioneers of Impressionism. Somehow, that doesn't fit the picture."

"Maybe the painting is only the starting point. Maybe we have to go from here to some subterranean chamber where Napoleon built his own personal shrine to Alexander," Cloutard said.

"Right now, I'm ready to believe anything," Hellen said. "Let's look for a hidden door."

"Good. We split up and check everything."

They began to scour the room.

"We can count ourselves lucky that the Senate is in session. We wouldn't be able to poke around here undisturbed otherwise," Hellen said, going to work on the countless wooden panels along the base of the bookshelves.

They spent the next hour and a half examining the place from floor to ceiling. They tried every bit of trim, every ornament for movement. Everything that could conceivably hide a button or switch was pressed, probed, and pushed. They knocked on every wall and every plank, testing for hollow spaces behind.

Hellen was on the verge of giving up when she suddenly heard a loud *click* followed by a triumphant whoop from Cloutard.

He was standing on one of the ladders and had pressed on one of the many, many volutes, the spiral-shaped ornaments gracing columns and consoles in any number of architectural styles. Cloutard had discovered something on one of the spiraled wooden consoles that graced the gallery at regular intervals.

Directly beneath Cloutard, a section of wooden paneling had sunk inward slightly.

Hellen hurried over to join him. The wooden panel could be moved. The entrance that appeared was only about three feet high. Hellen leaned in with her flashlight.

"I see stairs," she said, creeping farther inside.

"I hope it gets a little bigger than this," Cloutard muttered, following Hellen inside. "We are not all as pint-sized as Napoleon."

"Don't worry, François," Hellen said, already a few yards ahead. "It turns into a regular-sized passage. I can stand here."

"It is still claustrophobic," said Cloutard. Every few steps, the passage turned in a new direction. The went downstairs, climbed a ladder, and turned left, then right, then left again. This went on for several minutes until both had completely lost their orientation.

"What is this, the Minotaur's labyrinth?" Hellen wondered aloud. "Lucky for us the passage hasn't branched off. My sense of direction isn't great," she admitted.

"Look. Is that a door ahead?" Cloutard said. He was already digging his lockpicks out of his pocket.

But before he got a chance to try the lock, Hellen had turned the antique door handle downward, and the door opened easily.

They drew a sharp breath as they stepped into the room beyond. Neither had expected this.

CHAPTER 46
ANACOSTIA, WASHINGTON, D.C.

Akira kept looking back over her shoulder. She'd managed to shake off her pursuers, but for how long? Although she'd destroyed her phone, the two killers had tracked her to the museum. *It must have been when I scanned my museum pass*, Akira thought. *I hope Mr. Johnson is all right.* Looking back, she was angry at herself for putting the friendly old man in harm's way.

For the first time in her life, she felt alone and helpless. It was a sensation she had never known before—in general, she avoided people and was actually happiest when she was by herself. But the pain she felt now was more crippling, harder to cope with than a packed subway car. The only person she had ever allowed to get close had been taken from her. And professional killers were after her, most likely on government orders.

Gradually, her weariness was making itself felt. She was walking now along Martin Luther King Street in Anacostia. It wasn't the safest part of Washington, but it was the perfect place to hide. Her head ached—she hadn't drunk anything for hours. Her stomach was growling, too, and it was getting harder for her to think clearly. If she was going to do anything, she had to replenish her energy. She fished a few bills out of her jeans and looked around. The cash she still had wouldn't go far, but it was enough for a snack and a burner phone.

A few minutes later, she found a convenience store. She took a few power bars from the rack and two bottles of water from the fridge. At the cash register, she added a small cell phone, packed in plastic, from a rotating stand.

Her heart skipped a beat when she glanced at the TV on the wall behind the store owner. Her hands turned moist, and her pulse began to race. She saw a photograph of herself on the silent screen. Beneath the image, she read: "Wanted for murder." She quickly pulled her hood lower over her face, gathered up the food, phone, water, and her change, and hurried out again. Dashing around a corner into an alley, she sank to the ground behind a dumpster. She was struggling to breathe. It felt as if a lead weight was pressing on her chest. Sweat seeped from every pore. She tugged nervously at the neck of her hoodie, feeling as if someone was clamping down on her throat. Slowly, she forced herself to breathe. *Deeply, in and out*, she thought. Then she quickly unscrewed the cap from one of the water bottles and drank half of it. She closed her eyes and focused on her breathing. Within a couple of minutes, she had managed to calm down a little.

She needed help, fast. Hands trembling, she ripped open the packaging around the phone, threw it aside, and activated the phone. She tapped out a message on the tiny keys: *I need help. On my way to you.* She pressed "Send," put everything away in her backpack, and returned to the street.

Keeping her head low and moving fast, Akira darted along until she found a taxi. She jumped in the back. "1023 58th Avenue, Fairmount Heights," she said to the driver as she sank wearily into the seat. She took a power bar out of her pack and bit into it hungrily.

Half an hour later, the taxi pulled up in front of a small wooden house standing in the middle of a neglected yard.

"Comes to forty-eight dollars even, miss," said the driver, shutting off the meter.

Akira suddenly realized she'd just spent almost all of her remaining cash in the little store. "One minute. Hold on," she said, jumping out of the car. She opened the rickety front gate, ran to the house, and knocked on the door.

A morbidly obese young man wearing an almost knee-length hockey jersey opened the door.

"Can you lend me fifty dollars?" Akira said, looking at the man with her irresistible, tried-and-tested, puppy-dog look and nodding back toward the waiting taxi. The man grunted and rolled his eyes, but he put down the bowl of Froot Loops in his hand and dug a few bills out of his extra-extra-large shorts. "Thank you!" Akira said. She grabbed the money, ran back to the taxi, and paid the driver.

"So which hornets' nest have you been banging with a stick this time?" the man said as he descended the steps to the basement, closely followed by Akira.

"Thanks for helping me, Boba Fat," Akira said, sitting on the sofa.

"We're not online here, you know. It's Robert. Or Bobby, if you like," the young man said. He sat on his large leather armchair in front of a semicircular desk, above which six monitors were mounted in two rows. Beside the desk stood two water-cooled server racks and cabinets with shelves bending under the weight of hundreds of action figures. On the wall hung an eighty-inch flat-screen TV on which a zombie shooter game was paused. "I heard about your boyfriend. Man, I'm sorry. Why do the cops think you killed him?"

As briefly as she could, she explained to Bobby everything that had happened to her in the last few hours and everything she'd found out about the group that had been publicizing the Medusa cult.

"Are you totally crazy? Why would you work for *DARPA*? I thought you were one of us!" Bobby said. He sounded truly disappointed.

"It's complicated. And beside the point. All I know is that someone wants me out of the way because of what I told DARPA. And now I need your help. I need new papers and a new credit card. And you have to help me find out what's really going on."

"The papers are no problem. I can do all of that here. But what do you mean, exactly? How do you want to find out what's going on?"

"Simple." Akira smiled sheepishly and looked up at Bobby for a moment. "All we have to do is hack the server of a CIA and MI6 task force. Oh, and the DOD," she said, grinning from ear to ear.

Bobby's eyes widened and he almost choked on a spoonful of Froot Loops.

"Oh, well, if that's all it is."

CHAPTER 47

COMMISSARIAT DE POLICE, RUE BONAPARTE, PARIS

"I think I've lost count of how many times I've been arrested because of you and Tom," Hellen said.

"Who would have guessed that there was a secret passage connecting the library and the Senate hall, or that we would interrupt their session just before a crucial vote, or that we would literally step on the toes of one of the police on duty?" Cloutard said.

Hellen shook her head in feigned indignation. "I'd never even had a parking ticket before I met you two."

"On the plus side, we are not boring. I think you like hanging out with *mauvais garçons* like us—the bad boys, as Tom would say."

Hellen grimaced. "At least your fake cultural-ministry papers got us out of there. That's one good thing."

"Yes. And won't the ministry be surprised to get a written warning about their intrusive employees?"

Hellen pointed excitedly at the street sign mounted on the wall beside the station exit. "Seriously? The *commissariat* is on Rue Bonaparte? That must be a sign."

"Yes, especially knowing Mandalov's conviction that Napoleon is the lead we need to follow," said Cloutard.

"Unfortunately, we're not going to get back into the palace easily, not after being ejected so ignominiously. We need a Plan B."

"*Pas de stress*. First, I need a good cup of coffee," Cloutard said, and he marched away down Rue de Mézières. Fifteen minutes later, they were sitting inside Café Cassette. It had taken them longer than usual to cover the short distance—the Paris streets were also filled with demonstrators and disorder. The ripples of the Medusa cult were turning into surfable waves.

"Let us hope this whole Medusa-cult thing is over soon. It could destabilize all of Europe," Cloutard said, spiking his coffee with a shot of Louis XIII.

"Indeed. But right now, all we can do is focus on our task, and the two are undoubtedly connected. Let's go through everything we know," Hellen said. She took the first sip of her *café au lait* and her eyes widened in surprise. "My God, François, this coffee is divine!"

"Did you really think that only you Viennese could produce a decent coffee?" he said, a little affronted. "I, for one, am endlessly grateful that we no longer have to put up with that dishwater from the machine at Blue Shield. Their 'coffee' was a violation of the Geneva Convention." The Frenchman sipped from his cup, his little finger extended, and an expression of pure bliss appeared on his face.

"You are the absolute snobbiest of snobs," Hellen said with a laugh. "But seriously, what do we do now?"

"Any word from Tom? Perhaps he and Hagen actually destroyed the Medusa after all, and we are searching for something we no longer need," Cloutard said.

"No. Radio silence. I've called several times and sent messages, but all I get is the mailbox and no reply. I hope nothing's happened to him." She fell silent for a moment, then pushed the thought aside. "Which I can't imagine for a second."

"We are talking about Tom, *ma chère*! Nothing will happen to him," Cloutard said, and he raised his hand to signal the waiter. "I will order us a little something to eat. After all this trouble, I need food just to think straight."

Hellen nodded and reached for the menu.

"You won't need that," Cloutard said. "Trust me."

Hellen knew that Cloutard was not only a first-class thief, but an even bigger gourmet. She let him do the ordering.

"One thing right away," Hellen said. "Even if Tom has destroyed the Medusa, we need to keep looking for the two artifacts."

Cloutard nodded. He already knew which direction she was going. "Of course. This is the Golden Fleece and the Aegis of Hephaestus, after all." He sipped at his coffee and wiped the *crema* from his mustache.

"That, and we have to find Professor Richter's killer. Or have you forgotten that part, Monsieur Poirot?"

Cloutard frowned. "Hellen, have you never read Agatha Christie? Poirot is Belgian." He shook his head in dismay. "Belgian, *pour l'amour de dieu*! If you must compare me to a detective, please, at least make it a real Frenchman."

"Okay, Maigret," Hellen shot back.

"Not much better," said Cloutard.

"Do you actually trust Mandalov?" Hellen asked. "He comes across as an elderly gentleman with a chivalric sense of honor, but it wouldn't be the first time we've been taken in by a double agent."

Cloutard nodded, but slowly. "*Bien sûr*, that is true. But he takes anything to do with Alexander the Great very seriously. I know him well enough to say that he would not start making up absurd stories about Alexander. While we are sitting here, he may well be getting things moving to find the artifacts himself—or perhaps even to get his hands on Medusa's head. But if he says that Napoleon is the best lead we have, then I believe him. Honor among thieves, you know."

"*Madame et monsieur*," the waiter said just then, standing beside the table with two plates in his hands. Hellen and Cloutard leaned back, and the waiter placed the food in front of them.

"François, it looks amazing. What is it?"

"My two favorite dishes here, which we will share. We have avocado Benedict, a poached organic egg on a muffin, with avocado, bacon, arugula, and a hollandaise sauce..."

"Mmmmmm..." Hellen murmured, her mouth already watering.

"... and here a *risotto de coquillettes*, a mussel risotto flavored with white truffle oil, served with truffled white ham, arugula, and shaved parmesan. And we are drinking a Saint-Germain spritz—Saint-Germain liqueur, *Carmina Gin de Christian Drouin* infused with raspberry and elderflower, lime juice, Prosecco, and a shot of Perrier," Cloutard recited, as the waiter set the glasses on the table. He wished them "bon appétit," and departed.

Hellen was in raptures from the first bite, and for a few minutes they enjoyed the exquisite food in silence.

"I think we would do well to pay another visit to Luxembourg Palace this evening," Cloutard finally said. "I feel very strongly that we were in the right place."

"But how, François?"

"I have an idea," Cloutard said, and he took out his phone. He dialed a number, talked for a few moments, and a minute later ended the call. He looked satisfied.

"Did you just buy two tickets for the Opèra Garnier?" Hellen said with a frown.

"*Exactement!* They are performing Charles Gounod's *Roméo et Juliette*. And we are in luck: Juan Diego Florez is singing Roméo. Finally, a little culture on one of our adventures!"

Hellen looked at Cloutard expectantly, but he said nothing more and sipped at his Saint-Germain spritz, looking very pleased with himself.

"And? Would you at least tell me what we'll be doing at the opera?"

Cloutard looked at her in incomprehension. "We will be listening to Juan Diego Florez! Is that not reason enough?"

"François!" Hellen spoke so loudly that other guests turned and looked. "Tell me!"

"*Calme-toi, mon trésor.* We are also meeting Marquis Augustin Dieulafoy, the Grand Vizier of the French Thieves' Guild."

CHAPTER 48
A BAR IN ALAMOGORDO, NEW MEXICO

Lieutenant Colonel Weaver sat at the bar inside a small establishment in Alamogordo, not far from the base, and sipped at his bourbon. He felt he'd earned a drink, although it was still early. Soon enough, he'd have the head back safe and sound and be on his way to Arlington. He was angry at himself for letting two foreign agents rip him off so blatantly. But it wouldn't happen twice. The black-ops team General Horne had put at his disposal through the Pentagon knew their business. After discovering the crashed car, they'd quickly discovered that Wagner and Hagen were driving a stolen pickup truck.

Weaver smiled when he thought about that. How could you be stupid enough to steal a brand-new truck with GPS tracking? He quickly tipped back the last of the bourbon and rapped the glass back onto the bar, tapping a finger on the rim of the glass to signal a refill.

"It's gotta be after five somewhere, right?" a female voice suddenly slurred behind him. He turned to see a drop-dead stunning woman with shoulder-length copper hair stumble past. She wore tight jeans, boots, and a skin-tight top that made no attempt at all to conceal her assets—she would have put the waitresses at Hooters to shame.

She struggled to pull a up barstool beside Weaver, then slapped her handbag on the bar and took off her sunglasses. When the barkeeper refilled Weaver's glass, she signaled to him for one of the same. Weaver looked the woman up and down. *That's sure not her first drink today*, he thought. He noted the Band-Aid between her temple and forehead.

"So has your day been as crappy as mine?" the woman asked. She raised her glass toward Weaver in a toast. Then she threw the contents back in one swallow and immediately ordered another. "Lemme guess: Air Force?" she slurred.

"Marines," Weaver said drily, sipping at his bourbon.

"Wow," the woman said. She giggled and drained the second glass like the first. "So, you must have—how do you boys put it?—seen some action." She laid a hand on Weaver's shoulder and leaned close. "Were you down there with the ragheads in, uh, whatchamacallit?" she whispered.

Weaver ignored the slur and studied her face. This close, he could see that she was using makeup to hide more injuries than whatever was under the Band-Aid. In the dimly lit bar, he hadn't noticed that right away.

"What happened to you?" Weaver tapped his own forehead, then pointed at the Band-Aid.

She raised one hand a little gingerly to her head and tried to cover the injury with her hair. "Believe it or not," she said, "I had a fight with a horse's hoof." With no more explanation, she got to her feet and waved her hand in the air to get the barman's attention. "Hey! Who do I have to screw to get a drink around here?" she said loudly and staggered back a little. Weaver reached out to steady her.

"Oops," she said, grinning broadly, and she threw an

arm around Weaver's neck. He helped her back onto her barstool.

"What's the name?" he asked.

"What?" she looked at him questioningly. "The name of the horse?"

Weaver couldn't hide a smirk. "No. Of the guy who did that to you."

"I told you, a—"

"A horse? Bullshit. But more original than 'I fell down the stairs' or 'I walked into a door.'"

"What are you gonna do, Mr. Marine? Drive me home and beat up my ex? Yeah, now he's my ex." She looked at him with a serious expression on her face, but she couldn't hold it long. She burst out laughing and, still smiling, supported herself on Weaver's shoulder. She moved her mouth very close to Weaver's ear. "Wouldn't you like to come back to my motel and see if we can destroy the bed? Men in uniform turn me on like you wouldn't *believe*," she whispered, as her fingers softly stroked his buzzcut. She tongued his earlobe for a moment, then moved back from him and turned her attention to her drink, which the barman, grinning broadly, had refilled in the meantime.

Weaver, who was every inch a man, who feared nothing, and who'd ruthlessly done whatever he had to in countless battles, was speechless. He looked at the woman, and his eyes moved inevitably to her body-hugging top with the deep neckline. For a fraction of a second he imagined what it would be like to actually have this magnificent specimen of a woman share his bed.

"Well I guess that's a 'no,' Mr. Marine," she said, when Weaver said nothing. She finished her drink and started rummaging in her handbag.

"Forget it. On me," Weaver said.

"Then thank you for your service," the woman said, saluting playfully. "That's what you say, right?"

Weaver nodded and watched her stumble toward the exit. She tried to simultaneously put the strap of her handbag over her neck, pull on her sunglasses, and open the door. It was not a pretty sight.

Weaver stood up resolutely. He took a bundle of cash from his breast pocket, counted out the necessary bills, and laid them on the bar. Then he hurried after the young woman and held the door open for her.

"Come on. I'll get you home," Weaver said.

"Hey, he's a gentleman after all. I was starting to think these things had lost their charm," the woman slurred, and she grasped her breasts firmly and wobbled them up and down. Then she gave Weaver her nicest smile and hooked her arm into his.

CHAPTER 49
OPÉRA GARNIER, PARIS

"This looks almost like the foyer at the Vienna State Opera," Hellen said delightedly. She lifted the hem of her floor-length evening gown as she accompanied Cloutard up the grand staircase to the parterre. Cloutard was wearing a midnight-blue tuxedo and had gone so far as to add a top hat to his ensemble.

Both outfits were just a few hours old, bought earlier in the Louis Vuitton flagship store on the Champs-Élysées.

"He won't say a word about our expenses when we bring him the Golden Fleece," was all Cloutard had said, grinning as he paid the five-figure bill with the American Express Business Platinum card van Rensburg had given them. Their original mission to find Richter's killer and prove van Rensburg's innocence had since been overshadowed by their new quest. But both he and Hellen were silently aware that the one would lead to the other.

"What makes you so certain that your marquis is going to be here tonight?" Hellen asked, looking around excitedly. It had been an eternity since she and Tom had gotten dressed up for a night out. She loved the adventures they shared, but sometimes she missed "normal" life a little.

Cloutard handed her a glass of champagne and they clinked glasses. "The marquis is here every night. He is an opera freak and has led the opera's *claqueurs* for years."

"*Claqueurs*?"

"These days, for a band, you might call them 'groupies,'" Cloutard explained. "They are the most die-hard of fans, applauding and cheering for particular singers and raining boos on others." He leaned a little closer. "Of course, the *claqueurs* are not averse to a little financial motivation. It has been a custom of all great opera houses since the eighteenth century."

"And what about the thieves' guild you mentioned?"

"Later, *ma chérie*. I see the Marquis."

As the first bell rang to tell the audience that the performance would soon begin, Cloutard made a beeline for a man who might have been his brother—tall and slender and also wearing a tuxedo, with a regal bearing and an aristocratic face. With a mustache artfully turned up at the ends, he bore a certain resemblance to Salvador Dali. And to top it all off, he wore a monocle wedged over his right eye, with which he periodically scrutinized those gathered around him.

The marquis was flanked by two exceptionally beautiful women, both at least twenty years younger, and a man who, to Hellen's now well-trained eye, could only have been a bodyguard.

"Augustin!" Cloutard cried, raising his hand in greeting.

The marquis turned toward Cloutard and adjusted his monocle to see who might be calling his name. His face remained as stony as a statue's. Cloutard's steps slowed noticeably when he saw the marquis's notably cool reaction. The party gathered around the marquis had turned, too, and were also staring at Cloutard.

The bell rang a second time, and the passages and

entrances around the auditorium emptied, which only added more tension to the situation. To Hellen, the atmosphere felt far from friendly.

The marquis took a few steps in Cloutard's direction until the two men were standing eye to eye, staring at each other as if they were about to take part in an antiquated duel. Neither said a word.

All eyes in the parterre passage were now on the two men.

"You've got some nerve, showing up here after all you've done," the marquis said in a nasal voice. He spoke slowly, as if dedicating his entire attention to every word he said.

Cloutard raised his eyebrows and looked a little perplexed. He seemed uncertain about what the marquis was talking about.

Then, almost in slow motion, the marquis's face changed. The corners of his mouth turned upward, and furrows appeared around his eyes.

"François Cloutard! How long has it been?" the marquis said, laughing heartily as he embraced Cloutard. Cloutard was as surprised at the marquis's warmth as he had been at his feigned hostility. "What brings you to the opera? If I know you, this is more than mere coincidence."

Cloutard nodded. "You are right, as usual. I need a few minutes of your valuable time, Monsieur le Marquis."

The bell rang a third time. Marquis Dieulafoy looked around and realized that almost everyone had already taken their seats inside. "Whatever brings you back to your old homeland, and especially to my circle of influence, it will have to wait."

From inside the auditorium, they could hear applause. The orchestra had entered the pit and the conductor would be close behind. Without waiting for Cloutard to respond, the marquis turned away and disappeared with his entourage.

Hellen looked doubtfully at Cloutard. "That was weird," she said.

"You do not know the marquis. Weird is his trademark. It is time we went inside ourselves. We will only see him again after the performance."

Hellen and Cloutard made it to their seats just before the first martial notes of the overture. "Let us enjoy the show. There is nothing else to do, anyway," Cloutard whispered, earning a withering glare telling him to shut up from the man beside him. Cloutard raised his hands apologetically, leaned back, and sank into Gounod's masterpiece, among the pinnacles of French romantic opera.

CHAPTER 50
STATE ROAD 9, NEW MEXICO

"How the hell did they find us?" Tom yelled. He leaned halfway out of the open window and fired a few shots at the dark-blue helicopter that had appeared behind them.

"Keyless Go and alarm system, right? And this thing probably has LoJack, too," Hagen shouted back. "Four cars to choose from, and you steal the one with built-in anti-theft GPS. Well done." He shook his head.

"Okay, okay. Nobody's perfect. I let this beauty get the better of me. Sue me. Just make sure they don't catch us," Tom shouted. Wind and sand whipped him in the face as he emptied his second magazine at the chopper.

Several of his shots found their mark but had no visible effect. He dropped back inside the car to reload. Hagen was swerving on and off the road to avoid the bursts of gunfire from the weaving helicopter. The pickup's huge wheels kicked clouds of dust and sand high into the air. Suddenly, Hagen swung the wheel hard and headed due south, into open country.

"Where are we going?" Tom asked.

"I don't think they'll follow us into Mexico," Hagen

replied, a slightly insane look in his eye. "Fingers crossed they haven't finished this section of Trump's wall yet."

"You're even crazier than I am," said Tom. He turned and leaned over to the back seat. Pushing his duffel bag and Hagen's backpack aside, he rummaged through the owner's bags, which were also lying on the seat. Nothing. Then he looked up to the ceiling. Above the second row of seats was a custom-made flat case, color-matched to the interior.

Tom tried to climb into the back, but the bumpy desert and Hagen's unpredictable swerving didn't make it easy. Finally, he made it over.

"Hold on!" Hagen suddenly shouted, but before Tom could straighten up in the back, he realized why Hagen was shouting. For a brief second, he was weightless. Then the airborne car slammed down again before roaring on as usual, at least by the standards of the uneven desert.

"What are you doing back there? Shoot the bastards!" Hagen cried. He was struggling hard to dodge the repeated attacks from the chopper. Machine-gun fire rained down on them again and again, and now and then they heard a kind of nail-gun sound when bullets smashed through the steel body of the car.

When they reached the border, Hagen swung the wheel right. The helicopter pilot had realized in advance that he was heading for the border and now swung out in a wide loop to start a new assault without entering Mexican airspace.

"Shit! We can't get through here," Hagen said when he saw the massive, dark-brown beams driven into the ground side by side. The rusting steel wall seemed to cross the desert forever as they raced alongside it at sixty miles an hour.

Tom, meanwhile, had been working on the lock of the ceiling case with his pocketknife. "Got it!" he shouted abruptly. He swung the case open and found exactly what he'd been hoping for. In the open lid of the case hung a new American Tactical Omni AR-15-style rifle with a Millett scope. "Long live the Second Amendment!" he whooped. "I'd have been surprised if Bubba back there wasn't a gun nut," Tom said, freeing the rifle from the case. He clipped a magazine into place and racked the bolt. "All right. Let's see if we can't turn this thing around."

He rolled down the side window and leaned his entire upper body out of the car. In rapid fire, he emptied the semi-automatic's magazine at the helicopter. This time, his counterattack had an effect: one of his bullets hit the mercenary who was shooting at them through the open hatch on the port side. The man tumbled out, and the chopper briefly swerved away. Tom dropped back inside the pickup.

"Still sorry we didn't take Soccer Mom's Prius?" he said to Hagen, and he slammed a second magazine into the rifle.

"Don't get cocky. Just get that thing out of the sky," Hagen snapped back.

"Yes, sir," Tom said, and he pushed the last magazine into his belt. This time he didn't lean out of the window but opened the door instead. He tossed the rifle into the bed of the pickup, then climbed out and swung himself into the back after it. The helicopter had adjusted course for a new attack and was now flying behind them, just above the border wall. Another one of the mercenaries was leaning out of the hatch now, firing at the pickup. When Tom landed in the back, he was able to roll clear just in time as a burst of bullets slammed through the steel floor of the cargo bed. The back window exploded, and Hagen ducked. Tom picked up the Omni and returned fire, then reloaded and fired again. His bullets were certainly hitting the chopper, but it flew on undeterred. He had to think of something. He looked around. Shouldering the rifle, he opened the toolbox bolted to the bed and quickly found what he was looking for. He took it out and returned his attention to the helicopter.

It was close, just off to his right. So close, in fact, that Tom could almost read the name on the badge on the pilot's chest. Then he saw that the soldier in the hatch had pulled the pin on a grenade. He had no time to lose.

He hurled the fire extinguisher he'd found in the toolbox toward the cockpit, then swung the rifle up lightning fast and fired. The red, high-pressure canister exploded, covering the cockpit in white extinguishing foam. The pilot reflexively swung the joystick, and the soldier holding the grenade lost his balance and tumbled back inside. The grenade slipped from his grasp.

"St-o-o-o-o-p!" Tom bellowed. With no hesitation at all, Hagen stood on the brakes as hard as he could. Tom slammed into the back of the cab. Two seconds later, just as the helicopter shot past, the grenade exploded. The chopper swung into a left curve, and the rotors sliced into the top of the border barrier, sending sparks flying. The helicopter spun a hundred and eighty degrees and exploded in a huge fireball at the base of the wall, tearing a massive hole in it—just what Tom and Hagen needed. The gaping hole offered a glorious view of the late-afternoon sun hanging low in the sky.

Tom smiled, pleased with his handiwork. He rapped on the roof and looked in through the shot-out rear window.

"Nothing keeping us out of Mexico now."

CHAPTER 51
RAMP IN FRONT OF THE OPÉRA GARNIER, JUNCTION OF RUE AUBER AND RUE SCRIBE, PARIS

"Are you sure the marquis hasn't stood us up?" Hellen said, looking around doubtfully. "Everybody's left. We're the last ones."

"Trust me, *ma chère*. I know the Marquis. As *chef de claque*, he will always visit the dressing room of the *prima donna* and *primo uomo* to offer his congratulations, which naturally takes some time."

"Then why don't you tell me who he really is while we're waiting? And maybe add a little about this thieves' guild."

"*Bien sûr*," Cloutard said, and he took a swig from his ever-present flask. *Toi aussi?*"

He offered Hellen the flask, but she shook her head. "One of us needs to keep their wits about them," she said with a smile, knowing that Cloutard was far from being the alcoholic he often appeared to be.

"Marquis Augustin Dieulafoy is a scion of old French nobility, one of the few noble families that still exists."

"Your people put an end to most of that in the French Revolution," Hellen said.

"Be that as it may, there is more to the man than his

noble title. As I mentioned, he is also the Grand Vizier of the French Thieves' Guild."

Hellen reached out resignedly for Cloutard's flask, deciding that she could really use a shot of cognac after all. He smiled and opened it for her before handing it over.

"I have a feeling this will take some time," Hellen said, taking a solid swig.

"Not unlike the Assassins' Guild in 12th-century Arabia, thieves from many countries came together in Paris and formed a guild, which exists to the present day. From street pickpockets to forgers, from con men to safecrackers, it unites all men and women who have chosen to live a little ... outside of the law."

"You make it sound very dignified," Hellen said.

"In many countries, so-called *sukkursale* formed, something like franchises of the original Guild. Each of these was managed by a Grand Vizier."

"And here in France, that's the Marquis," Hellen concluded.

"*Correctement*. Augustin is also responsible for Belgium, the Netherlands, and Monaco."

"Well, he certainly won't get bored," said Hellen. She pointed beyond Cloutard. "You were right, by the way. There he is."

Cloutard turned around and the two men locked eyes again. They looked as if they were engaged in some sort of contest, eyeing each other like two fighting cocks before battle.

The marquis looked away first, turning to Hellen. "François, who, pray tell, is your charming companion?" he asked, placing an insinuating kiss on the back of her hand and, without waiting for Cloutard's reply, went on, "*Enchanté*, Madame de Mey."

"I knew perfectly well that you know exactly who she is," said Cloutard a little stuffily.

A dark-blue 1954 Citroën Traction Avant pulled up in front of the opera house. A man with the unmistakable air of a servant got out, walked around the immaculate vintage car, opened the door, and stood waiting for the marquis.

"Let's not loiter out here like common thieves," Dieulafoy said. "Allow me to invite you to my humble residence, where I can entertain your wishes in peace and quiet." Although excessively polite, his tone made it clear he was not asking.

They drove for ten minutes through the 2nd Arrondissement, along Rue du 4 Septembre, past Palais Brongniart and the Church of Saint-Nicolas-des-Champs, then turned into Rue Beaubourg and from there into the narrow Rue de Montmorency.

"This is Nicolas Flamel's house," Hellen whispered excitedly in Cloutard's ear. "He was the alchemist who was supposed to have found the Philosopher's Stone."

Cloutard grinned. "You and I both know that is not true. But you are right. Augustin lives in the Maison Nicolas Flamel. It is the oldest house in Paris, built in 1407."

Hellen and Cloutard were led into a salon by a servant and asked to wait. The marquis reappeared after a few minutes. He had changed out of his tuxedo and now wore a simple but still exceedingly elegant three-piece suit, with a bow tie colored dusty rose and a matching carnation in his lapel. He took a seat and watched as his servant opened a bottle of Bollinger. When all three had clinked glasses, they finally got down to business.

CHAPTER 52
WHITE SANDS MOTEL, ALAMOGORDO, NEW MEXICO

The White Sands Motel was a typical, cheap, just-off-the-highway place, familiar from a thousand road movies. A flickering neon sign at the roadside with a giant arrow pointing to the single-story building, and a noticeboard listing the usual amenities: air conditioning, cable TV, free HBO, truck parking, family rooms.

Weaver rolled the Humvee into the parking lot and pulled up directly in front of her room.

"Number 13, right?"

"Yeah. My lucky number," the woman slurred, her eyes half open, waving the room key in front of his face. "You're a real gentleman, Mr. Marine," she mumbled, cuddling close to him. Weaver had his work cut out keeping the woman's limp body vertical, even for the short distance from the car to the door of her room.

She only had three drinks at the bar, Weaver thought. *But who knows how much she had to drink before that*. He'd get her into her room and head straight back to the base. This little side trip had cost him enough time already. His phone could ring any moment, and he'd have to get on the road. But what was he supposed to do? He had a weakness for good-looking women. And while he certainly wasn't a paragon of morality, if there was one thing he hated, it was men who assaulted helpless women. For him, that was the epitome of weakness. And he was anything but weak.

He took the key, unlocked the door, and pushed it open to reveal small, shabby room, the air heavy with the smell of disinfectant. A coverlet, once brightly colored but now faded from too much washing, covered the queen-size bed. The room looked anything but inviting.

"You're a real sweetheart, you know that?" The woman stopped hanging off of him and pulled him into the room, only to throw her arms around his neck a moment later and start kissing him fervently. Weaver was taken by surprise, but didn't push her away. "If only there was some way I could show you my gratitude," she breathed into his ear, then nibbled at his earlobe. She wriggled around and gave him a push, and Weaver fell backward onto the creaky bed. Hips swinging, she went back to the door, removed the key that was still protruding from the knob, closed the door, and locked it securely from the inside.

Weaver studied the woman, his eyes roving over her perfect body. Despite her drunkenness, she obviously knew how to use it. *What the hell*, he thought. *Half an hour more or less isn't going to make a difference.* He started unbuttoning his uniform shirt. After all, it wasn't every day that a supermodel threw herself at him.

"Not so fast, soldier," the woman said. Suddenly her voice was steady and crystal clear.

Weaver looked up into the barrel of a Glock 44 with a B&T small-caliber suppressor. He felt no fear, just surprise. It wasn't the first time he'd had a gun pointed at him. He was just angry at himself—now he'd been duped twice in one day.

"Who are you? What do you want from me?"

"I could give you one of the cover names I use, but how would that help? Call me Mantis."

"Is that supposed to mean something to me?"

"Probably not. You're not my usual prey." She looked Weaver up and down with a lewd smile. He was still lying on his back, propped on his elbows on the bed. "A little old for me. But still in good shape, I'll admit."

"You still haven't told me what you want."

"True. Sorry. I was just thinking about making an exception for you . . . but I still need you. I guess I'll have to pass. Pity." Weaver looked at her, not understanding. "Where was I? Oh, yes," she went on, "I've discovered that you and I have a common interest, and I wanted to propose a deal. You're looking for something that I would also love to get my hands on."

"I have no idea what you're talking about."

"Don't be so coy, Lieutenant Colonel Weaver. I know exactly who you are and what you've let slip through your fingers."

Weaver's eyes widened. Was it possible that this woman, whoever she was and whoever she was working for, was talking about the head?

The woman had read his mind. She held her left hand about eighteen inches above the top of the table she was leaning on. "About so big? Pickled in liquid, snaky dreadlocks, ugly as sin, grim-looking, and answers to the name of Medusa?"

"I can't help you, sorry," Weaver said.

"Oh please. Don't do that. We're both professionals. Your military honor is out of place here. I don't want to take the Medusa away from you, I only want—"

The ring of Weaver's mobile phone interrupted her. He raised his hands and sat up.

She waggled the pistol, signaling for him to take the call. "No tricks. Put it on speaker."

Weaver did as she said. He withdrew the phone slowly from his pocket, took the call, and switched it to speaker. "What is it?"

"Sir, they've gotten away. Davis, Simpson, and Campbell are dead, the pilot too."

Weaver was suddenly furious. "What happened?"

"We don't know exactly, but Border Patrol found the burned-out wreck of our chopper on the Mexican border."

"Shit. What about the agents?"

"No sign of them, sir. Presumably, they're in Mexico. Sir, what do you want me to do?"

Weaver said nothing. He simply hung up and narrowed his eyes at the Mantis, trying to figure her out, which was anything but easy. She'd just played him for a complete sucker with her performance.

"Looks like the Medusa's gotten away from you again. As I was just about to say, I don't want to take the head away from you forever. But what I *would* like"—she paused for effect—"is to borrow it for a few days. After that, you can have it back. And I'll pay you handsomely for the favor. What do you say?"

Weaver thought it over. Could he trust this woman? Probably not, but right now he didn't seem to have a choice.

"How do you see this working? Hypothetically speaking, of course."

"Of course," the woman said. "Well, hypothetically, it's easy. We work together to retrieve the head. I've got some unfinished business with that Wagner myself." She stood up and strutted back and forth at a safe distance from Weaver. "After that, we both fly to Greece. Seventy-two hours later, you have the head back in your possession, along with a nice little nest egg, enough to spend the rest of your life somewhere warm. And best of all: no one ever has to know about any of it."

She looked at Weaver. She knew she had him.

"Okay, deal," said Weaver. "And I already know how we're going to get it back." He held out his hand to the woman.

She lowered her pistol, and they sealed the deal with a handshake. Weaver took out his phone and dialed a number.

"General Horne, I need your help."

CHAPTER 53
MAISON DE FLAMEL, PARIS

Cloutard quickly outlined the story behind Medusa's head, how dangerous it was, and the artifacts that, according to the expert Damjam Mandalov, they would need to destroy it. "Napoleon Bonaparte may have discovered Alexander's tomb and brought the artifacts he found in it back to Paris. We were inside Luxembourg Palace, where he lived after his Egyptian campaign, but we found nothing. Unfortunately, were unable to search further because the police caught us."

The marquis tsk-tsked, appalled. "The police? François, you seem to have lost your touch. All that work for UNESCO, all completely above board, and now working legally for van Rensburg . . . it is not doing you any good at all."

Hellen frowned. "But how do you know—"

Cloutard stopped her with a gesture. "Do not ask. He just knows."

"Am I right in assuming that you want me to get you back inside Luxembourg Palace to continue your . . . research?"

Hellen and Cloutard both nodded. Marquis Dieulafoy

sipped from his glass of champagne and looked thoughtfully first at Cloutard, then at Hellen.

"Madame de Mey, may I have a few minutes alone with François?"

Hellen was not particularly enthusiastic about the suggestion, but she knew she had no room to negotiate. "Where can I freshen up?" she asked, standing up. "'Powder my nose,' as they say."

When she returned ten minutes later, both men were smiling happily, and Dieulafoy's butler was refilling their glasses. Verdi's "Brindis" from *La Traviata* was playing in the background, almost as if someone had put the duet on especially for this moment.

"Augustin may have something even more interesting for us," said Cloutard.

Hellen tilted her head. "I'm listening," she said, and silently reminded herself to ask Cloutard as soon as she could about what the marquis had wanted to discuss so privately. It couldn't be good, she was sure of that.

"The Thieves' Guild, of which I am honored to be the Grand Vizier, has existed in Paris for many hundreds of years. Beneath this house is our archive, which dates to the days of Philip the Fair."

Hellen's expression brightened, but as so often on their adventures, she knew she would have no time to examine the treasures below in any detail.

"We happen to be in possession of a number of documents that may be of interest to you in this matter."

"Documents?" Hellen asked.

"Madame, Napoleon Bonaparte is one of the great personages of our nation. It is no accident, therefore, that I am well acquainted with the materials the guild possesses on the Corsican. And I believe that one of them, a certificate, will certainly meet with your approval." The marquis was on his feet now. "If you would be so kind as to follow me to the cellars."

Dieulafoy led the way downstairs, closely followed by Hellen and Cloutard. They went along a passage and through three old steel doors, each one with multiple locks, before reaching an ultramodern vault. The marquis tapped in a ten-digit code, pressed the palm of his hand to a touchpad, and held his right eye to a retinal scanner. The door opened with a hiss, and they entered a room of perhaps two thousand square feet, a state-of-the-art document archive. Many of the items were sealed inside airtight cabinets—similar to what Hellen had seen at the Vatican's secret archive.

Dieulafoy crossed to a computer terminal, where he tapped in a different code and called up a search program. Moments later, one of the airtight compartments opened. Dieulafoy pulled on a pair of white gloves and lifted an ancient leather folder out of the compartment. He leafed through the pages carefully.

"This is what I think you need to see," the marquis said, handing Hellen a pair of gloves. She pulled them on quickly and began to study the certificate, Cloutard leaning over her shoulder. "I do not believe I promised you too much," Dieulafoy said.

"This . . . this is sensational," Hellen said. She pointed to a line on the certificate. "If I hadn't seen this with my own eyes, I would never have believed it."

CHAPTER 54
CIUDAD JUÁREZ, MEXICO

"What did you say? The crime rate's lower than ever? Don't worry?" Tom said sarcastically, glaring at Hagen over the bed of the pickup.

"I never said it was zero," Hagen replied.

Hands raised, they stood on the left and right of the car, facing the scowling faces of five armed Mexicans.

After successfully crossing the border without being seen two hours earlier and a bumpy fifteen-mile drive through the desert below the border, they had finally come to a road. They had followed Ascensión Ciudad Juárez, as the road was known locally, almost all the way to the airport. But the brand-new Ford F-150 Raptor had been riddled with bullets, and they could hardly drive into the airport in a shot-up pickup. They would have drawn too much unwanted attention, so they'd decided to ditch the car as fast as possible and find another one.

"We don't just need a car," Hagen had said. "We need a phone, too. I need to contact my people urgently. Horne can't get away with this."

"Don't the CIA have people here in Juárez? A safe house?" Tom had asked.

"I'm sure they do, but it won't be in the phone book," Hagen replied snidely.

After another fifteen miles, they had seen the first outlying buildings of Juárez. The sun was below the horizon, and the moonlight doused the land in an almost mystical light.

Mexico, unlike much of the United States, didn't have a gas station or convenience store every fifty yards. A few commercial warehouses and a handful of dilapidated, boarded-up buildings covered in fading graffiti were all the outskirts of Juárez had to offer. They were still about six miles from the airport when they finally saw a bar and a small *tienda* on the right. "I'm pulling over there. They must have a phone," Hagen said.

He had turned into the parking lot and pulled up beside an old, rusty Toyota pickup. At this time of night, the place looked sketchy at best, and Tom didn't think it would look much better in daylight. Even he felt a little uncomfortable as they climbed out. They didn't even get as far as the entrance before a handful of men emerged from the darkness into the flickering light of the sole streetlamp and surrounded them.

"*Hombres*, what did you do to this beautiful car?" said one of the men, apparently the leader.

Ciudad Juárez, also known simply as Juárez or, until 1888, as El Paso del Norte—the northern pass—had had a reputation as the most dangerous city in the world for many years. The war between the Sinaloa and Juárez cartels had left thousands dead every year in the border city. Exactly why the crime rate had fallen in recent years was the subject of speculation. One theory was a peace treaty between the cartels, a kind of new "order among criminals." Another postulated that putting an end to corruption within the police force had helped bring the violence down.

"I knew we should have stopped at that taco stand a mile back," Tom hissed.

"Really? You want to get into that here and now? I think we have other problems to deal with," Hagen said. One of the Mexicans had planted himself in front of him.

"Your friend is a clever guy, *hombre*," the leader said, approaching Tom with his index finger raised and his head slightly lowered. "What are two *gringos* like you doing in a shot-up truck in my beautiful city?" Without warning, he grabbed his own crotch and shook it. "My *cojones* are telling me you guys are in deep shit." The man let out a laugh and the rest of the gang joined in. Tom and Hagen shared a look. Both still had their hands on their heads and were still standing left and right at the back of the bullet-riddled Ford. Tom glanced down at the bed of the pickup, where the rifle that belonged to the Texan from whom they'd stolen the car lay almost within reach. Hagen saw what Tom was thinking and shook his head very slightly. The five men were armed, sure, but they were just a clutch of street thugs. Two of them had chromed pistols in their waistbands, one was holding a length of chain, one a pry bar, and one a baseball bat. Starting an international incident now with an assault rifle would literally have been overkill.

"So tell me, *hombres*, what brings you to Juárez?"

Hagen was about to say something, but Tom spoke first. "I don't want to be difficult, but if I told you, you wouldn't believe it."

"What are you trying to say, *gringo*? You from the CIA or something?" The leader laughed again, took another step toward Tom, and looked up at him with an insolent sneer. He was at least half a head shorter than Tom and was wearing a stained tank top and a heavy chain around his neck. His trousers hung low on his hips, and a hairnet covered his oily black hair.

Tom met his gaze without flinching. This seemed to confuse the man a little—he and his compadres were the fearsome gangbangers, weren't they? Tom squinted, screwed his mouth sideways, and tipped his head from side to side.

"It's complicated," he finally said. He nodded across at Hagen. "He's ex-SAS, but he's been working for MI6 for years and right now he's on the CIA's payroll. I'm just an antiterror specialist and adventurer," he said shamelessly. Hagen looked at him in disbelief and shook his head.

For a moment, no one said a word. The only sound was the buzz of the defective streetlamp. At first, hairnet guy just stared at Tom in disbelief, but then fell into a fit of laughter. He took his eye off Tom for a split second.

His friends had begun to laugh, too, but the high-pitched shriek of their leader shut them up. Tom had kicked the man in the crotch as hard as he could and grabbed the chromed pistol from his waistband. He already had the man in a headlock. Hagen, just as quick, had disarmed the man with the baseball bat and knocked him out with it.

Tom shifted the chromed Beretta between the leader's head and the three remaining gangbangers. "Put it on the ground," he said to the one with the pistol, who had been thinking about drawing it. Slowly, the man did as Tom said. "Now fuck off," he said, and all three turned and ran.

"*Hijo de puta*," snarled the man Tom was still holding in a headlock.

"How can you say that? You don't even know my mother," Tom said. He let go of him, but kept the pistol aimed at his head. "I need your phone. You got a car?"

Hagen went to the man, who handed over his phone and car keys. "This one?" Hagen pointed to the dilapidated Toyota. The man, still not able to stand upright, nodded. Hagen loaded their things from the Ford into the Toyota, then took the pickup's code-key and tossed it to the surprised gang leader. "You only had to ask."

Tom put away the pistol and climbed in, and he and Hagen drove away.

Hagen ended his phone call a few minutes later. "There's light at the end of the tunnel. We've got a plane. In two hours, we can be on our way."

CHAPTER 55

BOBA FAT'S HOUSE, ANACOSTIA, WASHINGTON, D.C.

"I don't know about you, but I'm starting to think that whoever's pushing this conspiracy has a much bigger agenda," said Akira, her eyes on one of the six monitors, which was showing CNN with the sound off.

"Whaddya mean?"

"Look what's going on in the world." She pointed to the screen with the news program. "Not so long ago, people thought the whole thing was a bad joke. Now we're sitting on a powder keg. In practically no time at all, they've caused more trouble with a made-up cult than Q-Anon has ever managed to. And what drives me even crazier is that I can't find out who's behind it. They're real professionals, not just loonies trying to earn dollars for millions of views." Akira turned back to her laptop. "How far are you with the DOD?" she asked Bobby.

"Any second," he said, hammering out line after line of code on his keyboard. "Booyah! I'm in!" he shouted, raising his hands in the air like a piano virtuoso at the end of a masterful performance.

Akira jumped to her feet and peered over Bobby's shoulder.

"So, what are we looking for?" Bobby said.

"I'll only know it when I see it," Akira answered. "Look up General Jasper Horne. He's DARPA's Pentagon liaison."

Bobby nodded. He opened a search field and typed in the name. A second later, Akira drew a sharp breath. "What's this? Project Perseus?" she asked, pointing at an entry. Bobby clicked on the link and Akira quickly scanned the text.

"Looks like a bomb test," said Bobby. "Object successfully destroyed? What object? And why was it cc-ed to the UN Security Council? How are they involved with an Army bomb test?"

"No idea," Akira said. "Who authorized it?"

"The original order came from a CIA task force," Bobby said, which made Akira prick up her ears. "How's the CIA server going?"

"My algorithm's working on it, but it'll probably take another—" A *beep* interrupted her. "Never mind. We're in." She cracked her fingers and went to work. In a few minutes, she found what she was looking for.

"Very interesting. The head of the task force, Isaac Hagen, traveled to Vienna at short notice, just after I sent him my data package," Akira said. She returned to the keyboard and tapped away for a few seconds. "Let's see what he was up to in Vienna."

Half an hour later, a deathly pale Akira sank back in her chair. Everything suddenly made an absurd kind of sense. She'd discovered that the museum director had been murdered, that the billionaire she'd been eavesdropping on was sitting in a jail cell as the prime suspect, and that a parcel connected with the murder had turned up, which the authorities had initially thought was a bomb. After that, she'd hacked the surveillance camera system at Cobra headquarters and stumbled across a recording that showed that

Tom Wagner, Isaac Hagen, and Hellen de Mey were all involved.

"Look at this," Akira said, showing Bobby the video, which proved beyond doubt that the head of Medusa really existed. They saw the head revealed and the damage it had done when removed from its jar, then watched Tom unload a full magazine into it at point-blank range without leaving a scratch.

After the initial shock and a long discussion about deepfakes, Akira managed to convince Bobby that everything they had seen was real. The secret that had been kept faithfully by every director of the Museum of Fine Arts since the nineteenth century had been exposed, which also explained why DARPA was after the indestructible head.

"But it says here that the 'object'—which I'm assuming means Medusa's head—was destroyed," Bobby objected.

"Of course it does," Akira said. "If you're going to break an international treaty, you'll have to tell the UN something first. After that, you can take your time and do your experiments, and no one's going to say a word."

"General Horne might even be behind the conspiracy b.s. For generals and arms makers, nothing would be better for business than a new world war."

Akira nodded. "I'm pretty sure it was Horne who put those killers onto me, at least. Weaver had already tried to warn me off the project several times. It looks like Horne didn't want any loose ends, so he did it his way."

They kept on digging, and a few minutes later, Akira suddenly cried: "Ha! He was really there?" She turned her laptop to Bobby.

"Who was where?" Bobby asked.

"Tom Wagner. He was in White Sands at the same time as the bomb test." She tapped on the screen that showed the tracking data for a cell phone in New Mexico. Beside the words "Holloman Air Force Base" blinked a red dot.

"Who?"

"Do you live on the moon? The guy you just saw in the video. He saved the Pope's life a few years ago, and he and Hagen destroyed the Absolute Freedom terrorist group."

"Oh, *that* Tom Wagner," said Bobby, although he still didn't know who he was supposed to be.

"Whatever," Akira said. "If that old Blue Shield team is mixed up in this, then it's big."

Bobby turned back to his own screen and burrowed deeper into the DOD files. "Hey, check this. Isn't that your boss at DARPA? A Lieutenant Colonel Weaver showed up at Holloman Air Force Base with a black-ops team just before the bomb test."

Akira looked up.

"Weaver? Really?"

Bobby nodded.

"If Wagner and Hagen are really in New Mexico, and Weaver wanted to stop the Medusa from being destroyed, then something must have happened. From what I know about Wagner, he's not just going to let them take the head away."

"You mean something like this?" Bobby pointed at his screen. "I came across this news item earlier: a Blackhawk helicopter crashed on a training flight near El Paso, right on the Mexican border."

"Bingo," said Akira. "That means the head's still around, and maybe Tom Wagner has it."

"But the way things look, not for much longer. Look at this!" Bobby said.

Akira followed Bobby's finger as he pointed to a line on the screen.

"That's not good. That's not good at all."

CHAPTER 56

INSIDE A GULFSTREAM V, DESTINATION VIENNA

"Your CIA guys sure delivered fast," said Tom, after making himself comfortable in the luxurious private jet.

"Yes. Once I told them what General Horne and his flunkies did to get the head, things moved fast. The jet's actually FBI. They're in Juaréz meeting the local cops about ongoing cartel issues."

"Lucky for us. Most importantly, we get out of here fast."

Ten minutes later, they were in the air and heading for Vienna.

"I need a drink," said Tom.

"You really know your way around this thing," said Hagen, as Tom got up to fix himself a drink without asking where the bar was.

"We had this exact model at Blue Shield. They're all the same. Not as fancy as van Rensburg's jet, but still an awfully comfortable way to fly, right?" Tom asked, filling the cocktail shaker with freshly pressed lemon juice, Weller Special Reserve bourbon, and a shot of Monin cane sugar syrup. "With or without egg white?" he asked.

"Without, thanks."

Tom expertly shook the silver shaker of his favorite

drink, cracked it on the edge of the bar to loosen the lid, and poured the contents into two ice-cube-filled tumblers. He shaved off two thin slices of orange, twisted each above a tumbler to spread the aroma over the glass, then placed the slices on top as a garnish.

"You missed your calling," said Hagen as he accepted the glass and put his feet up.

Tom did likewise. "If you spent as much time in cocktail bars as I have, you'd learn a trick or two," he said. He raised his glass to Hagen and knocked back a mouthful of his whiskey sour. "Ahh, that's the stuff," he said, with a sigh of satisfaction.

"Cocktail bars?"

Tom laughed. "In my Cobra days, I used to play a little piano in a cocktail bar in the First District in Vienna. I must've played the Great American Songbook cover to cover. I've hardly found the time since then, though."

"So he plays piano, too, does he?" Hagen said.

Tom smiled sheepishly. "Mom taught me," he said, and a sudden sadness washed over him. The back-to-back adventures of the last few years had managed to keep his parents mostly out of his thoughts. They'd been killed in a bombing in Syria, and after their deaths he'd grown up in Vienna with his grandfather, Arthur Prey.

"You were seven, weren't you?" Hagen said. Tom nodded. "I'm sorry. I really am. But you got the guys who did it in the end."

"Yeah. Guerra's dead, but I still have no idea why they were killed. Guerra was just following orders, and the question's still open: whose orders? One day I'll find out," Tom said. "Um. Can we change the subject?"

For a moment, they both sipped at their drinks in silence. Then Tom asked, "So, how's office life?" Hagen glared back at him over the edge of his tumbler. "Not your favorite topic?" Tom said, and they both smiled. "Okay, then what do we do with this thing now?" he said with a nod toward his duffel bag, which they had buckled securely into one of the leather seats.

"I don't know. My master plan has gone down the drain. If Weaver and Horne were really acting on the president's orders—or at least with his tacit approval—then it'll probably be up to the UN Security Council to deal with it. I'm out of ideas."

"I'm also suspicious about these hackers and all the conspiracy stuff," Tom said. "Who's behind that?"

"My computer geeks at MI6 have run into a brick wall on that. They're getting nowhere."

"It's scary what you can do with a well-planned Internet campaign."

"Do you think Horne's part of that, too? Would he really try to start a war? Would he go that far?" Hagen asked.

"If you can believe my uncle's stories, I wouldn't be surprised. Horne was always the first to rattle his saber. His idea of problem-solving was to send in SEAL Team Six or order an air strike. Diplomacy was never of much interest to him. And I don't think for a second that they've given up."

"It's worth looking into, though. I'll have my team poke around a little in Horne's and Weaver's private lives. When they tried to confiscate the head from us, they definitely went too far. If I do it right, they'll be court-martialed for it. But that can wait until we land."

"Suits me. I should call Hellen, too. She worries when she can't reach me. If I'm not careful, I'll be the one getting court-martialed," Tom said with a laugh. "But a few hours one way or the other won't matter. I'm going to grab a little shut-eye." He swung the footrest out and made himself comfortable.

"Excellent plan," said Hagen, and he also stretched out and closed his eyes.

"Gentlemen," they heard the pilot say over the intercom twelve hours later. "We'll be landing in Vienna in a few minutes."

Tom and Hagen woke up with a jolt.

"Are we there already?" said Tom, still sleepy. He stretched and rubbed his eyes. A glance out the window confirmed the pilot's announcement. Below, Tom saw the familiar landscape of Lower Austria.

A short time later, the plane touched down safely on the tarmac at Vienna International Airport, and the pilot taxied to the private terminal in the northwest corner of the airport.

When the jet had come to a standstill, the pilot came back into the cabin.

"Mr. Hagen, I don't know what's going on, but the tower has instructed me not to open the doors until we get the okay."

Tom and Hagen, their gear already shouldered and ready to disembark, frowned and shared a look. This was extremely unusual.

Tom put his duffel bag down again and went to one of the windows.

"What the hell is this?" he said, when he saw Cobra vehicles pulling up. He could only stand and watch as his former comrades surrounded the plane. Hagen was also looking out a window.

Suddenly, they heard a voice over a megaphone.

"Tom Wagner. Isaac Hagen. This is the police. Exit the plane slowly, unarmed, and with your hands clasped behind your head."

"Honor guard?" said Hagen.

"I don't believe this," Tom said. He fished out the phone Hagen's people had given them in Mexico.

"What are you doing?"

"Calling my old boss to ask him what drugs he's on." He dialed Captain Maierhofer's number, but it went straight to voicemail.

"Tom Wagner. Isaac Hagen. We have an international arrest warrant. The plane is surrounded. Come out unarmed, with your hands up," the voice came over the megaphone again.

"Horne," Tom growled. "The asshole put out a Red Notice on us."

CHAPTER 57
EON VAN RENSBURG'S PRIVATE JET, APPROACHING VIENNA AIRPORT

Hellen de Mey, unlike Tom, was one of those unfortunate people unable to sleep on a plane. Not because she was afraid of flying, but because it simply wasn't comfortable enough. Even the luxurious private jet they'd been flying around Europe for the last few days couldn't offer her the feeling of "bed" that she needed.

Instead of sleeping, she mentally reviewed everything she'd discovered from Marquis Dieulafoy and in the archives of the French Thieves' Guild. Her reflections were accompanied by Cloutard's loud snoring. Like Tom, he had no problem napping anywhere or anytime.

But what she'd found in Paris would probably have kept her awake anyway.

Marquis Augustin Dieulafoy had shown her a certificate proving that Napoleon Bonaparte had been a member of the Order of the Golden Fleece.

The Order had been founded in Bruges in 1430 as a chivalric order of knights, and still exists today. Until the dissolution of the Austro-Hungarian Empire, the emperor had always dictated who could and could not be admitted to the illustrious Order. In Spain, home to another chapter of the Order comparable with the Spanish line of the Habsburgs, the Spanish king is still the grand master today.

Hellen was astonished to discover that Napoleon had been a member, because the honor of membership was normally reserved for nobles. She couldn't imagine why Emperor Franz II had accepted Napoleon at all.

The Thieves' Guild had more to reveal about Napoleon, however. Among their documents was an exchange of letters between the Holy Roman Emperor Franz II and Napoleon. And one of the letters had been crucial.

Although the letter contained nothing to explain why Napoleon was so eager to be a member of the Order, it did contain an agreement that Napoleon would hand over "certain artifacts" to the Order if he were accepted. Hellen could only surmise that Napoleon, not coming from a noble background, simply craved recognition among the nobility.

The artifacts in question—as the letter had also revealed—were the Aegis breastplate and the Golden Fleece itself. And since Napoleon had been accepted into the Order, he and the emperor must have reached an agreement, and the breastplate and fleece would have been duly handed over.

Which was why they were on their way to Vienna. Hellen remembered that, in Professor Richter's house, she'd seen a picture of Emperor Franz Joseph, Franz II's descendant, in the ceremonial garb of the Order. In the picture, he was also wearing the Order's ornate gold "collar" with its golden ram pendant, today on display in the Imperial Treasury collection.

The gentle bump when they touched down at Vienna International Airport shook Hellen from her deliberations and, at the same time, woke Cloutard from his nap. He looked around in a daze until he finally seemed to remember where he was.

"Can you finally tell me what the marquis wanted to talk

to you about privately?" Hellen said, looking hard at Cloutard. "Or is that a secret among thieves?"

Cloutard knew that look. No more weaseling out. He cleared his throat, sat upright, and straightened his shirt collar as if to gather his courage. "He asked me to be the Grand Vizier of the Vienna Thieves' Guild. The post has been vacant for years. He knows how much time I spend in Vienna and that I have a second residence at Tom's grandfather's apartment whenever Arthur goes off to Cuba."

"Grand Vizier of the Vienna Thieves' Guild? What does that mean? What will you have to do?" Hellen sounded a little dismayed.

"Practically nothing, in fact. It is an empty title. I will only be called upon for the international Grand Viziers convention. But Vienna is not on the list of upcoming events."

Hellen shook her head. So there was a global guild of thieves that organized international conventions. Incredible. Then again, she was now on the hunt for the golden fleece to destroy the head of Medusa. Compared to that and all their other exploits, an international thieves' guild seemed pretty tame.

From the airport, they headed straight for Professor Richter's house, arriving about an hour later. Cloutard put his skills to work and picked the lock on the front door with practiced ease. Hellen was already on her way to Richter's office.

"Madame Wagner, what are we actually looking for?" Cloutard asked, knowing that she hated being addressed by the surname "Wagner." Hellen had good reasons for insisting on keeping her—in Cloutard's opinion—delightful surname "de Mey."

"Careful, François, or I'll start drinking Coke when you cook."

Cloutard snorted. Coca-Cola could make cultivated French people see red. It was certainly not to be drunk when dining.

"But back to your question," Hellen went on. "I didn't think the picture of Franz Joseph was significant, but I do remember that it was lying on top of a folder of other papers."

The police had turned everything upside down, so Hellen and Cloutard had to start their search from scratch. But they quickly found what they wanted.

"Is this it?" Cloutard asked. He had a folder in his hand and was holding up a photo of Edmund Pölz's painting of the emperor dressed in the regalia of the Order.

"That's the one," Hellen said. She flipped quickly through the other documents in the folder. "It looks as if Richter was on the same trail we are. There's an application here for access to the Order's archives. It's addressed to Cardinal Lackner, Archbishop of Vienna. He's the current almoner of the Order of the Golden Fleece. The Order's archives are in the Archdiocese of Vienna, apparently." She thought for a moment, then smiled. "We'll get Father Giacomo to help."

Cloutard frowned. "And who is that, again?"

Hellen was already heading for the door. "Remember the priest in Barcelona, the one with our four nuns at the opening of the Sagrada Família?"

"*Bien sûr*. He loaned his cassock to Tom so he could sneak into the church."

Hellen nodded. "The nuns visited him in Vienna not long ago, while Tom and I were in the Caribbean. Father Giacomo Tramontano had the honor of being appointed Cardinal Lackner's private secretary."

Cloutard laughed out loud. "The poor man. And now he has to help us again. As I recall, he is not the bravest soul."

Hellen checked the time. "We have a few hours to think about how we can talk him around. Between now and then, I need a little sleep."

"Why didn't you sleep on van Rensburg's plane? *C'est extraordinairement confortable!*"

Hellen only sniffed.

Cobra base, Rossauer Barracks, Vienna

"Where's Captain Maierhofer? I demand to see him immediately," Tom shouted as the door closed and was locked from outside. A police officer had just put down two trays with microwaved ration packs on the table while two others had kept an eye on him and Hagen. Then the three officers exited together.

They had been sitting in the windowless room for hours. The only furnishings were two low beds and a table with two chairs.

"Do you know where we are?" Hagen asked, sitting down at the table and starting to eat.

"The Cobra base in Vienna, at the Rossauer Barracks. Actually, the Rossauer Bernadis-Schmid Barracks. They changed the name in 2020," Tom said, pacing restlessly.

The historic building around them had been completed in 1865 as a defensive barracks, able to house up to four thousand soldiers and three hundred and ninety horses. In imperial times, after the March Revolution of 1848, it provided an urban base from which to respond quickly to uprisings among the middle and lower classes. Crown Prince Rudolf Barracks, as it was originally called, had three inner courtyards, bases for the traffic police, the Cobra and WEGA special units, and the offices of the Austrian Ministry of Defense. The northern courtyard served primarily as a landing pad for military helicopters.

"Bernadis? Wasn't he the Austrian lieutenant colonel in the German army? That staff officer who was part of Operation Valkyrie?" Hagen asked, his mouth full.

Tom shrugged. "You've been spending too much time on Wikipedia again, haven't you? Is your job really that dull?" Tom said, snarkier than necessary. Hagen's frown made him pause. "Sorry, Isaac, I'm just pissed off." More resigned, he sat on one of the cots. "I have no idea where Hellen is or if she's okay. My boss is sitting in jail, and thanks to that psycho General Horne, my own people are holding me prisoner."

"Horne went too far with the Red Notice," Hagen said. "One hundred percent. The UN Security Council won't stand for it."

"But what's he planning? Okay, he's got us out of the way for now, but how does that help him?"

"No idea. I think he's just playing for time." Tom was back on his feet, pacing furiously. "Can you sit down again? Please? You're making me nervous, strutting around like that."

Tom stopped and looked at Hagen. "How can you eat at a time like this?" Tom said, and he pulled up the other chair. He sniffed at the indefinable mass of food the guard hat put on the table, screwed up his nose, and pushed the tray aside.

"In the SAS, we learned to eat when we could. You never knew when you'd get another chance. So eat something. Whiskey sours and peanuts don't exactly constitute a balanced diet," Hagen said, and he slid the tray back in front of Tom.

Tom looked at the bowl in front of him in disgust. "This stuff looks like somebody already ate it."

"Oooh, that year of luxury in van Rensburg's villa made you soft."

Tom snorted and forced a spoonful into his mouth against his will. "I was right," he said, choking it down. But he held his nose and managed to empty the bowl. "We should start thinking about how we're going to get out of here," he said. "We can't just sit around and wait until someone feels like they have to talk to us. At least the head's in a safe place for now."

"How do you see us getting out of her? There's an army out there, and most of them are like us," Hagen said.

"Right now, there aren't that many of them. Most of them are out at the demonstrations—I picked up that much when they brought us in."

"Fine, but then how, in the name of Zeus' butthole, do you want to get out of this cell?"

Tom grinned. "Nice line."

"I've been to the movies once or twice myself."

"Let's keep it simple. Next time that door opens, we overpower whoever comes in. I think we can take down three snakes between us," Tom said with a grin.

As if they'd talked it through in advance, Tom and Hagen jumped up, grabbed their chairs, and positioned themselves left and right of the door when they heard a key being pushed into the lock. They held the chairs over their shoulders like baseball bats. Tom held his breath. The door swung open, and Tom let fly.

CHAPTER 58

THE GARDEN OF HAAS & HAAS TEAHOUSE, STEPHANSPLATZ, VIENNA

"You want me to what?" Father Giacomo almost choked on the words. "*Madre de dios*, forget it."

Sister Lucrezia had told Hellen that Father Giacomo always ate breakfast at the lavish teahouse behind St. Stephen's Cathedral, and the nun was right. All the color drained out of Father Giacomo's face when Hellen and Cloutard sat at his table and laid out their plan. A chunk of butter croissant, spread liberally with apricot jam from the nearby Wachau, went down the wrong way and he had a coughing fit. The events in Barcelona were obviously still fresh in his mind, including being abandoned in his underwear in a car just a block from the Sagrada Família.

"A few hours at most, that's all we'll need. I doubt we'll need longer than that to search the archive. We know the time period we have to search pretty exactly," Hellen said calmly.

Beside her, Cloutard, amused at the poor priest's plight, was trying to conceal a grin behind his hand.

"A few hours?"

Guests had begun turning to look at them.

"*Monsieur l'abbé*, it is very easy," Cloutard said. "You take the key to the cardinal's archive, let us in, and let us out again a few hours later. No one will even notice we were there." He could barely contain himself as he watched the priest's face changing color.

"*Passare sul mio cadaver.*" Father Giacomo shook his head vehemently.

Hellen decided to bring out the big guns. "You know perfectly well that Sisters Lucrezia, Alfonsina, Renata, and Bartolomea trust us unconditionally, don't you? And you even helped Tom get inside the Vatican and disguise himself as a Swiss Guardsman so we could 'borrow' the Sword of Peter. How do you think Sister Lucrezia will react when she finds out you denied us this one tiny favor?"

The priest's expression instantly turned to stone. He seemed more afraid of the Mother Superior than of losing his job with the cardinal.

Cloutard decided to press the point. "If you do not help us, then imagine what will be waiting for you in the Holy City if you ever return to Rome. Dante's Inferno will feel like a vacation by comparison."

Father Giacomo gulped. Without a word, he fished a couple of euro bills out of the pocket of his cassock and laid them on the table beside the breakfast he had barely touched. "Let's go," he whispered. "His Eminence will not be in until early this afternoon."

His head hanging low, he shuffled across the back of Stephansplatz, turned into the passageway leading to the Cathedral Museum—part of the pilgrim Way of St. James through Vienna—then turned left onto the Wollzeile and led Cloutard and Hellen into the Archdiocese of Vienna's building. It was still early, and the upstairs offices were empty. Hellen and Cloutard could see that Father Giacomo was breathing fast. Knees quaking, he slipped into the cardinal's office and returned a moment later with a keycard.

"Follow me," he said flatly.

They returned to the ground floor and went out into the Archdiocese's inner courtyard, which was surrounded by arches. The priest opened an unassuming door, and they went down a few steps and stopped at a door with a card reader and an old push-button keypad. He slid the card through the reader, tapped in a four-digit code, and opened the door.

"You have two hours," he said, and he turned away and left them at the door.

Hellen didn't hesitate for a second. She quickly worked out the filing system and began searching the years from 1800 onward. Napoleon had become a member of the Order in 1804. She pulled out a few files and handed several of them to Cloutard, who frowned. Then they sat at a table in the center of the archive and began combing through the dusty documents.

For an hour, the only sound was repeated sighing as they went through the entire period up to Napoleon's death in 1821.

"Anything at all?" Hellen asked.

Cloutard shook his head. "No word of Napoleon, nothing about any artifacts, and certainly no mention of the Golden Fleece."

"But there must be something in the notes from the meeting. It would have been impossible for the Order to take possession of the Golden Fleece without recording it in the minutes, wouldn't it?" She shook her head angrily. She hated dead ends.

"Perhaps we should look at the years after he died," Cloutard said, although he did not sound confident at all.

But Hellen was staring into space and didn't respond to Cloutard's suggestion. She simply gazed at nothing. Cloutard waved his hand in front of her eyes, but she didn't react. Then he rapped his knuckles gently against her head. "Hello? Hello? Anyone home?"

She swatted his hand away like an annoying fly. "You're right: we should focus on the period from 1848 to 1916," she said absently.

"The reign of Franz Joseph?" Cloutard asked,

"Well done, François. A-plus. You may sit."

"Do you think you are the only one with a little historical knowledge? You are talking to a polymath."

"Of course—my humble apologies, Leonardo," Hellen jibed. "Seriously, though, Richter had the emperor in his research folder for a reason."

They soon found the files for the period in question. Twenty minutes later, Cloutard let out a cry: "Eureka!"

"What is it?"

Excited, he showed her at a letter personally written by the emperor.

"A planned meeting of the Order in Achilleion, Empress Elisabeth's palace on Corfu," Hellen said breathlessly, her eyes widening. "But it's known that the emperor never visited Empress Elisabeth on Corfu, not even once. So, if he never visited Sissi in Achilleion, it means the planned meeting could never have taken place."

"But the artifacts could still be there. Look here." Cloutard pointed at another page of the letter.

"'Certain artifacts' are mentioned here, too, and a debt of gratitude owed to the French emperor." Hellen exhaled loudly. "So the artifacts were taken to Greece, to Sissi's palace on Corfu. Apparently, everything was prepared for the meeting and Franz Joseph's visit."

Hellen had already jumped up and was about to leave the room, but Cloutard held her tightly by her arm.

"Not so fast. The letter says something else important. The emperor's aide-de-camp was tasked with taking care of the key. He was told very clearly not to forget the collar used to open and close the vault. The dying Achilles will show him the way, it says."

Hellen's heart sank.

"*Pas de probleme,* Madame de Mey. I have always wanted to break into the Imperial Treasury."

CHAPTER 59
ROSSAUER BARRACKS, VIENNA

The guard sat at his desk, eyes on the small TV beside the surveillance monitors. He shook his head in disbelief. The reports had been growing grimmer and grimmer. Demonstrations, terror threats, riots, street battles. Every day, all over the world, and all because of a conspiracy blog. But he could understand how frustrated people were. In reality, they were demonstrating for many reasons: for basic rights like freedom of expression, or out of fear of a surveillance state, and absolute control of the Internet, for instance. And even before the reports about the cult had appeared, people's frustrations had been close to the boiling point. General discontent, distrust of politicians, corruption, and ever-increasing inflation had already been sending people onto the streets. A conspiracy theory about some absurd cult that wanted to take over the world was simply the final straw. *Impressive, though, how a made-up story can bring truths to light*, the man thought as he slurped at his coffee.

He was glad he wasn't out on street duty with the other Cobras. There at the barracks, everything was calm and comfortable. Almost the entire force was out. Fearing riots or even direct attacks, the police had called for reinforcements from Vienna's emergency task force, WEGA, and the antiterror unit Cobra to help control the hundreds of thousands of people surging through the heart of the city.

Riveted to the news reports, he did not see the masked, black-clad figure that slipped from the shadows into the streetlight and edged toward the guardhouse. Only when the monitors suddenly showed a white-noise blur did he finally look up—in time to see the pistol pointing at him from outside the window. But he had no time to react. A heartbeat later, he was dead.

The Mantis lowered her silenced pistol and signaled to the man inside the van across the street. Lieutenant Colonel Weaver looked up at the fortress-like brick complex, in front of which the Mantis was now standing. Eight fortified defensive towers topped by battlements loomed in the night sky above the five-story historic building. The complex covered an area the size of five football fields. Weaver got out and retrieved a heavy black case from the back of the van, slammed the sliding door, and ran across the empty street.

"This is crazy, even by my standards. The place is a literal fortress, and it's protected by one of the best special forces units in the world," Weaver said, pulling his ski mask over his face as they passed the boom gate.

"Not today. And if you want your ten million, then don't think, just follow my orders. Didn't they drill that into you in the Marines?" the Mantis said.

Weaver was not used to being ordered around by a woman, but he found it highly arousing in a way—apart from the small insult at the end.

"If we survive this, you and I should have a little celebration," Weaver said, his eyes on the woman as they turned left after the breezeway and entered the courtyard, where a few cars were parked. There was no one in sight there, either.

"Is that your best pickup line?" Weaver swallowed. "Believe me, you wouldn't survive a night with me," the woman said with a smile. She reached out her hand. "The bag."

Taking cover behind a car, she put away her pistol and unzipped the large bag. From inside it, she took out two Steyr AUG A3 assault rifles and passed them to Weaver. His adrenalin was pumping harder than it had in a long time, but to his own surprise, he felt calm and composed. He missed this kind of action. His eyes widened when he saw what lay beneath the rifles.

"That's your idea of a distraction?" he whispered, when he saw the two dozen blocks of C4 packed together. But the woman ignored him. She activated the bomb and took the remote detonator. Zipping the bag closed, she pushed it under the car.

Keeping low and staying close to the wall, rifles at the ready, they moved swiftly to the northwest wing of the building and found cover inside a doorway a safe distance away.

"Time for you to earn your pay," the woman said. "Whenever you're ready." She handed him the detonator and pressed her hands over her ears.

CHAPTER 60

COBRA BASE, ROSSAUER BARRACKS, VIENNA

Tom was able to check his swing just in time. "Woah, could you make an announcement next time? I almost bashed your head in," he said when he saw his old boss, Captain Maierhofer.

"Is this how you greet old friends?"

"Sorry, sir," said Hagen, as he and Tom put down the chairs.

"What are you doing here?" said Tom as Maierhofer entered the cell. He was carrying a duffel bag over his shoulder.

"What does it look like? I'm here to get you out." Tom stared at the captain in disbelief. The man who once would have loved nothing more than to fire him into outer space was here to help him escape? "I got a tip-off. The Mantis, or whatever she calls herself, is on her way here to get the head back."

"And because we're the only ones who can stop her—" said Tom, but Maierhofer cut him off.

"Don't get too full of yourself, Wagner. You're not the only one I've trained."

"Yes, but I'm the best," said Tom with his cheeky grin.

"Well, as much as I don't want to admit it—"

The explosion was more than deafening—they also felt it. The walls trembled and bits of plaster dropped from the ceiling. All three reflexively hit the floor and covered their heads.

"Sounds like she's already here," said Tom. He stood up and helped Maierhofer to his feet.

"Thank you. As usual, Wagner, nothing escapes your eagle eye," Maierhofer said. "Didn't you promise me there'd be no explosions?"

Tom looked at the captain in confusion. "I . . . we're . . . I've been here since . . . this wasn't me!" Tom stammered helplessly.

Maierhofer grinned at him. "I never thought I'd see the day. Tom Wagner, at a loss for words," he said. "And the way things look, I'm just in time." The captain heaved the heavybag onto the table and returned to the door, drawing his pistol as he moved, and checked the corridor outside. "You both have to get out of her as fast as you can. I didn't think they were going to blow up half the city. There's the Mantis and a Lieutenant Colonel Weaver, and they aren't just here for Medusa's head. They want your heads, too. They want you out of the way," he said.

"Weaver and that bitch are working together?" Hagen said in surprise.

"It looks like it. She tortured my assistant and found out you were headed to White Sands. She met Weaver there," Maierhofer said.

"How do you know all this?"

"I'll explain later. Right now, our objective is to keep the head out of their hands. And Wagner? Do me a favor and get rid of that horrible thing once and for all." Tom could practically feel Maierhofer's frustration and pain. They had all seen what the head did to his son. Lukas had been in a coma ever since.

"Aren't you going to be in trouble for this?"

"Let me worry about that, Wagner. My career will survive."

In the meantime, Hagen had opened the bag. Inside were two bulletproof vests, two holstered Glocks, and a couple hundred rounds of ammunition. A phone, too, which Maierhofer indicated was for Hagen. He slipped it into his pocket and pulled on one of the vests and strapped the holster to his leg. "Heads up," he snapped, tossing the second vest to Tom. In seconds, they were ready to go. Almost in unison, they each chambered a round in their Glock. They joined Maierhofer at the door.

"We'll meet at the side entrance on Maria-Theresien-Strasse. I'll be waiting there with a car."

"Where's the head?"

"In the northwest wing, in one of the air-raid shelters. And Wagner—and this goes for you, too, Hagen—avoid collateral damage, please. I've lost enough men already." Maierhofer's voice almost broke at the last sentence. He struggled, but managed to swallow his fury and sadness. "Go! Do you need a written invitation?" he barked. Tom had to smile when he heard the old man's commanding tone. It was a voice he knew well.

"Yes, sir," Tom and Hagen said together. Maierhofer disappeared in the opposite direction.

CHAPTER 61

IN FRONT OF DIRECTOR RICHTER'S OFFICE, MUSEUM OF FINE ARTS, A FEW HOURS EARLIER

"I'm not comfortable with this at all. The poor woman has just lost probably the most important person in her life. Director Richter was everything to Mrs. Gabi. And now I'm supposed to distract her so we can steal from her?" Hellen stared at the floor like a little girl ashamed at having broken her grandmother's favorite vase. "It just doesn't feel right. Taking something from someone who deserves to lose it, someone we don't know, is one thing. But Mrs. Gabi was always good to me when I worked here."

Cloutard seemed a little impatient. "I understand, Hellen. But we have come so far, jetting across half of Europe just to find these two artifacts. And Tom's message confirmed what Mandalov told us: the only way to tackle the Medusa is with the Golden Fleece and the breastplate. That is our task." He looked intently into Hellen's eyes. "And yes, to do that, we may need to depart from the truth a little. Besides, you have the simpler part of the job—you only have to distract Mrs. Gabi. I have to steal the key to the display cabinet and take the gold collar of the Order from the Treasury in broad daylight."

"How do you think you'll do it, François?"

"I have a plan. I have not worked out every detail, but it will do. *Alors*, it is time to get to work."

Without waiting for Hellen to respond, he knocked on the door and pushed her into the reception area outside the director's office. Mrs. Gabi was packing things into boxes. Richter's successor had probably already been named, and Mrs. Gabi's days as the director's secretary were numbered.

Hellen saw immediately that she'd been crying. Her eyes were red, and she looked miserable.

"Oh, Hellen! How lovely to see you again. What brings you here, now that Director Richter is . . .?" Mrs. Gabi's voice faltered. She fought back her tears, but quickly lost the battle and broke down sobbing.

Hellen went over and hugged her, using the poor woman's weakness to her own benefit. Her bad conscience was getting worse by the second. While Mrs. Gabi pressed her face into Hellen's shoulder and bawled, Cloutard slipped as quickly and silently as a ghost through the room and disappeared a second later into the deceased director's office. Hellen, who had worked at the museum for several years, knew that the director insisted on looking after all of the keys personally. She had told Cloutard precisely where he would find the keys for the Treasury's display cabinets.

With his superlative lock picking skills, he silently and swiftly unlocked one of the drawers in the director's huge, antique desk. The large drawer was lined with velvet and divided into compartments of different sizes like a jewelry box, each compartment containing a bunch of keys. Cloutard quickly found the one he needed and crept back to the door. Mrs. Gabi was still crying her heart out. Spying through the keyhole, he saw Hellen gently lead the poor woman out of the office. She had managed to talk her into taking a short stroll with her across the plaza between the twin museums, in the center of which stood the proud monument to Empress Maria Theresia, unveiled in 1888. Mrs. Gabi dutifully locked the door behind her, but that meant no more to Cloutard than a short delay. He waited for a minute before leaving the director's office, then unlocked the door to the reception area, locked it again behind him, and hurried downstairs. As he left the museum, he could see Hellen and Mrs. Gabi standing by one of the four Triton and Naiad fountains.

The clock was ticking. He had the key to the display cabinet, but despite what he had told Hellen, he had not the faintest idea how he was going to get his hands on the gold collar while the museum was open.

CHAPTER 62

COBRA BASE, ROSSAUER BARRACKS, VIENNA

Flames filled the courtyard, and a column of black smoke billowed into the sky. When Tom stepped into the courtyard, he was hit by a wall of heat that almost took his breath away. The devastation was immense. A massive crater gaped in the center of the courtyard, exposing the underground garage below the complex. Its roof had fallen in and burning cars had slipped into the crater. Dozens of alarms were blaring.

"Which way?" asked Hagen, who had emerged into the yard just behind Tom. He raised his left arm to protect his face.

Tom nodded toward the far side of the courtyard. "Through there," he said.

Pistols raised, they rounded the blaze, turning constantly, scanning their surroundings with every step. Almost all of the hundreds of windows that opened onto the courtyard had been shattered in the explosion.

They stopped momentarily when they heard gunshots in the distance and took cover behind one of the few cars left relatively undamaged, aside from its blown-out windows.

"That way," said Hagen, when another salvo rang out.

For a second, the muzzle flash had illuminated a corridor that they could see from the courtyard.

They moved on rapidly. When they reached the northwest wing, they pressed close against the wall beside the entrance. "Shit," said Tom when he saw the unmoving bodies of two of his old comrades lying in front of the door. A fire extinguisher lay beside them—Tom guessed that they'd come running outside after the explosion, only to be cut down by Weaver and the Mantis.

He checked both men's pulses while Hagen kept him covered. Then he stood up slowly, shook his head as he looked at Hagen, and raised his Glock. He nodded toward the door. Hagen cautiously turned the handle and pulled it open, and Tom darted inside.

Glancing left and right, they moved quickly in the direction from which the shots had come, Hagen keeping a constant watch on their rear. Tom stopped at the corner and risked a quick peek. He saw the body of another fallen Cobra, but to Tom's relief the man was still alive.

"They went down there," the man groaned, and he pointed to the stairs descending just around the corner.

They heard another explosion, this one considerably smaller.

Tom and Hagen shared a look. "They've found the head," said Tom.

"I'm okay," said the man on the floor. "Go!"

Tom nodded to the man, and he and Hagen edged down the stairs, backs to the wall, guns pointing downward.

The bullets slammed into the plaster wall, missing them by a hair. Splinters and dust flew around Tom's head as he ducked back behind the corner at the bottom of the stairs, just in time.

Hagen was behind him, pressed against the wall. "Are we too late?" he asked.

Tom nodded. "They've got the head." He slid down the wall into a crouch and risked another quick look. As before, several bullets flew an inch past his head and buried themselves in the wall.

"Forget him," Tom heard the Mantis yell after Weaver's last burst drove Tom back into cover. "We've got what we came for. Time to go."

To Hagen's surprise, Tom suddenly pushed his gun blindly around the corner and squeezed off several rapid shots. Hagen, leaning over the top of Tom, followed his lead. Their bullets flew haphazardly into the walls, exposed pipes, and ceiling of the basement. A sharp cry rang in the corridor. Tom grinned and peeked around the corner. A scalding jet of steam hissed from a pipe where Weaver had been standing.

"Come on!" the woman yelled again. She grabbed Weaver by the collar and pulled him after her, away from Tom and Hagen.

"I want to see that bastard dead," Weaver snapped, firing again at Tom even as he followed the Mantis out.

Tom saw a map pinned on the wall opposite the bottom of the stairs, showing escape routes and emergency exits, and a large "H" inside a circle in the center of the northernmost courtyard caught his eye.

"I think I know where they're headed," he said, jumping to his feet. "You stay on their tail. I'll try to cut them off." As Tom raced back upstairs, he saw Hagen from the corner of his eye, disappearing around the corner to take up the pursuit.

Back on the ground floor, he didn't return to the hallway they'd come from but turned instead to the southeast, into the wing that separated the northern and central courtyards. Through the windows, he could already see the olive-green Bell OH-58 Kiowa helicopter standing in the middle of a small area demarcated by a row of small trees.

Then he spotted them. Weaver and the Mantis ran out through a doorway on the far side of the courtyard, heading for the Kiowa. But Tom also saw that the woman, wearing a large, black backpack, was now driving Hagen ahead of her, her rifle aimed at his head. Tom didn't hesitate. He knew what would happen to Hagen if he didn't act. He took aim and fired through the closed hallway window. Outside, all three instinctively ducked. The moment of confusion gave Hagen a chance. He whipped around, knocking the Mantis's rifle aside, then punched her in the face. Blood poured from her nose as he dropped and rolled nimbly beneath the helicopter, and he was able to throw himself over the hood of a parked car just as Weaver opened fire. The bullets missed their mark, slamming into the car instead.

In the meantime, the Mantis had tossed the backpack onto a bench in the back of the chopper. She jumped in after it, her nose still pouring blood. Tom was racing down the hallway when he heard the helicopter's engine start up with a high-pitched whine. Giving Hagen a chance to get to safety had cost Tom valuable seconds, but he finally reached the door out to the courtyard. He kicked it open and ran out firing. The rotors had almost reached takeoff speed—the engine whining ever higher, the rotors beginning to make their familiar clattering sound. Weaver was inside the chopper now, too. The skids rose clear of the ground as the Kiowa took off.

Tom sprinted straight at the helicopter. Jamming the Glock back into its holster in mid-stride, he jumped and managed to grab hold of the skid. But not for long. Weaver jerked open the side door and fired his revolver down at Tom. A bullet found its mark, hitting Tom in the chest. The shock as the bullet cracked into the bulletproof vest made him lose his grip. He tumbled ten feet and crashed onto the hood of a parked car, the windshield shattering under the sudden impact.

Tom twisted in pain. Every inch of his body ached. Lying on his back, he drew his pistol again and emptied the magazine at the rising helicopter. He dropped the empty mag out with a click of his thumb, slid a fresh one into place, and kept firing.

Even as he emptied the second magazine, he was remembering his and Cloutard's escape from Tabarka Fortress. Of course, the difference then was that they'd been the ones in the helicopter, fleeing AF.

The Glock's slide clicked open. Tom had fired his last shot. Grimacing with pain, he looked along the barrel of his empty Glock, helplessly following the helicopter's path as it vanished into the night sky.

CHAPTER 63
MARIA-THERESIEN-PLATZ, ON THE RING,
A FEW HOURS EARLIER

Cloutard crossed the Ring to Heldenplatz. As usual, *fiakers* trotted up and down the busy square, with tourists taking photos in all directions: the National Library, the Hofburg, the president's office, and the two equestrian statues of Prince Eugene and Archduke Karl in the center of the plaza. It was all terribly picturesque, as if especially designed for tourists' cameras. But Cloutard was not there for the sights. He was looking for something else entirely. He crossed the large plaza and moved through the breezeway to the inner courtyard, from where the Swiss Gate led to the Swiss Court and the entrance to the Imperial Treasury.

Diagonally opposite the memorial to Emperor Franz II was a café, and Cloutard's face brightened as he stepped into the garden area. Sitting inside was a group of young men, laughing loudly. Even from a distance, Cloutard could see that the alcohol was flowing freely, and the group had long since left sobriety behind. He approached them confidently, and his suspicion proved correct: it was a bachelor party. The Frenchman spoke with them for a few minutes, and they quickly came to terms.

Then he left, but not before comparing watches with the

groom-to-be, who was still the most sober of the group. A few minutes later, he went to the Treasury, bought a ticket, went upstairs, and began casually strolling around the exhibition. The Treasury had only recently reopened. A few years earlier, Tom had wreaked havoc inside while trying to stop Jacinto Guerra from stealing the Holy Lance. Ironically enough, Cloutard was now going in to steal something—but with far less noise and no bullets.

When he reached the room that contained the Order's golden collar, he stopped and waited. When he heard the group of loud young men coming a few minutes later, he had to smile. When the bachelor party entered the room, Cloutard signaled with a slight tip of his head to where the security camera was located. It wasn't long before the group was in position. The groom began peeling off his clothes. Cloutard had told him that a buddy of his worked for the security company and that he was going to prank him. Slowly, and obviously hampered by alcohol, the drunks formed a human pyramid that would completely blot out the camera's view. When the naked bridegroom began climbing onto his friends' shoulders and waving like a lunatic into the camera, Cloutard didn't hesitate. His activity also spared him from the sight of the drunken groom performing a helicopter dick for the camera. The Frenchman calmly and easily opened the display cabinet. Seconds later, he had the collar. No one took any notice. Everyone was laughing at the human pyramid and the bridegroom's dubious—if acrobatic—performance.

It wasn't long before the guards appeared. Even the security officer ran up from the front desk.

But Cloutard was not yet finished—he had made a promise to the marquis, without whom they would never have gained access to the archives of the Thieves' Guild. In exchange, Cloutard had promised to liberate something for the marquis from the Treasury. Or rather, to replace it with a copy. Specifically, the Emerald Unguentarium. Made from a single enormous emerald discovered by Spaniards in Columbia in 1558, the Unguentarium had been carved into a container by Dionysio Miseroni at the request of Emperor Ferdinand III. Cloutard did not know exactly why the marquis wanted that particular artifact, but he had given Cloutard the fake to replace it with, and Cloutard exploited the general chaos in the room to make the switch.

With the collar and the Unguentarium in his small backpack, he quickly left the Treasury behind and flagged a passing taxi on Heldenplatz. He had no time to lose.

Hellen had checked in on WhatsApp that everything was all right, and sent him an address where they were to meet afterward. But why it had to be all the way on the other side of Vienna, he had no idea.

Before he could meet with Hellen, however, Cloutard made a quick stop at Tom's grandfather's apartment, close to the Belvedere. He needed a safe place to stash the Unguentarium.

CHAPTER 64
MARIA-THERESIEN-STRASSE, VIENNA

Breathing was hard. His chest hurt. A few ribs were definitely bruised and probably broken. The sirens of the approaching emergency vehicles wailed louder and louder. With a huge effort, Tom managed to sit up. He slid forward on the hood and dropped to the ground in front of the car. Still sitting, he carefully loosened the Velcro fasteners and threw the vest aside. A shock of pain rocked his body. Groaning, he pulled his t-shirt up and saw a hand-sized bruise spreading across his chest. He coughed. Hagen, in the meantime, had run over to him. He held out his hand to Tom.

"Come on. We have to get out of here."

"You *cannot* imagine how this aches." Tom took Hagen's hand but couldn't stop himself from screaming when he pulled him to his feet. "Easy, you bastard, easy."

"Sorry I let them catch me," Hagen said as they headed for the side entrance they'd agreed on with Maierhofer.

"Don't sweat it. It can happen to the best of us. You're still among the living, and that's what counts, right?" said Tom, clapping him on the shoulder. But in his head, a very different train of thought was running. Had Hagen allowed them to catch him? Had it all been a distraction to make sure the mission succeeded? Could he and the Mantis be allies? It was Hagen, after all, who'd identified her. An international killer, someone not even on Interpol's or the FBI's radar . . . on top of which, he'd turned up in Vienna at just the right time.

Tom stared at the back of the Briton's head as Hagen stepped onto the street ahead of him. *Bullshit*, he thought, dismissing the thought.

The buildings around them flashed with pulses of red and blue light. A hundred yards up the street, police, ambulance, and fire department vehicles were already blocking the thoroughfare. Cops, paramedics, and firefighters were running in all directions. It was chaos.

Then Tom saw a flash of headlights at the other end of the street: a car parked in a dark corner. Maierhofer was at the wheel—and to the amazement of both him and Hagen, a young Asian-looking woman was sitting beside him.

As Hagen and Tom approached the car, Maierhofer climbed out.

"You look like you're traveling light," the captain said.

"Yes," said Tom drily. "They were one step ahead of us, literally, the whole way. That bitch is good, but she won't get away from me next time," Tom said.

"Not so fast, Wagner." Maierhofer held out a phone. "For you," he said. Hagen's phone rang at the same time. Both men raised their eyebrows in surprise and answered the calls.

A few minutes later, Tom said goodbye to Hagen and shook his hand. Then Hagen climbed into a dark van that had just pulled up. Tom watched briefly as the van drove away. He had to admit that he'd begun to trust him. But after what had happened in the last hour, the question had to be asked: whose side was Hagen truly on? Probably his own, when it came down to it.

What bothered him more, however, was that he'd just been forbidden—from the very top—from going after the Medusa again.

Tom snorted with disgust as he climbed into the back seat. Maierhofer was back behind the wheel. He hit the gas and they sped away along Franz-Josefs-Kai, the street running parallel to the Donaukanal, a historic arm of the Danube.

"What did the chancellor say?" the captain asked.

"The UN Security Council, the EU, and the U.S. have been holding talks about the Medusa for days. Top level. And guess who had the final say? The Americans, of course. No surprise there. The chancellor told me loud and clear to stay out of it. He also said he could have taken care of the arrest warrant, but you springing me from that cell put an end to that. The last thing he said was that, if Hagen and I take on DARPA and all the rest again, and the Americans catch me, he won't be able to bail me out." Tom sighed and laid his head back. "Hagen's been officially withdrawn, too. So that's that." He could not hide his exasperation. He was exhausted, and every inch of his body ached.

"Are you hurt?" Maierhofer asked.

"Just my pride." Tom raised his head again with a groan. "I'll live. The vest took the bullet." He rubbed his chest. "Who's your friend, by the way?" he asked, looking at the young woman who'd been sitting silently in the passenger seat the whole time.

Before Maierhofer could reply, she turned back to Tom.

"I . . . I'm . . . " she began shyly and a little self-consciously. "I'm Akira Seki. I'm a big fan," she finally said, with more strength. But she seemed to find it hard to hold Tom's eye. She reached a hand back between the front seats.

"I've got a fan? Tom Wagner. Nice to meet you." Tom glanced curiously into the rearview mirror as he shook her hand and his eyes met Maierhofer's.

"Miss Seki contacted me and told me quite an incredible story," Maierhofer said. "At first, I admit, I thought she was putting me on, but considering everything that's happened lately, I listened."

"It was you who contacted Hagen, wasn't it?" said Tom.

Akira nodded. Then she told them both about her work for DARPA, how she'd become aware of Richter through van Rensburg, what she'd discovered, and that two men had tried to kill her. "And when I listened in on a call between Weaver and that woman and found out about the Red Notice, I flew here and contacted your old boss. My hacker friend Bobby got me some new papers. But this hasn't been easy for me, I can tell you. I'm not very good with people, you see, and—"

"Slowly, slowly. You need to take a breath now and then," Maierhofer said. Despite her initial timidity, the more Akira talked, the faster the words came pouring out.

"Hold on," said Tom. "Rewind. You tapped our phones?"

Akira blushed. "No, no. Not yours. Just Mr. van Rensburg's. On Lieutenant Colonel Weaver's orders," Akira said, her voice softer.

"What's the latest on van Rensburg?" Tom asked Maierhofer.

"No change. His lawyers haven't gotten very far. The district attorney is stonewalling everything. It looks like he wants to make an example of your boss. He thinks it'll advance his career."

"And your son?"

"Also no change," Maierhofer said after a pause.

"Sorry to hear it. But maybe Hellen's made some progress. I haven't spoken to her at all since we flew to the

States. That reminds me, I should call her. Can I borrow your phone again?" Tom gazed out the window. "Where are we going, by the way? My houseboat's in the other direction."

"You can't go home now, Wagner. I just broke you out of jail, remember? Which means the Red Notice is active again. Not even the chancellor can intervene now. Your houseboat is the first place we'd look."

Tom nodded. "Wonderful. So, what now?"

"I've taken the liberty of organizing a little assistance. We're going to see some old associates of mine," Maierhofer said.

"Great. Wake me when we get there." With a groan, Tom laid his head back again and closed his eyes.

CHAPTER 65

IN A HELICOPTER ABOVE VIENNA, NIGHT.

Weaver peeled of the ski mask and pulled on the headphones dangling in front of the copilot's seat. "Why did you stop me from killing Wagner?" he said angrily into the microphone. But the Mantis didn't react.

She guided the helicopter at high altitude over the city, heading northeast, but didn't say a word. Weaver was boiling inside. He was still acting within the scope of his orders. *You have a free hand. Bring me the head of Medusa! Whatever it takes, collateral damage included*, Horne had said, but Weaver was no longer so sure that he wasn't going too far. Yes, the woman had come through. She'd even promised him a substantial sum of money. But if they'd been caught, he'd be spending the rest of his life rotting in a dark hole—or maybe even find himself on the wrong side of a death sentence. And then there would be the international scandal . . . and they weren't out of the woods yet.

"Anybody ever tell you you're batshit crazy?"

The woman still did not react. Weaver turned around furiously and threw the ski mask and the assault rifle onto the seat in the rear, and the black backpack containing

Medusa's head caught his eye—the reason they had dared to attempt this suicide mission at all.

"I know why DARPA wants the head, but do you mind telling me what you want it for?"

The woman finally turned and looked at him. "That, my friend, is something you'll find out soon enough. Right now, our only priority is to land this bird in one piece and get out of the country."

Weaver looked out the window. "Okay. And how are we going to do that?"

"You soldiers . . ." She let out a scornful laugh and shook her head. "Blindly taking orders, never thinking for yourselves. Do you really think I'd carry out a mission like this without a damn good exit strategy?"

Among the glittering city lights below, directly beside the Danube, was a dark patch—the Lobau floodplain, part of the Danube-Auen National Park. An urban recreational area with no cars and—at night—no people. Weaver saw headlights come on in a small open area. The helicopter flew toward the lights, then turned. Against the glowing night sky, Weaver could still see the distant column of smoke rising from the barracks. The chopper bumped down on the small meadow and the Mantis shut down the engine.

"Watch your head," she said, as she climbed out and moved toward the four men waiting beside two black SUVs. In black designer suits and wearing the usual headphones, they reminded Weaver of Secret Service agents. They stood motionless in the headlights, hands crossed in front of them. The high-pitched whine of the engine died, and the rotors gradually slowed to a stop. Weaver shouldered the backpack, grabbed his rifle, and jumped out of the chopper behind the woman, discreetly confirming that the rifle was loaded as he approached the men.

He stopped and swung the rifle up to his shoulder when

the men suddenly pointed their pistols at him. He switched his aim from one man to the next.

"Hey, sweetheart! What the hell is this? We had a deal," Weaver shouted.

The Mantis turned back and signaled to her men to lower their guns. "Easy, boys. He's with me." She turned away again, circled her hand in the air over her head, and headed for one of the cars. "Let's go."

The men holstered their pistols. One of them held the door open for the woman. She nodded to him and climbed in, but the man continued to hold the door open.

"Come on, Lieutenant Colonel. Or do you really want to get up close and personal with a Cobra team?" he heard her say from inside the vehicle.

Only now did Weaver lower the rifle. He approached the car slowly. As he drew near, the waiting man held out his hand. Weaver looked at his stony expression and handed him the backpack. The man's silent glare shifted to Weaver's rifle. "I guess I don't need this anymore," he murmured, looking down at it. A barely visible smile appeared for a moment on his face, and he tossed the rifle aside. He climbed in beside the woman.

"The plane's waiting. We're ready to go," said the man in the passenger seat.

An hour later, they reached the small border crossing at Schrattenberg in northern Austria. Weaver looked nervously out the window as the two SUVs passed through the unmanned crossing.

"Being in the EU has its advantages," said the woman, grinning at Weaver, who relaxed again.

After another hour they reached the small suburb of Brno-Tuřany. They followed the main road through the town before turning right onto a smaller road that took them to Brno–Tuřany Airport. They stopped at a guarded entrance near the end of the runway. The driver handed the sentry an envelope and they were allowed to pass. Not far from the fence, at the western end of the runway, stood the first of several hangars that seemed to blend seamlessly into the surrounding area. Situated close one beside one other, each was about a hundred and fifty feet long and overgrown with grass and bushes, like small hills in a landscape. The SUVs turned into the second hangar and stopped, and the two men in Weaver's car jumped out and opened the back doors. Weaver and the Mantis climbed out. Before them stood a small private jet, a Hawker 750, with a range of about 2400 miles and seats for eight passengers.

"All good with the flight plan?" the Mantis asked one of her men.

"Yes, ma'am. The rest of the team is waiting for us there," he replied as they made their way toward the Hawker.

"When do I get my head and my money?" Weaver asked. He was still standing beside the car, looking at her stubbornly. She stopped and turned around.

"Patience, Colonel. If everything goes as planned, in forty-eight hours you'll be a rich man and your government will have a new toy to play with. Feel free to update your boss if it makes you feel better," she said.

Weaver watched her as she disappeared inside the plane. He quickly tapped out a message on his phone and sent it off before trotting to the plane himself. He was the last to board, behind the man carrying the pack that contained the head.

"So tell me: who are you working for?" Weaver said as he dropped into a seat across the aisle from the woman.

"Don't even go there, Colonel," she began, shaking her head. She accepted a glass of champagne from one of her men. "This isn't the sixties anymore, and my name isn't Pussy Galore. Can't a woman have her own world-changing ambitions without working for some chauvinistic supervillain who's always stroking a white cat? Have some champagne and enjoy the flight."

The twin engines howled to life, and the plane began to taxi.

Confused and still a little skeptical about the whole operation, Weaver nonetheless did as the Mantis suggested. He accepted a glass and raised it to her in a toast. Then he leaned back and thought about which country to settle in with his ten million.

CHAPTER 66

AMONG THE VINEYARDS OF VIENNA, NEAR LEOPOLDSBERG

Maierhofer parked the car beside a hedge. Below them, Vienna glittered under a starry sky.

"We're here," said Maierhofer. He got out and went to a small gate that led through the hedge to the property beyond.

"Where the heck is 'here'?" Tom asked, following him through the gate.

"We're meeting an old counterterrorism contact of mine from the DSN. He's bringing new passports. Now you're back on the most-wanted list, you need to get out of Austria as fast as you can."

"Specifically, we're on our way to Corfu," Tom heard a woman's voice say. Hellen.

Tom and Maierhofer, with Akira behind them, walked further into the rather unkempt-looking property. An old Airstream stood beside a half-built house. Tom loved the old American travel trailers and immediately felt right at home, although the rest of the property was far less inviting.

Hellen and Cloutard had been sitting on camp chairs beside the Airstream along with a man and woman Tom didn't know. When Tom came through the gate, she was already on her feet and ran to meet him. She threw her arms around his neck, but when she went to kiss him, he drew a sharp breath and pulled away.

"What is it? Are you hurt?" Hellen said when she saw him touching his ribs gingerly.

"Nothing serious. A bad bruise. It only hurts," Tom said. He pulled her close with his other arm and kissed her carefully.

Hellen could tell that it was more serious than the other times he'd been injured. It was not like Tom to admit to being in pain. Arms around each other, they joined the small party.

Cloutard raised his hip flask in greeting. Tom grinned at the Frenchman, clapped him on the shoulder, and took the small, silver flask out of his hand.

"*Excuse-moi*," he said, and took a gulp.

Cloutard grimaced. "Please do not speak French, Tom. It hurts my poor old ears."

"Right, introductions," said Maierhofer when the unknown couple stood up. The man held out his hand to Tom. "Leo Gardner, Tom Wagner."

"My pleasure," said Tom.

Gardner nodded but said nothing. The man made an unusual impression on Tom—none at all. Usually, Tom could get the measure of someone quickly, but Gardner, at least at first sight, was inscrutable.

"And this is his business partner, Lara Weiss. They're in the process of setting up a private detective agency."

"You're the ones who tracked down that serial killer, right?" Tom said.

"Which one? The cut-off-your-feet-and-mail-them-back kind, the bag-over-your-head-and-bash-your-brains-out kind, et cetera—take your pick," Leo said blandly.

"And you keep saying *we're* the violent ones," Tom said, grinning at Hellen.

"Have a seat," said Leo, pointing to a pair of camp chairs. So far, Akira had stayed in the background, but now she went around and shook everyone's hand, too. She was hugging her backpack shyly.

"Why are we going to Corfu? Now that the chancellor's reined me in, I was hoping to rest up a bit."

"We found a clue about two artifacts we'll need if we want to destroy the Medusa," Hellen said.

She quickly filled him in on what she and Cloutard had discovered: the lead that took them to North Macedonia, the Napoleon connection, the Order of the Golden Fleece, and Cloutard's pilferage from the Treasury.

Tom grinned. "We're going to make them close that place for good."

Leo Gardner, meanwhile, had gone into the Airstream and now returned with a bottle of straw-colored Wiener Gemischter Satz from Mayer am Pfarrplatz, and a clutch of long-stemmed glasses. Lara poured a glass for each of them.

"God hardens, reviews, and disciplines those whom he approves," said Gardner, raising his glass.

"Um . . . all right," said Tom.

"He is quoting Lucius Annaeus Seneca," said Cloutard. "The Stoic philosopher. A little of that might do you good, *mon ami*. Maybe there would be fewer explosions."

"Are we really going to let them get away with the Medusa? Just like that? Even if we have the artifacts, how can we destroy the head if we don't even know where it is?"

"I can help," said a voice from the background.

Akira had made herself comfortable sitting cross-legged on the ground beside the caravan. She was playing with her phone, trying to stay inconspicuous, and was so unobtrusive that Lara had neglected to give her a glass of wine. She hastily made up for it, pouring another glass and handing it to the slight young woman.

"These people . . . I mean, one of them . . . one of the ones with the Medusa . . . I might be able to . . ." But she faltered and shook her head, as if she had to rearrange her thoughts.

"J.J.," said Maierhofer suddenly, and he stood up and greeted a man who'd just arrived.

Tom sensed immediately the old friendship between Maierhofer and J.J. He guessed they had been through quite a lot together.

The newcomer handed a bundle of passports and paperwork to Maierhofer before turning to Gardner. "Sorry," he said, "but your Opel GT took a couple of scrapes. I'm not as young as I used to be, and my reflexes aren't what they were before the war."

Tom turned around to Gardner. "You drive an Opel GT?"

Gardner showed no emotion, but looked calmly back at J.J. "That's what I get for lending my car to the bingo champ of the nursing home."

Silence fell for a few seconds. Everyone stared from Leo to J.J. and back until, as if in slow motion, a smile formed on each man's face and they suddenly burst into laughter—an infectious laughter that soon had the others laughing, too.

"You wanted to say something a minute ago, Akira." Hellen approached the young hacker once the mirth had settled. Suddenly, all eyes were back on Akira, which made her visibly uncomfortable.

"To make it short, and so everyone can understand, I have Lieutenant Colonel Weaver's phone ID. He's the guy who just stole Medusa's head. It's a DARPA phone, so most hackers would take ages to unlock it, but that stuff's super easy for me. And locating the phone's even easier." She turned her phone around to show a map with a red dot blinking in the middle. "I don't even need a laptop."

"Sorry, but I think Corfu will have to wait," said Tom. "We have no idea what they're planning with the head. We can't just let them run around loose with that thing."

Everyone nodded, but Maierhofer spoke up: "The chancellor's pulled you off the job, remember? He made it crystal clear that you're to keep your nose out of it."

Tom tilted his head, and he flashed a smile for a second.

"As if you've ever done what you're told," Hellen said, reading her husband's mind. "So you're not too concerned about this, either, are you?"

"Right as usual," said Tom. "If we'd stuck to the rules, we wouldn't have found half of what we have in the last few years."

"And we would probably be dead, too. Many times over," added Cloutard, who was demonstrably not a great fan of rules and regulations himself.

"The artifacts are probably safe where they are," Tom said, looking at Hellen and Cloutard. "That woman and Weaver aren't interested in them, anyway. And now that Hagen's out of the picture, you two are back on duty. First, we have to stop whatever Weaver and the Mantis are planning. Who knows what they're up to with the Medusa? It's no use looking for the artifacts now while the two of them might be trying to destroy half the world."

"That which is not good for the hive cannot be good for the bees," Gardner quoted.

Tom looked at Leo in incomprehension.

"Marcus Aurelius," said Cloutard.

It took a few seconds, but then Tom sang: "Sugar, oooh, honey, honey."

And the others joined in with, "You are my candy girl, and you got me wanting you."

Gardner rolled his eyes, but there was a trace of a smile on his face, too.

Hellen nodded to Gardner. "He plays piano better than he sings."

"Okay, what's the plan?" said Tom, bringing them back down to earth. He looked eagerly at Akira.

"I think they've reached their destination," Akira said. She'd been staring intently at her phone the whole time.

"Where are they?" Hellen asked. Seven expectant pairs of eyes were on Akira now, and she squirmed in discomfort.

"Uh, they . . . they're in Sicily, close to Syracuse."

CHAPTER 67
NEAR SYRACUSE, SICILY, ITALY

In the course of his military career, Weaver had been part of many black-ops missions, first as a rank-and-file soldier on the front lines and later as leader of multiple operations. But what he saw here far exceeded his expectations. The woman who had introduced herself simply as the Mantis and who had talked him into this extraordinary partnership truly left nothing to chance. After a ninety-minute flight and a drive of similar length, they had reached their destination. Weaver had always wanted to visit this beautiful country but had hoped it would be under more pleasant circumstances.

The small farm lay just twenty minutes outside the nearby city of Syracuse. The barn itself was not particularly impressive, but the operation itself certainly was. Another eight men joined the four who'd met them in Vienna. And while he'd initially believed that the Mantis was no more than an aide to someone higher up, he was now forced to admit that she was the one calling the shots.

He ran his hand over the shoulder-high hood of one of the three armored vehicles standing side by side inside the barn while the men were loading them up. The Knight XV, modified by Conquest from a Ford F150 base to the point of being unrecognizable, was an impressive creation. Powered by a 6.8-liter V-10 engine, the vehicle could withstand not only automatic rifle fire, but could shrug off hand grenades and even RPG attacks. The off-road beast looked more like a futuristic military vehicle from a sci-fi blockbuster than a car designed for personal protection.

Weaver left the car and crossed to a long row of tables set up on the other side of the barn. All around stood construction-style floodlights mounted on tripods, bathing the dusty barn in a cold light.

Assault rifles and other weapons were laid out in neat rows on the tables. Beside the tables, two men were picking up metallic cylinders, each about ten feet long and with a kind of doughnut-shaped head and carrying them to one of the Knight XVs. Weaver counted eight cylinders in total.

What that's all about? he wondered. The cylinders reminded him a little of something that had fascinated him as a child. If you pushed iron bars into the sand at a beach ahead of a storm, and if lighting struck one of the bars, then later you could dig a hunk of glass out of the sand. The intense energy of the lightning, conducted by the iron bar into the sand, melted the sand crystals into an abstract glass sculpture.

Laptops, tablets, and countless documents lay on a separate table in the center of the barn. Next to the paperwork stood an antique amphora about eighteen inches high. Beside the table stood a whiteboard on casters. A plan sketched on it looked like the diagram drawn up by a football coach in advance of a big game.

Weaver studied the whiteboard and the layout of the area that he believed was their next destination. The plan told him the location, at least, if not what the Mantis was intending to do there.

The woman was standing beside the table, studying a copy of an ancient document.

"You've got a hell of an operation here," said Weaver, coming up beside her.

She looked up from the document, but not at Weaver. "That sounds like a compliment, but that undertone of surprise doesn't make me feel like a compliment *should* make me feel," she said. She turned to face Weaver, and her face was so cold that it sent a shudder even down his spine. "You men are all the same. You all want a strong woman, but when you finally meet one, you can't believe she's got things under control without a man's help."

Weaver held her gaze. She smiled at him and returned her attention to the document.

"Have you got what I asked for?" she said.

Despite her spellbinding looks and almost hypnotic charisma, he had to keep reminding himself that this woman was a stone-cold killer. The proof of that lay just a few steps away, in a corner of the barn. Lying side by side were five body bags: the farm's owners. From the shape of the sacks, Weaver could see that at least two of them contained children. That disgusted him. As a rule, he had no problem with killing, but he had always drawn the line at kids. He tried to keep his revulsion hidden from the others, and especially from her.

"I should be getting the confirmation in a few minutes," Weaver said.

"I hope so. For your sake," the woman said, and an instant later she was pressing her silenced pistol to his forehead. "Because I can end you any time I want, and you can join that nice family over there." Weaver didn't flinch. "And I'd save myself a shit-ton of money, too." She smiled at him, lowered the pistol, and returned it to the holster strapped to her thigh over her form-fitting black unitard. "But I still need you. Besides, we have a deal. And if there's one thing I hate more than chauvinist bullies, its people who don't honor their deals."

Weaver's phone pinged. He slipped it out and read the message. "May I?" he said, nodding to one of the tablet computers on the table. The Mantis nodded. He switched the tablet on, called up a website, and entered some information. "For you. Live satellite images of the target area, with real-time weather."

The Mantis picked up the tablet and smiled. "You're starting to grow on me, Lieutenant Colonel Weaver. I think this is the beginning of a beautiful friendship," she said, returning the tablet to the table. Then she picked up the amphora carefully and placed it inside a small flight case with a matching recess carved in its foam lining. She rolled up the copy of the antique document, wedged the tablet under her arm, and carried the case to the second of the three Knight XVs.

"Are our on-site men ready?" the woman asked one of her mercenaries. He nodded.

"Then we're go for Project Trinitas."

Weaver, standing with his back to the vehicle, quickly tapped out another message on his phone. Then he climbed in beside the Mantis.

CHAPTER 68
GREEK THEATER, SYRACUSE

The sun had set an hour earlier behind the hills on the far side of the expansive harbor. Weaver peered out the open car window. The convoy of armored Knight XVs moved rapidly uphill along the winding Viale Giuseppe Agnello. Aromatic cypresses, pines, and olive trees swept past on both sides. Over the rush of the wind, Weaver thought he could hear distant singing. The music grew louder as the XVs pulled to a stop on the short, dusty access road. The Mantis's men jumped out.

Sitting at the makeshift fence surrounding the property, the bored security guard barely had time to look up from his phone. A faint *pfft* from the Mantis's pistol and the man slumped to the ground with a bullet in his head. A mercenary dragged him clear while another opened the gate in the chain-link fence. Weaver, standing to one side, looked on as one of the men set up a collapsible satellite dish on the hood of one of the XVs. He ran a cable from the dish to a laptop on the passenger seat and typed in a few commands.

"We're online and the mobile jammer's active," the man said. He left the car door ajar to avoid damaging the cable connecting it to the dish. The Mantis holstered her pistol and picked up the tablet showing the live satellite images.

"You two take care of the security here . . . and here," she said to two of her men, pointing to the map on the display, and they ran off in different directions to find and neutralize the remaining security guards. She turned to a third. "And you keep an eye on the area and tell me as soon as the cavalry gets here." Then she handed the tablet to another and stalked away, eight of the men following. The last two began unloading the cylinders. Weaver decided to stick with the woman.

They crossed a small rocky plateau and stopped at the other side. Illuminated by dozens of stage lights set up on large tripods at the top, the theater looked like a densely populated island at night.

Weaver's eyes widened when he saw where the music was coming from. Below him, in the glare of the spotlights, lay a Greek amphitheater. It was perfectly aligned north-to-south and overlooked Syracuse harbor and Isola di Ortigia to the southeast. Weaver was surprised to see that the semicircular rows of seats carved into the stone—which became progressively smaller toward the center, like the concentric rings of a tree—were clad entirely with wood.

A fifty-piece orchestra was playing in front of and a little below the stage, while on the stage itself, before a blazing, ten-foot-tall cross, stood a man in costume singing "Di quella pira" from Giuseppe Verdi's *Il Trovatore*. As the song and accompanying music reached the crescendo, a large number of men suddenly ran from the darkness onto the brightly lit stage, brandishing rifles and machine pistols.

The Mantis's mercenaries, and Weaver, too, tensed at the sight of the weapons, but they realized in the same instant that it was simply part of the opera.

They were standing above the tiered seats from which

the wealthy would have watched the performances below, centuries upon centuries ago. The Mantis, eyes closed, was savoring the music that rose, with the help of the 2500-year-old amphitheater's incomparable acoustics, to where they stood. Weaver stood beside her like a cowboy, his right hand resting on the revolver in its belt holster.

The music stopped abruptly. The Mantis opened her eyes and stared down at the stage. A man, no doubt the director, had been sitting with a small group in the front rows. Now, he jumped to his feet and stormed onto the stage yelling and waving his arms. Gesticulating wildly, he hurled a barrage of Italian at the male choir.

"Wait here," the Mantis said without looking at Weaver, and descended into the tiered rows of seats. Composed but purposeful, she moved down the stone staircase that cut through the center of the semicircular terraces. Single file, like hunters on a safari, the mercenaries followed their leader down, each a few feet behind the man ahead. The director stopped shouting when he noticed the sudden restlessness in the orchestra, and he turned to see the new arrivals backlit by the stage lighting.

He was building up to another verbal volley, but never got to open his mouth. The Mantis casually drew her pistol and shot him dead as she stepped onto the stage. "I hate bullies," she murmured. "Round them up," she shouted to her men, who instantly obeyed.

Weaver, who had watched things unfold below from his raised perch, watched the five men and women who had originally been sitting with the director, and whom the Mantis had initially ignored, jump from their seats and try to flee. He drew his revolver and ran down the stairs. He fired a warning shot into the air, then took aim at the escaping group and herded them, panicked and distraught, onto the stage.

The initial shock of the tenor and the men's choir gave way to growing panic and helplessness. The men and women of the orchestra stumbled in fear back toward the stage. Instruments fell to the ground, and music stands and chairs tipped over. Screams and whimpering could be heard all the way to the top row of seats as the musicians were rounded up like cattle. Tied with cable ties and gagged with gaffer tape, they were forced onto the ground behind the tree-ringed stage.

Two men were set to guard them, while several others ran back to the vehicles to help with the final preparations. Returning with the large cylinders that Weaver had been unable to identify back in the barn, the men used a cartridge-powered driver to fasten the ten-foot-high devices into the stonework around the stage.

Weaver, who had helped tie the hostages, now positioned himself beside the Mantis, who was standing in front of the anxious prisoners.

"*Signore e signori. Sono terribilmente dispiaciuto . . .*" she began in accent-free Italian. "We don't want to keep you from your rehearsal any longer than necessary. If you stay quiet and do what my men tell you, you will go home tonight alive. If not, you will share your director's fate. *Capito?*" She pointed to where two of her henchmen were dragging the director's lifeless body off the stage. They threw him callously into the bushes.

Weaver saw the fearful faces, some streaked with tears, nod timidly.

"Come with me," the Mantis said to him. "I'll show you why we're here." They returned to the stage, and she slipped the rolled-up copy of the old document out of her unitard. She studied the sketch on the paper, comparing it to her surroundings. "Here," she said, and she pointed to where the burning cross was standing.

Two of the mercenaries ran over and extinguished the fire, then pushed the cross over and hauled it clear. Weaver and the Mantis stepped back as another of her men began breaking open the wooden stage with a crowbar.

"As you may know," the woman said, turning to Weaver, "according to legend, anyone who looks the Medusa in the eye will turn to stone." Weaver nodded. "But Medusa's head also hides a very different secret, and I am the only one who knows what it is."

Weaver looked at the woman doubtfully. Just then a clap of thunder shattered the otherwise quiet night. The Mantis raised her head to the sky, as if to welcome the first drops of rain.

CHAPTER 69
TEATRO GRECO, SYRACUSE

"Are we too late?" said Hellen when they stopped the car a safe distance from the theater. Cloutard sat beside her, and Tom sat with Akira in the back. On their way to the theater, seemingly from out of nowhere, a thunderstorm had gathered. Within moments, the clear night sky had vanished behind grim clouds, and the windshield wipers had begun to battle the heavy rain. They had turned off the main road into Via Luigi Bernabò Brea and driven past the Latomie del Paradiso quarry when Hellen spotted a patrol car from the local *carabinieri* in the darkness fifty yards ahead. It was parked across the entrance to the Teatro Greco, Syracuse's ancient Greek theater.

"*Putain de merde*," said Cloutard, nipping as usual at his flask.

"If the cops were really responding to a call, there wouldn't be just one patrol car standing here with its lights off," Tom said.

"We're definitely in the right place," said Akira. "In the last message Weaver sent to Horne, he named the theater. Also, it looks like there's someone up there." She pointed up the small, forested hillside where, beyond the trees, a bright glow was visible.

"It might just be a coincidence," Hellen said. "If you think about everything that's going on in the world right now, I wouldn't be surprised to find a bigger police presence here, too. According to the Internet, they'll be performing a Verdi opera here in a few days. Maybe the cops are just watching the site?"

"We should play it safe, either way," said Tom. "We can't afford a run-in with the authorities, not when we're so close. There's still an international arrest warrant out on me, remember, and I've spent too much time locked up in the last few days. He grimaced in pain as he leaned forward between the seats. "If Weaver and the insect are up to something here, then I don't believe in coincidences."

"Something's happening over there," said Hellen. Tom looked up to see one of the men climb out of the police car and move a few steps in their direction.

"Couldn't we just ask?" said Akira meekly. Tom looked at her. Suddenly, he snapped his fingers and turned to Cloutard.

"Rentals always have a road map," he murmured, mostly to himself. "François, check the glove box. See if there's one there," he said, excited but resolute, and Cloutard opened the glove box and began poking around.

"Why do you need a map? I've got everything right here on my laptop," Akira said.

Tom winked at her. "Google Maps has saved my ass more times than I can remember, but sometimes analog beats digital. Unless you want to lend me your laptop as an umbrella." Akira just looked at him in confusion.

Tom got out in the pouring rain and opened the driver's door from the outside. He and Hellen shared a smile as he reached between her legs and popped the hood. Then he quickly went to the front of the car, lifted the hood, and propped it open.

"What's that for? What are you going to do?" Hellen asked when he got back into the car.

"Me? Nothing. I'm on the run, remember? You and François are going to go and talk to the *carabinieri*," Tom said, patting them both on the shoulder.

"*Pas encore*. You know how much I hate storms. My clothes haven't really dried out since that deluge last year in Innsbruck."

"Don't be like that, François. All you need to do is act like dumb tourists who've had a breakdown and try to find out what's going on," he said, gesturing for them to climb out.

Cloutard muttered a few more complaints in French, but then he unfolded the city map and held it over his head. He left his beloved Panama hat in the car. Arm in arm, the map spread out over their heads, Hellen and Cloutard walked toward the patrol car.

"Are you going to let them do that alone? What if those are the bad guys?" Akira said meekly, almost stammering.

"You don't know me, so I'll let that slide," Tom said with a smile. "Of course I'm not going to let them do it alone. Wait here, and if you see anything, honk." Without waiting for a reply, he got out of the car and immediately ducked behind a tree. He glanced ahead quickly, then jumped over the low wall alongside the road, into the grounds surrounding the ancient quarry. Keeping out of sight among the trees and bushes, he moved away from the road before turning and sprinting ahead. Jumping down over another wall, he ran on until he reached the old building that stood at the entrance to the theater, which bordered the quarry. A set of steps led back up along the side of the building to the street, and he had to stop for a moment at the foot of the steps and hold his side.

"Shit," he hissed through his teeth. The point-blank shot that his vest had stopped and the subsequent fall had taken a serious toll. His chest was one huge bruise. Any abrupt movement hurt. Even breathing hurt. But he had to put that aside.

"*Fermatevi, non potete andare oltre*," Tom heard one of the *carabinieri* shout, telling Hellen and Cloutard they couldn't go any farther. The man inside the car had switched on the patrol car's headlights.

Keeping low, Tom moved up the steps. Across from him, beyond a low wall and a hedge, sat the patrol car, blocking the theater entrance. Tom crept up to the wall and watched the scene from there.

Hellen and Cloutard were playing their roles to perfection. They were waving the big wet map in the man's face and talking loudly and rapidly in a chorus of French and German. The second man was still sitting in the car. Tom watched him carefully. The unexpected tourists seemed to be making him nervous. Tom's gut was telling him something was off, and he didn't have to wait long for confirmation—the man in the car began screwing a silencer onto his pistol.

Tom peeked around the corner of the wall and his eyes met Cloutard's. He drew his finger across his throat, and Cloutard understood that they had to take out the two fake *carabinieri*. Cloutard gave him the slightest of nods and made sure the "cop" in front of him didn't turn around. Tom crept out from behind the wall and around the car.

Then things moved fast. The man in the car got out, ready to shoot Hellen and Cloutard, but Tom was on him in a split-second. Simultaneously, Cloutard used the blustery wind and his feigned clumsiness to send the map flying into the other man's face. Then he punched him hard several times and he went down.

"Not cops at all," said Tom, holding up the "officer's" silenced pistol. Hellen looked with relief at the unconscious body of the man Tom had overpowered.

"Give me a hand," said Tom, grimacing again as he dragged the man to the back of the car. They stowed the two bodies in the patrol car's trunk, first taking away their guns, ammunition, phones, and radios. Tom locked the trunk and threw the keys into the bushes.

Suddenly, an ear-splitting clap of thunder made all three of them freeze. Multiple bolts of lightning crackled down at the same instant toward the theater, which was still out of sight. They exchanged a look.

"To answer your question from before," Tom said to Hellen, "I think we got here just in time."

CHAPTER 70

TEATRO GRECO, SYRACUSE

The sight was disconcerting, to say the least. From their hidden vantage point, Tom, Hellen and Cloutard could clearly see what was happening in the theater below.

In a semicircle around the "orchestra"—the circular stage that formed the center of the theater—the eight metallic cylinders had been set up vertically. Each pylon was about ten feet high, with a metal ring resembling an oversized doughnut about two feet in diameter on top. The pylons had been bolted into the stone, one at the foot of each of the stairways that segmented the seating area and converged on the stage, like the spokes of a wheel.

In the center of the stage, where the wooden floor had been torn open, a metal column about four feet high had been set up, with a plate-like platform mounted on top of it. The structure looked a little like a high circular café table. Opposite this, on the outer edge of the orchestra, two men were setting up a second small column, on top of which was a claw with four small arms.

The men stepped back as the Mantis and Weaver approached. Lightning flashed and thunder rumbled.

Weaver had the flight case in his hand. He lifted it up, opened the lid, and held it toward the Mantis.

Hellen drew a sharp breath when she saw what the woman removed from the case. "It's the amphora from the photo in Richter's house," she whispered.

Weaver closed the case and handed it to one of the men. Then he folded out the four arms of the claw on the platform.

Hellen pressed a hand over her mouth to stifle a scream when the Mantis smashed the amphora on the stonework. The Mantis knelt down and, from among the shards of clay, retrieved an elongated lump of stone about the size of a beer bottle. She set this up inside the claw, the arms holding it in place, then crossed to the "café table."

"Maybe the Medusa cult isn't a figment of everyone's imagination after all. It looks to me an awful lot like they're carrying out a ritual down there," Tom said.

"*Étrange*. Very strange. I wonder what they are trying to do?" said Cloutard.

"Whatever it is, we have to stop it. We can't let them use their mumbo jumbo to create a weapon, or worse," Tom said impatiently. Despite his pain, he would have liked nothing better than to take out the mercenaries, one after another—Weaver most of all. The Marine had been a thorn in his side from the start. His fingers wrapped around the grip of the pistol he'd taken from the fake cop.

Hellen, seeing his impatience, put her hand on his and pushed the gun down again.

"If you go storming down there in your condition, you won't help anyone, least of all yourself. There's too many of them. And we don't even know where the head is."

Tom's grip relaxed a little.

"*Oui oui*. She is right. We have to solve this one with our heads, not our fists," said Cloutard with a wink at Tom, making him smile.

"Okay, then what—"

But he was cut off in mid-sentence. Rustling and crackling behind them, followed by the clack of rifle bolts, made all three spin around. They found themselves staring along rifle barrels into the cold eyes of two masked mercenaries.

CHAPTER 71

CLOSE TO THE TEATRO GRECO, SYRACUSE

Akira was still sitting by herself in the rental car, not far from the entrance to the Teatro Greco. Rain rattled onto the roof. It was half an hour since Tom had left her there, and her uneasiness was growing. She was in a foreign country with a trio of people who were basically strangers, and she didn't know what she was supposed to do. Half an hour earlier, she'd seen Tom, Hellen and Cloutard take care of the "*carabinieri*" and hide their unconscious bodies in the trunk of their own car. But then they had disappeared up the road and she had lost sight of them.

Had they forgotten about her?

No. No way.

From what she'd learned about the former Blue Shield team, she knew they just wanted to keep her out of harm's way.

Whatever. Waiting in the car like a sitting duck wasn't a solution either.

Maybe she should just take off? She didn't owe these people anything. Her life had gone off totally off the rails already. Because of her, her boyfriend had been murdered.

And if Weaver ever got his hands on her, she'd end up the same way.

She climbed out, pulled her hood over her head, and ran to the front of the car to close the hood. Then she climbed in behind the wheel. The key was still in the ignition. She started the car, turned it around, and drove away.

You have to get away, she told herself. *With Bobby's papers, you can start a new life somewhere else, somewhere no one will find you.*

When she reached the intersection of Via Luigi Bernabò Brea, where they'd turned off earlier, she stopped and thought about where she should go. But a profound sense of guilt came over her. Exhaustion and despair filled her body. Tears flowed down her face and her head sank forward onto the steering wheel. What was she supposed to do? For the first time in her life, she felt completely alone. She had hidden behind computers all her life, and if she hadn't forced herself to visit the museum once a week, she never even would have met Jamie. Jamie . . . the love of her life, and now he was dead. And one of the men responsible for his death was here.

She lifted her head and wiped away her tears. Then she turned the car around and stepped on the gas.

CHAPTER 72
TEATRO GRECO

"Ah, Mr. Wagner. And your loyal companions, too," said the Mantis when she saw Tom, Hellen and Cloutard, their hands clasped behind their heads, being led up onto the stage. "I've been expecting you. You're right on time." She raised her arms to the sky and gazed upward. "The show's about to begin."

Overhead, lightning flashed through the dark, ominous clouds that seemed to have gathered only over the theater and the area immediately surrounding it. Tom looked around. Off to his left, he saw the hostages sitting at the edge of the row of trees that grew around the lowest section of the theater. The rain was hammering down mercilessly. Soaked to the skin, Tom, Hellen and Cloutard stood in front of two of the Mantis's men next to the eastern *parodos*—the entrance used by the actors and extras to access the stage from the sides.

"In just a few minutes," the Mantis said, looking at her watch, "you will see for yourselves the true power of the Medusa."

Tom, Hellen and Cloutard were not the only ones to duck low when a deafening crash, like the crack of a pistol inches away, rang through the theater. Weaver and the Mantis's men ducked, too. A bolt of lightning had slammed into one of the pylons. Blue and violet sparks crackled around the ring at the top of the pylon and leaped across to a neighboring pylon, briefly causing both of them to glow.

"Those things remind me of Tesla coils," Hellen whispered, nodding toward the metal structures. "She's trying to capture the energy of the lightning, but why?"

Then they saw one of the men bring up a cylindrical metal container. The Mantis took it from him and set it atop the small platform in the center of the orchestra. She turned the container forty-five degrees until, with a loud *click*, it locked into place on the base.

"That must be the head," Cloutard whispered.

"Probably," said Tom. "But that's not the container it was in before."

"It's you!" Hellen suddenly yelled, taking a thoughtless step toward the woman. "You're behind this absurd cult. What are you doing? Do you really think your stupid ritual is going to reawaken the Medusa? Do you think you can use her to take over the world? Are you willing to sacrifice all these people to find the right host?"

One of the mercenaries holding them at bay already had his rifle butt raised, ready to beat Hellen with it, but he stopped when the Mantis laughed loudly and signaled to him to stand down.

"Doctor de Mey, please. You're an intelligent woman. Do you really think I share the same archaic ambitions as all the power-hungry men out there? Of course I want to change the world, but believe me, it's got nothing to do with bringing it to heel or destroying it."

"No matter what you do here today—and who knows, you might even get away with it—you should remember one thing," Tom began, with a coldness in his voice that made even Hellen shudder. "If I live through this, I will find you. I will become your worst nightmare. And when I find you, may God have mercy on your soul."

Cloutard frowned and leaned a little toward Tom. "A mediocre interpretation. I have seen you do better," he whispered. Tom shrugged.

"Mr. Wagner, I have to admit, your reputation and your skills are familiar even to me. And yes, you caught me in Vienna. But you could not hold me for long, as you can see. Like so many men, you, too, have underestimated me. Believe me when I say that you have never encountered anyone like me. So do your worst. And in any case, my partner here will be the one to decide whether you live through this or not." She patted Weaver on the shoulder. "He's just dying to break your neck."

Weaver's eyes seemed to flash for a second as he stared at Tom.

With a wave of her hand, she signaled to her men to take up their positions. Followed by Weaver, she moved clear of the orchestra, leaving the stage area completely empty. A few feet behind each of the pylons stood one of the Mantis's men. She herself, with Weaver, Tom, Hellen, Cloutard, and the two mercenaries guarding them, stood at the edge of the stage.

An ear-splitting roar of thunder rolled through the night. Overhead, the clouds seemed to be literally charging up, like enormous batteries. They began to spiral, as if forming a tornado. Her hands raised high, the Mantis gazed into the sky. Tom, Hellen and Cloutard exchanged a look. They had never felt as helpless as they did then.

"Today marks the beginning of a new world," the woman cried. She pulled on a pair of sunglasses and pressed a button on a remote control.

. . .

Not far from the Teatro Greco, at the same time

Out of sight, Akira peered at the historic structure through a pair of binoculars she had found in Tom's duffel bag. She could hardly watch—the situation seemed hopeless. She wondered briefly whether running away wasn't perhaps the better choice after all. A dozen heavily armed mercenaries, an out-of-control Marine, and a cold-blooded assassin were holding eighty hostages, as well as the three people whose exploits she'd been following for some time. Tom Wagner was good, but he was hurt. He was no match for the mercenaries in his condition. And while Dr. Hellen de Mey might be a brilliant scientist, she wasn't a trained soldier like Tom. As for the old French snob, he was surely out of his depth, too. Besides, he seemed like he was half-drunk most of the time.

Never meet your heroes, she thought. How could this team ever have taken down an organization like AF?

Akira was jumping at the slightest out-of-the-ordinary sound, but she stayed where she was and watched events unfold. She took out her phone to alert the police, but discovered she had no signal. Turning the binoculars to the north, toward the upper part of the theater, she saw the three XVs in which Weaver and the rest must have arrived.

A sly smile crept over her face when she noticed the small satellite dish on the hood of one of the vehicles. Suddenly, she knew how she could help. She stowed the binoculars and her phone in her backpack and took out her stun gun, which had proven itself once already. And while she had only managed to knock out her poor neighbor in a fit of fear and panic the first time, the stun gun gave her at least a slight sense of security in this situation.

She got to her feet and crept back down the path she'd

come up. To her left, a stairway lined with trees and bushes led upward, probably for the audience to reach their seats. Keeping low, she ran up the steps, climbed quickly over the railing at the top and hid in the bushes on the other side. She looked around. She couldn't see into the theater from there. To her right was the adjoining quarry, a hundred feet deep. Some distance ahead, she saw a small house, or maybe more of a tower. She couldn't say exactly what it was. The building was the only thing between her and the Grotta del Ninfeo—long ago, an aqueduct had transported water from the small artificial grotto to the theater, allowing the stage to be flooded and plays to be performed in the water. Beside the grotto, which lay fifty yards beyond the building, a set of stairs led up to the street above, where the three vehicles stood.

Between her and the tower, and again to the trucks, there was no cover at all. No bushes, no place for Akira to hide. A hundred and fifty yards of open space. She was breathing fast, and her hands were trembling, but she also felt excited, invigorated. For the duration of a heartbeat, the space in front of her lit up brightly when a bolt of lightning hit the theater. Thunder rolled. The way ahead was clear.

Now or never, she thought, and she jumped up and ran. She had never been a fast runner in school, but she was a lot more motivated here and now. She ran as hard as she could, and although it couldn't have been more than fifteen seconds to the tower, it felt like minutes. The fear of being caught had given her muscles an extra burst of strength.

She pressed back against the tower wall and caught her breath. She risked a peek around the corner—nothing—and crept onward, the stun gun in her outstretched hand. She sneaked a quick look around the next corner, too. Still nothing. Ten seconds later, she reached the steps beside the grotto. Warily, she climbed to the top. She saw the XVs and, to her relief, just one man in the rain at the edge of the terrace, his eyes glued to the spectacle in the theater below. Another five steps, and she reached the bushes separating the access road from the street. As silently as possible, she crept on all fours through the bushes to the side of the XVs away from the theater. As gently as she could, she opened the driver's door and climbed inside. She pulled over the laptop, glancing up repeatedly at the man who was standing thirty feet away, still staring into the depths.

She saw in an instant what she was dealing with. On the screen was a live satellite feed of the entire area that was being sent on to other devices on its own secure network. Thanks to Weaver, no doubt, they had a direct link to one of the countless spy satellites used by the U.S. armed forces. A jamming signal was also being transmitted, blocking the local phone networks. She retrieved a USB drive from her backpack, plugged it into the laptop, and opened a small software package she'd written. Within a few minutes, she had taken complete control of the system. First, she deactivated the warning system that was monitoring the local police frequencies, then set a ten-minute delay on the satellite images. Finally, she shut down the jammer. Then she removed the thumb drive, closed the laptop, and climbed out of the car as quietly as she'd gotten in. The continuous rumbling of thunder covered the click of the car's door—not even the man standing just yards away heard it.

Akira looked up at the sky, barely able to believe her eyes. She had only ever seen something like this in the movies. A vortex seemed to have formed directly over the theater. The clouds glowed as if they were about to explode. But she could not allow herself to be distracted. She had one more thing to take care of.

CHAPTER 73
TEATRO GRECO

Like everyone else at the theater, Tom, Hellen, and Cloutard gazed at the sky overhead. Hellen had just seen something in Tom's eyes she had not seen in all their years together—not fear, exactly, but helplessness. She could tell just by looking that he was hurt worse than he was willing to admit. And it was also true that they had been in far more desperate situations but had always managed to escape at the last instant. This time, though, they were caught up in something they could never have foreseen. They had stumbled blindly into the lion's den, without backup, without a plan. And Tom was injured.

The Mantis pressed the button on the remote control, and it was as if time stood still. Everything moved in slow motion, as if in a dream. Dust, small stones, leaves, and sheet music were all sucked into the air and danced in a circle above the stage. The container in the center of the stage opened outward, like a flower blooming. Medusa's head appeared, its gaze directed at the black stone pinned in the claw just a few yards away, on a pedestal of its own.

As if Zeus himself had focused all his wrath on that one point, the energy bundled in the clouds suddenly discharged. As they watched, several bolts of lightning crashed at the same instant into the pylons. Bolts of electricity flew, arcing not only between the metallic rings on top of the pylons, but also striking the mercenaries stationed behind them. Lightning surged through their bodies. They did not scream, but their faces convulsed in pain. Their eyes gleamed brightly, then faded to charred hollows as the men collapsed. One ring after another began to glow, like streetlamps at night. The flickering lightning, like a nightclub strobe, lit up the entire area and reflected in the puddles. Unable to move, unable to do anything, Tom, Hellen and Cloutard could only stand and watch the gruesome spectacle. Weaver and the two mercenaries behind them were as stunned as they were.

Simultaneously, the arcs from the eight pylons discharged and created another connection, eight bolts of lightning crackling into the head of Medusa. The serpents covering her head jolted to life, her eyes glowed red, and her mouth gaped. Her eyes opened and two red beams of light shot from the eyes toward the black stone they faced, like Superman activating his heat vision.

Like a white-hot chunk of coal, the stone vibrated for a few seconds, glowing brighter and brighter. Tom had to press his hand over his face to protect his eyes from the dazzling light as it shifted through the colors of the spectrum.

The pain was intense as a blast wave swept him and the others off their feet. He tried to pull himself together, but it was some time before his disorientation faded and his senses started working again. He could not tell how many seconds or minutes had passed. His head was buzzing. Every breath hurt. Every sound, every voice, everything sounded as if it was coming from far away. He blinked several times and rubbed his eyes, trying to clear the blinding stars dancing in front of them. Through the sparkling colors, he could make out Hellen. She was struggling in the mud beside Cloutard, trying to regain her senses, fighting the same shock as Tom. But he was relieved to see that his friends did not seem to be otherwise hurt.

When he finally managed to get back to his feet, he looked around. Eight smoldering corpses lay behind the pylons. Weaver and the two mercenaries were still on the ground. Tom stumbled toward the stage. Medusa's head, still perched on its stand, was undamaged. The claw that had been holding the black chunk of stone, however, was empty. To make matters worse, the Mantis had vanished.

The rain had stopped, and the sky was free of clouds. Tom went back to his friends and was just reaching down for a rifle when something knocked him off his feet. Weaver, still on the ground, had stretched out and with a quick twist had kicked Tom's feet from under him. Tom hit the ground hard beside Hellen but pumped full of adrenalin, he was back on his feet in a second despite his injuries.

"Let's finish this once and for all," Weaver snarled.

Tom let out a scream of fury and pain and charged at Weaver. He grabbed him by the collar, driving him backward until they crashed into the small platform that held the head. They crashed to the ground as the platform tipped over, the head rolling across the stage before coming to rest face down.

Hellen made it to her feet before Cloutard. The explosion had hit him hardest of all, and he was nowhere near as young as he once had been. "Watch out!" he shouted. Hellen spun and snatched up a rifle. One of the mercenaries was just getting to his feet, but she clubbed him with the rifle. He fell to the ground, unconscious.

"Where's the other one?" she growled in rage as she straightened up again, adrenalin flowing. She heard a rifle bolt slide back and snap forward behind her. She dropped the gun she'd been holding by the barrel and turned around. Thousands of details of her life, many absurd, flashed before her inner eye as she stared down the barrel of the assault rifle the second man was pointing at her. He could barely stand.

"Hellen!" Cloutard shouted, but there was nothing he could do.

Hellen closed her eyes, but the shot never came. When she opened them again, she saw Akira. The young woman had appeared as if from nowhere, running in from the parados and incapacitating the man from behind with her stun gun.

Perplexed, Hellen could manage only a single word: "Thanks."

Akira smiled.

"*Merveilleux.*" Cloutard, who had struggled to his feet, sank back onto the ground, exhausted but smiling.

"I thought we might be able to use this," Akira said, holding up the head's original container.

"The Medusa!" Hellen cried, and she wheeled around. She saw Tom grappling with Weaver on the ground, both men punching wildly at one another. Then, looking a little farther, she saw the head. "Over there," she said, and ran to it, Akira close behind.

Tom was on his feet now, but he doubled over and groaned in pain when Weaver landed a solid blow to his ribs. His arms crossed over his head, Tom parried blow after blow. As Hellen and Akira ran past them, Weaver was distracted for a fraction of a second, and Tom managed to land an uppercut. Weaver's head jolted back, and he lost his footing, but the force of the punch triggered a shock of pain, hurting Tom almost as much as Weaver. With one hand protecting his ribs, Tom dropped on top of Weaver, his knee on the Marine's chest, and swung at him one-handed.

Tom didn't hear the shot, but he felt the singeing heat. He clambered up and stumbled back a few steps. Looking down, he saw a red stain spreading on his shirt around a small hole. Then he looked at Weaver, on the ground in front of him, the revolver in his hand.

"Tom!" he heard his wife scream as more bullets found their mark, one in his chest and another in his stomach. He toppled over backward.

CHAPTER 74
UNKNOWN LOCATION

The man could not express how deeply grateful he was to the developers of drone technology.

In his present circumstances, limiting as they were, a drone kept him almost at the very heart of things, with the distinct advantage that he was in no danger of getting shot.

As if on a Netflix binge, the man had been watching events unfold at the Teatro Greco for quite some time. At first, he'd thought that the story about the Medusa was complete humbug. But it didn't matter to him, anyway. The Medusa was just one topic among thousands, interchangeable, there to generate clicks, and useful for organizing demonstrations, triggering mass unrest, and winning elections.

Whether the story behind it was actually true was completely beside the point.

But when Tom Wagner and his friends appeared on the scene, everything suddenly got more interesting. Two birds with one stone, so to speak.

Originally, the plan had been to use the bizarre Medusa story to destabilize the global balance, no more than that. After pandemics, wars, and the advancing climate crisis, the world was already on a knife edge. Under normal circumstances, in a more stable world, an ugly Greek monster wouldn't have worked at all, but the state of things at the moment certainly made things easier.

But the whole affair had taken on a life of its own and an energy he had hardly dared to dream of. Now Tom Wagner and DARPA were involved, along with heads of governments around the world, the CIA, and a slew of other three and four-letter organizations. Even old Mandalov had jumped on board. It was almost like winning the lottery. *Sometimes, life throws you curveballs you just can't plan for*, he thought.

He also had no interest in the outcome, because he would win either way. Global stability had taken a hard blow once again—another piece of the puzzle that, with events unfolding as they were, was coming together faster than expected. He had already mentally checked off the Medusa box, and now he could devote himself to other things. His gaze fell on the file that, with a little effort, he been able to make his own. The UNESCO and Blue Shield logos were emblazoned on the cover, and the title beneath the logos read: "Blue Shield: Abandoned Projects." Two of the projects it contained had particularly caught his attention.

The man looked up in amazement at the screen. Something had happened, something he knew he would truly enjoy.

He guided the drone expertly, changing the angle and zooming in.

Yes. Tom Wagner had been shot.

Let's see that again! the man thought, and he rewound a few seconds. A smile played on his lips when he saw the man on the ground fire several shots into Wagner.

Finally. This is my kind of action, he thought to himself, zooming in a little closer still, to see the desperation on Hellen de Mey's face. Things could not have gone better if he'd been there himself.

Unfortunately, he hadn't been able to get any popcorn. That would have made the moment perfect.

The man watched closely as Hellen de Mey leaned over the injured Wagner and tried desperately to keep him alive.

To hell with Netflix. This was better. Far better.

CHAPTER 75
TEATRO GRECO

Hellen knelt beside Tom and pressed her hands onto his wounds, but blood streamed between her fingers and would not stop. The last few minutes felt to her like hours, and the sound of the gunshots still resounded in her head. She had been lifting Medusa's head into the jar of greenish liquid when the first shot rang out. At first, she hadn't understood what had happened. Then came another shot, and another. How many were fired, she did not know. Then Weaver had stood up and aimed at her, and she had been certain that the next bullet was hers.

"Give me the head!" he'd bellowed, his face bloody from Tom's blows.

"Over my dead body," Hellen had said, moving in front of Akira, who had the jar in her hands.

"Fine with me," Weaver had replied coldly, and he squeezed the trigger without hesitation. But the only sound was a *click* as the hammer landed on a spent cylinder. He'd pulled the trigger again and again, pure rage contorting his face, only stopping when a dazzling light fell on him from above. He turned his face to the sky.

"*Questa è la polizia, abbassate le armi!* This is the police.

Put down the gun!" he heard—a police helicopter, the voice coming through a loudspeaker. Officers were swarming into the theater from all sides.

"It is your choice," Cloutard had suddenly shouted from the edge of the stage, a rifle pointed at Weaver.

"This isn't over," Weaver, still furious, had snarled back, and with a final glare at Hellen, he disappeared into the darkness in the general chaos that followed. Cloutard watched him go. Right now, saving Tom was more important.

"Hold on," Hellen sobbed. "Help is on its way." Cloutard was kneeling helplessly beside her, with Akira standing a short distance away, her arms wrapped tightly around the container with the head.

"*Merde, merde, merde*," said Cloutard, running his fingers through his hair. He took a long swig from his flask.

"Don't worry. It's just a scratch," Tom gurgled, looking into Hellen's eyes. A smile briefly crossed her face. Tom coughed, and blood swelled from between his lips.

"*Sacrément*, where are the medics?"

Tom lost consciousness for a moment.

"Tom, no! Tom!" Hellen cried, shaking at him. "You have to stay awake."

His eyes opened again, and he groaned. Hellen laid her bloody hand on his cheek.

"Three bullets," Hellen murmured weakly, looking pleadingly at Cloutard. "One in his stomach and two in his chest, near his shoulder. We have or to hurry or . . ." Her voice faded.

"Did I miss something?" said Tom, momentarily coming to again. Hellen looked at her husband. Tears poured down her cheeks.

"No. No," she said, smiling, trying to give him hope.

"We'll get you to a hospital soon and everything will be good." She stroked his forehead tenderly.

"*Temps!* We will never get him to a hospital fast enough. We need more time!" Cloutard suddenly snapped. He turned to Akira. "And we can give him all the time in the world," he said, waving Akira closer. Cloutard looked first at Hellen and then at the jar in Akira's arms.

"No! We can't do that!" Hellen protested.

"Why not? You told me that Maierhofer's son is still alive, that he is only in a catatonic state. His system is dialed down to the absolute minimum. That is what we need right now. That can give Tom the time he needs to pull through."

Hellen could not think clearly. So many thoughts were racing through her mind. She tried to say something, but no words came.

"We are out of time. Get behind me," said Cloutard. He reached out to Akira for the container. Akira looked at Hellen, and at a short nod from her she handed the jar to Cloutard. Tom, drifting in and out of consciousness, was aware of nothing.

Cloutard opened the lid and reached inside. His face twisted in disgust as he lifted out the head. At first, the snakes hung slack, but they suddenly hissed, rose as if to strike, and stared down at Tom.

Hellen shook at Tom's legs to bring him around. "Tom. Tom! You have to wake up. Wake up for me." Barely noticeably, he opened his eyes. The snakes hissed again as Medusa's eyes opened. A tremor shook Tom's body, and suddenly his eyes opened wide.

The snakes fell slack again. Cloutard slipped the head back into the green liquid, and Akira closed the lid.

"You can't leave me alone. You have to fight. Do you hear me?" Hellen cried. After that, she perceived what happened only vaguely. Paramedics came running and crouched over

Tom. At first, Cloutard had a great deal of trouble explaining to them what had happened to him, but when they saw Medusa's head floating in its tank, they did as he asked. When the helicopter took off, carrying all four of them to the nearest hospital, they looked down to see the police and medics tending to the distraught hostages. None had been hurt. But there was no sign at all of Weaver, the Mantis, or the remaining three mercenaries.

CHAPTER 76
UMBERTO I HOSPITAL, SYRACUSE

Hellen could only watch helplessly as the gurney trundled through the double doors. The police helicopter had landed in the parking lot beside the hospital, and they had rushed him inside. Warned in advance, doctors and nurses had quickly descended on Tom and whisked him away. Cloutard put his arms around Hellen, and she began to cry uncontrollably. Now that all the tension, excitement, and danger of the last few hours was over, everything came pouring out.

Would she ever see Tom again? Deep inside, she knew that Cloutard had made the only possible decision, but a trace of doubt remained. Even if the operation went well, they still had a major problem: while the condition that Medusa's head had induced in Tom had given him the time he needed to survive, there was still the question of how they could snap him out of it.

"Signora Wagner?" she heard a man's accented voice say. A doctor had approached her hesitantly. She looked up from Cloutard's chest as the doctor handed her a tissue. She blew her nose. "I have spoken with my colleagues in Vienna, and we are now fully informed about this . . . unusual situation. We will be starting the operation as soon as possible. It is true that his catatonic condition has saved his life for now. Now we have to remove the bullets. Not a simple task. Go home, please. There is nothing you can do here. Your husband is in good hands."

"*Grazie, Dottore*," said Cloutard. Hellen only nodded. The doctor hurried away, and Hellen took a seat beside Akira, who was sitting quietly on a visitors' bench and holding three cups of coffee. She handed one to Hellen.

"From what I know about Tom Wagner, well, he's strong. He'll make it," Akira said calmly.

"Thank you. You really were a tremendous help," Hellen said, forcing herself to smile. Akira only nodded. She handed a cup of coffee to Cloutard.

"*Merci, ma chère*," Cloutard said. He fished out his flask to add a little spice to the horrible coffee-machine brew, then turned to Hellen. "It is true that we can do nothing here, but we can still be useful somewhere else. I know you do not want to leave Tom alone right now, but he would want us to do everything we can to bring this to an end. And if Mandalov's claims are true, it is our only chance to save him. We need the artifacts. We need to destroy the Medusa and lift her curse.

"I'll keep an eye on things here," said Akira.

Hellen sipped at her coffee. Her eyes were glued to the floor. Then she looked up and nodded gratefully to Akira. "You're right," she said after she had thought it all through. Her voice sounded uncertain, on edge. Cloutard could see how hard the decision was for her. "We have to get rid of the Medusa once and for all. We can only pray that Mandalov knows what he's talking about. Tom's life depends on it."

CHAPTER 77
EON VAN RENSBURG'S PRIVATE JET, ON APPROACH TO CORFU, GREECE

Hellen hadn't said a word since the plane took off in Sicily. She sat in silence, gazing out the window, an empty stare into nothing. She simply didn't want to acknowledge what had happened.

Cloutard had tried repeatedly to start a conversation, asking her for details about Empress Sissi and why she had always sought refuge on Corfu. He knew that Hellen had always been fascinated by the Habsburgs and was trying to distract her from what had happened to Tom.

But he failed miserably. She said nothing. She simply sat and stared out the window. Her face was like a mask, betraying no emotion, no tears, no grief. Cloutard knew that a person who felt nothing was suffering more than one openly battling their emotions. Despair would take over, and the downward spiral was fatal. It almost seemed as if Hellen had truly given up. The few words he had heard her say since Tom's had been shot leaned dangerously in that direction.

"Did we do the right thing? What if Mandalov turns out to be a charlatan?" Hellen had said desolately when they left the hospital. "François, our odds have never been this bad.

What if the artifacts Mandalov spoke about no longer exist? What if we can never find them again, not on Corfu or anywhere else in the world? And what if the Golden Fleece and the Aegis can't really hurt the Medusa? What if she survives them, too? What if we destroy the Medusa and Tom *doesn't* recover?"

All of her protests were justified. She knew it, and Cloutard knew it, too.

So he had taken matters into his own hands. He had contacted Mandalov and told him what had happened. The Medusa was back in their hands, and he could assume that they would soon find the artifacts . . . at least, Cloutard hoped they would.

Mandalov was happy to hear that the Medusa was safe again, and he assured Cloutard that he would be available if needed. He did not want to explain in detail how to destroy the Medusa—he, Mandalov, would have to do that himself, he said.

They reached Corfu in the late afternoon, and the plane touched down gently on the tarmac. Cloutard immediately disabled flight mode on his phone, and a moment later was reading a message from Giorgos Topol, a good friend of his from earlier days—better days, Cloutard thought. Days when he and Topol had now and then relieved Greek excavations of an artifact or two. But something else made those days better—back then, Cloutard had not suffered from his olive-bloom allergy. As soon as he stepped off the plane, his nose began to prickle, and the first sneezing fit hit him.

"*Merde*," he swore. "Here we go again."

His expression was so miserable that it drew a small smile even from Hellen. "Bless you," she murmured, but she instantly returned to her somber frame of mind.

"Frangikos!"

Cloutard hated the Greek version of his name, and Topol

knew it. The stocky Greek man met them on their way to the arrivals hall, grinning so broadly he could have fit a banana in his mouth sideways.

Giorgos Topol was a nondescript figure. Barely five-foot-three, balding, overweight, unshaven, and bow-legged enough to straddle a keg of beer, he looked like a Greek version of Danny DeVito. No one would have suspected him of being one of the greatest smugglers and antique dealers in the entire Aegean region.

"Thank you for coming so soon, Giorgos," Cloutard said, and the two men embraced. Topol actually lived on Lesbos and had heard every bad joke there was about his home island, but Cloutard's call had caught him hopping among the Ionian Islands. "This is Hellen de Mey," Cloutard went on after another bout of sneezing. Hellen shook the man's hand without the slightest sign of emotion. Cloutard had already outlined the situation to Topol, so he was not surprised at Hellen's cool reception.

"Have you thought of a way for us to explore Achilleion without being disturbed?" Cloutard said, sniffing furiously as they climbed into Topol's car and pushed their way into the usual dense traffic around the capital city, also called Corfu. "Honestly, I do not know what Achilleion is used for these days," said Cloutard. "As I recall, Empress Sissi was never happy when she had to leave her beloved palace. After her, it was owned by Emperor Wilhelm II. In the First World War it was a military hospital, in the second it was the headquarters of the German occupying forces. Then it was a kindergarten, and at some point, it was also a casino."

Topol laughed loudly. "Yes, it certainly has a checkered history. They shot a James Bond film there too, you know. Nowadays, it's a museum, and they use it occasionally to host EU summit meetings." He cleared his throat. "Which brings me to our biggest problem—right now, a meeting of

EU heads of government is taking place. Security is very tight."

Cloutard sighed and wiped his nose. Hellen stared out the window.

"That was the bad news. But I have found a solution." Topol said, and he turned to Hellen and Cloutard and grinned confidently.

CHAPTER 78

GASTOURI, A SMALL MOUNTAIN VILLAGE ON CORFU

They had passed through the small mountain village of Gastouri and now followed a bumpy mountain road up the hill to Achilleion. Night had already fallen, and, because of the miserable condition of the road, the drive was something of an adventure in itself. Just before they reached the palace, Topol turned left. He stopped and pointed to a house. "Villa Pascalia," he said. "Achilleion's grounds are extensive, but the villa is right next door. Nice place, all luxury. You can rent it on Airbnb. Right now, some of the security people are staying there. It gives you direct access to the property."

Cloutard grinned. He already knew what Topol had set up.

"Right now, the house is empty. All the security people are working." Topol climbed out and went around to the trunk, where he took out two garment bags. "I went ahead and got you the same suits the security companies use." He eyed Cloutard. "I hope I've got you the right size. You've put on a little weight since we last met," he said with a grin, pointing at Cloutard's paunch.

"*Tais-toi,*" Cloutard snapped, managing to draw another smile from Hellen.

"The dying Achilles is supposed to show the way, remember?" she said abruptly. "Do you know what that could mean?" Cloutard looked at her in amazement. He was delighted that she was getting involved but kept that to himself.

"There's a statue called 'Dying Achilles' in the palace garden," Topol said.

Hellen shook her head angrily. "Fuck. I'm really not on top of this," she said. "I knew that. I should have thought of it."

"Follow me," said Topol, and he waddled off toward the villa. He picked the lock on the door in seconds, and Cloutard nodded, impressed. Hellen followed close behind. She was wearing the backpack that contained Medusa's head and carrying her own small pack in her hands.

"Here are your security passes. There are dozens of security people patrolling the grounds, and several security companies have been enlisted, so they do not all know each other. You should have some peace and quiet for a while. I've arranged a little distraction to get you onto the premises."

Cloutard thanked Topol, who left, promising to return very soon.

"All right so far?" Cloutard asked Hellen. "Can we make a start?"

Hellen nodded, and they started changing into the security-company suits.

"What do we do with the head?" Hellen asked, pointing toward the backpack.

"Topol will keep an eye on it when he comes back."

Hellen frowned. "Do you trust him?"

Cloutard nodded. "He is one of the few people in the world I would trust with this backpack."

Ten minutes later, they were ready, and Topol had also returned. He had five men with him. Hellen did not think they looked exactly trustworthy.

"Yannis, Vassilios, Stephanos, Dimitrios, and Nikolas are the advance party. They will storm the palace entrance and keep the two sentries busy catching them."

"But they'll get arrested," Hellen said.

"Yes, but this is Greece. They'll be out again in the morning, and no one will ever think about it again."

Cloutard grinned. "Put it on our tab, Giorgi."

The men exchanged a few words in Greek, then trooped off toward Achilleion. The two gate guards, deep in conversation, looked up in surprise as the five men sprinted out of the darkness and directly toward them. All five made it onto the grounds, and the guards ran after them. The entrance was left unguarded, and Hellen and Cloutard were able to enter the grounds unnoticed.

"I have to say, the EU heads of government are not in particularly safe hands here," Cloutard remarked drily. They were well inside the gardens when Cloutard suddenly succumbed to another fit of sneezing. Two security guards on their rounds eyed them briefly, but noted the passes on lanyards around their necks, nodded an acknowledgement, and moved on.

"Our camouflage seems to be working," said Hellen. "Now let's find this statue."

Immediately in front of the terrace, which offered an impressive view of Corfu's coast, they found the Dying Achilles. Created by the German sculptor Ernst Herter in 1884, the marble Achilles stared into the sky, as if transfigured. He lay on a pedestal surrounded by an iron fence three feet high.

Hellen immediately climbed over the fence and began inspecting the statue and the pedestal on which it lay. Cloutard looked around, worried that someone might spot them. If they were caught now, their forged passes would not save them. Hellen was kneeling at the pedestal and using her phone as a flashlight, looking for anything that might be a clue. Cloutard's nose began to tickle again, and he took hold of it with his fingers and shook it, trying to make it stop. He even slapped himself, knowing that the brief pain could neutralize his urge to sneeze. Hellen, in the meantime, continued her examination. She had moved up from the pedestal to the statue itself, now—more specifically the right hand, which seemed to be pointing to the ground in a certain direction.

Just then, her phone rang—loudly. Momentarily startled, it slipped out of her hand and fell among a row of ornamental plants that lined the pedestal. She rummaged among them nervously.

"Why did you not switch it to silent?" Cloutard hissed.

"Because the hospital could call at any time. They're operating on Tom right now, remember?" she snapped back.

Hellen recovered the phone and checked the number on the display.

"The hospital," she said, louder than Cloutard was comfortable with, and she took the call.

Cloutard, distracted, forgot to slap-treat his allergy and was on the verge of a major sneezing fit. "What do you mean, 'complications'?" he heard Hellen say as she straightened up.

Just then, four security staff appeared on the terrace and looked in their direction.

"Damn it. We are done," said Cloutard between sneezes.

Seconds later, they were surrounded. "What's going on here?"

"But you're getting them under control, aren't you? He has to get well again," Hellen said, distraught. She ignored the security guards completely. One of them climbed over the fence. "What does that mean . . .?" she asked, holding up her index finger to the security man to tell him to wait. Tears filled her eyes. The guard, ignoring Hellen's distress, grabbed her by the arm and pulled her toward him. The sudden jerk made her telephone fall out of her hand. She tried desperately to catch it but missed, and the phone cracked, display first, onto the edge of the pedestal. She looked down. The screen flickered a few times and died.

"No!" she cried in despair, her tears flowing down her cheeks.

CHAPTER 79
GARDEN OF ACHILLEION PALACE, CORFU

The next thing they knew, they were in handcuffs. The security officers hauled them roughly into the palace through one of the rear doors, then on through a series of hallways and storerooms before finally marching them through the kitchen and outside again through the service entrance at the other end.

Cloutard, normally quite a reserved person, actually yelled at the men several times en route, between bouts of sneezing. He couldn't remain silent at the way they were mistreating Hellen.

Hellen was obviously at the end of her rope. Her husband was dying and she was clutching at straws, grasping at an old legend that a dubious expert on ancient Greece had told her about in his underground hideaway. And now it looked as if even this last window of hope was about to slam shut. Achilleion would be forever closed to them. He saw no way for them to get back into the palace—not soon, anyway—to find the Aegis or the Golden Fleece.

Hellen didn't protest. Her gaze was vacant, and she seemed to have lost all her strength. Two men escorted them out through the delivery entrance to where a police van was waiting. Just then, a convoy of limousines began pulling up in front of the palace—the evening reception of the summit meeting, where numerous informal talks would take place, was starting soon.

Heads of government, wearing tuxedos and evening gowns, exited the vehicles to a storm of camera flashes, microphones, cameras. In all the excitement, none of the waiting journalists noticed the two prisoners being behind led out a side entrance.

"Doctor de Mey?"

Cloutard heard the call, but Hellen didn't react. She had given up.

"Doctor de Mey?"

He heard the voice more clearly now. A man who had just climbed out of one of the limousines was looking in their direction, puzzled. He saw that they were in handcuffs, and immediately strode in their direction.

In the glare of the spotlights and camera flashes, Cloutard could not immediately see who it was. But then he recognized the Austrian chancellor, Konstantin Lang, the man whose life Tom had once saved in Jerusalem and with whom Hellen and Tom had found the Florentine Diamond, the Habsburgs' "Stone of Destiny," in Schönbrunn Palace.

"What's going on here?" the chancellor demanded, clearly unhappy at what he was seeing. Two Cobra officers flanked him, and they also seemed to have recognized Hellen.

"These two are under arrest," one of the security men said in halting English. "We caught them by the 'Dying Achilles' statue."

Lang looked first at Hellen, then Cloutard.

"We can explain," Hellen said, her voice barely audible. "It's about Tom. His life is in danger."

The chancellor seemed perplexed. "But I spoke to him on the phone just recently. He was alive and well."

"*Monsieur le Chancelier*, a great deal has happened since then," Cloutard sniffed. He asked an indignant-looking security guard for a tissue.

Skipping the details, Hellen and Cloutard explained what had happened and why they were there. A spark of hope flashed inside Hellen. She had known that Konstantin Lang was a history buff ever since the first Habsburg exhibition she'd curated at the Museum of Fine Arts.

"So, you think the Golden Fleece is hidden somewhere here?" The chancellor's enthusiasm was palpable.

"We hope so," said Hellen. She looked down at her hands, still in handcuffs.

"Get those things off immediately," the chancellor growled at the security men. After a brief radio exchange with the head of security, in which Chancellor Lang's Cobra guards took a vocal role, one of the frustrated security men unlocked the cuffs.

Hellen and Cloutard rubbed their wrists and felt like they could breathe again. "We're back in business, aren't we?" Hellen whispered, her spirits slowly reviving.

"Do you really think there's something to be found at the statue?" Lang asked as the three, with the Cobra officers hovering close by, made their way back through the palace gardens. Along the way, Chancellor Lang waved to the German chancellor and the French prime minister, who were watching them with some embarrassment. Cloutard heard Lang's German counterpart whisper, "These Austrians . . . strange people"—a statement Cloutard could absolutely agree with.

"The letter to Emperor Franz Joseph's aide-de-camp left no doubt about the Dying Achilles," Hellen said. She suddenly recalled her broken phone. "François, can you try to reach the hospital in Syracuse?" she asked.

Cloutard immediately took out his phone. "*Bien sûr.*" He knew she didn't need his help anymore. She was on the scent of an old legend. There was no holding her back.

"Look there," the chancellor said, and he pointed to a corner of the pedestal that had been dislodged an inch or two.

"That must have happened when that gorilla dragged Hellen away," Cloutard murmured, rubbing his nose as he searched for a number for the Umberto I Hospital.

Hellen jumped over the fence and braced herself against the plate that topped the pedestal on which Achilles lay. To their surprise, it proved far easier to move than they would have guessed. They all looked on, wide-eyed, as the front of the pedestal sank into the ground, revealing a narrow stairway.

"I want your job. This beats being chancellor by a mile," Lang said, but he quickly remembered the seriousness of the situation. Hellen ignored his flippant remark. She took a flashlight from her backpack, where she was also carrying the collar from the Treasury, and carefully began the descent.

CHAPTER 80

BENEATH THE "DYING ACHILLES", GARDENS OF ACHILLEION, CORFU

The cone of light from Hellen's flashlight swept over the walls of the passage she was descending into. Above her, she heard the chancellor discussing the situation with his Cobra bodyguards.

"You stay up here," Lang said. "What do you think is lurking down there? Terrorists waiting for someone to find the entrance? Ancient Greek monsters? The Hydra? Cyclops? I'm going down. If you want to stop me, you'll have to shoot me."

Considering that the Medusa actually existed, Hellen felt the chancellor's words were perhaps not so wisely chosen. Nevertheless, she refrained from commenting as he climbed down after her. Cloutard had decided to stay aboveground to try to reach the hospital.

"Have you already found something?" Lang asked, as excited as a child on Christmas Day.

"Not yet, not really," Hellen said, searching the small room, just six feet square, with the flashlight. "But it goes on." She shone her light toward a narrow passage that continued underground.

"What are we waiting for?" the chancellor said, and he nudged Hellen toward the opening.

Cautious but determined, Hellen entered the passageway. It was too long for her flashlight to illuminate the far end, and the farther they went, the narrower the corridor became, or so it felt.

"The Italian prime minister would struggle down here," Lang said. "Too much pasta."

If Tom's not here to spout nonsense, the Austrian chancellor takes over, Hellen thought, pushing forward through the now extremely tight passage. This was no place for the claustrophobic.

She almost stumbled when she suddenly found herself standing at the top of a stairway leading deep into the earth. Here, too, her flashlight was not strong enough to light the bottom.

Without hesitation, she continued down. She thought briefly of the steps beneath St. John's Co-Cathedral in Malta, which had suddenly collapsed beneath her, but that danger did not exist here. These steps had been carved directly from the stone.

The air was stuffier down here and smelled of mold. Bugs large and small crawled on the walls, disappearing into cracks when the light fell on them. Behind her, the chancellor sounded a bit more out of breath than he had a minute or two before. She turned around and looked up at him.

"All good," he said. "Just a little out of the ordinary."

Hellen shook her head. What did it say about her and her life if what she was doing counted as "normal" for her? But even if it wasn't, she was there to save her husband's life. She quickened her steps. Deeper and deeper she went, mentally blocking out any danger that might be lurking. The chancellor panted behind her, struggling to keep up.

Hellen's light finally hit the floor below, and she could see the end of the stairway. She descended the last few steps even faster, and a few seconds later she was looking around inside a much larger room.

"We're in the right place," she said, shining her flashlight around for the chancellor's benefit.

In front of them was a large table surrounded by about thirty chairs. At the head of the table—not placed there but carved directly out of the surrounding stone—stood a throne, no doubt intended for the grandmaster of the Order's use. A thick layer of dust covered everything. On the wall beyond the table hung a painting with the insignia of the Order, which also contained a stylized figure of a golden ram. Against the wall on the right was something resembling the altar in a Catholic church.

Hellen moved past the table and shone her light over its surface. She stopped and leaned forward when she noticed several uneven points. Then she took a deep breath and blew the dust away, revealing quotations in Ancient Greek carved into the surface. They were etched around a ring-shaped recess in the center of the table. Hellen knew immediately what she had to do.

She set her backpack down quickly on one of the chairs and carefully removed a velvet cloth, which she unfolded on the table. The golden collar of the Order appeared, gleaming in the flashlight beam.

"Doctor de Mey," the chancellor said, stepping closer when he recognized the chain. "Unless I'm mistaken, that should be under lock and key in a cabinet in the Treasury."

"That's true," Hellen said with a sheepish smile. "We . . . had to borrow it. Only temporarily."

"I see," Lang replied, not without a sardonic edge to his voice. "Don't worry, I won't spill the beans. This is the most exciting thing I've done since that whole Florentine Diamond escapade. Your secret is safe with me."

Hellen, with the collar in her hand, handed her flashlight to the chancellor and leaned over the table. "Shine the light on this ring," she said, and Lang knew immediately what she was about to do.

"The collar fits the recess perfectly, doesn't it?" he said.

Hellen nodded and began pressing the collar link by link into the tabletop. The last link was the ram pendant. She paused for a second.

"Moment of truth," she said. Using her thumb, she pressed the small ram pendant down and heard a familiar sound, a kind of *click*. Somewhere in the room, something had opened.

"Over here," Lang said, pinpointing the source of the sound. A section of the base of the throne, a kind a drawer, had slid outward. The chancellor turned the flashlight onto the drawer, which Hellen carefully opened wider.

A golden glow from inside told them that they'd found what they were there for. It was a cape spun from golden thread and attached to a breastplate, in the center of which, at the level of the solar plexus, was a highly polished bronze plate—the mirror they would need to protect themselves from the Medusa. Hellen carefully lifted the fleece and breastplate out of the drawer, stopping for a moment to admire the ornate workmanship. Then she took a large cloth bag, similar to Tom's duffel bag, from her backpack and stowed the armor inside it.

She took a deep breath. The first step was behind them. The artifacts existed and were now in her hands. Hope was still alive.

"What's next?" the Chancellor asked.

"We contact Damjam Mandalov. He knows how to use

these to destroy the Medusa and lift her curse. We may have to spirit these out of the country."

"Let that be my concern. My position has to be useful for something," Lang said proudly.

They quickly made their way back to the surface, where Cloutard was waiting for them. But when Hellen saw his face, she was suddenly afraid. A knot formed in her chest.

"I have spoken with the hospital. He is still on the operating table," Cloutard said. "His condition is still critical. The problem is that the catatonic condition that gave us more time has become the problem. Because his metabolism—indeed, his entire system—is almost at a standstill, his wounds are unable to heal. It is only a question of time until . . ." Cloutard's voice faltered. He did not want to say any more.

Hellen swallowed her horror and summoned up as much composure as she could. She closed her eyes and took a deep breath, then held up the duffel bag with the artifacts. Cloutard's face brightened, but not for long. In Hellen's eyes, he could see that she knew there was only one road for them to follow. She nodded to him.

"*Alors.*" He gathered himself. "I have also contacted Mandalov and told him—presumptuously, I know—that we have everything. He sent me the coordinates for the place we are to take the Medusa and the artifacts."

"Where?" Hellen and the Chancellor asked as one.

"To Crete, to the cave where Zeus was born."

CHAPTER 81

PSYCHRO VILLAGE, CRETE. TWENTY-FOUR HOURS LATER

"Gesundheit," Hellen said with a smile.

Cloutard, red-eyed, sniffling, nose dripping, just looked at her miserably. He was a pitiful sight.

Hellen's mood had improved considerably in the previous few hours. Hope had taken root, and Mandalov had proven himself a man of his word. The old man had won Hellen's trust from the start with his wisdom and dignity. She believed absolutely that he would be the one to break Medusa's spell, destroy the head—and save Tom's life.

"*Merde*, it is worse here on Crete than anywhere else," Cloutard panted. "What kind of evil olive trees grow here? *C'est un désastre.*"

"Which makes me all the more thankful that you're here, François."

Cloutard shook his head. "That goes without saying. It will take a little more than pollen from hell to kill me." Another sneezing fit shook him. "At least, I hope so," he added ruefully.

Hellen parked the car in the parking lot at the "Greek Mythology Thematic Park." It was a tourist attraction of the worst kind, dripping with kitsch. On the drive, Cloutard had shown her pictures of the park on Google Maps, shaking his head and muttering "*terriblement.*" As they got out of the car, the sun was already starting to set, and the theme park and adjoining caves had closed for the day. They were alone. In the distance, they heard the sound of an approaching helicopter.

"Mandalov. He is right on time," Cloutard said when the helicopter was in sight. The empty parking lot served well as a makeshift landing pad. The door slid open and the old man with the long white hair climbed out slowly but not unsteadily, supporting himself on a walking stick with one hand and waving with the other.

Hellen opened the trunk and took out the backpack containing the head and the bag she'd packed with the Aegis and the Golden Fleece. Then, to Cloutard's amazement, she also produced a small pistol that Topol had given her on Corfu. She racked the slide and pushed it into the back of her trousers.

"Tom isn't here, and I don't want to take any chances," she explained, handing the bag to a speechless Cloutard while she shouldered the backpack. She closed the back of the car and went to meet Mandalov.

"Thank you for coming so quickly," she said.

"It is not far from here," Mandalov said, and he pointed upward between two buildings, where a dirt track led up the thinly forested hillside.

"Will you make it?"

"I'll be all right. It is a quarter of a mile, a little more, and not especially steep." Slowly and deliberately, he set one foot in front of the other. "At my age, however, it may take a while," he added.

They walked together in silence. After about fifty yards, they came to an ornate iron fence that enclosed the area around the caves. Hellen and Cloutard watched as

Mandalov reached into his jacket pocket, fished out a bunch of keys, and opened the old padlock on the gate.

"You seem well prepared," said Hellen.

"I have been waiting and preparing for this day for many, many years," Mandalov said, wheezing a little. He opened the gate and continued on. Hellen had to make a real effort not to race ahead—she could hardly wait to see the Medusa destroyed once and for all, hoping fervently that by doing so they would save Tom's life.

Cloutard, walking a few steps ahead, turned back with a frown.

"But why?" he asked, then sneezed. "*Je ne comprends pas.* Why have you been waiting to destroy the Medusa?"

Mandalov stopped and took a few deep breaths. "Hay fever?" he asked sympathetically.

"The mother of all hay fevers," Cloutard replied.

"Ah. Well, to answer your question . . ." Mandalov turned a little to address both of them, ". . . I am the oldest living member of the Ptolemaic cult of Alexander the Great, which has existed since the death of the great commander himself."

Hellen raised her eyebrows. A few years earlier, she would have been astonished, but not anymore. She had seen too much, and too many purported legends had turned out to be true.

"Our only task is to destroy the Medusa," Mandalov said, moving off again. "Only Alexander himself, as a demigod, was able to control the monster. After his death, Medusa's head disappeared, and the Alexander cult was created to find it and destroy it."

"But didn't you say that the Medusa could be controlled with the artifacts?" Hellen said with a trace of doubt.

"Not entirely. Only Alexander was capable of that. When he was protected by the cloak and the Aegis breastplate, the

Medusa feared him. In the end, he was the one who cut off her head. These artifacts will simply help us to destroy her." He stopped again to catch his breath. "I will tell you the rest up there." The old man was clearly having some difficulty, and he needed all the strength he had to make it up the road.

I hope he doesn't keel over first, Hellen thought, as Mandalov took her arm and they traversed the last few yards to the cave entrance together.

Cloutard pointed back down toward the parking lot, where a few people had gathered.

"Your helicopter has drawn some attention," he said. "I think I should wait outside and make sure you are not disturbed." He passed Hellen the bag containing the artifacts.

Mandalov reached inside his jacket and took out a Maglite flashlight. "Come. We should not lose any time," he said, switching on the flashlight and leading the way inside. "Follow me, I know the way. I've been here often enough."

Cloutard watched until they disappeared from view.

Moss-covered rock formations rose thirty feet and more in the entrance area, and Hellen supported the old man as they descended a wooden staircase into the depths. It was almost completely silent inside, the only sounds an eerie dripping and the creaking of the stairs reverberating inside the mountain.

"How are you going to destroy the head?" Hellen asked. "Is there a ritual or something? I mean, are you really sure you can destroy it?" Hellen gulped. "My husband's life depends on it."

Mandalov laid his hand reassuringly on Hellen's arm. "Trust me," he said. "I have everything we need to destroy her and break the curse."

"Speaking of rituals," Hellen said, a thought suddenly

occurring to her, "I have a question." She told him what they had seen in the amphitheater in Syracuse.

The old man listened with interest. His expression grew grim, and his reply was something that Hellen had not even remotely counted on.

"I'm sorry, my dear, but I don't know what you witnessed. I know Greek mythology better than most experts, but even I have never heard or read about a ritual like that." He looked down in resignation. "The world of the Greeks contains so many wonderful things. It has fascinated me since my youth. I have tracked down many of those wonders myself, but I'm afraid I will never be able to answer the questions raised by the ritual you saw. But maybe you will, one day."

"Maybe we can do it together," Hellen said, smiling at the old man.

Mandalov turned and looked deep into Hellen's eyes. "I don't think so, my dear. I will die here today."

CHAPTER 82

IN THE CAVE OF ZEUS

They pressed on in complete silence for a few moments. Hellen began to understand. At a cleft in the wall. Mandalov stopped and stared into the darkness.

"I, as a mortal man, am able to bring the Medusa and the artifacts to the only place where she can be destroyed, but she will take me with her into death. It is unavoidable."

Hellen was torn. She did not want the old man to sacrifice himself, of course, but at the same time she knew with sad certainty that it was the only possible way to save Tom. But Mandalov raised his hand, as if anticipating her objection.

"Don't be upset, my dear. This is my destiny. I have spent my entire life—and it has been a full one—preparing for this moment. Believe me, it is the only way."

He held out his hand to Hellen in farewell, but when she took his hand in his, she realized he was holding something in it. A key. "This is the key to a safe deposit box at the Private Bank in Skopje. Inside it you will find my will. After you visited me, Dr. de Mey, I made the decision to leave all of my possessions, everything you saw in Samuel's Fortress, to you. In the box you will also find the contact information for my lawyer. He will take care of everything for you."

Hellen stood with her mouth wide open, at first unable to utter a word. "Why me?" she finally managed to squeak.

"Because you, my dear, have your heart in the right place. You won't use the information you find there to the detriment of humanity, nor to make yourself rich. You have demonstrated that often enough in your career."

Hellen felt herself flush. Mandalov smiled and squeezed her hand firmly. But before she could say a word of thanks, Mandalov turned away.

"It is time. Destiny is calling. I have a date with a Gorgon." He smiled. "Go. Make sure you get yourself and Monsieur Cloutard to safety. This place will be utterly destroyed. The destruction of the Medusa is a cataclysmic ritual. Few things can withstand it."

Hellen embraced the old man warmly. She felt as if she had known him forever. Her eyes grew misty. Mandalov gave her a final hug, then shooed her back toward the exit.

"Farewell," he said. Then he took the bag with the artifacts and the backpack containing the head. For a moment, Hellen stood and watched the old man until he was no longer visible in the darkness. Then she turned away. A few minutes later, she was back upstairs.

But when she stepped outside, her heart almost stopped.

"I am sorry, *ma chère*," Cloutard croaked nasally. Weaver was standing close behind him, his revolver pressed to Cloutard's temple.

"Where's the Medusa?" he growled.

Hellen said nothing but glared back coldly. Not only had he almost murdered Tom, now he was threatening Cloutard. She knew she could not let him enter the cave.

"My patience is at an end," Weaver said. "Talk. Talk, or I'll kill him. Believe me, I don't give two shits about your friend's life." He pressed the gun even harder against Cloutard's head. The skin around the end of the barrel turned white. "If you don't talk right now, then in a few seconds, he'll be dead. And then you'll talk. Enhanced interrogation is a specialty of mine. Sooner or later, you'll talk."

Hellen knew they were out of time. Mandalov would soon destroy the Medusa, and God alone knew what that would unleash. At the same time, she knew she had to take Weaver's threats seriously. She looked at Cloutard but had no idea what to do.

CHAPTER 83
OUTSIDE THE CAVE OF ZEUS

Then Hellen saw it: Cloutard's face started to pucker, as if he'd bitten into a lemon. The muscles around his nose began to twitch wildly. He closed his eyes slowly. Weaver's attention was on Hellen, and he didn't notice what was going on with Cloutard.

Suddenly, there was a kind of explosion, and Cloutard let out the most violent sneeze Hellen had ever heard. His head snapped forward. A shot rang out but missed the back of his head by a hair's breadth. The violence of the sneeze had caught Weaver completely off guard. Quick as lightning and as hard as he could, Cloutard snapped his head back again, cracking into Weaver's nose and breaking it. Weaver stumbled back, and Hellen took her opportunity. She was ready, and she'd seen Cloutard's sneeze coming in plenty of time. She didn't stop to think as she reached for her pistol. Three shots followed in quick succession, each one striking Weaver in the chest. He staggered back a few steps as blood streamed from his mouth. Then he toppled backward, his head crashing onto a rock, and died on the spot.

"Gesundheit, François," Hellen said, adrenalin surging through her.

"You are more like your husband every day," Cloutard said, shaking his head. "I never expected my allergy to save my life."

Hellen smiled, but a moment later turned her eyes to Weaver, suddenly conscious of what she'd done. She looked down at the gun in her trembling hand. It took a few deep breaths for the trembling to settle, then she clicked on the safety and returned the pistol to her waistband.

"Where is Mandalov?" Cloutard asked.

Before Hellen could reply, they heard an ominous rumbling. The earth shook and stones broke loose above the entrance to the cave. "Later," Hellen said. "We need to get out of here."

"*Une bonne idée*," Cloutard agreed. The rumbling was quickly becoming a roar.

They ran. The stony path they'd come up along, already rough, suddenly became almost unpassable. Gaps opened between their feet. Large sections of the hillside began to slide, and solid ground underfoot was hard to find. They jumped and ran, zigzagging down the hill to escape the ever-growing fissures.

Hellen risked a quick glance over her shoulder as she ran. Shocked, she saw half the mountain collapse, as if Hades himself were pulling it back into the underworld.

Cloutard stumbled and fell but managed to roll and got back on his feet with impressive spryness. He ran on. The widening crevasses were hard on their heels, but they ran and ran, literally for their lives. Then, without warning, a small avalanche of earth and rubble hit them, knocking both of them off their feet. Flailing wildly, they did their best to avoid being buried in the landslide.

And suddenly, from one second to the next, it was over. Hellen was seeing stars. Real ones, because she and Cloutard were lying on their backs, staring up into the clear night sky. They were half-covered in soil, branches, and loose stones, but for the most part were unhurt. Hellen raised her head. A few stones bounced past, but the whole terrifying event seemed to be over.

"That was close," Hellen said. She was on her feet now, slapping the dirt from her clothes. "Are you all right, François?"

"Yes, *tout va bien*."

"Good. And for your acrobatic performance just now: ten out of ten for style. Well done." She grinned and threw her arms around Cloutard, happy they had made it out in one piece.

"I suspect that Mandalov did not make it," Cloutard said. Hellen nodded.

"He knew he would die here," she said. "He sacrificed himself, and—"

But just then, Cloutard's phone rang. He looked at the display and smiled. "It is for you," he said, clicking the green button and passing the phone across.

"Hey, sweetheart." Hellen let out a squeal of delight when she heard Tom's voice. He sounded weak, but he was alive. "Did you guys take care of that son of a bitch with the buzzcut?" Hellen sobbed, still unable to find any words. Tears of happiness trickled down her face. "I had the strangest dream. Can someone get me out of here? You know I hate hospitals."

Hellen laughed with joy—her brash, brazen, cocksure Tom was back.

CHAPTER 84
ULTRAMODERN SKYSCRAPER, SINGAPORE

The express elevator stopped with a *ping* at the penthouse and the wood-paneled doors slid open. Wearing a skin-tight black dress and a pair of Louboutin high heels, the Mantis stepped out into the penthouse foyer. Her copper-colored hair was slicked back against her scalp. A pair of sunglasses by London designer Oliver Goldsmith modeled on Audrey Hepburn's in *Breakfast at Tiffany's* hid her steel-blue eyes, and a Hermès Birkin 35 handbag in Bordeaux alligator leather, easily worth fifty thousand dollars, dangled from her elbow.

She nodded to the two security men in Brioni suits flanking the large double doors. One of the men pressed his hand to a scanner on the wall, and the doors swung inward almost silently.

They returned her nod without a word as the woman swept past.

"Welcome home, Your Ladyship. Was your trip a success?" said the butler, a man of about sixty.

"Yes, thank you, Barkley. Extremely successful, in fact."

"Is there anything I can do for you?"

"No, Barkley. Thank you. I do not wish to be disturbed."

The butler bowed and exited again as unobtrusively as he'd appeared.

She crossed the marble reception area. Twin stairways curved up to the floor above them, with a small fountain splashing between them. She went around the fountain to an arched double door. Pulling both doors open, she stepped into a dark room. Indirect lighting came on automatically on all sides. The windowless circular office was big enough to easily contain a gymnasium. The most striking piece of furniture in the room was an antique desk. Paintings adorned the walls, among them Van Gogh's "Poppy Flowers," Vermeer's "The Concert," and one of Claude Monet's "Charing Cross Bridge" series. The three paintings, all of which had been stolen and were officially still unrecovered, had cost her a fortune.

Sideboards extended halfway around the walls on both sides of the entrance, and on top of these was a collection of weapons from various historical epochs. Swords, shotguns, pistols, daggers, and knives. The pride of her collection was the "Sword of Islam," a ceremonial blade that had once belonged to Benito Mussolini, but which disappeared after Il Duce was toppled in 1943.

She slipped out of the high heels and kicked them away, tossed the sunglasses onto a large sofa, and went over to one of the sideboards. Beneath a concealed panel was a palm scanner. She placed her hand on it and a section of the wall paneling slid aside.

Behind the paneling was an illuminated set of shelves. On the upper shelf, an ancient, wood-bound folio decorated with rich carvings and an elaborate clasp lay open. Ornate metal hinges held the antique document together. The folio was open to a hand-drawn map. On the shelf below lay three white velvet cushions.

The Mantis opened her bag and lifted out the amber-colored crystal, about six inches long, created by Medusa's gaze in the ritual in Syracuse. A yellow light shimmered over her face as she examined the semitransparent crystal from every side.

She smiled, satisfied, and laid the crystal gently on one of the cushions.

She closed the paneling again, then crossed to a small serving cart that held several Baccarat-crystal whiskey decanters. She poured herself a drink, then picked up a remote control and pressed a button.

As if by magic, sunlight suddenly burst through a gap in the wall. The gap gradually widened until a third of the wall had opened to reveal huge windows, while a third of the roof also slid back. Beyond the windows was a stunning rooftop garden. The Mantis stepped outside and strolled to the end of the garden.

She gazed out over the breathtaking skyline of Singapore and raised her glass as if to toast the entire city.

"One down, two to go."

CHAPTER 85
VIENNA GENERAL HOSPITAL, AUSTRIA

". . . if you want to stop me, you're going to have to shoot me? He actually said that?"

Tom was sitting upright in bed. He grimaced and held his chest. Laughing still hurt, but he was otherwise back to his old self. "At least I don't feel the bruised ribs anymore," he joked.

"You should have seen him. He was like a kid in a candy store," Hellen said. She held his hand in both of hers and couldn't take her eyes off him. She had her beloved husband back, the Medusa had been destroyed, and everyone was well. When Mandalov destroyed the head, Maierhofer's son had woken from his catatonic state in Vienna as if nothing had happened, almost at the same time as Tom.

"And let us not forget that your wife saved this old Frenchman's hide," said Cloutard, standing at the foot of the bed. He raised his hip flask to Hellen, who was sitting on a chair beside the bed, and took a swig.

"Thank you, François. I can't tell you how much that means to me," Tom said, looking gratefully at Cloutard. Half a dozen balloons bobbed from the ceiling with their strings hanging down, and Cloutard was trying persistently—but in vain—to sweep a string out of his face. Finally, he pulled it all the way down and clawed at the balloon until it popped.

Tom flinched and turned deathly pale. He broke into a sweat. Hellen was on her feet instantly and bombarding him with questions when she saw the change.

"What is it? Are you all right? Should I call the nurse? Where does it hurt?"

"It's okay. Don't worry," Tom said, waving it off. "A spasm, no big deal."

Hellen reached for the jug of water beside all the get-well-soon cards on the nightstand. She poured a glass of water and handed it to Tom, who gulped it down, hardly pausing to breathe.

"All good, really." He put the glass down, wiped his forehead, put on a smile.

"So, what about van Rensburg?" he said. "How did you prove he was innocent?"

Hellen and Cloutard looked at each other.

"Ah, well..."

"We..."

"...we were doing research in Prague..."

"...and we checked the CCTV and then it..."

"...so many clues..."

"...things got kind of carried away..."

"...yes, and then we learned..."

"...we got dragged out of the palace..."

"...correct, and..."

Hellen faltered. She looked at Cloutard and finally summoned up enough courage to put an end to their poor attempt at an explanation.

"We didn't. We got too caught up in all the history."

"Then... what's going on with him?"

"Well, Akira was good enough to stay with you in Syracuse until they transferred you here," Hellen continued.

"And she was getting bored, so she wrote a program that scoured the Internet for videos from the Volksgarten. And finally, on TikTok or Instagram or somewhere, she found one from a tourist in the Volksgarten that backed up van Rensburg's story. Maierhofer's sorting out the formalities right now to get him out of jail. They should be here soon. Akira's on her way, too."

"So someone actually posted something useful on a social media platform," said Tom.

"*C'est vrai*," said Cloutard.

"And what about that other guy, Apostle Ibis?" Tom asked. Hellen and Cloutard laughed.

"A-pos-to-los Ibis," Hellen corrected.

"Whatever his name is, what did you find out about him? Is *he* behind this stupid cult? And was the bug lady working for the cult, too?"

"To be honest, so far we haven't been able to find out anything about him at all," Hellen admitted. "Not even Gardner's friend J.J. at the DSN could find anything. Apart from the check in Richter's office and the suite in Prague booked in his name, we have nothing to go on. He may be no more than a straw man."

Tom shook his head. "No leads on the Mantis, then?"

"*Non, mon ami*," Cloutard said. "But you do not need to worry about that now. Get well first."

"The Medusa cult, by the way, is already old news," Hellen said. "The group behind it has moved on to other things. But the whole world will be suffering from the aftermath for a while yet."

"*Alors*, we have not walked away completely empty-handed," said Cloutard, prompting Hellen with a jab to her side.

"Oh. That's right. My inheritance," she said.

Tom, surprised, sat up straighter, but a second later he

had to hold his chest and screwed up his face in pain. "Your inheritance?" he groaned.

Hellen eased him back onto his pillows and told him about Mandalov's estate. "Maybe we'll discover in there what the ritual in Syracuse was all about," she said thoughtfully.

There was a knock at the door, and van Rensburg and Maierhofer came in. Close behind them was Akira, who was holding another balloon on a string in her hand. She was a little taken aback by the scowl on Cloutard's face.

"Hey, come on in," said Tom.

Handshakes and hugs followed, and the usual "good to see you," "glad you made it," "I hope jail wasn't too bad," and "hope you're back on your feet soon" platitudes did the rounds.

"By the way, Wagner," Maierhofer said, "Chancellor Lang has sorted out that Red Notice for you. And Isaac Hagen sends his apologies. He says he's got his hands full investigating General Horne."

"Thanks, Captain."

Silence settled for a moment, until van Rensburg cleared his throat. He looked from Tom to Hellen and finally to Cloutard. He rubbed his hands, apparently struggling to find the right words.

"Mr. Wagner, Ms. de Mey, Monsieur Cloutard," he began. "I'm very glad to see you all here safe and well again, and to be able to thank you in person. So, thank you for risking your necks to prove my innocence. How can I ever repay you?"

The three shared a look, and it was Hellen who spoke. "Well, actually, we didn't have anything to do with it. It was Akira who got you out of jail."

"Who?"

"Me, sir. Akira Seki," Akira said meekly, stepping out

from behind Maierhofer. She let go of the balloon and held out her hand to van Rensburg.

"Oh, yes. Captain Maierhofer told me about you on the way here. Then it's you I have to thank." He shook her hand warmly in both of his. "How can I show my appreciation?"

She grinned sheepishly at van Rensburg, while Tom, Hellen, and Cloutard nodded to her encouragingly.

"Um . . . I'm sure I'm not welcome at DARPA anymore, and I could use a job . . ." she said, with a little more strength in her voice.

Van Rensburg looked to Tom, Hellen and Cloutard, who all nodded. Then he turned back to Akira with a broad smile.

"All right, Ms. Seki. Welcome to the team!"

The End of
"The Medusa Secret"
Tom, Hellen and Cloutard
will return in
„The Gifts of the Three Kings"

GET THE FREE PREQUEL TO THE
TOM WAGNER
ADVENTURES

ROBERTSMACLAY.COM/EN/START-FREE

THE TOM WAGNER SERIES
BY ROBERTS & MACLAY

The Stone of Destiny

The Sacred Weapon

The Library of the Kings

The Invisible City

The Golden Path

The Chronicle of the Round Table

The Chalice of Eternity

The Sword of Revelation

The Lost Treasure

The Medusa Secret

The Gifts of the Three Kings

Coming soo

The Shadow of Nostradamus

The Tesla Formular

The Tibetan Shrine

The Pope's Ring

The Treasure of the Templars

THRILLED READER REVIEWS

"Suspense and entertainment! I've read a lot of books like this one; some better, some worse. This is one of the best books in this genre I've ever read. I'm really looking forward to a good sequel. "

"I just couldn't put this book down. Full of surprising plot twists, humor, and action! "

"An explosive combination of Robert Langdon, James Bond & Indiana Jones"

"Good build-up of tension; I was always wondering what happens next. Toward the end, where the story gets more and more complex and constantly changes scenes, I was on the edge of my seat"

"Great! I read all three books in one sitting. Dan Brown better watch his back."

"The best thing about it is the basic premise, a story with historical background knowledge scattered throughout the book–never too much at one time and always supporting the plot"

"Entertaining and action-packed! The carefully thought-out story has a clear plotline, but there are a couple of unexpected twists as well. I really enjoyed it. The sections of the book are tailored to maximize the suspense, they don't waste any time with unimportant details. The chapters are short and compact–perfect for a half-hour commute or at night before turning out the lights. Recommended to all lovers of the genre and anyone interested in getting to know it better. I'll definitely read the sequel."

"Anyone who likes reading Dan Brown, James Rollins and Preston & Child needs to get this book."

"An exciting build-up, interesting and historically significant settings, surprising plot twists in the right places."

ABOUT THE AUTHORS
ROBERTS & MACLAY

Roberts & Maclay have known each other for over 25 years, are good friends and have worked together on various projects.

The fact that they are now also writing thrillers together is less coincidence than fate. Talking shop about films, TV series and suspense novels has always been one of their favorite pastimes.

M.C. Roberts is the pen name of an successful entrepreneur and blogger. Adventure stories have always been his passion: after recording a number of superhero audiobooks on his father's old tape recorder as a six-year-old, he postponed his dream of writing novels for almost 40 years, and worked as a marketing director, editor-in-chief, DJ, opera critic, communication coach, blogger, online marketer and author of trade books...but in the end, the call of adventure was too strong to ignore.

R.F. Maclay is the pen name of an outstanding graphic designer and advertising filmmaker. His international career began as an electrician's apprentice, but he quickly realized that he was destined to work creatively. His family and friends were skeptical at first...but now, 20 years later, the passionate, self-taught graphic designer and filmmaker has delighted record labels, brand-name products and tech companies with his work, as well as making a name for himself as a commercial filmmaker and illustrator. He's also a walking encyclopedia of film and television series.

www.RobertsMaclay.com

Printed in Dunstable, United Kingdom